A
FIGHT
IN
SILENCE

A FIGHT IN SILENCE

MELANIE METZENTHIN

TRANSLATED BY
DEBORAH RACHEL LANGTON

LAKE UNION
PUBLISHING

This is a work of fiction. Names, characters, organizations, places, events, and incidents are either products of the author's imagination or are used fictitiously. Any resemblance to actual persons, living or dead, or actual events is purely coincidental.

Text copyright © 2017 by Melanie Metzenthin
Translation copyright © 2019 by Deborah Rachel Langton
All rights reserved.

No part of this book may be reproduced, or stored in a retrieval system, or transmitted in any form or by any means, electronic, mechanical, photocopying, recording, or otherwise, without express written permission of the publisher.

Previously published as *Im Lautlosen* by Tinte & Feder in Germany in 2017. Translated from German by Deborah Rachel Langton. First published in English by Lake Union Publishing in collaboration with Amazon Crossing in 2019.

Published by Lake Union Publishing, in collaboration with Amazon Crossing, Seattle

www.apub.com

Amazon, the Amazon logo, Lake Union Publishing and Amazon Crossing are trademarks of Amazon.com, Inc., or its affiliates.

ISBN-13: 9781542093682
ISBN-10: 1542093686

Cover design by Ghost Design

Printed in the United States of America

First edition

A FIGHT IN SILENCE

PART ONE

The Weimar Republic 1926–1932

Chapter 1

Hamburg, 1926

Days like this unfailingly reminded Paula that Hamburg's university was still in its infancy and taking its first baby steps, a long way off from catching up with its older siblings, the renowned Faculties of Medicine for which the German Empire was famous. Her father, the distinguished psychiatrist Dr Wilhelm Engelhardt, had repeatedly advised her to do her medical studies at the highly respected University of Göttingen, where he himself had been a student. He had emphasised over and over to her that those with the means to do so studied in Berlin, Heidelberg or Göttingen. At a proper university hospital.

But Paula loved Hamburg, this big, wealthy city which had so swiftly recovered after the war and regained its former glory – a cosmopolitan, Hanseatic port with a spirit of fun. Why go any further afield when Hamburg had founded its first university just seven years earlier? No matter that it lacked a recognised university hospital and had hastily given professorial status to a few doctors from Eppendorf General to give the appearance of having a Faculty of Medicine – Paula had not regretted her decision.

Days like this, however, made Paula wonder if she should have followed her father's advice after all. Days when students had to queue outside the lecture halls of the impressive main building at Dammtor to hear lectures by respected guest academics from well-known universities, academics who wouldn't usually find themselves in Hamburg.

For weeks now, she'd been looking forward to today's evening lecture by Professor Habermann from the University of Munich on the nature of mental illness and the state of mind of sufferers. Her friend Leonie, also a doctor's daughter and medical student in her second semester, had come along with her. Dressed in the latest fashion, her hair stylishly bobbed with a few rebellious curls peeping jauntily from beneath her cloche hat, her skirt short enough to draw attention to her silk-stockinged legs, Leonie looked more the starlet than the student.

An innocent observer might easily gain the impression that Leonie was using university less to develop her knowledge than as a shop window where she could assess the worth of potential husbands. But Paula knew better. The image she portrayed was Leonie's personal weapon in the battle of the sexes, because an attractive appearance could turn male students into true gentlemen. Today was a case in point, as the men had let the two girls go straight to the head of the queue while they all stood in line for the caretaker to open the doors to the lecture hall.

This was one of the few benefits of being a woman, but it didn't remotely compensate for the disadvantages all the girls encountered throughout their studies. Academic staff frequently went in for ambiguous remarks and disrespectful jokes. While Paula's approach was to fight back with hard work and high achievement, Leonie simply laughed it all off as though she had no idea that the pointed remarks were aimed at her. Having seen her do this on numerous occasions, Paula eventually asked why she didn't put up more resistance.

Leonie was dismissive. 'Weak men are scared of intelligent women and only weaklings crack stupid jokes at the expense of others. If they choose to think I'm naive and simple-minded, what do I care? I'm here and I'm allowed to study and that's all that matters,' she said.

Paula had thought about this for quite a while. Did it really make life easier, or was Leonie doing herself and other women a disservice by behaving so superficially and thus confirming all prejudices towards women students?

But today Leonie's easy-going attitude to life had paid off. The lecture hall doors opened and they were the first in. Paula wanted to head straight down to the front, but Leonie grabbed her arm and drew her towards the middle rows.

'The handout said there'll be slides. We don't want to have to lean our heads back as though we're in a barber's shop, surely?' Leonie bent her head right back as if trying to watch a film from the front row in the cinema, then winked conspiratorially at Paula, who giggled. She'd known Leonie a long time now, but couldn't say with any certainty whether she was genuinely interested in this lecture or more in the men attending alongside them. Whatever the case, Leonie was clearly pleased to see how fast the adjacent seats were filling up. The young gentlemen who'd let them go in first were also keen to enjoy female company, during the lecture at the very least. Conversation initially revolved around whether certain seats were free and Leonie's gracious nod of the head in reply was embellished by her fabulous smile.

To begin with, Leonie listened attentively, then she turned to Paula and whispered, 'It's more like a cabinet of curiosities than an academic lecture, don't you think?'

Paula nodded, but she also shushed her friend.

'. . . and so the recurring question is what distinguishes man from beast?' The professor's voice echoed around the hall. 'There are many who say it's the creative mental energy, the desire never to give up and to set ourselves major objectives. I've brought some images with such power of expression that they speak for themselves.' He gestured towards the hapless lecture hall assistant charged with the awkward task of operating the huge and ungainly projector. The picture now displayed against the wall showed a lunatic with no hair and the grin of a simpleton.

Leonie gasped audibly. 'Told you – freak show. Like at the fairground!'

Paula took no notice. As the daughter of a psychiatrist who had never concealed his work from his family, she had known people like this as a child. At first sight, they could be frightening but behind that was often a naive trust that had intrigued Paula right from the start.

'Here we see a classic case of dementia praecox,' the speaker went on. 'A form of schizophrenia. Notice the staring eyes and the vacant smile. Many tend to speak of an empty shell, of someone mentally dead. A being devoid of all humanity.'

Applause came from somewhere in the hall but faded the moment Professor Habermann looked sternly in its direction.

'So, what constitutes humanity? The second image, please.'

The projector hummed, then displayed the next slide. This time it was a drawing of two faces which merged into one another.

'Professor Wilmanns of Heidelberg University Hospital has kindly made these portraits available to me,' Habermann explained. 'They have been collecting the work of the mentally ill for many years. Sadly, I can't show you the colour original, but even this monochrome photograph gives you an impression of the power of expression inherent in this poor soul.'

'And proves that he's truly insane,' murmured Leonie. 'Nobody of sound mind paints anything like that.'

'It's reminiscent of Surrealism,' came a male voice from the row behind them. Paula turned. In the half-light she couldn't see much, only that the man had dark hair and was clean-shaven.

'Surrealism?' she asked.

'A style of painting that makes everything dream-like and unreal.'

'I haven't heard of it. Is that—?'

Before she could finish the sentence, she received a prod from Leonie. 'Just look at that! Puts any theatre of horrors in the shade.'

Paula turned back. A new picture flickered against the white wall with another male face, another smile. But this was not the classic picture of the mentally ill. The man's skull was deformed: the left half of the head looked completely normal while there was an odd sort of dip on the right, as if the cranial bone were missing, leaving only hirsute skin to cover it. For a moment Paula wondered whether the man had been born like this or whether it was the result of injury, but unlike Leonie she didn't find his appearance shocking, more something that aroused the deepest sympathy in her.

'Here we have a particularly interesting case. As you can see, part of the skull, the calvaria, is missing. The few babies born like this do not usually survive the first few days of life. This person graduated from art school but then sustained a serious head injury during the war. It borders on the miraculous that the man survived. He demonstrates only minor motor deficiency, such as, for example, a discrete paralysis in the left side of the body, but this places little restriction on him. There has, however, been a sustained personality change that means he is unable to control his natural urges or live unsupervised among other people because his every physical need must be met instantly. Unfortunately, these needs are not restricted simply to social norms, such as enjoyment of food, but include an uncontrolled libido which means he cannot be left in the proximity of a woman.'

A gasp of outrage rippled through the hall but ceased as soon as Professor Habermann continued speaking. 'This personality change is apparent in the style of his art. Before this young man sustained his horrific injury, he had been an exceptionally gifted artist, probably destined for enormous success. I'll now show you one of his pictures, created before he sustained mental and physical damage.'

The projector clattered, and they saw a portrait of a young woman that was so true to life that at first sight it could have passed for a photograph.

'As you can undoubtedly see, the young man showed a real flair as a portraitist. From what his relatives have told us, art was his whole purpose in life and, even now, painting is the only way in which he can remain calm without being forcibly restrained. When he picks up his brush, he demonstrates a level of perseverance and patience not seen in any other interaction, even though the results are somewhat modest.'

The next picture appeared.

It was another portrait, this time of a man smoking a pipe. It lacked all naturalness and softness of line, but in spite of the harsh qualities and rough brushstrokes that gave it the feel of a caricature, it still demonstrated the artist's innate talent.

'There are many explanations as to why his art changed. The current school of thought among psychiatrists is that his brain is no longer able to perform complex operations, to perceive things with accuracy and then reproduce them. What is interesting is what happens when these works are shown to art experts who know nothing of their provenance, only that the first came before a young man's wartime experience and the second, after,' the professor said. 'The critics praised a strength of mental energy that this poor soul no longer enjoys in actual fact. His acquired deficiencies are celebrated as the honesty with which he removes the gloss from things to reveal the true horror experienced. His work has been compared with that of Max Beckmann, an artist with whom some of you will be familiar.'

Paula couldn't help but turn and whisper to the young man behind them. 'Does this Beckmann mean anything to you?'

'No, but I've noted the name.'

In the half-darkness she could just make out the gentle smile on his face.

'Are you really a medical student? You seem more like an art student passing through.'

He laughed softly. 'Doctors are allowed a feeling for art, surely?'

Before Paula could think up a clever reply, she felt Leonie dig her in the ribs and heard the unmistakable hiss of her friend telling her to be quiet. Paula felt a flash of irritation. Since when had Leonie been so diligent? It was usually the other way round in lectures, with Paula asking her friend to pipe down. But then she realised why – someone wanted to ask a question from the floor. Revolutionary behaviour. Paula could not call to mind a single occasion of a student daring to disturb the flow of a professorial lecture, and by an esteemed guest at that, with a banal question. But Professor Habermann was unperturbed and permitted the interruption.

'Looking at these pieces of work, which so clearly show the subject's deficiencies, could we apply the idea of a reverse conclusion and use the painting as a diagnostic tool in the discovery of early-stage mental illness, as yet undetected?'

'An interesting question, to be sure,' replied Professor Habermann, 'but the findings would be very non-specific as there are modern art forms using similar styles and techniques without the artists in question having any mental illness at all.'

'But that's precisely the question,' retorted the student. 'Are not modern art forms in themselves an expression of the disturbed, created in the first place in the depths of a troubled or broken mind and then taken up by a society shaken to its foundations? Surely this decadent art is already an expression of a sick society? And the artists creating it are then, by definition, to be assessed as mentally ill, or at the very least neurotic in the Freudian sense?'

There was unease in the lecture hall, and murmurings rippled throughout the room until Professor Habermann raised his right hand and regained calm. 'I fear this is a philosophical question which has little to do with the clear objectives of the treatment of the psychologically ill. It's important to decide just how insanity is defined,' he said. 'With these pictures we are delving into illness that is comprehensible and unambiguously described, the symptoms of which are not limited to art. Look at the two patients whose pictures I showed you. In both cases we are dealing with people who are seriously ill, are unable to participate in normal social interaction and can no longer support themselves. Art therapy gives people the opportunity to express themselves and, in doing so, enables us to learn more about their minds so that we can develop different treatments. New methods of treating schizophrenia are on the scientific horizon and could help in the future to cure this illness, or at the very least give a normal life to those affected, in so far as it is possible.'

Professor Habermann paused. No further questions came and so he continued his lecture.

'That was August Lachner,' Leonie whispered to Paula. 'He's very strange.'

'D'you know him?'

'A little,' Leonie whispered in return. 'I once made the mistake of taking up his invitation for coffee.' She rolled her eyes. 'He told me all about his doctorate and then spent ages enumerating how much it costs the German people to care for the mad and the idiotic, and how there ought to be ways of releasing the mentally dead as this would help the whole of society.'

'You'll have to be more careful in your choice of companion.'

'And you'll end up an old maid,' shot back Leonie.

'Better that than with August Lachner,' hissed Paula, and was gently elbowed in the ribs in return.

Professor Habermann presented several more case histories, but Paula retained little after the unsettling story of the painter maimed by war. One memorable exception was the work of a nineteen-year-old schizophrenic whose depiction of cows and horses Professor Habermann said was on a par with Stone Age cave paintings.

While the speaker had the pictures flashed up on the wall, Paula looked over at August Lachner in expectation of another interruption, but he said nothing.

By the time the professor was concluding his lecture to general applause, Leonie was already deep in conversation with the young man to her left as he tried to talk her into spending what remained of the evening in some fashionable café. Leonie feigned hesitation, her usual trick when flirting, but her body language indicated that she'd already agreed. A second young man seemed hopeful that Paula would join them but, unlike Leonie, this empty coquetry wasn't her style. She stood up and turned to the man in the row behind them, now busily packing away his pen and lecture notes in a brown briefcase of grained leather. Paula faltered. She hadn't brought anything to write with as she'd seen the lecture less as work and more as an interesting pastime.

'May I ask you another question?' she said, wanting to take a closer look at him once the curtains had reopened and let in the light.

'Of course.' He gave her a nod of encouragement. 'What would you like to know?'

He had dark brown hair, which, unlike with most of the men she knew, was not smeared with pomade. She liked that. But it was his eyes that intrigued her the most, their bright blue reminding her of a lake in a summer storm.

'Those art movements you talked about, they don't mean much to me, although I'm often at the city art gallery.'

'That's not so surprising,' he said. 'In the mainstream galleries, they really only have the Expressionists to represent the whole of modern art, alongside the regular Old Masters. A while back I went to the Museum of Fine and Applied Arts, and I often look in at the Galerie Commeter in Hermannstrasse, even though I can't afford anything at the moment!' His momentary smile softened his features, although his face remained manly. 'Anyway, my name's Richard Hellmer. I'm in my seventh semester.'

'Paula Engelhardt,' she said, extending her hand. 'I'm in my second.'

'And already interested in psychology?' His handshake was warm and friendly.

'The burden of heredity, you might say. My father is Wilhelm Engelhardt, psychiatrist.'

'And that's why you aspire to this particular field?'

'Could be. And you? What prompted you to come this evening? Art or psychiatry?'

'Both. I'm writing my dissertation on different ways of treating mental illness and am intrigued by what people are capable of, even when others have called the value of their lives into question.' His face grew serious again and his gaze turned disdainfully towards August Lachner, who was just leaving the hall.

'That interruption surprised me,' said Paula, seizing the opportunity to keep the conversation going. 'Art as a means of diagnosis to detect mental illness?' She shook her head.

'Our colleague is a devotee of the theories of Professor Alfred Hoche at Freiburg.'

'I don't know the name.'

Before Richard could respond, Paula got a gentle push.

'Paula, are you coming? Eckehard and Felix would like to treat us to coffee.'

'No thanks, I still have lots to do today.'

'Pity,' Leonie said, winking at her, then left the lecture hall with both young men.

'Looks as though we're the last to leave,' commented Richard.

'Yes, it looks like it. And the caretaker's keen to lock up. I'd love to continue this conversation, though.' This time she smiled at him.

'I know you're busy, but if you could spare some time . . . ? I know a little café near here.'

'An hour either way shouldn't matter,' she replied, and followed him out of the lecture hall into the foyer, where they collected their coats from the cloakroom.

The café, located a couple of streets behind the faculty building, was in an incongruous little brick structure that seemed to squat crookedly behind a magnificent late-nineteenth-century villa.

'Every time I see this place I feel sorry for it,' said Richard, 'all alone among the showy villas – that's why I keep coming back here, and, besides, they have very good cake. Let's hope they haven't sold out already.' He fished out his pocket watch. 'Ten past seven: touch and go. They close at eight.'

'Coffee and stimulating conversation are enough. We don't need cake as well.'

'Then I shan't worry about letting the side down if it's all gone.'

Once inside, Paula found the café to be far bigger than she'd expected. First came the inviting high-ceilinged interior, while at the back it was altogether smaller and more cosy. She guessed they must have knocked through to the house behind to create this size and effect. Bumps and ridges beneath the ornamental burgundy rugs indicated where the old divisions between front and back had once been. There were little round walnut tables throughout with elegantly turned wooden chairs to match, the seats upholstered in dark red velvet. The daily newspapers hung from racks around the walls.

Most tables were still occupied, even though the café would be closing shortly. Many of the students present, some of whom Paula knew by sight, sat over their books and notes, while quite a few men played chess and a group of older ladies talked animatedly.

Richard led the way to one of the few empty tables at the back then helped Paula out of her coat and hung it on a rack along with his own. He'd only just sat down when a waitress arrived, ready to take their order. She was a pretty blonde with a pout that didn't quite go with the prim black dress and white lace apron.

'We'd like two coffees, please,' said Richard, 'and do you have any cake left?'

'But of course – what would you like? Sponge cake or almond?'

He looked at Paula. 'The almond cake here is superb, I have to say.'

'I can't resist the idea of almond cake.'

They sat in silence once the waitress had gone. Paula tried to remember what they'd been talking about when they'd set off after the lecture, but before she could ask him, Richard picked up where they'd left off.

'You wanted to know about Professor Hoche. A few years ago, he and the lawyer Binding published a work on the destruction of life unworthy of life.' Richard's face had taken on a serious expression, similar to the one he'd directed at August Lachner.

'Life unworthy of life?' asked Paula. This was a term she'd never come across.

He nodded. 'I read their publication. It starts with the completely understandable call to make it possible for the terminally ill or gravely injured to have a humane death in the form of a mercy killing as a Christian act towards one's fellow human beings. A high dose of morphine, for example, when nothing further can be done.'

He fell silent for a moment, as if something had taken him back to a sombre past. Paula wondered whether he was old enough to have served in the war. But before she could find out, he was off again.

'While the first part makes complete sense from a humanitarian standpoint, in the second he deals with those referred to as the "mentally dead". These, according to Hoche, among others, are the type of people whose drawings we've just had the opportunity to appreciate, and who have no grasp of what they're living for. He describes it as an act of mercy to kill them and calls for new legislation making it possible for a doctor to do this within the bounds of the law – out of common humanity and for the good of the people, as he puts it.' Full of revulsion, he shook his head. 'But that's not all. Do you know who else he includes among the mentally dead?'

Paula was taken aback, and yet fascinated by the vehemence of his feelings on the subject. She'd actually hoped for an inspiring conversation about art but at the same time was flattered that, instead of sticking to the usual banalities, he was sharing his innermost feelings with a woman he'd only just met. 'No, but I can see you're going to tell me.'

He hesitated. 'My apologies,' he said. 'I did get rather worked up there but it's something that means a lot to me.'

'You don't need to apologise. I'm very interested, and where would we all be with no humane attitude to life? Please, do go on.'

'Are you sure?'

Was that a flicker of unease in his eyes?

'Quite sure, or else I wouldn't have asked.'

Before he could reply, the waitress had brought the coffee and cake, and Richard took a sip of coffee while Paula tried her almond cake. It was excellent.

'So,' she said to encourage him, 'you wanted to tell me more.'

He nodded but the passion he'd just demonstrated for the subject had gone. 'I'm not sure it's appropriate in such a pleasant environment.'

'Where else is there? Or do you feel it's inappropriate because subjects like this don't usually play a part in conversation when a man and a woman are sitting together in a café?'

He dropped his gaze as if caught out. 'Well, it might be like that with other women,' he conceded, 'but I appreciate the chance to talk about something serious instead of wasting time on trivia. I think this is an important subject and would be so grateful if you could broaden my view on it.'

'Really?' Paula smiled. 'Would it help if I told you that I fobbed off my friend with an excuse so I could sit here now with you?'

'Probably not,' he admitted, and his uncertain expression turned into a smile so subtle it showed only in his eyes.

'When I read Hoche's publication, what shocked me in particular was his inclusion of elderly people with senility among the mentally dead, as well as people like the artist wounded on active service who

Professor Habermann mentioned. That's a clear case of someone who fought for his fatherland, paid for it with his mental and physical integrity, and in return gets labelled mentally dead while someone tots up what he's costing the nation – the very same nation he was protecting when he sacrificed his health for ever.'

It was back, that bitter look in his eyes, and Paula wondered again if he was speaking from personal experience, so she asked the question.

'Were you in the war?'

'No, I was too young, and that was probably a good thing.'

'Would you otherwise have volunteered?'

'Absolutely not.'

'Not many men would admit that today.'

'Are you disappointed in me now?'

Paula took a sip of her coffee. 'Why should I be? It takes far more courage to stand by an opinion that's unpopular with broad sections of society, because you end up lumped together with the unpatriotic types.'

'Don't tell me you mean the Social Democrats?'

'Aren't they generally viewed as unpatriotic?' Her retort was brisk, only to see how he'd react.

'Is someone deemed as unpatriotic simply because he rejects war? Isn't it another, very special form of patriotism to want peace and prosperity for the homeland? And without the need for weapons and fighting?'

Paula nodded. 'I most definitely didn't mean to insult you. I simply wanted to hear how you'd respond.'

'And was it what you expected?'

'It was no less than I'd expected. I was quite simply curious. Most of the graduates and students that I know are types who remain loyal to the Kaiser and mourn the good old days and have little faith in the Republic. You're quite different.'

'Different in a good way or shockingly different?' His eyes twinkled, as though he knew what she'd say.

'Different in a nice way,' she acknowledged. 'I think it's refreshing that you can talk so openly on such difficult subjects, even though I'm a woman.'

'Why shouldn't I talk openly with a woman?'

'Yes, why indeed? I've asked myself that very question over and over again. It seems to inhibit a lot of men, as though a woman needs only a pretty face, a good child-bearing pelvis and no brain.'

'Oh well, as a woman trained in anatomy, you can easily parry that by telling them that it's not the external dimensions of the pelvis that help in childbirth but its inner diameter, something which is not visible from the outside.'

His eyes were twinkling again, and Paula tried hard to stay serious but finally had to laugh. 'You're impossible, Herr Hellmer. Now I beg you . . .'

'Please, call me Richard, Fräulein Engelhardt.'

'Oh, so I'm to call you Richard and you're sticking with Fräulein Engelhardt?'

'I'd like very much to call you Paula, if you'll permit me to do so.'

'I hereby grant you permission, Richard.' She took another sip from her cup. 'And now you have to tell me why you're so different from all the other students I've met.'

'It could be because I'm the first person in my family to have the privilege of going to university.' He paused, as if he were watching to see the effect his words had on her. 'My father's a master carpenter. He has a big workshop in Rothenburgsort with three journeymen and two apprentices.'

'Didn't your father want you to take over the family business?'

'No, my older brother was supposed to do that.'

'Supposed to?'

'He was at Verdun.' The brevity of his reply was such that Paula didn't like to ask more. The mention of Verdun reduced everyone to silence – the final resting place of countless young men, the place of nightmares – a subject not discussed in the presence of young ladies, or not in her usual circles at least.

'I'm so sorry,' she said gently.

'So am I. He was a magnificent young man but not cut out for war. His death affected everything.' He took a deep breath. 'I know that certain things can no longer be changed. We can but try to make the future better.'

'Is that why you're studying medicine and are so interested in psychiatry?'

'Among other things.'

It was clear to Paula that he didn't want to talk about it and she respected that, even though she was desperate to know what drove him on. She finished her coffee. Richard noticed her empty cup and asked if she'd like another.

'If there's still time then yes, please.' She looked at the large clock on the wall as she spoke. It was a quarter to eight.

'Oh, is that the time already? I hadn't realised.'

'Nor had I,' she said. 'It was very good to talk with you on such serious and weighty issues, Richard.'

'Would you like to do this again, Paula?'

'Very much. And I'd like to know more about the art movements you mentioned before.'

He hesitated and Paula noticed how he swallowed hard before speaking, as if he were having to summon up all his courage. 'Would you be interested in going to the city art gallery with me this Saturday, and then on to the Galerie Commeter?'

'I would be very interested indeed,' she said, beaming at him.

'Would you like to pick me up on Saturday at two?'

'If you'll give me your address.' He began to reach for his briefcase to find something to write with, but Paula quickly put her hand on his arm.

'I thought you might see me home this evening to be sure nothing happens to me on the way.' Even as she spoke, she was amazed at her own daring. That was more like Leonie's approach to men.

'Forgive me for not having suggested that myself. Of course I'll see you safely home.' He called over the waitress and paid and then helped Paula into her coat.

When they said goodbye a little later at her father's front door, Paula didn't know what to make of her emotions. Even though not a hint of romance had passed between them her heart was pounding, and whenever she closed her eyes, he was there in her mind. She was touched by the candour with which he had treated her as an equal and shared his feelings, thoughts and beliefs, and perhaps that was why she felt so elated.

Chapter 2

Over the next few days, Paula caught herself constantly looking out for Richard on campus, but with no success. Although she knew this was because of the way their new university was organised, she was still disappointed. The old-established institutions had lecture halls and libraries, while Eppendorf General Hospital had only one lecture hall and that was still under construction. For the time being lectures were held in the main building at Dammtor. Students in later semesters spent most of their time at Eppendorf General, while those less far on in their studies went there only for anatomy presentation and dissection, and thus Paula moved largely within the confines of the main university, where lectures in natural sciences took place.

'You can't get him out of your head, can you?' In a gap between lectures, she and Leonie were sitting in the café Richard had introduced her to. Since then Paula had become quite a regular. She'd told Leonie it was the delicious cake and welcoming atmosphere that attracted her to the place and was close to believing this herself, except for the fact that every time the door opened she felt an irresistible urge to look over and see who was coming in.

'Who on earth d'you mean?' Paula said, doing her best to look indifferent, but she knew it was useless. Once Leonie was on the scent, there was no escape.

'Hey, you know exactly who I'm talking about! The nice-looking one with the dark hair and blue eyes – the one you talked to for ages after that lecture. Did he take you out somewhere after I'd gone?'

Paula gave a tactical cough, wondering why she was being so evasive. Nothing further had happened between her and Richard. They'd simply had an interesting conversation with no ulterior motives. Why on earth did she feel as though Leonie's harmless question might break the spell?

'He brought me here to this café – that's how I know about it,' she replied eventually.

'Aha. I've been wondering why you've been heading so determinedly in this direction the last few days. And? Are you hoping to find him here? A little tête-à-tête in a familiar environment?' Leonie gave her a conspiratorial wink.

'No. I like the cake.' As if in confirmation, she speared a small piece of almond cake with her dessert fork and lifted it to her lips with great relish.

'Oh, of course, the cake. So aren't you going to see him again?'

'That's not what I said.'

'Now we're getting somewhere. Any details?'

'I'm afraid you'll be disappointed, as my kind of detail will definitely bore you. But tell me instead how you got on with Felix and Eckehard. One woman escorted by two men – didn't you feel like a princess with a pair of eager courtiers?'

'Paula darling, don't change the subject. Felix and Eckehard were absolutely charming but overdid the wooing. It was rather like being a princess watching her jousting knights aiming to dent each other's shining armour. They were more interested in outdoing one another with witty remarks than in paying any attention to me – it was exhausting. You should have come along to give me some support. But you had something more worthwhile of your own, am I right?'

'Compared with what happened to you, then yes, you could say that. We had quite a serious discussion, and it really opened my mind.'

'Right, now I'm really curious! You mean that men can actually talk about something serious in female company?'

'Richard can.'

'So it's Richard – Richard who?'

'Richard Hellmer.'

'Oh yes, I've heard about him. The remarkable Richard, the man who divides opinion.'

'In what way "divides opinion"?'

'Did he tell you his father's a carpenter?'

'Yes, but I don't see what that has to do with anything . . .'

'What?' Leonie cut across her. 'Come off it, Paula! It's considered so shocking that women are now allowed to attend university, but at least you and I come from the right stratum of society, even if there are certain elements who want to ruin it for us and send us off to be wives or nurses instead.' She reached for her handbag, took out her cigarette case together with an elegant ivory cigarette-holder and lit up. Paula knew it wasn't the smoking that Leonie enjoyed, so much as the disapproval of the tight-lipped married ladies nearby as she sat there posing like a flapper. 'And now that even the proles are sending their children to university'—she paused for effect and drew on her cigarette—'then the red revolution isn't far off. And the people who go on about all this probably fear the red revolution less than their fathers' wrath if a carpenter's son should turn out to be the best student of his intake.' Leonie sat back, her cigarette-holder poised between index and middle fingers, looking relaxed, elegant and seductive all in one go.

'So you're really saying he fits in well with us? He certainly doesn't act like he's trying to provoke, quite the opposite. And anyway, what a student's father does for a living is irrelevant as long as it's a respectable trade that pays the fees.'

'And shouldn't it also be irrelevant whether we're male or female? Have you been swotting for your anatomy certificate? It'll be very interesting to be examined by Professor Hempel on the internal pelvic organs. Knowing him, he'll ask us idiotic questions about the uterus. Then he'll repeat that ridiculous line about the atrophied uterus and its effects on a woman's intellect. Or was it the other way round? Is it intellect that causes the uterus to atrophy?' Leonie sent a smoke ring to the ceiling.

'But you'll still smile sweetly rather than giving your actual opinion?'

'Indeed. As a psychiatrist's daughter, you'll know that when dealing with idiots it's best to say, *Yes, absolutely, you're quite right*, and give them a kindly smile to stop them throwing a fit and leaping around like crazed monkeys.'

Paula giggled. 'It's a shame he doesn't know what you really think of him.'

'It's just as well that he doesn't! Unlike how the remarkable Richard sees us, in Hempel's eyes we're mere women. Not class warriors.'

'He's the son of a respectable master carpenter, not a class warrior. His father's business seems to have weathered our period of rampant inflation well, given that he's keeping three lads and two apprentices busy in his workshop – that's something to be proud of and far from proletarian. It's a solid professional trade, no different, as far as I can see, to the practice of a general practitioner.'

As she spoke, she was also thinking of the husband of a cousin of hers, a consultant in general medicine, who'd lost all his inheritance to inflation and had hanged himself in the attic. Malicious gossip had it that he'd been too broke even to afford a pistol to finish the job in style.

'I realise that,' said Leonie good-naturedly. She smiled. 'And the more you say about him and the more you defend him, the more curious I am. So what's this about your discussion that opened your mind?'

Paula hesitated before relating her conversation with Richard and describing his views on life. Leonie listened attentively, her light-hearted mood giving way to solemnity, something she hid as a rule behind the mocking face she showed in public.

'I envy you,' Leonie commented. 'I don't mean for the subject matter but for the fact that with you he felt at liberty to treat you as an equal. No wonder you're thinking about him all the time.'

Her reaction surprised Paula.

'But if this is what you're looking for, why do you make do with those shallow flirty types? What's preventing you from seeing the chap opposite as a human being first and a man second?'

'Maybe I don't want to come across as icy.'

'Charming. Is that why you smoke? To seem fiery?'

Leonie, taken aback for a moment, burst out laughing. 'Touché, my love. Now tell me, when are you seeing Richard again?'

'Saturday. He's picking me up after lunch and we're going to the main city art gallery.'

'How very elegant! Just make sure that all the cultural chit-chat doesn't make him forget you're a woman.'

'I don't think he'll do that, and if he did, I'd know how to remind him.'

'Paula dearest, you really are a dark horse! People whisper about me, saying I'm out to catch a husband when I'm only flirting, but the truth is you'll catch one long before I do. But that won't be too difficult because I'll probably never marry.'

'You can't be serious!'

Leonie took a last puff on her cigarette. 'Oh, but I am! The times we live in offer so many opportunities: we've got the vote, we're allowed to study, but the moment we marry we're nothing and not even allowed to work without the express agreement of the dear spouse. And because men want to hold on to their power over us, nothing will change. There's only one thing that makes us superior and that's our brain. A saucy wink, a bit of a wiggle in all the right places and they're panting after us like lovesick puppies, and we can get them to do whatever we want, provided they believe they still have something to conquer. For a while, it's an entertaining and harmless way of making up for all the other indignities.'

'Is that why you seek out men who can't compete with you? Isn't that terribly boring?'

'Mostly it's amusing, and it proves again and again that I'm right. Men aren't good for much more than that. Still, I'll see how it goes with you and Richard, and then I'll either envy you for finding something quite special, or I'll pity you if it turns out to be a fantasy and all men are in fact the same; if they appreciate your femininity, they overlook your intellect, or they appreciate comradely intellect and overlook the femininity.'

This gave Paula plenty more to think about. Her father had always told her how much he'd appreciated her mother's excellent mind, first as a nursing professional and then as a married woman sitting in on lectures in medicine as a guest and, to general astonishment, successfully completing the course of study. Paula remembered her father's description of the obstacles encountered by her mother, who, purely on the grounds of her sex, was refused a licence to practise medicine in spite of passing all the examinations. She had nonetheless worked with him in his surgery until Paula was born, although only rarely thereafter. Paula had never had the chance to ask her mother why, as she had died from diphtheria when Paula was only six.

From that moment on, Paula's father had tried to take on her mother's role as well as his own, to encourage and support her. It was only much later that she realised how she had helped to fill the gap in his own life. Although there had been quite a few ladies only too willing to become the new Frau Engelhardt, he had never remarried because he wanted to devote himself to his daughter. And in any case, no other woman came close to Paula's mother in his view, while not one of them was anything like good enough so far as Paula was concerned. She was aware of her power over her father and was not prepared to share him with some stranger, neither as a child, nor as she grew up.

Only as a grown woman could she see how her relationship with her father had influenced the way she herself dealt with men. She had never felt excluded and had always believed that her views and opinions would be taken seriously as a matter of course. She wondered what her father would make of Richard Hellmer.

Chapter 3

Richard hated the operating theatre but knew how to conceal his loathing. It would never have occurred to Professor Wehmeyer that his model student experienced profound revulsion at every operation.

Because he could name every artery, nerve and muscle like a shot but opened his mouth only when asked, unlike his friend and fellow student Fritz Ellerweg, who was forever asking questions, Richard was regularly given the honour of holding the clamp while the professor performed the procedure. Fritz, meanwhile, who definitely wanted to be a surgeon, had to content himself with a place in the second row, behind the theatre sister. He knew that Richard would gladly have made way for him and so felt no resentment, especially as Richard had told him the real reason for this silence that the professor valued so much. He battled with nausea, not because of what he could see – that didn't bother him, quite the opposite. In fact, Richard found the positioning of the inner organs, nerves and blood vessels absolutely fascinating, particularly as no two bodies were quite the same and the varying courses taken by arteries and veins were remarkable. Consequently, he had always been enthusiastic about dissection in anatomy classes, although that was all about dead bodies that had been drained of their blood and kept in formalin for months before their use on the anatomy course, when they were stripped down little by little over the course of a whole semester.

No, for Richard it was because of the odours. He struggled with this mix of disinfectant, blood and other body fluids. Even worse was when a suspected stomach ulcer turned out to be a malignant growth that had eaten into the gut. This gave off an absolutely vile odour. Eventually, his sister had suggested that he sprinkle a few drops of eau de cologne on his surgical mask beforehand and this at least had helped him deal with the smell, but did nothing to address the nausea. To distract himself, he would silently recite the name of every artery and nerve he could see, and as a result, when the professor asked a question, Richard generally knew the answer immediately, whereas Fritz found he was still thinking about it.

Richard had tried to get Fritz to practise with him, so that the role of the professor's favourite could go to his friend, but in vain. Fritz was so fascinated by the precision and practicalities involved in making the incisions that he paid far more attention to the professor's hands than to the human body in front of them.

'Can I really not persuade you to devote yourself to the right part of the medical profession?' Professor Wehmeyer asked him yet again on the day Richard had correctly named the branches leading off from the *truncus coeliacus* and the various arteries leading away from it. 'You have real talent, more than most others.'

'Thank you, Professor.' Richard kept his reply short and wondered how Professor Wehmeyer could possibly have formed this opinion, as he'd never yet used a scalpel. For sure, the professor had twice left the stitching to him, but in Richard's view stitching was quite different from the art of surgery itself.

'I gather you're preparing a dissertation on mental illness,' continued the professor. 'Do you really want to squander your talents by becoming a mad-doctor?'

'I fear you overestimate my capabilities, Professor. Anyone can hold the clamp.'

'But it's not just anyone who can perceive beauty in the bodies placed before us and feel so immediately at ease with such a complex anatomical structure.'

Richard said nothing. He didn't want to go any deeper into this, particularly as the professor had only recently witnessed another student making insulting comments about Richard's family background. The professor had kindly but firmly informed the culprit that a trade is the best of foundations for a good living and that the grandfather of the famous surgeon Professor Sauerbach had been a cobbler. 'Never forget,' he'd said, 'that we're skilled craftsmen too, and it's the medical trade that we put to practical use for the good of humanity.'

A further question from the professor cut across Richard's recollections.

'Where are you with your thesis?' he asked as he deftly tied ligatures on the adjacent blood vessels before performing a resection of the stomach.

'I've completed about half of it.'

'That's a shame.'

'Sorry, sir?'

'I meant it's a shame for me. I would have liked to make you part of my working team but it wouldn't be right to make you an offer if you're already so far into your PhD work.' He sighed.

'No, sir.'

As with the two previous operations, Professor Wehmeyer left the stitching to Richard and once more praised his manual dexterity. Meanwhile, Fritz stood silently in the background. He remained silent long after they'd left the operating theatre and got rid of their masks, gloves and gowns.

'What's wrong?' asked Richard in the changing room as he put on his outdoor shoes and tied the laces. 'Are you annoyed he asked me about moving up into his team?'

'Yes,' Fritz admitted. 'For months I've been wanting to ask him if he'd take me on as one of his PhD students, but he barely notices me and would rather promote someone who's not really interested.'

Richard straightened up. 'Then don't go on waiting. Speak to him about it.'

Fritz was staring at his shoes. 'I don't think I'd have much success. You know how he looks at me whenever I ask him a question.'

'Listen, I've told you so many times, he doesn't want to discuss how to perform the incision and other surgical technicalities, he wants to test your knowledge. The rest comes later.'

'Well, what should I say to him? What can I offer him now?'

Instead of answering, Richard said, 'Why d'you want to be a surgeon?'

'I don't know how to explain it,' Fritz said, rising to his feet with a sigh.

'Try. Explain to me why this is the only thing in life you want to do, why it's the dream that possesses you day and night.'

Just then the doors to the changing room flew open and two other students came in to gown up for the next operation.

'Let's talk about it outside,' Fritz said, reaching for his coat and briefcase.

Richard nodded, packed his bag and casually threw his coat over his shoulder.

It was a beautifully warm October day with more than a trace of summer still, even though yellowing leaves had begun to drift here and there around the hospital grounds. Aside from a nurse pushing a man in a wheelchair along the neat sandy pathway, there was nobody to be seen.

'I always wanted to be a surgeon,' Fritz said at last. 'My father's a general practitioner and I've seen all too often how he's the one to make the right diagnosis but then has to leave the rest of the treatment to hospital-based colleagues. I want to do more than just prescribing pills and potions, taking temperatures and offering the right tincture for every little ache and pain. Right from the very first time I ever stood in an operating theatre I realised how fascinating it is to explore the human body anew every time. Yes, there are fixed structures, but you can't ever be sure what else you're going to come across, and then you have to find a complex solution, and fast. I love the challenge and feel sure I'd be up to it.'

'But that's precisely what he's testing for every time he asks how quickly we recognise which artery or nerve we're looking at. Why d'you always take so long to answer?'

'Maybe because I spend too long thinking it through. For me, it's not just about coming out with the Latin as fast as possible, it's because I want to weigh up what it might mean for the course of the whole operation. And by then you've already given the answer,' Fritz said, giving his friend a playful cuff on the arm.

'You already know why I do that – to try and take my mind off how ill I'm feeling in there.'

'Yes, of course, and that's why I'm not angry with you about it. But it still annoys me sometimes.'

'I'm sorry. But I still think you should explain all that to Professor Wehmeyer. Best do it today.'

Fritz lowered his gaze.

'Hey, Fritz, no one who earns his living cutting open bellies or sawing off legs can afford to be a coward.'

For a moment Fritz was taken aback but then he gave a shout of laughter. 'You do realise you're a complete crackpot, don't you?'

'I can live with the insult if you're a budding surgeon, but to be called a crackpot would be really worrying if it came from a psychiatrist.'

'And you say that with a straight face.' Fritz couldn't stop laughing.

'Now you're in a good mood, seize the moment. As far as I know, Professor Wehmeyer's always in his office around two o'clock.'

And so Fritz sought him out the same day. Quite how the conversation went, Richard never knew, but when they both walked into the operating theatre the following day Professor Wehmeyer asked Fritz to hold the clamp and asked him very specific questions about the operation and incision procedures, all of which Fritz, after brief consideration, was able to answer to the complete satisfaction of the professor.

'It seems to me I have underestimated you, Herr Ellerweg. I'm going to keep my eye on you, and if you continue to prove so convincing, I can well imagine bringing you on to my professional team.'

He turned then to Richard. 'I hope you will not consider it disrespectful regarding your own ability if Herr Ellerweg takes your usual place during the next operation.'

'Absolutely not, sir,' Richard answered soberly, pleased that his surgical mask concealed his smile of relief.

Chapter 4

All week Paula had looked forward to seeing Richard again and to going to the gallery with him, but the closer the minute hand on the wall clock in her father's front room crept towards the two, the more restless she felt. It certainly didn't help her nerves to hear their housekeeper, Frau Koch, remarking repeatedly that she welcomed seeing Paula turn her attention to nice young men rather than just studying.

Her father had lowered his newspaper and looked at his daughter with a mixture of scepticism and amusement.

'So is that how it is?' he asked.

'Hardly! We're only looking around the city art gallery together. I've told you he knows a lot about modern art movements and hopes to become a psychiatrist when he finishes.'

'I'll tell you one thing,' observed Frau Koch as she poured coffee for Paula's father, 'he seems to be a thoroughly nice young man and Fräulein Paula would do well to consider him. Cultured, and a budding doctor at that . . .' She looked enchanted at the very thought.

'I presume he looks the part too?' her father said with a broad smile.

Paula felt cornered by the pair of them and had a response on the tip of her tongue, but held back when she realised that, although it would have amused her father, it would have shocked Frau Koch. And so she kept her counsel and watched the big hand approach the hour. Only a few more minutes to go . . .

She took another look at her dark blue, calf-length dress. With it she was wearing dark blue silk stockings and black patent shoes. Her dead mother's pearl necklace was the only jewellery she'd permitted herself, aside from her plain gold earrings.

As soon as the hour hand reached two, there was a ring at the door. Frau Koch was, Paula noticed wryly, a good deal faster in answering than she normally was.

'On the dot,' her father remarked, with a note of irony in his voice that bothered her. Perhaps he didn't like Richard coming here to collect her, she wondered, but then pushed this out of her mind as Frau Koch returned with Richard. She had taken his hat and coat, and he was carrying a bunch of flowers. Paula and her father stood to receive him while Richard presented her with the flowers, his face grave and respectful but his eyes full of smiles. There were five white roses and four pale pink.

'Thank you so much,' she whispered, then remembered they were not alone. 'Papa, this is Richard Hellmer, a fellow student. Richard – my father, Dr Engelhardt.'

'How do you do?' said Paula's father, extending his hand.

'How do you do, sir?' replied Richard, returning the handshake. For a moment Paula thought she saw a sceptical frown on her father's forehead, but before she could look more closely, Frau Koch had returned with a vase.

'At least he knows the language of flowers,' she whispered in Paula's ear. 'White for youth, beauty and innocence and pink for the ties that bind.'

Glaring at the housekeeper, Paula handed her the flowers so she could arrange them in the vase.

Her father then asked Richard, 'Would you like a cup of coffee? As far as I know, the next tram leaves in quarter of an hour.'

'That would be nice, thank you, but we don't need the tram. My father has been so kind as to let me use his car today.'

Paula was all ears. A car? Even in their circles this was unusual. Her father seemed to be thinking something similar.

'Your father has a car?' His voice gave away his surprise.

'Well, er, yes . . .' Richard gave an awkward cough.

'Please, do sit down,' said Paula's father. Frau Koch had already brought a cup for Richard and busied herself with pouring his coffee.

Richard accepted the seat offered him.

Paula's father wanted to know more. 'What type of car is it?'

'An Opel 4 PS. But it's a delivery vehicle.'

'A delivery vehicle? That's unusual.'

'Papa, I hadn't got around to telling you that Richard's father owns a large carpentry workshop in Rothenburgsort.'

'A carpentry workshop?' Dr Engelhardt said, raising his eyebrows, and Paula finally acknowledged to herself why she hadn't previously mentioned Richard's family background. In her mind, she'd never have admitted her father's prejudice but she knew deep down that, in spite of his apparent tolerance, he could be highly critical of the company his daughter kept. Tradesmen were, of course, decent people but they didn't belong to the professional elite that surrounded her father. Everybody admired their skill and, if satisfied, recommended them on to others, but one didn't invite them to social occasions.

'Ah, yes, of course. Your father's business must be doing very well for him to see a car as a worthwhile investment.'

'The investment has certainly been worth it.' Richard sounded more confident now. 'Two years ago we still had a cart and a couple of horses, but the car is more economical to run and freeing up the stables meant we could extend the work area and still use part as a garage.'

'Well, that sounds like a truly flourishing business. Didn't your father have plans for you to take it on one day?'

'No. I had an elder brother and that would have been his future but now my father's hopes are pinned on his grandson, my sister's son. Karl has just turned nine. As soon as he's home from school, he's straight in the workshop.' A fond smile played on Richard's lips, making it obvious how attached he was to his nephew.

Paula's father saw that Richard had finished his coffee. 'Well now, I won't delay you any longer,' he said as he got to his feet. 'You have quite a cultural afternoon ahead, from what my daughter tells me.'

'That's right,' said Richard, standing up now too. 'We want to go to the city art gallery and look at contemporary work compared with the Old Masters.'

'An unusual hobby for a young man from your sphere.'

'Is it?'

'Well, you know, I thought the modern place to go was the picture house.'

'Maybe we'll do that another time.' Richard smiled politely as he said this, but this time the smile was only on his lips, not in his eyes.

Paula stood as Frau Koch brought in Richard's hat and coat.

'I wish you both a pleasant afternoon,' her father said to them. Paula understood straight away what lay behind this seemingly trivial friendly remark. She was to spend only the afternoon with Richard. Her father expected her back for the evening. Glancing at Richard, she wondered what he thought of her father's behaviour. Had he been offended by her father's attitude towards his family background, or did he simply see it more as a father's concern for a daughter stretching her wings?

But Richard didn't give anything away. As soon as he and Paula were out on the street, he stopped next to a green vehicle. From the front it looked like a normal saloon car and it was only the absence of rear windows and the presence of a tailgate that gave away its other function.

'What an unusual colour! I've never seen that before.'

'It's classic for this model – that's why people call it the tree frog.'

'That's original!' she said with a laugh.

'The French think Opel's guilty of copying the Citroën Type C. That only ever comes in yellow, so people say this is the same car but in green. It's fine by me – I like green.'

'It's good that it's green, so nobody can confuse us with the post van.'

They both laughed and Richard ushered Paula into the passenger seat before climbing in behind the steering wheel.

As they set off, Paula wondered whether the car was called the tree frog not only on account of its colour but also the way it hopped and skipped over the unmade road. It wasn't until they had turned on to the asphalted road that it felt as if the car had suspension.

'My father toyed with the idea of investing in a car,' Paula said as they drove towards the city centre. 'He took me with him when he went to look at a vehicle that a colleague of his had used for years on house visits and wanted to replace with something newer. It was an open-topped two-seater.'

'And why did he decide against it?'

'He realised it would have been nothing but a vanity purchase because he doesn't actually need a car. The tram stops right outside our door and he rarely does house visits, and you can take an awful lot of taxi rides for the purchase price of a car.'

'That's true,' Richard conceded. 'Although since Opel moved to assembly line production, their cars cost a lot less, and automobile clubs are springing up all over the place. If I were a betting man, I'd say the future belongs to the motor industry.'

'But it's still an exception to be picked up by a young man with a car,' she said cheekily.

'I should hope so!' he replied. 'Though I'm afraid your father wasn't too pleased.'

'Not at all. He was surprised, that's all, precisely because it is so unusual.'

Richard only nodded. Paula wondered whether she should say anything further on the matter but decided to let it rest. A lot of things could turn into problems if given too much importance.

When they reached the gallery, Richard parked and came round to open the car door for her.

She was already a regular there and knew much of the collection well, tending to spend her time on the Old Masters. These, in her father's view, nicely rounded off her education in the humanities, whereas he saw the Expressionists as nothing more than a variation within the modern art movement and something that wouldn't last.

'True art,' he liked to say, 'is demonstrated through its ability to command our admiration of the artist's skill in capturing reality in its most honest form.'

She repeated these words to Richard as they looked at the Expressionist pieces.

'In many ways, he's right,' Richard acknowledged. 'It's admirable the way painters have over the centuries so successfully portrayed the realities of their times in an idealised form. As artists, however, they've outlived their usefulness.'

'Why is that?'

'Because of the arrival of photography. Why would a painter bother depicting something as it is, when any halfway decent photographer can do that with a camera? Surely an artist with any credibility at all would want to go beyond the old boundaries and stand apart from what the lens can capture?'

'So you're saying that photography has ruined the concept of fine art?'

'No, it's simply liberated art from being forced to portray every detail of reality.'

Paula thought about this for a while before saying anything further. 'Where does your interest in art come from?' she asked eventually. 'And for modern art at that?'

It took him a while to respond, but finally he swallowed hard and said, 'It's . . .' He faltered for a moment, and then went on. 'It's to do with my brother.'

'Who fell at Verdun?' Her voice was full of sympathy.

'He didn't fall there. He died after the war.'

'From war wounds?'

'That's an interesting question with several different answers depending on your views.'

He didn't say anything further, leaving Paula confused. She was about to ask him another question, but the suffering and pain written across his face made her keep her silence. The self-confident, cheerful young man, never at a loss for an intelligent answer to every question, had vanished. Now she was seeing a very different side to his personality: solemn, perhaps even melancholic. It made her wonder whether she'd met the real Richard yet, and how many sides there might be to his character.

For a while they went on from one painting to the next without speaking, until Paula could no longer bear the silence.

'Are we still going to the Galerie Commeter?' she asked.

Richard took out his watch. 'It's just closed, unfortunately, but we could see what's in the window if you like.'

She noticed with relief that the melancholia had disappeared, and it didn't occur again all day, neither as they strolled hand in hand along the lakeside path to the Galerie Commeter, nor when they looked at the art in the window and Paula saw a Surrealist painting for the first time in her life, not even when they walked on to the Alster Pavilion to sit over an ice cream sundae and watch the steamboats.

In fact, it could have been the perfect afternoon, had not August Lachner and two men unknown to Paula stepped inside the Pavilion just behind them. Paula noticed how Richard tensed as they entered, all the more so when the trio spotted him and headed straight for their table.

'What a charming coincidence,' enthused Lachner. 'Delighted to see you here, Richard. And you are Fräulein . . .?' He smiled at Paula, while Richard's mouth hardened.

'Paula Engelhardt,' she said, introducing herself.

'It's a pleasure to meet you. August Lachner, and these are my fellow students, Peter Watuscheck and Johannes Möller.'

His colleagues briefly acknowledged Paula. Watuscheck was red-haired, tall, thin as a rake, while Johannes Möller was more of a Greek athlete.

'May we join you?' August Lachner asked Richard, who gave a slight nod in reply, although his face indicated he'd much rather throw them out of the building. The three men seemed not to notice, or if they did, they deliberately ignored it.

'Forgive the interruption, Fräulein Engelhardt,' Lachner went on after taking a seat. 'Richard's one of our fellow students and I didn't want to miss an opportunity once again to try to persuade him to join our organisation.'

'I'm still not interested,' replied Richard with exaggerated politeness.

'But surely no right-thinking man could possibly reject what we stand for? Perhaps you could persuade him.' Lachner smiled at her once again, and if she hadn't already formed an impression of him at Professor Habermann's lecture, she wouldn't have minded him joining them at all. The image she'd previously had of him was quite different from the one he presented now. Opposite her sat a youthful figure, blond-haired and freckled, little more than eighteen by his appearance, although he must have been in his mid-twenties.

'What's this all about?' she asked, curious to find out what had happened between Lachner and Richard.

'First, may I enquire, Fräulein Engelhardt, whether we have had previous acquaintance?'

'Fleetingly, yes, at Professor Habermann's lecture.'

'You were there? As a guest?'

'No, I'm a registered student.'

August Lachner nodded in recognition. 'Very good. I greatly appreciate seeing a woman as an equal companion to a man.'

'Is that a quote from a Wagner opera?'

'No, it's my own opinion. Our movement respects the role of women, because a woman is the nucleus of the family. Without her, the people cannot exist, and in my view women are predestined to work in gynaecology and midwifery, where they are wholly superior to men.'

Paula stared at Lachner in some confusion, not sure whether she was flattered or discouraged by his remarks.

'Forgive me, Fräulein Engelhardt, I digress. You wanted to know what this is about.' He reached into his inner jacket pocket, took out a pamphlet and placed it on the table.

Emblazoned across the front in Gothic script were the words *National Socialist German Students' League*.

'A league? Why are you showing me this? That'll be an organisation for men.'

'As far as membership goes, you're right, Fräulein Engelhardt. But the ideals we espouse are the same as yours. We believe that access to study can no longer be the preserve of the affluent elite, but should be for everyone with the ability, regardless of family background. One of the founders of our student league, Wilhelm Tempel, is the son of a master cobbler and represents the conviction that National Socialism must fight against the entrepreneurs' obsession with profit and in favour of the betterment of workers and, if need be, do so shoulder to shoulder with social democracy.'

'So why the National Socialism? Why not go straight to Social Democracy?' asked Richard.

'Because the SocDems lack the guts to fight for the concerns of our people. All we see is their cringing servility towards foreigners and their squandering of everything we own.'

'Harsh words,' said Richard, breaking in.

'True words,' Lachner corrected him. 'Our army was unbeaten in the field, and what happened? Our unpatriotic leftie friends stabbed the military in the back and negotiated a shameful peace that even our grandchildren will have to pay for. And then there's the massive sequestration of land!' His previously boyish face had now taken on the look of a grown man's. 'A quarter of our agriculture now lies in Polish hands, but even that isn't enough for our enemies. Think back to the breach of international law when the Frenchies occupied the Rhineland three years ago. Doesn't it enrage you to see our wounded war veterans, who sacrificed their health for our people, begging on the street? And what do the Social Democrats and the German People's Party do? They bow and scrape, then tug their forelocks at the people who've ground us into the dust instead of standing tall and opposing them like real men. It's high time Germany woke up and gave thought to its greatness. Our research is the best in the world – no other nation has achieved so much in the field of science and medicine. And yet we're supposed to go on kowtowing to neighbouring countries instead of looking them straight in the eye?' As he spoke, Lachner had become increasingly worked up, and Paula had to concede that he'd touched a nerve for her too. The unfairness of the Treaty of Versailles and the occupation of the Rhineland had upset her father as much as it had Lachner.

'If you remember,' Richard remarked, 'all the parties fought side by side against the unlawful occupation of the Rhineland, because here there were only Germans – no communists, no other lefties, no Nazis. Everyone took part in the sabotage and it was a Social Democrat government that called the general strike. At the same time the Minister for the Exterior, Stresemann from the German People's Party, played a crucial role in peacefully bringing about an end to this occupation and a review of the tough conditions set at Versailles. He's said to have been nominated for this year's Nobel Peace Prize.'

Lachner sniffed in disdain. 'Nobel Peace Prize? Don't make me laugh. A mere sugar lump for a well-behaved donkey who wants to persuade us that he's fighting for the German people, while the truth is he's prostrating himself before the occupying powers and letting them lead him by the nose, when what he should be doing is banging the table like a real statesman.'

'August, our opinions are so far apart, and not only on this, that there is no organisation in which we could possibly stand side by side, so leave it now, please.'

Lachner glanced at his pair of supporters and they both nodded almost imperceptibly. 'As you wish,' he said to Richard. 'I fear you're failing to read the sign of the times. Social Democracy has reached the end of the road and will be swept away by the same storm that'll set the German flagship back on course and help our people regain their old greatness.' He stood up and his two friends immediately did the same, then he turned to Paula again.

'Fräulein Engelhardt, may I wish you a pleasant day, and perhaps you'll think about the company you keep. National Socialism also offers opportunities for development to intelligent young women such as yourself.'

'Good evening, Herr Lachner.'

Once the three men had gone, Richard screwed up the pamphlet they'd left on the table.

'Would he have annoyed you so much if he shared your opinion on the mentally ill?' asked Paula. 'I found some of his observations perfectly reasonable. The Treaty of Versailles and the Rhineland occupation were unjust – our people have had to let too much go.'

Richard nodded slowly. 'That's true. But realistically, what do we have apart from the negotiating table? We've lost the war, we have no power and have nothing more than diplomacy to keep matters in balance. And personally, I think Stresemann's doing a good job.'

'You seem to know a lot about politics.'

'Only what's in the papers.'

'So what is it that you dislike most about these new kind of socialists?'

'National Socialists,' Richard corrected her. 'They reject democracy. Everything they do is organised in accordance with the authoritarian leader principle, and this requires unconditional obedience to that leader. There are strange things going on. Apparently, the latest absurdity is that they greet each other by lifting their right arm and bawling, 'Heil Hitler!' – that's their leader's name.'

Paula burst out laughing. 'You're joking!'

'No, I'm absolutely serious.'

'That's one of the silliest things I've ever heard. I don't believe we need to waste any more time in thinking about these nutcases. No one will take them seriously.'

She expected Richard to nod in agreement, but he seemed remarkably worried and withdrawn, as if his thoughts had taken him far away.

'Tell me something, Paula,' he said at last. 'What would you have thought of Lachner if you'd met him for the first time today and not known his other views, especially as you agreed with some of his theories? Isn't it rather beguiling to hope there are simple solutions to our international and economic difficulties?'

'What's the matter, Richard? Are you completely against any such ideas?'

'No,' he admitted, 'but there are too many points where this ideology clashes with my own world view, even if I do share a few of Lachner's opinions.'

Paula gazed across Alster Lake. The setting sun bathed the water and the passing pleasure boats in a red-gold light. The afternoon her father had granted her was over, but everything within her fought against letting it end too soon. Richard seemed to read her thoughts.

'When does your father expect you back?'

'Does that matter?'

'It does to me. I don't want him to think badly of me.'

Paula let out a sigh. 'Then it's time for us to be leaving.'

Richard gestured to the waiter for the bill.

Slowly, they made their way back to his car, taking time to enjoy the sun going down and the glimmer of the gas lamps bordering the Alster as they lit up one by one.

'That new picture house is opening on Hoheluftchaussee next week,' said Richard when they reached the car. 'The Capitol. They say it has twelve hundred seats. Would you please . . .?' He hesitated then said in a low voice, 'Would you let me take you there, Paula?'

This new intimacy made her heart race. 'I most definitely would!'

'And what would your father say?' There was that smile again, but only in his eyes, while the set of his mouth appeared quite serious.

'As long as they've chosen something intellectually demanding for the premiere, he'd approve.'

'In that case, he'll welcome their choice of *Faust* with Emil Jannings as Mephisto.'

For a moment he stood very close to her, so close that Paula wondered whether he was expecting something more from her, but then he opened the passenger door to allow her to take her seat.

Although it was only seven thirty when Richard dropped her off at her front door and bid her a polite farewell, her father was already showing his impatience.

'That was a very long afternoon,' came his greeting. 'I hope you enjoyed it.'

Paula took no notice of the reproach in his voice and replied with deliberately exaggerated courtesy. 'Have you already eaten, Papa?'

'No, I've been waiting for you. Frau Koch has finished for the day but left everything ready.'

'That was very thoughtful of her.'

'That's her job, my child.'

'Of course, Papa. Shall we go through to the dining room?'

He accompanied his daughter in silence, and her stomach tensed. Her father never admonished her directly, and certainly never said any harsh words to her. Nevertheless, he had his own special way of expressing displeasure, and it had the power to sour a beautiful memory. She wondered whether this was because she had come home after seven, or had something to do with Richard himself, or was simply that Richard was a man. Her father was never like this when she went out with Leonie, and would even give her extra money for a taxi in case they were late.

She decided to confront the matter head on, so as soon as they'd taken their seats at the table, she said, 'Richard's invited me to go to the Capitol with him next week for the opening night.'

'I assume you've politely turned him down?'

'No, I was delighted to accept.'

Her father noisily cleared his throat. 'And you think he's the right sort of company for you to keep?'

'He's the best student in his semester, he's polite, kind, intelligent and his father runs a successful business that brings in more money than many general practitioners earn. What's so wrong with company like that, Papa?'

'I'm not yet sure what to think,' her father retorted. 'I've asked Frau Koch to find out about his family.'

'Why don't you send in a detective instead, Papa? Who knows – maybe the family aren't carpenters at all and the workshop is a façade for counterfeiters?'

'Paula, you're being childish.'

'Yes, Papa,' she said with sigh, thinking privately that she wouldn't be the only daughter having this sort of conversation with their father, but she was wary of voicing such thoughts. At least he hadn't been able to raise any real objections against Richard, which confirmed her suspicion that this was less about Richard's background and more about the fact that he was worried Richard would come between them.

Chapter 5

Richard loved his family and the chaos they generally created, but on this particular evening he was relieved he could avoid being quizzed by his sister, Margit, in the main living room, by retreating to the converted attic room he'd lived in since becoming a student. Margit was even nosier than his mother and had waylaid him at the front door. Fortunately, Margit's youngest, Lottchen, the pet name for eighteen-month-old Charlotte, pushed in between them, howling over some trifle, distracting Margit sufficiently for the moment that he was able to quickly sneak past.

As he hurried up the narrow wooden stairs he could still hear the children's voices clamouring for his sister and couldn't help but smile. Since their hasty wartime wedding ten years ago, Margit and Holger Mathieson had had five children: four boys and then Lottchen. Richard hoped that the blessing of babies had run its course now that Margit had her longed-for daughter at last. Without the backing of the family business, Holger and Margit would never have been able to afford such a large family.

Soon after their marriage Holger had returned to the Front, where he had been so badly wounded that his right lower leg had had to be amputated, which restricted the sort of work he could do in the carpentry workshop. It was because of this that Richard's father had found him jobs that did not require him to stand on his feet for too long, including taking on the bookkeeping. This had turned out to be a smart move, as Holger had quickly demonstrated a good ability with figures and a shrewd business acumen. Even six years earlier he had warned against keeping too much liquidity in the accounts because of creeping inflation, and thanks to this advice and a number of sound investments, including the purchase of a large area of land used for forestry outside the city, the carpentry business had come through the bleak times relatively unscathed.

This success had helped Holger come to terms with his disability, because without it, he would never have turned to bookkeeping and they would certainly have fallen victim to the crippling inflation and been forced to declare insolvency, along with so many other businesses. Richard and his father were of one mind on this – Holger was a godsend for the family, not only for the successful running of the business but also for his positive outlook on life: he always made the best of every stroke of fate, even when it was hard, and never more so than after the death of Richard's brother, Georg.

All this was racing through Richard's mind as he stepped into his attic room and set about lighting the stove, as the nights were already turning cold. As always, he paused to look at the framed photograph on the wall near the stove. He remembered all too well the day it was taken. Twelve years ago: September 1914. He'd been thirteen, while Georg had just turned nineteen and received his marching orders. The photo showed the whole family: from the left, his father, then Georg in uniform – his face proud and happy because he had no inkling how little honour there truly lay in dying for the fatherland – then came Richard, with seventeen-year-old Margit to his right, and finally, on the end, Mother.

Richard sighed deeply, closed the lid of the stove and sat down at his desk to study, but he couldn't concentrate on his books.

If his brother hadn't died, he probably wouldn't have studied medicine. Instead, on completing his carpentry apprenticeship straight after school, as his father had wanted, he would probably have studied history of art, as he'd always hoped. But Georg's agonising death had made Richard determined to play a part in preventing anything like this from happening again in the future. He was astonished that his father had made no protest when he'd announced that, instead of qualifying as a master craftsman and later taking over the business, he wanted to study medicine.

'I know you'll do the right thing,' his father had said, giving his son a warm pat on the shoulder. 'We'll find other ways of keeping the business in the family, and I'll be very proud of you. Show those smug doctors' sons the kind of material the Hellmers are made of!'

'Solid mahogany,' came Richard's swift response, making his father shout with laughter.

He'd known from the very first day that he'd made the right decision. Medicine meant something to him, as did the contact with people, so it was easy to ignore his fellow students' mockery and the silly remarks about his background. He kept quiet about his own carpentry training but lent a hand in his father's workshop when the business needed him.

After registering Dr Engelhardt's reaction, he was glad he'd kept this secret, even though he couldn't help being offended that he had to hide his skill at this respectable trade, as if it were some kind of flaw in his character. He wanted to be judged on all of his achievements, not just his academic background.

Fortunately, Paula seemed quite different. She saw him as he was, shared his opinions, but was also able to put forward her own views, and do so eloquently. He'd never met a woman he could talk with so openly, a woman with whom he had so many interests in common. On top of that she was exceptionally pretty, with her dark blonde hair and emerald eyes. He'd met her only a week ago, but already he knew this was a woman worth courting and fighting for – that had been clear to him right from their first visit to the café together, when he'd seen her eyes light up and reflect his own passion as he talked of art and psychiatry. From that very first evening he'd had to admit to himself that he'd fallen head over heels like a schoolboy. Her image had stayed in his mind and their outing today had further strengthened his feelings. No matter how much Paula's father looked down on him, he would show Dr Engelhardt that he was worthy of his daughter in all respects, of that he was absolutely determined. And anyway, the Hellmers were fashioned from solid mahogany and that was more noble, more enduring and harder than any German oak.

Chapter 6

For Paula the next few days passed in a mixture of euphoria and guilt. Every thought of Richard filled her with a joyful anticipation and sense of excitement that stole her appetite and left her in a daze, and yet at the same time she saw her father's uncertainty growing, not so much because of Richard but because of his fear of change. Since the death of his wife, his beloved daughter had become his entire life and now here she was, working towards her professional independence as well as making room in her heart for another man. Paula had to acknowledge that her feelings for Richard were making her father jealous. This became increasingly obvious when his scepticism persisted in spite of the fact that Frau Koch's investigations had revealed only the best about the Hellmer family.

'This is a hard-working, well-respected family of craftsmen,' she related on the evening prior to the film premiere Paula was so excited about. 'They have a lot of customers, and if the young Herr Hellmer can take time away from his studies on a Saturday, he works alongside them so they can fulfil all the orders.'

Dr Engelhardt's eyebrows raised more than a little. 'That doesn't say much about the quality of the work. Everyone should stick with what they're trained for. An aspiring doctor cannot do the work of a carpenter's lad – that can't possibly produce a decent result.'

'Well now,' said Frau Koch, leaning forward in an almost conspiratorial pose, 'so far as I can gather, his father insisted that he complete his apprenticeship before starting at the university, so he's actually fully qualified.' She lowered her gaze before continuing, 'And what an advantage that would be! He'd be able to do a few useful jobs around the house later, in his own home, wouldn't he?'

Paula stifled a smile. Frau Koch was clearly on her side and continually sang Richard's praises. Dr Engelhardt only rolled his eyes, as he'd long seen through his housekeeper's remarks.

'I suppose you're telling me I should be grateful that in Richard Hellmer I'm getting the perfect son-in-law?'

'Father, it's really not like that yet,' Paula said, hastily intervening. 'I'm only going to the cinema with him!'

'That's how it always begins. With your mother and me, it was the opera.' He heaved a sigh. 'Are you at least seeing something sensible?'

'But I've already told you – it's *Faust* with Emil Jannings as Mephisto. You can't get much more sensible than that.'

Her father murmured something and then, looking rather bored, reached for his newspaper. 'You should know.'

Paula hesitated, wondering if she should leave it at that, but then decided not to let him get away with it so easily.

'Papa, which opera did you visit with Mama when you realised how you felt about her?'

A smile lit up his face. 'I already knew when I bought the tickets for our box. It was the premiere of *Gernot*, by Eugen d'Albert, one of those typical German stories of tragedy, heroism and glory, but your mother loved it.' His expression softened at the memory. '*Faust* with Emil Jannings seems far more fitting and highbrow.' Then he turned back to his paper, while Frau Koch gave Paula a victorious little thumbs-up sign from behind his back.

The following evening, Richard collected Paula in the car again. Half of Hamburg seemed to be out on the town, and Richard had to hunt around for somewhere to park. In some ways the tree frog looked rather forlorn amid the superior black saloon cars that flaunted the wealth of their owners, but in others it seemed to Paula a perfectly suitable vehicle for them both: the tree frog symbolised her and Richard's fight for their place in society, based on merit rather than gender or background. And as a motor car, it was just as good as the fancy models delivering men in cashmere coats and women in mink stoles.

The newly opened Capitol on Hoheluftchaussee was one of the most extraordinary buildings Paula had ever seen. The Expressionist façade was decorated in terracotta, while inside it was as high and wide as a cathedral. The foyer, too, clearly showed that no expense had been spared by its creators. Silesian marble, artistic wood panelling in walnut and extravagant gold decoration invited closer examination. Even more impressive than the foyer was the auditorium itself, with over twelve hundred seats. Red was the dominant colour: a red curtain concealed the huge screen, the orchestra pit and the stage; all the seats were upholstered in red with gleaming gold frames, while every box was decked out in ebony and embellished with magnificent panelling.

'Impressive, eh?'

'Wonderful,' said Paula. 'Where are we sitting?'

'We're in a box.' He smiled at her in a way that made her heart beat faster. He'd got tickets for a box! She couldn't help but recall her father's words about what he'd felt years before when buying opera tickets for a box for himself and her mother.

And this box, still redolent of new wood and fabric, competed with any at the opera, that was for sure. But despite this magnificence, all that mattered to Paula was that she was here with the man whose presence she now craved.

The performance was sold out. More than twelve hundred people, Paula said to herself over and over, enjoying the thought of so many people gathered together to celebrate the joy of being alive. She rested her hand on the armrest, and no sooner had the lights dimmed than she felt Richard's hand slip protectively over hers. The tingle of excitement she'd been experiencing all week grew as his warmth seeped into her. It seemed an innocent enough gesture and yet said so much more than words, all the more so when his fingers began gently to stroke hers. She had never realised the magic of something as simple as two hands touching. They had often held hands, but this was different – a moment of intimacy that never went beyond what was proper but still kept her spellbound. These were his hands, then, with their story of gentleness and strength – not the fine hands of a surgeon but of a man who could knuckle down to manual work when needed, but who also had a soft side. Paula realised this was more than a crush. This was love.

When he delivered her home safe and sound later that evening, he brought his face close to hers, and just before their lips met he hesitated, so as to let her be the one to take the final step. And then there was no doubt. Her lips found his, a delicious combination of the restrained and the demanding, and just like his hands, they told her of a man who was both strong and sensitive. Paula knew then that she never wanted to be apart from him, that she wanted to revel in his warmth and closeness for always.

As they let go of one another, he whispered to her, 'You do know I love you, my wonderful Paula?'

'And I love you too,' she whispered back, as she started to kiss him all over again.

That evening her father lost the battle for Paula's heart once and for all. He would always be her father but now he would have to learn to enjoy his future son-in-law and perhaps grandchildren. After all, her mother had always told her that love is the only thing that's bigger when it's shared.

And on that same October evening, Paula knew that her future lay ahead, glowing and beautiful, and that, regardless of what fate might have in store, nothing in the world could change it.

Chapter 7

Just as autumn yields to the onset of winter, so Dr Engelhardt had no choice but to submit to the inevitability of sharing the love of his dearest daughter with Richard Hellmer. Paternal jealousy and paternal love battled it out until love prevailed and Dr Engelhardt started to see Richard through Paula's eyes. He was baffled by the ease with which he eventually slipped into this, but it was because he saw so much of himself in the young man and also noticed many characteristics that he admired. Everything that had once filled him with doubt now came across as evidence of Richard's determination. Paula was sure that Frau Koch had played quite a role in this, as their housekeeper had an inimitable talent for highlighting Richard's strengths in her various anecdotes.

In addition to all this was Richard's unconditional support for Paula's medical studies. Whenever they were together, they shared not only a growing romance but also a mutual passion for their subject, and Paula gained a lot from Richard being five semesters ahead of her. She found she had nothing to fear in viva examinations, even when faced repeatedly with the ingrained disrespect of most senior academics, all of whom were men. A case in point was the final anatomy examination with Professor Hempel, a man who made no secret of his view that women should be allowed entry to the medical profession only as nurses or midwives. With a self-satisfied leer, he questioned Paula on the function of erectile tissue in male genitalia. Paula gave anatomically accurate answers without appearing remotely flustered.

'You have very good knowledge in this matter,' Professor Hempel had to concede. 'I assume you have already carried out extensive research, as is now to be expected of a women's movement that no longer stands by morality and decency.'

'I'm sorry, I don't understand what you're suggesting. Could you perhaps clarify further?' She looked him straight in the eye, as she'd practised with Richard after telling him about the professor's ambiguous remarks during previous examinations.

'Just go all shy and quiet like a little fawn,' Richard had advised her, 'and look him innocently in the eye, exactly how you've done with me, then I'd lay good money on him being properly embarrassed.'

'Oh Lordy, I can't do that,' she'd replied. 'I'm not Leonie, after all. I'd rather flash him a fierce look, like a cat.'

'Yes you can. Come on, show me your inner fawn.'

And so something they'd once laughed over was now put to serious use. This fawn was determined. Professor Hempel had to content himself with a muttered 'Typical woman' at the end of the session.

When she recounted this to Leonie, her friend sighed with envy. 'You really have the most incredible luck! The extraordinary Richard is more than a dream, he's the perfect combination of good friend and good man. Now, tell me, has he got a brother you could introduce me to?' She tilted her head and gave a saucy wink. Paula knew she was only teasing but felt a pang of emotion. For the first time since their art gallery trip, she recalled that Richard had once had an older brother he'd loved very much and whose death he never talked about. She recalled the invisible shell that had enveloped him as soon as the conversation had turned to his brother.

'His brother's dead. He was at Verdun,' was all she said.

'Oh, I'm so sorry.' There was real empathy in Leonie's voice, and they never discussed the matter again. The moment Verdun was mentioned, Richard's dead brother seemed to fade from conversation and memory. Paula remembered what Richard had told her about how he hadn't died at Verdun, but later on. What he really meant by this she still didn't know.

◆ ◆ ◆

In December, Richard's father invited Paula and her father to the Hellmer family's Christmas dinner. After they'd all enjoyed a thoroughly festive meal, the family settled around the Christmas tree in the main living room and happily exchanged news and stories, while Richard and Paula seized the opportunity for a little time alone together. It was the first time Richard had shown Paula his attic flat, as they had usually met either at Paula's home or at the university. Anything more would have been a step too far for Paula's father and Richard was careful not to do anything that would make Dr Engelhardt think badly of him.

Paula was admiring the wood panelling on the walls when she spotted the framed family photograph near the stove.

'Is that your brother?' she said, pointing to the young man in uniform.

Richard nodded and it struck her how quickly his expression changed. His face was so sad that she felt tentative about broaching the subject.

'Yes, that's Georg. The Georg we all knew and loved.'

'Do you prefer not to talk about him?' Her voice was timid.

He took a deep sigh. 'The memory is too painful.'

'You don't have to tell me if it hurts too much.'

'I know.' He sat on his bed and gestured for her to sit next to him. He held her hands tenderly between his. 'It's time I told you about Georg. Seeing as our getting to know one another owes something to his tragic end.'

Questions flooded into Paula's mind but she stayed quiet and waited.

'You already know he was at Verdun. It must have been sheer hell. Blood and death everywhere, shelling all day, gas attacks, muddy trenches – I can hardly bear to think of it. Many men came home crippled: my brother-in-law, Holger, for one. But it was worse with Georg. Physically he was unscathed, but he had shell shock.' Richard paused. 'You know what that means, don't you?'

Paula nodded. Her father had treated some of these cases, the easier ones that could still be helped. But there were others: men who had no control over their bodies, who constantly had outbreaks of 'the shakes', who couldn't hold a weapon, who were inwardly destroyed, the war still raging inside them with no one providing any support – men whose suffering and desperation were not recognised and resulted only in their being branded cowards and shirkers. The more severe their shell shock, the more brutal the treatment methods that were supposed to return them to fighting strength.

'Georg was one of those who could barely react when spoken to. First he was sent to an army field hospital, but they couldn't do anything for him there. Then he came home. We felt desperate when we saw the trembling, lifeless shell he had become. He didn't speak at all, not even to me. He refused all food and lost so much weight that he was nothing more than skin and bone. We tried for three months but nothing worked, absolutely nothing. And then'—here he swallowed hard—'we made the worst possible mistake, because we knew no better. What's that saying – the road to hell is paved with good intentions? That's what happened in our case.'

The corner of Richard's mouth was working as he struggled to maintain his composure. She said nothing, just gently squeezed his warm hands.

'We took him to a regional psychiatric institution which supposedly specialised in the treatment of shell shock. They subjected him to treatment that was nothing short of torture. Then on top of that they tried something with a combination of insulin and electric shock therapy. That's how he died. I saw his body when he came for burial. It wasn't my brother. It was an emaciated, starved and tortured corpse. We should never have left him at the mercy of the unscrupulous doctors at that place. We should have been more willing to give it time, but we didn't know any better. We thought it was the best thing to do.'

A single tear ran silently down Richard's face.

'I'm so deeply sorry,' Paula whispered, 'but as you said, none of you could have known. Most bad shell shock cases spend the rest of their lives being cared for.'

'A lot of psychiatrists believe they can do whatever they like with these patients and that if they die, at least they stop costing anything to society. It's like that booklet by Hoche, *Allowing the Destruction of Life Unworthy of Life*.' Richard's tone was full of bitterness.

'And so this is why you want to be a psychiatrist. Because you want to make a better job of it.'

He nodded. 'I want to help those without a voice. And if I can't help them, then I want to be sure they live in dignity at least, and are not robbed of their individuality and humanity. There must be an end to describing them as parasites and an expensive burden on society. That's why I would always oppose people like Hoche, and anyone else who estimates human worth in numbers and productivity. I owe that to Georg, as well as to all the sick who are now being treated like lepers were in the Middle Ages. And I don't want to hear anything more about mercy killing, about it being kind and charitable to kill someone who can't make their own decisions.'

'And that's what you'll do, Richard. We'll do it together. You and I.'

She kissed him tenderly, but his mind was still tangled up in those stark memories and at first his response was muted, until his natural passion took over.

'D'you know what I'd like you to give me for Christmas?' he asked her once they'd let go of each other.

'Didn't the Stefan Zweig anthology appeal?' She was teasing him now as she knew perfectly well how much he admired Zweig's work.

He didn't pick up on that, saying instead, 'My parents keep an allotment in Moorfleet with a cherry tree. When it blossoms next spring, and if you're not tired of me by then, I want us to get engaged under that tree.'

Paula's heart leapt. 'You seem to be proposing? Suggesting we get engaged in the spring?'

'That's right. Or am I supposed to get down on one knee, like in a bad Rudolf Valentino film? That's not my style!'

'Definitely not. You'd rather stay firmly on your feet.'

'Exactly, or else I can't carry you over the threshold!' He gave her a glorious smile and the sadness that had consumed him earlier vanished. The past might have left him wounded, but wounds can heal and Richard was positive enough in outlook to learn from bitter experience and make the best of the future. Paula remembered another thing her mother used to say: *We can't change the past, but we can shape the future.*

'I guarantee I'll never tire of you. I love you and I'll always love you, even if the world collapses around us. But why should we wait until May?'

'For two reasons. First of all, we don't want to rush things with your father, and second, what could be more perfect than an engagement party among the cherry blossom, with the first breath of spring brushing your cheek?' His gentle caress down the length of her back made her shiver with pleasure.

'That does sound pretty enticing,' Paula whispered.

A knock at the door broke the spell. It was Margit.

'I was just wondering where you'd both got to.'

'Are you playing chaperone, big sister? There's really no need!' Richard said with a wink.

'I realise that. There's cake, but if you don't want any . . . Lottchen will be delighted if I tell her she can have Uncle Richard's slice as well.'

'Absolutely not! That's exactly what Lottchen's after. Keep her away from my cake – we'll be down directly.'

Margit laughed and went back downstairs.

'My mother's Christmas cake is absolutely not to be missed!' Richard said to Paula. 'The only thing finer will be our engagement cake in May!'

Paula laughed, feeling protected and secure in a way she hadn't for a very long time.

Chapter 8

It was 21 May 1927 and chilly for the time of year, but dry at least. In the late afternoon, rays of sunshine managed to break through the grey skies and gave a hint of summer so that the preparations for the party could be made outdoors. The big cherry tree was in full bloom, exactly as Richard had hoped, and stood protectively over the long table adorned with a spotless white cloth, now covered with a host of delicious treats lovingly baked by his mother, sister and Frau Koch. There were all sorts of fruit tarts and cakes, including a seasonal version of Richard's favourite Christmas cake, as well as almond cake, strawberry flan, apple cake and a huge cream gateau, all worthy of a wedding feast. Placed between the cakes were plates of home-baked biscuits, the biggest temptation for Margit's brood of youngsters, who were already purloining goodies from the table to nibble before the party started.

'The devil take you, you bunch of rascals!' Margit called out as the four lads and little Lottchen launched yet another rearguard attack on the table. 'You'll all feel my hairbrush across the seat of your shorts in a minute!'

'Why so angry, sister dear?' Richard said, smiling across at Margit as he and Paula stood side by side to greet the other guests. He looked very handsome in his dark blue suit, plain white shirt and tie. Paula's short-sleeved summer dress was pale blue, showed off a little more leg than usual and complemented her dark blonde hair, which was drawn back at the temples and fell loose over her shoulders. It had been well worth the two hours Leonie had spent taming and styling her friend's unruly locks with curling tongs.

'Little hooligans!' Margit was at her wits' end. 'What do I do with them?'

'Too late to ask that now,' replied Richard. 'If you'd consulted me a few years back, I'd have given you some timely tips on birth control.'

She glared at him. 'Shall I go after you with the hairbrush too?'

'Well, I'm not exactly dressed in shorts,' retorted Richard, looking at his suit trousers with a mischievous grin. 'No point in shooting the messenger. That's simply what it's like when you have five children.'

'You're such an idiot. You should be grateful that Paula's willing to waste her life on someone like you.'

'I am, believe me,' he said, smiling fondly at Paula, who returned the smile with absolute certainty in her eyes. 'But we certainly won't be having five children.'

'Here's Fritz!' Leonie was calling from the garden gate, where she'd been talking to Paula's father and his friend Dr Stamm, the most senior consultant at the children's hospital in Rothenburgsort.

Paula and Richard turned to welcome the new arrival.

'You're cutting it fine!' Richard said in greeting to his closest friend.

'In what way? The feast hasn't even begun yet! And where's the band I was promised?'

'The musicians will be here after the coffee and cake. But if my sister doesn't watch out, the table will have been laid bare long before anyone sits down.' He glanced at his ten-year-old nephew Karl, who, together with eight-year-old Jürgen, and with no regard to their mother's threats, was instructing Lottchen on how to distract their mother while the next raid was carried out.

'Hard-working Fritz looks as though he lingered a little too long in the operating theatre, am I right?' said Leonie, twinkling playfully at Richard's friend. 'Getting promoted to surgery takes up your time, eh?'

'Ah, Leonie Hirschthal, infallible prophetess and the sharpest tongue in the faculty, a feature belied by her pleasant exterior,' Fritz said with a grin. 'What actually happened is that we had a bad accident to deal with and Professor Wehmeyer permitted me to assist with the operation. A manual worker fell off some scaffolding earlier on today and suffered broken bones as well as damage to a number of internal organs. He—'

Leonie interrupted him in mid-flow. 'Thanks, but you can spare us the gory details. We're looking forward to lots of cake and speeches from two happy fathers whose offspring are getting engaged, even though I can't for the life of me understand what's supposed to be so desirable about a marriage on the horizon.'

'That's most commendable of you, Leonie,' commented Fritz.

'What do you mean by that?' she said with a puzzled frown.

'That you want to spare the male population the prospect of being tied to you for all eternity and suffering the torment of your moods.'

'Oh, charming!'

'I mean it!' His grin grew broader.

'Richard, why do you spend any time with this man?' asked Leonie. 'He's not a bit like you.'

'I like honest men.'

'Oh, I see, and so I'm a beast with moods, am I?'

'That's not what I said,' Fritz shot back, 'although you are of course a lady with moods.'

'That sounds about right, so you may sit near me today.'

'May I, or must I?'

'That's for you to decide.' With a knowing smile, Leonie went off to mingle with the other guests. Fritz gave a little cough.

'Just watch yourself there,' observed Richard. 'You could still end up as the man on the receiving end of her moods.'

'Thanks for the tip, but don't worry, I can look after myself,' Fritz said, clapping Richard on the shoulder, and then vanished among the assembled company.

'What do you think?' said Paula. 'Another engagement on the horizon?'

'Leonie and Fritz, d'you mean? No, never. They're too similar, and that's why they're always niggling. Anyway, I know Fritz has got an eye on a nurse, Dorothea, and she seems to have both her pretty eyes on him!'

'Why didn't he bring her along, then?'

'Too soon, otherwise I'd have suggested it.'

He smiled adoringly at Paula and kissed her lightly on the cheek.

Once the final guest had arrived, the festive table was officially declared open. The sun had brightened the sky and the rich aroma of coffee and cocoa, the latter a treat for the children, now mingled with the sweet scent of cherry blossom.

Richard's father opened the formalities. 'We're gathered here today to celebrate the engagement of my son, Richard, to the charming Paula Engelhardt. It is always a very special occasion when the finest from two families unite, by which I mean of course their children. And so we celebrate Richard and Paula's commitment to marry as soon as Richard graduates, to set up home together and raise a family.' He paused. 'You all know me – I'm not much of a talker, more of a doer and a man with a love of good baking, so without further ado, I'll hand over to Paula's father, Dr Engelhardt, so that everyone else with a sweet tooth – and I know that includes my grandchildren – won't have to wait too much longer for this wonderful spread!'

Everyone laughed and applauded.

'Thank you, Hans-Kurt,' said Paula's father. 'I've thought a great deal about what I could say today, have written a few words and then rewritten them, as I want them to mean something to you all. But what more can I possibly add to what Hans-Kurt has already said? He has summed it up to perfection and so I'll keep it brief. I'll admit that I was highly sceptical when I met first Richard. This wasn't because of you, my dear Richard, but quite simply because a father needs time to feel sure that his daughter is giving her heart to the right man. If one day you have a daughter of your own, you'll understand. Every young man poses a potential threat to your child's happiness until one of them wins over the father's heart too. And that's precisely what you have done, through your inimitable patience, your faultless behaviour and your reliability. I cannot think of anyone I'd rather see by Paula's side. And now let us enjoy at last the wonderful delights on offer!'

More laughter and even more applause. Leonie whispered to Paula. 'Now that's what I call two really good speeches – I hope they do the same on your wedding day. But do you really both want to wait until Richard finishes?'

'Yes,' Paula whispered back. 'Richard wants to be financially independent when we're married.'

'So he's prepared to go without the marital pleasures?'

'Leonie, you're so indiscreet!'

'You already know that. So? Are you waiting, or . . .? You know what I'm getting at.'

'Would you prefer a slice of the cream gateau or the strawberry flan? I can also really recommend the almond cake and I know you love Frau Koch's apple cake.'

Leonie rolled her eyes. 'You're being evasive.'

'Do have the cream gateau, Leonie – it's a dream.'

'OK, so I take it that no answer is the answer, then.'

Paula smiled.

The promised band turned up a little later and as the allotment garden was now too small they spread on to the pathway as well. First came the standard dances, especially the waltzes so beloved by all age groups. Then, during the break, Paula spotted Leonie whispering with the musicians, before tapping a silver spoon against some crockery to get everyone's attention.

'In my family we have a wonderful dance for engagements and weddings,' she announced. 'It's a round dance for everyone to take part in, and so it's a way of sharing our joy. I've just asked the band, and they know the piece – it's called "*Hava Nagila*". Who's done it before?'

Several couples on Dr Engelhardt's side indicated that they knew it. Paula noted they were all her father's Jewish friends.

'Good, we'll show you!' said Leonie, asking everyone who knew the dance to join her in a little demonstration of the steps.

'The music's slow at first, then gets faster and faster, but don't worry – it's great fun!' Leonie reassured them after the demonstration. 'So now we have to line up, man, woman, man, woman, alternating and holding hands.'

Richard was laughing with delight, but Paula noticed that Fritz only sighed.

'What's wrong? Don't you like dances like that?'

'I've got two left feet, and it could all go horribly wrong!'

'Yes, there's no doubt you're about to ruin everything and take us all with you,' remarked Richard drily. 'You'll slip and we'll go down like dominoes, but it'll be highly entertaining at least.'

'Never mind!' Leonie was back with them again. 'Come on, Paula, let's look after this man with the peculiar feet.'

'Richard! Can't you save me from this?' Fritz implored him. 'Don't you need someone to watch over the cake – make sure it doesn't go stale, or something?'

'Be a man, Fritz! Anyone who can cut open people's stomachs can manage this!'

'So much for empathetic psychiatrists,' muttered Fritz, as he obediently held hands with Paula on one side and Leonie on the other.

Once they'd all lined up and the music had started, Fritz showed himself to be no more inept than anyone else trying the dance for the first time. And as soon as it had finished, he was among those calling for a second round.

'There, you see. Feet cured?' asked Leonie.

'Well, you know, I clearly underestimated my ability yet again.'

'You're modest enough to be a future Professor Sauerbach!' Richard liked teasing his friend.

Fritz grinned. 'Save your breath for the next round – the music could well be a lot faster.'

He was right there, and a few of the older guests got quite puffed out. But before the next dance round had ended, angry voices in the main street reached them, so loud they carried from beyond the little railway line. The band stopped playing and all the guests listened hard to what was happening up on the embankment. It sounded like a brawl between two rival groups.

'It's those Nazis against the communists again,' Paula heard Richard's father, Hans-Kurt, say. 'It happens here more often now. People call that part of the allotment gardens Little Moscow, and the Nazis can't help but come over all the time in their joke of a uniform to strut around and cause trouble.'

'And if there's a decent fight to be had, the communists don't need asking twice,' remarked Richard. 'With so many idiots around, psychiatry has a golden future.'

'I fear it's surgery we need here first,' said Fritz. Three young men in work overalls had just broken away from the melee, carrying a fourth man to safety; he was bleeding from the head.

'We could do with some first aid!' one of them called out. 'They've beaten him half to death.'

'Bring him here!' commanded Fritz. 'I'll take a look at him.'

The three did as they were told and placed their comrade carefully on the grass.

'Is there a telephone anywhere around here?' asked Fritz. 'We need the police.'

'The bar at the station has a telephone,' replied Margit. 'I'll go. It's better they don't see any of you men up there. I reckon they'll leave a woman in peace.'

Meanwhile, Richard's mother had brought over a pile of white serviettes for Fritz to bind the wounds with.

'Really sorry we've disturbed your party,' one of the young men said apologetically, 'but we couldn't let that shower of Brownshirts go parading around like that without doing something. You've got to show them who's boss.'

Nobody spoke. Paula watched Fritz tending to the wound with a makeshift bandage as the injured man slowly came to.

'He doesn't look too bad,' concluded Fritz as he finished the job. 'There's probably no concussion, but he ought to go home and get to bed and let his own doctor take a look at it.'

The brawl was still in full flow, and Paula was wondering whether Margit had managed to get to the station without mishap when four men in brown shirts broke away from the fight and followed the path down towards the Hellmers' allotment. They stood in front of the assembled guests.

'We're looking for four agitators who attacked us for no reason,' said the eldest one, twenty at most, a wiry lad with a pleasant enough face but for his hostile expression.

Richard's father stepped forward. 'This is a private party,' he explained. 'We have no knowledge of agitators, only of an injured man to whom we have given first aid.'

'We'll look after him,' said the young man in the brown shirt. 'Hand him over to us.'

'I'm not handing over anything to you. Disputes between rowdy youths are of no interest to us – that's a matter for the police. What we do know is our duty as German citizens to offer first aid to the injured. Do you understand?'

'They're commie swine!'

'I don't care who they are.' Richard's father was emphatic. 'I would like you to leave, because this is a private party. As for the rest of it, it seems to me that the party whose badge you're wearing is very much in favour of protecting German blood so please leave now before any more German blood is spilt.'

'Is that a threat?'

'No, it's a request for you to leave and to stop beating people who have taken refuge here. If you choose to disregard my request, you'll soon find out that our guests include a large number of strongly built manual workers who know only too well how to use their fists and would have no hesitation in showing any troublemakers it's our right to be here.'

Before anyone could say another word, there was a sound of police sirens. Paula heaved a sigh of relief – Margit had made it.

'All right, we'll go,' said the young man, giving way. 'But I'm warning you not to engage with any more communists.'

Richard's father stared at him in silence, then turned away. The four Brownshirts took themselves off.

'Thank you,' said one of the young men.

'I didn't do it for you,' replied Richard's father in a stern voice. 'I only wanted to stop more heads getting smashed in. Street fights make no sense to me whatsoever, regardless of what they're about or who's involved. Now gather up your comrades and get out of here.'

'You should show us more understanding – those Nazis are dangerous.'

'When I see what your political idols are getting up to in Russia, I'd say they're equally dangerous,' retorted Richard's father, his expression fierce. 'And now I bid you good day.'

Once the four communists had left, Richard's father asked the band to play another waltz, saying, 'I need something to calm me.' Then he took his wife by the hand and danced with a vigour Paula would never have thought possible for a chap of his age.

'So how about us?' asked Richard, following her gaze. He held out his hand.

'My pleasure,' she said. 'It would be shameful if we didn't have the staying power of our parents!'

Chapter 9

Saturday 6 August 1927 was the first time Richard deliberately entered false information on an official document. This was the registration form at a little guest house in Binz on the island of Rügen, where he wanted to spend a few carefree days with Paula. He registered them as a married couple, Richard and Paula Hellmer. He knew from Fritz that a serious-looking couple would never be asked for their marriage certificate, but back then it still required some courage. Fortunately, nobody noticed his hesitation, least of all Paula, who hadn't needed much persuading and was ready at his side for any new adventure.

The guest house was so near the water they could enjoy the smells and sounds of the sea and the cries of the seagulls that woke them in the morning.

Richard hired one of the numerous wicker beach chairs, big enough for two, with a striped awning to protect against the bright sunshine – which had of late almost entirely overtaken the traditional bathing machine in popularity. The one next to them was already occupied and surrounded by an imposing sandcastle. King of the castle was a short, red-faced man on the wrong side of fifty with a Kaiser Wilhelm beard that seemed far too large for his face. A red checked handkerchief with a knot at each corner adorned his head. He was wearing an old-fashioned one-piece gents' swimsuit and made no secret of his opinions, his sandcastle being decorated with a mosaic of mussel shells that formed a row of swastikas. The king's fair wife, clad in a full-length blue and white bathing dress with long sleeves, took a long and disparaging look at Paula's deep red modern swimsuit which left her arms and legs uncovered, while Richard had to put up with the red-faced man's discourse on how a decent German man should wear a respectable one-piece instead of going around in newfangled swimming trunks looking like Friedrich Ebert, although he made no comment on Paula's outfit.

'You've just got to know how to wear it,' Richard said casually. He called to mind the photograph of the former President of the Reich on the beach wearing poorly fitting bathing trunks with the caption created by his political opponents, 'A republic exposed', something which had done the rounds hundreds of times and given rise to a number of satirical songs. But nothing had stopped the triumphant progress of swimming trunks, and when Richard cast his eye around the beach, he realised that he and Paula were far less conspicuous than their conservative neighbours.

'I think we need our own sandcastle in this hostile environment,' he whispered to Paula. 'I'll get hold of a toy bucket and a watering can while you go and collect some shells and little pebbles to make our own mosaic with.' He gave her a conspiratorial wink.

'What kind of mosaic do you have in mind?'

'One that'll drive this Nazi mad.'

'You can't leave it alone, can you?' She gave him a playful nudge then went down to the water's edge to fetch what he wanted.

While Paula went looking for shells, Richard built a wall as high as their neighbour's, using the watering can to moisten the sand and patting it down with the spade. Once Paula had returned with her bucket nearly full, she settled down in the beach chair.

'D'you know, I could sit here for hours watching you do that?' she said to Richard. 'With your lovely athletic body all glistening with sweat.'

'And now we've got to listen to this smut!' hissed her virtuously veiled neighbour. 'Whatever next!'

Richard burst out laughing and took a while to get back to work as a result. Their neighbour shook her head in disgust.

Her displeasure increased when she saw that Richard and Paula were decorating their castle with pebbles placed in such a way as to bear a suspicious resemblance to the Star of David that Leonie sometimes wore as a pendant.

'They're Jewish stars!' barked out the king of the castle. 'Don't tell me you're Jews!'

'What on earth are you on about?' Richard's face was a picture of innocence. 'They're only a few starfish and other little finds from along the shore. But as you're from India, I expect you're not familiar with German customs.'

'India?' the man said, bristling. 'Have you quite lost your mind?'

Paula struggled to conceal her mirth as Richard continued, with a deadpan expression on his face.

'Well, you know, you're wearing a turban of sorts and you've decorated your sandcastle with the swastika, the Indian symbol of good fortune, so that's why I thought, you know . . . Oh, so you're not from India, then? That does explain why you speak such good German, of course.'

Paula could no longer contain herself and screamed with laughter.

'That is the last straw! Running around half naked like a jungle savage, flaunting Jewish symbols and insulting decent German citizens! I'll be reporting this to the lifeguard.'

'You're free to do that, of course. But I really wouldn't know why a man can't be permitted to decorate his own sandcastle with little bits and pieces from the beach, and what is really so exceptional about my style of swimming costume, which, as you so rightly mentioned, was considered fitting eight years ago for the President of the Reich and is now being worn by most of the men here?'

'Or at least by those men with the figure for it,' added Paula as she ran her hand over Richard's shoulders and planted a kiss on his cheek.

'I cannot allow this! I'm getting the beach superintendent!'

'Willibald, do calm down,' said his wife. 'Don't waste your time on these vulgar people.'

Willibald carried on mumbling to himself for a while then settled back in his beach chair.

Richard drew Paula towards him. 'How about a well-deserved cooling dip in the Baltic?'

'Lovely,' she whispered to him. 'Otherwise, these two will have heart attacks!'

It was a wonderful summer's day with a cloudless, brilliant blue sky. The waters of the Baltic shimmered a beautiful shade of green that for Richard invited comparison with Paula's eyes and yet also were so clear he could still see his feet when standing shoulder-high in the sea.

Not even their neighbours on the beach could spoil a day like this for them, particularly as Willibald was now contenting himself with unintelligible grumbling whenever he looked over in Richard and Paula's direction.

Early in the afternoon a family with two children came to occupy the beach chair to Willibald's other side. As the boys played boisterously in the sand, they destroyed much of Willibald's castle by tumbling against it in their free-for-all.

'Pesky kids!' shrieked Willibald. 'Can't you keep control of your brats?'

Willibald's reaction had quite an impact on the father, who immediately called his sons to order and with Prussian sternness instructed them to rebuild the good gentleman's sandcastle.

Richard and Paula looked on in amusement at the untroubled way in which the two boys set to work, effortlessly heaping up the walls of the castle once more but struggling to put the swastikas back together. This made Willibald splutter with anger again as he explained how these 'ham-fisted lads' should know how to put together a presentable swastika, and then he delivered a monologue about the magnificent party that the symbol represented. The boys seemed uninterested, but their father listened intently. Willibald, delighted with this audience, cheerfully continued his little speech.

'The National Socialist movement has one purpose, and that is to serve Germany and to help the German people regain their ancestral position among other peoples. The disreputable policies of previous governments has resulted in Germany becoming the plaything of foreign powers. It is time to secure Germany's position in the world and to push forward with our foreign policy with our heads held high. The National Socialist movement is for the people, for social justice and against the sequestration of private property as preached by the communists. Our salvation lies with this social and national movement so that our children and our children's children will not suffer the debts of Versailles and enslavement to foreign powers.'

'That sounds reasonable,' commented the father.

'Yes, it's actually a remarkable movement,' chipped in Richard. 'To take just one example, did you know that members of the National Socialist Party don't greet each other with "Hello", like normal people do, but instead fling their right arm high in the air and yell, "Heil Hitler"? This has the great advantage, of course, of ensuring that everyone knows the name of their leader. But it would be hard if he had a name with more than three syllables – suppose that someone of Polish ancestry were to become leader at some point and were called Kotowskowski?'

'Polacks and their sort have no place in the movement!' shrieked Willibald.

'Ah, I see,' said Richard very casually. 'Well, that's all right, then.'

'You like to badmouth everything, don't you?' Willibald said, looking at Richard with disdain. 'But even you will eventually understand where Germany's salvation lies.' He left it at that.

'Thank God he didn't finish up saying "Heil Hitler",' whispered Richard to Paula.

'But he's made quite an impression on the boys' father,' whispered Paula back. 'And this movement's getting more and more followers. Doesn't it worry you?'

Richard shook his head. 'You'll get a few malcontents running behind the Nazis, but they won't become a real force in parliament in the May elections – the Social Democrats and the German People's Party have too firm a seat in the saddle. To be honest, it's the communists I'm more concerned about. My father's worried they've got links to the Soviets.'

'But they're already unelectable,' retorted Paula. 'Frau Koch was telling me about some shooting that went on in the street between Nazis and communists in Hamburg, in broad daylight! We can't vote for any of that lot!'

'You're right. And that's why I'm not going to waste any more time today on Willibald and others like him. Shall we go in the water again?'

'I'd like nothing more. I just want to watch those droplets of saltwater dripping off that beautifully formed torso of yours,' Paula said, twinkling at him without a flicker of self-consciousness.

'And I always thought that only a man could devour a woman with a single look!'

'If you don't like it, then you'd better start wearing a swimsuit like Willibald's.'

'There's only one way to protect my body from your eyes!' he said, taking her by the hand and leading her down the beach and into the waves.

Chapter 10

The uplifting memory of those heavenly summer days of August 1927 gave Richard and Paula the buoyancy to get through the cold winter. This was a tranquil period for them both, with Richard completing his thesis and Paula passing her medical preliminaries and starting the search for her doctoral supervisor. She really wanted to study for a doctorate in psychiatry but received several rejections on the grounds of her sex, because no one believed a woman capable of handling the unpredictable behaviour of the mentally ill.

Finally, in spring 1928, she gave up the exhausting battle against the system and, as a way of showing her adaptability, decided to start her doctorate in gynaecology, although she remained determined to achieve her aims somehow. Once she was qualified, no one would be particularly interested in the subject of her doctoral research in any case. The very fact of becoming a medical doctor in her own right and not simply being a doctor's wife should be a triumph in itself. On top of that, she loved the practical research on 'post-partum infection' that she was carrying out with young mothers and took pride in the immediate usefulness of her obstetrics work as she discovered and swiftly eliminated sources of infection.

Her father felt that she had a distinct advantage over men in obstetrics and gynaecology and should consider making this her specialist field but Paula still cherished the dream of becoming a psychiatrist, although only her father and Richard thought her capable of it. Even Leonie considered it an unsuitable profession for a woman. She felt that constant contact with dangerous and often foul-mouthed lunatics would be quite unsuitable and advised Paula to leave it all to the men because they could physically defend themselves if the need arose.

'That's nonsense! What's to happen to mentally ill women?' retorted Paula. 'Women who can't open up to a man because they've had such appalling experiences and would rather be treated by a female doctor? And how come female nurses are allowed to work in asylums with male patients? They seem able to manage!'

'But you'd be much more respected as a gynaecologist.' Leonie didn't give up easily. '"Mad-doctor" is not an impressive title.'

'And what's your own specialisation going to be?' Paula said, quickly changing the subject. It pained her to discuss anything with Leonie if all she got back was the same reactionary outlook as she did from the old fossils in the faculty.

'I want to work in paediatrics.' Leonie was very clear on this point. 'I stand a really good chance of Dr Stamm taking me on when I graduate, without having to do a full doctorate.'

'A medical doctor without a PhD?' Paula raised her eyebrows.

'Why not? I'm not after an academic career – I just want to help people.'

'But why children when you've always been so clear about never getting married?'

'That's more to do with a married woman having no rights. It doesn't mean I wouldn't want children. Who knows, maybe when the time is right, I'll seek out the ideal father – one with all the right hereditary requirements.' She gave Paula a meaningful wink.

'That sounds rather like the political party we're not keen on,' commented Paula. 'What would be the right hereditary material for you, then?'

'Someone who looks like a film star. All he has to do is be thoroughly seductive. I'm the one with the brains.'

'Leonie darling, you're incorrigible!'

'I know that. But are you and Richard any better, with your regular jaunts to nice little guest houses in remote places?'

'We're engaged.'

'Precisely – engaged, not married. Doesn't that mean you're doing something sinful and forbidden?' Leonie gave Paula a good-natured pat on the shoulder but said nothing further.

◆ ◆ ◆

A fresh round of elections was held on 28 May 1928, almost exactly one year after Richard and Paula's engagement. While Paula herself and Richard's family voted unanimously for the Social Democrats, her father had for some time been undecided between the Centre Party and Gustav Stresemann's liberal DVP. In the end he chose the DVP, the German People's Party, saying this meant he could continue to support Stresemann's successful foreign policy.

As usual, Richard's predictions turned out to be right. The SPD won 29.8 per cent of the vote, the communists retained 10.6 per cent and Gustav Stresemann's DVP came in with 8.7 per cent. The National Socialists disappeared into near oblivion with only 2.6 per cent of the vote and twelve seats in parliament.

Hermann Müller became Chancellor of a grand coalition made up of Social Democrats, the German People's Party, the Bavarian People's Party, the German Democratic Party and the Centrists, and all the signs pointed to a decline in support for Hitler, much to Paula and Richard's relief.

A few days after the election, they were studying together as usual in Paula's room.

'So how does it feel, now that you've nearly finished?' Paula said, beaming at Richard.

'It's not over yet.'

'But you've registered for your final exam today! In four months' time you'll be a doctor and then we can get married!'

'Yes, but first I've got to do the compulsory six months of surgery before I can do what really matters to me. I'm dreading that.'

'You won't be on your own. Fritz will be in the operating theatre with you.'

'Only if he gets down to his revision and doesn't fail.'

'You mean because he's spending so much time with Nurse Dorothea?'

'He hasn't called her "Nurse Dorothea" for quite some time. It's been "honey pie" and "Doro" for a while, and they've recently got engaged on the quiet.'

'What – with no party or cake for us? And you're telling me only now? How can we forgive your best friend something like that?'

'We'll forgive them. Fritz has just told me he's off to the registry office tomorrow to have the banns called and wants me to be witness next month.'

'Why are they in such a rush?'

'Why do you think?' Richard said, rolling his eyes. 'Because they've slipped up, whereas we've been really careful! That's why I've got two jobs coming up: witness at next month's wedding, then godfather around the end of January.'

'Oh dear, you'd think that being a medical student and a nurse they'd have been more careful. What has Fritz said in his defence?'

'Nothing, but then I didn't ask him for the detail.'

'I see, so you don't give your best friend the same treatment as your sister, then! You're always telling her she should have taken more precautions!'

'I only started saying that when she was expecting number four.'

'So Fritz still has three shots before you take him to one side and stick a condom in his hand? In which case, he'd better make time to study and get fully qualified so he can feed his growing family.'

'You're pretty sharp-tongued sometimes.'

'Yes, but never so much as you, my dearest,' she said, kissing him lightly on the cheek.

Smiling, he put his arms around her. 'You're right – sometimes I can't keep my mouth shut either. Now tell me, isn't your father out today?'

'That's right, and he isn't back until tomorrow afternoon.'

'So how about giving Frau Koch the rest of the day off?' He gave Paula the seductive look she could never resist.

'But you've got to revise, Richard. You don't want to let me down, do you?'

'Oh, but I do want to revise. I was thinking of a detailed study of anatomy, with your help. You'll dispatch Frau Koch?' he said, grinning broadly.

'Richard, you're quite impossible,' Paula said with a laugh. 'You're right, though. Frau Koch will be delighted to take the afternoon off.'

Chapter 11

The party to celebrate the marriage of Fritz Ellerweg and Dorothea Schwabe took place in a pretty village guest house in the stunning Altes Land area, where the apple trees were in full blossom. The couple had opted for a registry office wedding and Dorothea wore a simple yet elegant summer dress of pale yellow, while Fritz went for a cream summer suit instead of the traditional black.

'I expect you wanted to keep your costs down, didn't you?' Richard whispered to Fritz, but the latter shook his head.

'We're both pretty pragmatic, to be honest. A church wedding would have been complicated – Doro's family is Catholic, mine is Protestant – so we've opted for the registry office.'

'And what'll the baby be?'

'Doro would love the child to be baptised a Catholic. I'm not the religious type, so it's Doro who should decide, and then her family will hold a nice little church ceremony later.'

Once the two fathers had made their speeches and the celebratory meal was over, the band struck up. Richard noticed it was the same one that had played at his and Paula's engagement party.

'I really liked their music,' Fritz explained, 'as well as that dance Leonie showed everyone. We must include it in the party repertoire!'

'So says the man who once lamented his two left feet!'

'I just underestimated my own ability.' He winked at Leonie, who was sitting next to Dorothea. 'Are we ready?'

Leonie flashed a smile at Fritz, got to her feet and explained the steps for '*Havila Nagila*' to all the guests. Her enthusiasm was catching, just as at Richard's and Paula's engagement party, and the wedding guests entered fully into the spirit of the dance and the music.

As Richard drove Paula home later that evening, he said, 'D'you know, maybe we should do something like Fritz and Dorothea – no big church occasion, just the registry office and then away for a couple of days afterwards.'

'My father wouldn't object: he's no great churchgoer,' replied Paula. 'Where could we go away to?'

'Three cities are tempting me: Paris, London, or Rome – you choose.'

'Hmm, I'm not sure. Paris is the city of love, it's always raining in London, and in Rome it's always sunny. Paris or Rome. Which one's better for you?'

'We have plenty of love ourselves, so we don't need the city to supply that. Yes, I'm wavering between the Louvre and the Sistine Chapel, but to be honest I'd prefer Rome and all its wonderful sights. And its weather, as you said.'

'Sounds wonderful – I can hardly wait!'

'My exam's on 4 September, so why don't we book the wedding for Friday 7 September and catch the train to Rome on the Saturday?'

'Perfect!'

Days where everything was perfect and went off without any major hitches had been few and far between for Richard since the death of his brother, Georg. But since he and Paula had been together, everything had felt right. This summer at Paula's side had been heavenly, his revision had gone smoothly and he passed his final viva with top marks on 4 September. Fritz had faced his on the previous day and had also excelled. Unlike Richard, though, he was keen to get going with the compulsory six months in surgery, starting on 1 October.

On 7 September, good fortune continued to smile on them. It was as if summer wanted to make a late guest appearance for the couple, bringing exceptional sunshine and warmth as its wedding gift.

The reception, arranged by Paula's father, followed the civil ceremony and took place in an exclusive Harvestehude garden restaurant.

Paula and Richard had taken their cue from Fritz's wedding and shunned expensive outfits, something both Paula's father and Frau Koch had happily accepted, somewhat to the bride's surprise.

'Spending a lot of money on a dress you wear only once in your life is a waste,' agreed Frau Koch, who was usually more romantically inclined.

Richard's father's behaviour was out of character, too, as he had started to find excuses not to lend his son the car. The garage key had suddenly gone missing, and when Richard asked where on earth it was, he got a terse reply about it being lost but that the locksmith had been informed. As Richard was so busy with the final preparations for his exam, he'd accepted the explanation and thought nothing more of it.

Once all the guests had arrived, Richard's father rose and began his speech. 'Dear Paula, dear Richard, you know I don't go in for a lot of words and like to get straight to the point. I wish you a marriage that is happy and blessed and that brings you everything you both seek. We want to give you the best possible start at this new and important time in your lives and have done a lot of thinking about what would give you the greatest pleasure. We all know it's customary to give the bride and groom a dinner service and items for the house, but it's a matter of taste and can go embarrassingly wrong. My wife and I can tell you a few stories about that! The dinner service we were given when we got married was so ugly that we kept it in case we ever had guests we didn't want to stay for too long. I'm pleased to say we've never had to use this secret weapon.'

Everyone laughed.

'As parents, we've always seen it as our duty to protect our children, so we've decided to spare you both a bad choice in crockery. Instead, we've collected contributions from all your relatives and friends so we could give you something you'll really enjoy – and for many years, we hope.'

He raised his glass towards Paula's father. 'Wilhelm, over to you.'

'Thank you, Hans-Kurt.' Dr Engelhardt cleared his throat and then took a small box from his pocket.

'Dear Richard, dear Paula, I know that I promised to buy you the train tickets for your honeymoon trip, but I've had to break that promise, because now you won't need them.'

'Oh Lordy,' Richard whispered to Paula. 'I think I can guess what it is.'

Paula's father handed him the little box. 'This is part of our gift. The other part wouldn't fit through the door!'

Richard's hands were shaking as he accepted the box and held it out to Paula for her to untie the red ribbon that kept it secure.

Inside it were some car keys.

'I . . .' Richard swallowed hard. 'I don't know what to say.'

'Well, if you don't know what to say now, what on earth are you going to say when you step outside?' Fritz said, clapping him on the shoulder.

'Yes, go on – go out and look at it for yourselves,' urged Leonie, giving Paula, who was as lost for words as Richard, a nudge towards the door.

Outside stood a gleaming, black Adler Standard 6. Richard knew this model was the best saloon car, held the road like no other and was very much in vogue with the upper middle class.

'That must have cost a fortune,' he stammered. 'Thank you all so very much! That's the most magnificent present you could possibly have given us. I'd never have dared dream of such a gift.'

'Well, we got rather a good deal and it's not absolutely brand new,' said his father, 'but there's a fair bit to celebrate this week. You're a doctor now, with the most charming wife.'

On the verge of tears, Richard hugged his father warmly, only just managing to keep his composure. Paula, on the other hand, couldn't stop crying and was grateful for the handkerchief Leonie passed her, saying, 'Everyone cries at a wedding.'

'You know what you need to do,' Richard said, turning to Paula. 'As soon as we're back from Italy, you must get a driving licence too.'

Paula just nodded, lost for words, as she wiped her eyes with Leonie's hankie.

'That's a fantastic vehicle,' said Fritz. 'It could practically take on a racing car. It does a good ninety kilometres an hour.'

'You can get lots of luggage in it,' added Leonie. 'You can take half your household to Italy with you!'

'And a car will give you far more pleasure and for longer than some shamefully expensive bridal gown, don't you think?' observed Frau Koch.

'It's a comfortable drive for a woman, you know,' added Margit. 'Clara Stinnes has been touring the world in a car just like that for over a year. I've been reading everything I can find about her. She's an incredible woman.'

'It looks as though our newly-weds are speechless,' said Paula's father. 'Perhaps we should all go back in and let them recover!' he said with a laugh.

'Yes, come on – it's time to cut the cake,' said Fritz. 'I'm starving.'

'You're right, go ahead,' said Richard, touched to the core. And then it was just him and Paula standing on the street.

'Paula, we've got our own car.' It still hadn't sunk in. 'A car we can drive to Rome.' He shouted out loud, 'To Rome!' and then swept his new wife off her feet, lifting her as high in the air as he could. 'We're driving to Rome in our own car!'

Chapter 12

September 1928 etched itself into Paula's memory as a month of luxurious freedom. Sitting at Richard's side in their new car as it hummed towards Italy, the windows rolled down and the air cool against her face, she felt sheer happiness and promised herself she would try to preserve this feeling in her heart for ever, whatever the future might bring.

They stopped overnight in a number of beautiful Italian towns along the way and Richard discovered a new enthusiasm. On their earlier trips to the Baltic coast he had taken a lot of photographs with his box camera, but in Italy he couldn't put it down. Paula teased him about submitting his photo collection to Baedeker for their travel guides.

'I hope my photos are a lot better than the ones in Baedeker!' He said this with such a serious expression on his face that Paula couldn't be sure whether he was joking or not.

By the time they got to Rome, Richard had snapped so many of the sights that he'd almost finished the film and their first job was to find somewhere to buy some more. Their landlady couldn't help as she spoke only Italian, and Richard's efforts with bits of Latin didn't get him very far. The language of Julius Caesar lacked the necessary vocabulary.

'Oh well, we'll find somewhere,' said Richard. 'There's bound to be someone selling film near the Colosseum.'

They were staying on the outskirts of the city, so they drove in to enjoy the sights. Richard parked within sight of the Colosseum and asked Paula to sit on the car bonnet.

'I'd love a picture of you like that with the Colosseum in the background. For posterity – proof we were really here!'

Paula slid up on to the bonnet.

'Can you go a bit more to the left, darling?'

She did.

'No, not that far, more in the middle.'

She sighed but did as he asked.

'And now look a bit more cheerful.'

She attempted a big smile.

'Not like that. You look as though you're going to bite someone. A little more pleasant.'

'Richard . . .'

'Yes, darling?'

'Just take the picture or it'll be you getting bitten.'

He got on with it.

Once Richard had used up the rest of his film at the Colosseum, they once again went off in search of a place to buy more. His knowledge of Latin didn't help this time either, and modern Romans were at a loss as to what it was he wanted. Richard would point at his camera and get puzzled looks in return. Paula had to stifle her laughter at the sight – Richard and the locals, all equally stumped. At last an elderly man made his way through the little crowd that had by now gathered around the honeymooners.

'You're from Germany, are you?' He spoke excellent German.

'Yes, from Hamburg.' Richard sounded delighted. 'I'm looking for somewhere to buy a film for my camera.'

'Oh, Hamburg – the Alster. What a lovely city!' The elderly Italian was rapturous. 'I haven't been to Germany since the war. My daughter married a German fellow; they live in Hannover.'

He led them to a small shop a few streets away and called out something in Italian. The only word Paula caught was 'Luigi' as the old chap pointed at Richard and at his camera. Luigi nodded and showed Richard his stock of film. When Richard heard the price, he bought the whole lot on the spot and was given a heart-warming farewell by Luigi and his seven children.

'Film like this costs three times as much in Hamburg,' said Richard happily, once they were outside.

'And you've put bread on the table for the whole family,' came Paula's dry retort as he stashed his hoard in the boot of the car. 'At least you refrained from giving them unsolicited advice on birth control.'

'The Italians love a large family. It's quite normal for them to have seven children. It wouldn't occur to me to try and talk people like that out of it.'

'You just save that for your sister, then.'

'That's right. Talking of big families and rejecting birth control . . . we haven't been to the Vatican yet. I absolutely must take some photos there.'

'Now there's a strange line of thought,' Paula observed with a shake of her head, then she linked arms with her camera-mad husband as he led her in pursuit of yet more marvellous pictures. The September sun shone down so warmly on their way to the Vatican that Paula treated herself to a broad-brimmed straw hat to protect her fair skin from any sunburn.

They didn't get even a glimpse of the Pope, of course, but Richard managed to persuade one of the uniformed Swiss Guards to allow him to photograph him alongside Paula. Then Richard explained to the helpful man how the camera worked and got him to take a picture of him and Paula in front of St Peter's. The guard was very willing and even ended up taking a picture of Richard and Paula standing among all his colleagues, also in the distinctive uniform.

By the end of their trip, Richard had taken a huge number of photographs as a permanent memory of their honeymoon and to give the folks back home at least an impression of the beauty of Rome in the September sunshine.

Chapter 13

On 31 January 1929 Richard stood alongside Fritz in the operating theatre for the first time since their student days. As a rule, only one of the two operated with Professor Wehmeyer, but on this particular day he had brought them both in because this was an unusual case. There had been more shooting between communists and National Socialists and the victim had been hit several times in the abdomen. In wartime this was a common injury, but in peacetime it was very rare and the professor wanted them to have the experience of seeing something of this kind.

'Let's hope that operations like this remain the exception, but it is important that every surgeon knows what to do in case it becomes part of our daily work in the future.'

It was on the tip of Richard's tongue to say that he would be working in psychiatry after April and had no intention of ever setting foot in an operating theatre again, but he remained silent, as he valued and respected Professor Wehmeyer's insightful approach to their work.

The bullets had left devastating wounds. One had entered the liver, one had ripped the spleen and three others had torn into the digestive system. In the end they had to perform a lobectomy on the liver and cut out part of the small intestine, remove the spleen and patch up the stomach in a variation of the Billroth Operation in order to retain any functionality at all.

Fritz did the major part of the work.

'You're on the right path to becoming a magnificent surgeon, Herr Ellerweg,' said Professor Wehmeyer. 'I wouldn't be at all surprised if your name isn't linked one day with a new surgical technique.'

'Thank you, Professor.'

In spite of the surgical mask Fritz wore, Richard could tell that his friend was flushed with pride.

In the changing room after the operation Fritz was still buoyed by the professor's praise. There was a knock at the door.

'Is Dr Ellerweg in there?' It was a woman's voice.

'Yes, I'm here.'

'Frau Hellmer has telephoned from Finkenau. Your wife went into labour early today; she's been delivered but something's not right with the baby.'

Fritz hurriedly finished buttoning his shirt and flung the door open to find a nurse standing outside. 'What else did Frau Hellmer say? How is my wife? And what's wrong with the baby?'

'Your wife is well, but you should go to her immediately, just as soon as you are ready. Frau Hellmer gave no further details.'

'Thank you.'

The nurse nodded and left.

'I'll drive you straight there,' said Richard, trying to sound calm in spite of feeling quite the opposite. It was hard watching Fritz make three attempts to tie his shoelaces.

It had started to snow while they'd been in the operating theatre and Richard had to clear the car windscreen before they could set off. Fritz stood by helplessly, clenching his fingers inside his coat pockets, biting his lip and not saying a word. He stayed like that for the whole journey. Quarter of an hour later Richard was parking the car right outside the maternity hospital at Finkenau. Paula was waiting for them in the entrance.

'What's happening?' Fritz called out. 'How's Doro, and what's wrong with the baby?'

Paula waited until Fritz and Richard were with her.

'Doro is fine physically; it wasn't a difficult birth. But... but seeing the baby was a shock.'

'Why? For goodness' sake, tell me what's wrong,' begged Fritz.

Paula took a deep breath. Richard's belly tied itself in knots as he watched her try to keep her composure.

'It's a little boy and he has a severe deformity.' She spoke quietly, quickly wiping a tear away before it could spill from the corner of her eye. 'He's anencephalic.'

Looking horrified, Fritz stared at her. 'What does that mean? He's been born with no head?'

'No, not that, but he's been born without the cerebrum: much of the skull has not developed and the midbrain is exposed. It's a miracle he was born alive. He'll die in the next few hours – days, at most.'

Fritz gasped, clenching and unclenching his trembling hands. 'Where is the baby now?'

'With Doro. She was hysterical directly after the birth and both the midwife and the doctor advised her against seeing the child again because it's too upsetting. But when I talked to her, she'd calmed down and said that he was her child in spite of everything, and even if he were to live only a few hours she wanted to care for him herself.' Now Paula reached for her handkerchief, unable to hold back her tears. 'She wants you to be there, with her and the child.'

'Of course I'll be there. He's my son too.'

'We've swaddled him and put a little bonnet on him to make him look a little more like a normal baby,' whispered Paula.

'So where's Doro?'

'I'll show you.'

Dorothea was pale but more composed than Richard had expected, given what Paula had told them. She held the baby in her arms and at first glance everything seemed all right, but when he looked the baby in the face, the deformity was very clear. Yes, the white knitted bonnet concealed the small, misshapen, flat skull, but the child's eyes bulged like those of a frog, while the shape of the head was strangely reminiscent of that of a toad. It was no wonder that Dorothea had been so shocked straight after giving birth. Richard realised that he was breathing faster than usual, but he couldn't slow it down. The sight was so awful that he found it hard to believe what he was seeing. This couldn't be true. It simply couldn't be true. He recalled how Fritz had planned everything for the nursery and had asked his advice for the best wood to use for a cradle. Walnut, Richard had told him.

'Walnut, yes, I like that. As soon as the baby's born, your father and his lads can get to work. Then in the same wood I'd like a chest of drawers to use as a changing table.' Had it not been for his mother-in-law's warning that it was bad luck to get the nursery ready before the birth, Fritz would have done all this months before . . .

Remembering this conversation brought a lump to Richard's throat, and he struggled to keep his emotions in check, blinking hard to get rid of the telltale pricking of his eyes. By contrast, and much to Richard's admiration, Fritz remained extraordinarily calm and composed, comforting first his wife with a gentle embrace, then taking the child in his arms and making the soft cooing sounds that people make with any newborn. He stroked the tiny, perfectly formed hands that gripped his fingers the moment he touched the little palms.

'He's lovely and strong,' said Fritz gently. 'There's so much life in him. Can it really be true that he's going to die so soon?'

'That's in God's hands,' replied Doro, her voice soft. She placed her own hand over those of her husband and son. 'The chaplain will be here any moment to baptise him.'

Richard realised Paula was shedding silent tears next to him and put his arms around her.

'And what'll you call him?' he asked, desperately trying to bring some normality to the distressing scene.

'We'd decided to call our first son Harald,' said Dorothea, sounding astonishingly collected. 'But I'd like to call him Gottlieb, because every child is loved by God, even a child not expected to live.'

'That's a very good name,' Fritz agreed, wiping his own eyes. 'Our little Gottlieb.'

There was a knock at the door. It wasn't the chaplain, as expected, but a doctor.

'Good morning. My name is Brandes, Dr Brandes. You're the spouse and father?'

Fritz gave a silent nod.

'You're a colleague of ours, is that right?' Dr Brandes said, holding out his hand in formal greeting.

'Yes,' said Fritz, returning the handshake.

'Good. That means I can be candid with you.'

'I know my son's going to die.' Fritz sounded hollow.

'It's inevitable with a deformity like this. This is a Gamper's midbrain being. Have you read the work of Eduard Gamper?'

Fritz shook his head.

'Dr Gamper produced a comprehensive paper on the matter in 1926 and, as far as I know, that was the first academic publication to describe this abnormality. I've never seen a presentation like this myself before, only drawings. As a doctor yourself, you'll know how important research is to us. For that reason, I wanted to ask whether you would hand over the body to us for anatomical research. It is, after all, a very rare abnormality.'

'I'm sorry?' Fritz looked back at Brandes in disbelief.

'Naturally, no one will be aware of the background: that's of no relevance. You'll definitely still have plenty of healthy children – abnormalities like this are whims of nature and not hereditary, I can assure you of that. I've brought a form for you to sign, showing that you're handing the specimen over to us.'

Fritz leapt to his feet. 'This specimen, as you're so charmingly calling him, is my son, and he's still alive at the moment. And I have no intention of putting him in formalin and letting him end up as a showpiece in some anatomical collection!'

'I understand, of course, that you are upset, but if this anencephalic dies here in the hospital, we have in any case a claim over the corpse for autopsy.'

'Is that how it is, then? Right. Paula, please would you help Dorothea to pack? There's nothing to keep us here. Our son will come home with us and die there, where he belongs, and that's in his parents' arms. And he won't end up in some lab jar – he'll be given decent burial at Ohlsdorf Cemetery.'

'Think about it. If you leave this child to research, his time on earth won't have been in vain.'

'His time on earth isn't in vain in any case!' Richard's tone was icy.

Dr Brandes grimaced angrily but said nothing further as he left.

Paula was still gathering up Dorothea's things when the chaplain arrived to perform a rapid baptism ceremony for little Gottlieb.

An hour later Richard and Paula set down Fritz, Dorothea and the child outside their home.

'If you need anything, please do let us know,' said Richard to Fritz as he got out of the car.

Fritz nodded then helped his wife step out of the car with the baby.

Gottlieb Ellerweg passed away peacefully in his mother's arms four days later and was laid to rest at Ohlsdorf Cemetery in the presence of his loving family and their friends.

Chapter 14

After Gottlieb's burial, Fritz didn't talk about his son, but he and Dorothea wore black for the next few weeks. He put on a show of normality but Richard knew how much his friend was suffering, and it wasn't just because the baby had died. Somehow, the baby's condition had become known and the hospital was full of gossip. Although it couldn't be established exactly who had started it, Paula's frequent visits to Finkenau for her doctorate led her to suspect Brandes. The doctor had been angered by the way Fritz, a fellow professional, of all people, had been so stubborn and sentimental – as he disparagingly referred to it – that he had deprived the anatomical collection of a valuable specimen. The worst of it was that a lot of his colleagues agreed with him. Yes, it was a tragedy to have a baby with an abnormality, but let's face it, the child hadn't been right and death was a release. Some viewed it as provocation that not only had Fritz chosen to let 'the being' decay in the ground instead of handing it over to the noble cause of research, but that he continued to dress in black, even one week after Gottlieb's burial. As far as they were concerned, Fritz and Dorothea should have been relieved that the child hadn't survived to become a dribbling idiot.

Richard did all he could to support his friend, as did Professor Wehmeyer, who was one of the few who respected Fritz's need to mourn and protected him from the latent criticism of other colleagues. Fritz himself was single-minded and held his ground against the underlying hostility until eventually the news about his son lost its novelty and people turned their attention to other things. Richard, however, never forgot how other doctors had criticised his friend for the decision he had made and even attacked him for it. He was certain that Fritz would never forget it either.

◆ ◆ ◆

At the end of March, Richard completed the compulsory period working in surgery and then started as a junior doctor in psychiatry on 2 April 1929. He'd originally applied to the hospital at Friedrichsberg, easy to reach from Rothenburgsort, where he and Paula had found their own flat very soon after their wedding. However, the vacancy he'd been offered was at the Langenhorn asylum in Ochsenzoll, an outpost of the hospital at Friedrichsberg. Richard hadn't been very enthusiastic about this at first, mostly because of the long journey to work and the bad transport connections. His father-in-law consoled him with the fact that the Langenhorn facility was very modern and offered far more opportunities for promotion for a committed young doctor than the Friedrichsberg hospital. And as Richard had a car, the twenty-three-kilometre drive was not an insurmountable obstacle.

On his first day, Richard reported to the lead consultant, Dr Sierau, and was immediately impressed with the place. 'You won't find any caged beds and straitjackets here now,' Dr Sierau had explained. 'Last year we managed at long last to put an almost complete end to those archaic modes of treatment and we now treat all our patients with understanding and care. The switch to new methods was hard and the first few nights were both disturbing and disturbed, but it took only a few days for most of our patients to adjust to the new ways of doing things. Now they conduct themselves as calmly as before but without the old means of enforcement. They're quite easy to deal with, and less prone to violent and destructive behaviour.'

Dr Sierau looked through Richard's references. 'I can see you completed your doctorate on different treatment methods for the mentally ill, Dr Hellmer. You would be a real benefit to our secure unit. Make yourself known to Kurt Hansen, the senior nurse there, a very experienced man who'll be able to tell you a great deal. As will Dr Morgenstern, the senior consultant, and a genuine supporter of our new approach to caring for the insane.'

The pathway to the secure unit took Richard diagonally across the grounds, and his first impression was of the sheer size of the whole estate. It was a village in itself. It boasted fields of vegetables, orchards full of fruit trees, some livestock, as well as its own church to cater for the patients' spiritual health. The patients themselves lived in small pavilion-style buildings which were run along the lines of an open country house, albeit fitted with the necessary security measures. The secure unit where Richard was to work was surrounded by a high wall and bars had been fitted to the windows.

Kurt Hansen was a fatherly man in his mid-forties with a bit of a paunch and nerves of steel, and Richard found him immediately likeable.

'It's like raising children,' he commented as he took Richard around the building. 'Do you have any children, Dr Hellmer?'

'Not yet.'

'Then you'll get some good experience here until such time as you do. Our patients need understanding because there's so much they can't grasp for themselves, but at the same time they need an iron hand, as plenty of them know perfectly well what the rules are and want to break them. They can be absolute rascals.' He gave a gentle laugh. 'Don't be fooled by them – some of our friends here are up to every trick in the book and are remarkably shrewd. Come on, let me show you around our home.'

'Thank you.'

'My pleasure.' He opened one of the doors. 'This is your office. If you need anything, just tell me. As you can see, you even have your own telephone.' Kurt Hansen gestured towards the dark wooden desk, the gleaming new device ready and waiting. 'Our senior consultant is very proud that every doctor has his own telephone.'

'Well, I hadn't expected that! My wife and I are still waiting for our own line to be put in at home. We should be getting one in a couple of months' time.' Richard hung up his coat and put on the white coat that had been left out for him, then followed the nurse through the unit.

'The patients here are in observation rooms because they have to be watched at all times. Here in this unit we've got two observation rooms, each with twelve beds.'

Hansen opened the door to one of these rooms. Three male patients lay in their beds, but otherwise the room was empty. 'The garden's open at this time of day,' he explained, 'and we do encourage as many of them as possible to get some fresh air. It doesn't work with all of them. You just accept them as they are.'

Richard noticed how light and brightly decorated the room was. The walls were painted a pale yellow and matching curtains hung at the windows.

Hansen continued through the room to a door at the back. 'These are bathrooms for the long soak.' Inside were a pair of glazed enamel bathtubs that were used for calming any highly agitated patients and which, if necessary, could be closed over with a canvas cover so that only the patient's head was visible.

'A long soak is a good way to calm someone, but in the last couple of weeks we've barely needed them. Of course, we have normal baths too – they're at the other end of the hallway.'

Richard nodded.

He was then led to the day rooms, also used for games. The walls were decorated with landscape paintings, lending the place the air of a comfortable living room rather than a stark institution.

The last stop on Richard's tour was the garden, which was surrounded by a high wall. Most of the patients were out here, sitting in the sun or simply walking round and round. Some were playing board games with the nurses.

'It's got the feel of a sanatorium, don't you think?'

Richard nodded again. 'Very peaceful,' he said.

'We try to build relationships with the patients, but it's always precarious. Eventually, the plan is to transfer them to supervised living in the open country houses when they're ready. But don't go thinking it's always like the first days of spring around here! It gets pretty wild at times, and that's when we really have to roll our sleeves up and get stuck in.'

'I'm not afraid of that,' said Richard.

'Nor should you be. That's not for top brass like you, that's work for the foot soldiers,' Kurt Hansen said with a good-natured smile.

◆ ◆ ◆

Richard learned a lot about himself in those early weeks. He had approached his work full of ideals, driven on by his determination that no patient should ever suffer the pain his brother, Georg, had endured. The humane approach and the widespread rejection of restraint in Langenhorn fitted well with his vision for modern psychiatry.

A young schizophrenic called Herbert, suffering from an advanced form of dementia praecox at the age of twenty-one, reminded Richard of his brother, although he bore no particular resemblance to Georg. Perhaps it was because of his helpless expression and agitation whenever he didn't understand what was happening around him. Richard didn't quite know why, but he felt sure he could work with Herbert and help him reach a degree of stability that would allow him to move into one of the open houses and take up a useful occupation. Kurt Hansen repeatedly warned him that Herbert would only take advantage of this goodwill and eventually break any promises made, but Richard was unwavering in his opinion. From then on, he gave Herbert plenty of attention and one day took him for a walk through the grounds to show him the herd of dairy cattle. His face trusting and childlike, Herbert followed him, pointing at the rhododendrons in bloom along the main pathways and looking pleased when they met other people.

They reached the cows just at milking time and an elderly man with Down's syndrome gave Herbert a slightly clumsy explanation of how to do the milking. Herbert was quickly fired up and wanted to have a go straight away. Richard had no objection and was surprised to see how deft the young schizophrenic could be.

'I'd like to do that all the time,' he said to Richard on the way back. 'May I try it again?'

'We'll see,' said Richard, finding it hard to quash the young man's enthusiasm.

Once they were back, he spoke to Kurt Hansen and asked what conditions had to be met by inmates before they could live in an open house and work on the land.

'You really want to do that for Herbert?' Hansen was sceptical. 'Nothing'll come of it. Today he'll think it's wonderful, but tomorrow he'll lose all interest and make a run for it, get drunk somewhere and get into trouble.'

'Have we tried?'

'Last autumn he was sent out to help with the harvest. It didn't go well. He kept it up for two days, then cleared off and the police brought him back. Dr Morgenstern thinks it's too soon to try it again. The lad's too hot-headed.'

Richard spoke to Dr Morgenstern about Herbert during his rounds and related the milking episode.

'And now you believe he'll really stick at it, Dr Hellmer?'

'That I don't know. But I do know I saw a childlike joy in his eyes instead of the dull stare we see him with in here. Wouldn't it be worth a try?'

The consultant removed his spectacles and polished them as he observed Richard from the corner of his eye.

Putting his glasses back on, he said eventually, 'You have a big heart, but you wouldn't be doing the lad any favours. He won't keep it up.'

'Because he failed at the autumn harvest?'

'Yes. He lacks the necessary seriousness. He sees something, wants it, but equally fast he loses interest and goes looking for the nearest distraction.'

'Maybe taking some responsibility for the animals would bring him an inner sense of structure. After all, living creatures demonstrate their feelings, unlike harvested fruit.'

Dr Morgenstern smiled indulgently. 'You're new here, full of idealism and the desire to make the world a better place. I value characteristics like these in our young doctors – one can lose that all too quickly. Carry on with Herbert's excursions and you'll see how he soon loses interest.'

'And if he doesn't?'

'Then we'll discuss the matter again in two weeks.'

'Thank you.'

'Don't thank me yet, Dr Hellmer. I'd rather you show me that you can motivate Herbert in the longer term to take a lasting interest in some occupation.'

Kurt Hansen seemed unconvinced and gave an almost imperceptible shake of the head, but Richard was confident that Herbert would be the first of many whose lives could once again become worthwhile with his help.

After two weeks of regular excursions with Herbert, Richard saw his efforts rewarded when Dr Morgenstern agreed to Herbert's transfer to one of the open country houses. Richard was triumphant at having made such a significant breakthrough and drove home that evening thoroughly elated.

When he arrived at work the following day, however, he learned that Herbert was back in the secure unit. Immediately after his transfer, he had climbed over the fence and absconded. The police had brought him back in the middle of the night after he'd got drunk in a pub nearby, not paid for his drinks and then had a punch-up with other customers.

Richard was thunderstruck to find Herbert, the very picture of misery, sitting on his old bed in the observation room, his face bruised from the brawl and his eyes bloodshot from the alcohol to which he was so unaccustomed.

'What was the point of all that, then?'

'Oh, Doctor, I had a real thirst on me and I hadn't been there for ages.'

'But you promised me you would keep to our agreement.'

'Yes, I will do that. Promise. Can I go back to see the cows now?' He looked at Richard with a trusting expression like that of an abandoned child. This time, however, it had no effect on Richard. He was so disappointed and angry with himself for not heeding the warnings of more experienced colleagues and for thinking that he knew better.

'Sorry, no more excursions to see the cows for the time being.'

'Why not?'

'You broke the rules. You ran off, got drunk, didn't pay your way and you got into a fight. And all that on the first night. I am bitterly disappointed.'

'I'm sorry. I'll never do it again. Promise.'

Richard didn't waver. 'No more cows for the time being. You need a bit more time. Dr Morgenstern was right.'

Kurt Hansen greeted Richard with an encouraging clap on the shoulder. 'Don't take it too much to heart, sir. You were well intentioned, but we know what we're dealing with here. It was clear from the start.'

'But why did Dr Morgenstern agree to the transfer if he knew all along that Herbert would abscond? This could have had terrible consequences.' He swallowed hard when he imagined all the things that could have happened.

'I want to be quite open with you, Dr Hellmer. You believe in the goodness of every patient and your heart's in the right place, but our patients are only human. They're neither angels nor devils. Unlike those doctors who see the patients as wilful devils to be subjected to constant discipline, you've got the makings of a good psychiatrist. But even those who think like you need to recognise that idealism doesn't always achieve the right end and can have serious consequences. And the sooner you experience this for yourself, the better. Herbert has only ever run off in order to get drunk and sometimes he gets a punch on the nose, like last night. Nothing worse than that has ever happened because Herbert's actually a very nice lad.

'That's why Dr Morgenstern was prepared to let you have your way. So you could find out at first-hand how easy it is to fall for a patient's trusting looks and promises that are genuinely meant at the time – Herbert really means it and that's how he persuaded you. But when it comes down to it, he just can't do it. We all knew it wasn't going to work. Dr Morgenstern gave you the chance to find out this way because he thinks a lot of you, so consider it a compliment, but you've still got a fair bit to learn.'

'So you wanted to bring me down to earth with a bit of a bump.' Richard forced a smile, although inside he felt ashamed of himself. Had he really been so pig-headed that nobody trusted him to listen to the facts? Yes, apparently. He remembered how happy he'd felt the evening before when he'd related his first big success as a budding psychiatrist to Paula. She'd been so proud of him, and yet now he had to tell her that his supposed great success had actually been a hard lesson. He sighed.

It was with mixed feelings that Richard went into the doctors' canteen. How on earth was he to keep his credibility with colleagues after this incident with Herbert? He took a deep breath, gathered himself and took a seat on the same table as Dr Morgenstern and Dr Krüger. Krüger was around Richard's age and had started at the asylum just before him. They'd crossed paths now and then and had greeted one another, but Richard had had little to do with him so far.

As Richard sat down at the table, Krüger observed him with not a little amusement.

'I hear you may just have experienced your first personal Waterloo?'

Richard was not usually short of a riposte, but his sense of shame went so deep that he couldn't summon a suitable reply.

'If that's what you want to call it,' was all he said.

'"Waterloo" seems rather harsh,' observed Dr Morgenstern. 'It's something we've all had to go through once.'

'I haven't,' said Krüger. 'Naivety and unrefined compassion are not appropriate when treating the mentally ill.'

Still no response from Richard, as he focused on the goulash on his plate.

'You're right,' said Dr Morgenstern. 'An indiscriminate sense of compassion is not appropriate, but then neither is a complete lack of compassion. What the former has in excess, the latter is woefully lacking. And learning to balance these out is part and parcel of our professional development.'

Richard listened to this exchange with interest. Was it his imagination, or had Dr Morgenstern just discreetly rebuked Dr Krüger? He looked hard at Krüger and saw that his lips were now pursed in anger.

'Yes, it was an error,' acknowledged Richard. 'I was convinced I was doing the right thing because that's what I wanted to believe. It will never happen again.'

Dr Morgenstern contradicted him. 'Yes, it will. It'll happen again at some point. It would be a bad thing for it not to happen again. We can't do our work without a sense of trust. And it takes professional experience to weigh up with comparative certainty when trust is to be brought to bear, and when not.'

'Where there is any doubt, I trust no one,' said Krüger. 'And if we look at Herbert's case, this unwarranted trust brought unnecessary risk to a number of innocent bystanders. He failed to settle his bill and involved harmless pub-goers in a brawl.'

'I read the police report,' retorted Richard. 'It's true that Herbert failed to pay and someone confronted him and one thing led to another. But who actually started the fight is unclear. These so-called harmless pub-goers were not the ones who reported him, which makes me suspect that they themselves started the fight.'

'The fact is that this would never have occurred, had you not been taken in by this lunatic.'

'Yes, you're right, and I'm extremely sorry, but I can't undo what's happened. I can only try to do better in future.'

Richard's admission merely irritated Krüger, while Dr Morgenstern gave a little smile.

Chapter 15

Over the next few months Richard became increasingly confident in dealing with his patients. At the same time he developed a strong aversion to his colleague Krüger, who considered it a waste of time trying to understand the minds of the mentally ill and simply responded to any bad behaviour with disciplinary measures. Richard quickly realised that Dr Morgenstern also viewed Krüger's approach with some scepticism, but Krüger did not let this bother him and threw his energy into making his mark with the success that his methods undoubtedly showed. For a while Richard was tempted to wage a quiet war against him, but decided against it. He would rather expend his energy on his patients than on feuds of that kind.

The men in the secure unit were often bored so Richard put his mind to the idea of establishing some simple forms of work on the wards, rather like in prison, where men would make paper bags with glue and paper. He put forward his idea to Kurt Hansen, who had no objections at all, so together they started to plan. One week later they had a concrete proposal to put to Dr Morgenstern. Every morning for three hours the games room on the ward would now be turned into a workroom. Soon a good proportion of the men were busy sticking the bags with an unexpected enthusiasm, but the disadvantage was that patients who were not able to work with that level of concentration felt excluded. Richard couldn't think what to offer these men as an alternative until, one evening when he was talking it over with Paula, she reminded him of Professor Habermann's lecture, where they'd met. 'How about letting them draw pictures? If the psychiatrists in Heidelberg can do it, so can you.'

'I don't think Kurt will be too keen. The paint would make a horrible mess on the ward.'

'Yes, but you don't need to give them ink or watercolours. What about coloured pencils or wax crayons?'

'That's a real possibility.' Richard was grateful for the idea and spoke to Kurt Hansen the very next day. Convinced by Richard's infectious enthusiasm, Kurt made arrangements to bring in all the necessary materials. Wax crayons turned out to be too expensive and the patients could do a fair bit of mischief with them, so Hansen went for coloured pencils.

Dr Morgenstern and the senior consultant, Dr Sierau, were quite taken with Richard's commitment and urged colleagues to take a look at what he'd managed to achieve in such a short time. Even Krüger, never one to stray into the secure unit, was among the visitors.

'Making paper bags isn't a bad idea in itself,' he said, 'but handing the mentally ill high-quality paper and expensive pencils only to have them ruined'—here he held up a pencil that had been snapped in half and then sharpened at both ends—'doesn't seem particularly productive to me. Do you actually believe the world has been waiting for scrawls like these?'

'The French are earning a lot of money at the moment with work by the Cubists, you know, so I thought our patients could do a bit of Cubist work too. Why should people spend a lot of money on paintings by some Frenchman when German pieces of work can be acquired instead? Especially if the pictures are painted by men who can't do anything else, freeing up the more productive chaps so they can work. And as we're more efficient, the art dealers will bite our hands off, you mark my words.'

Krüger looked at Richard with a mixture of irritation and anger. 'You're not serious, surely?'

Richard laughed. 'And you have no idea about art, surely?'

'Do you really believe someone will buy this scrawl?'

'No. Which is why I said you have no idea about art, otherwise you'd have known I was being ironic.'

'This project is a total waste of time and money.'

'Nothing that brings people joy is wasted. You can't put a price on joy and happiness.'

Krüger harrumphed with disdain then left.

◆ ◆ ◆

At the beginning of September 1929, Richard's father invited his son, together with Paula and her father, to meet him at home. He said it was to discuss urgent business.

It was different from the usual family gathering, as this time it was Margit's husband, Holger, who had called everyone together. He addressed the group.

'As you all know, I keep a close eye on the economic situation worldwide. There are a few things I've noticed. The stock markets have been rumbling for a good year. The fact that we were able to give you the car for your wedding was a result of that. Its original owner had made a few miscalculations and had to sell it off at less than its value. But I fear this is only the beginning. At the New York Stock Exchange, rates are constantly falling. It's all going to go belly-up at some point, I'm pretty sure of that. As soon as that happens, the Americans will call in their war loans to the English and the French, who will in turn have to recoup their losses by demanding the Versailles reparations from us in order to pay off their own debts. We could make repayments only through new loans, but if the banks fail, then there can be no loans, everything will collapse and we'll have another 1923. Cash won't be worth the paper it's printed on.'

Richard cut in here. 'But what about the Young Plan that's being negotiated in France at the moment? That's likely to fix the debt repayment, isn't it? Even if it does mean the debt won't be paid off until I'm eighty-seven.' His tone was bitter.

'I wouldn't count on that,' replied Holger. 'As I said, it's very like the situation back in 1923. And we must see to it that we make sensible investments in case inflation returns.'

'What do you suggest?' asked Paula's father.

'Before the last period of inflation we bought that large piece of forestry land beyond the city boundary. That's what's now supplying us with our wood. We've made no losses to speak of and have come through the hard times unscathed. Land always holds its value. On top of that, it means we always have the raw material for our work. I've noticed that the woodland next to ours is for sale. The current owner can't afford the land tax any more. I'd like us to make the purchase, but we don't have enough liquid assets. Wilhelm, I wanted to ask whether you would contribute – as our business partner, you might say. Then we can make use of the wood ourselves or sell it. Or rent out the land. The advantage is that woodland holds its value. Unlike property, there's no rental bond to pay and trees don't deteriorate. The longer they stay standing, the more valuable they are.' Holger smiled at the thought.

'And how much would I need to put in?'

'We're short of seven thousand marks.'

'That's a tidy sum. How much time have I got to think about it?'

'We've got a week.'

Richard could see his father-in-law doing the sums in his head.

'All right, then,' said Dr Engelhardt after a while. 'I'm with you, provided my name appears in the land registry as a stakeholder.'

'Consider it done,' said Richard's father. 'That'll apply both to the registration and the valuation of the wood. There are only two safe investments at the moment – land and precious metals. I'd always go for land – at least it can't be stolen.'

'At worst, they can impose state levies like forced mortgages, as they did during the last inflationary period, but we would still have the land,' added Dr Engelhardt.

Holger nodded in full agreement. 'And that's why we're buying 73 hectares at 316 marks per hectare. In an emergency we could sell enough land to pay off any forced mortgage, if it came to it.'

Paula's father silently ran through the figures again. 'So I'm in with about twenty-two hectares?'

'That's it,' said Holger. 'The owner urgently needs to sell, but I can only push through that price per hectare if we buy all of the land, and on our side we have only sixteen thousand marks.'

'Only sixteen thousand marks?' Paula's father chuckled quietly. 'What's that old saying about a trade in hand finds gold in every land?'

'We're doing all right,' said Richard's father, 'but you've always known we're not exactly poor.'

'Certainly since you suggested the car as a wedding present,' conceded Paula's father. 'As I've said, count me in. Feel free to prepare the papers for me to sign over the next few days, and I'll transfer you the money.'

Less than a month later, after Holger had completed the land purchase, it was clear that he'd once again found a way to get them through hard times. On 24 October 1929, the New York Stock Exchange collapsed, resulting in a severe economic crisis for Germany too. Businesses couldn't cover their costs, exports declined and countless people became unemployed. With the onset of winter, there were more beggars on the street than in recent years. Whole families were unable to pay their rent and became homeless. Soup kitchens and charitable food supplies struggled to meet the need.

Thanks to Holger's foresight, Richard's family remained untouched by the crisis, by and large, and the same went for Paula's father. In addition, Richard had advised Fritz to spend the cash that he and Dorothea had saved and so he bought a car, his father adding a couple of hundred to help out.

'Best way to blow your funds before they're worthless!' Fritz was beaming with delight as he showed his new Opel 10/40 PS to Richard. 'It can do eighty-five kilometres an hour.'

'It's really sleek. Great choice! So is Dorothea going to get her licence now?' Paula had passed her test three months earlier.

'Dorothea's not quite as modern as your wife. She enjoys me chauffeuring her!'

'Oh yes, Paula likes that too. But it's important she can drive herself if she has to.'

'In case you want to take a nap next time you go to Italy?' Fritz smiled broadly at his friend.

'Something like that,' Richard said, smiling back.

'Let's hope fuel stays affordable. At least in our line of work, we don't need to worry. Professor Wehmeyer thinks I'll qualify soon as a specialist and can be considered for a senior position if Dr Winkler feels he's ready to step down next year.'

'You're climbing the ladder fast!'

'It's important to me. I think what convinced Professor Wehmeyer is that night I saved the life of a suicide case. Isn't he in your care now, over at the Langenhorn?'

'Oh, you mean Heinrich Ahlers, the one who shot himself in the head after losing all his money in the crash?'

'That's him. Wasn't an easy operation, and at one point we didn't think he was going to pull through.'

'A case like that leaves me wondering if it really was a blessing for him that you're such an outstanding surgeon. He's paralysed down one side and his personality has completely changed. I don't think he'll ever move on from the secure unit.'

'Am I supposed to have let him die?'

'No, of course not. I'm just saying how it is. Sometimes modern medicine can be a curse too.'

'Maybe,' conceded Fritz, 'but I'd do the same again. I'd have clutched at each and every straw available if it had meant saving Gottlieb, even though he was severely deformed and would never have led a normal life. I don't care what anyone else thinks.'

This was the first time since Gottlieb's burial that Fritz had spoken his son's name.

'If it had been your son, what would you have done?'

'The same as you. I thought you'd know that.'

Fritz nodded weakly. 'Yes, I do.' He let out a sigh. 'Dorothea's afraid of having another child. She's scared another one could have a similar abnormality.'

'But that's highly improbable.'

'I know, but the fear's there.'

'Are you afraid too?'

'No. I've made a careful study of academic papers on this malformation. There are no indications of anything hereditary, nor any descriptions of more than one deformity of this type occurring within the same family. But that doesn't change Dorothea's mind about saying no to a second pregnancy.' He sighed once more. 'So, we're getting a dog soon.'

Richard's jaw dropped. 'A dog?'

Fritz laughed. 'You should see your face! Is that so absurd?'

'As a child substitute? Yes, somehow it is.'

'I'd like a German shepherd, but Dorothea's keen on a dachshund.'

'So, a dachshund it is?'

'You know me too well, Richard! But joking aside, Doro just needs more time, and a dachshund's ideal. On the one hand, it'll appeal to Doro's maternal instinct, and on the other, her husband can fool himself into believing he's got a true hunting dog.'

'You'll be trudging through the woods with the dachsie after foxes, then?'

'No, I'll be strolling by the Alster with him and Dorothea. Typical German family – man, wife, dachsie.'

They laughed at the picture this conjured up, and Richard was relieved to see his friend hadn't lost his sense of humour, in spite of the tragedy he'd suffered.

Meanwhile, the consequences of the economic crisis were making themselves felt in the asylum. Funds were short and the first casualty was the art therapy in the secure unit. The menus became less interesting, but thanks to their institution's self-sufficiency they were still more varied than in many other hospitals.

The economic crisis was a constant topic of conversation for the doctors and nurses, and not only because of the financial restrictions placed on them. Cases like that of Heinrich Ahlers were no longer the exception, even if most failed suicides were in far better physical shape than he was.

The issue of prevented suicide brought controversy to many a medical discussion. Richard and Dr Morgenstern took the view that every suicide should be prevented because it was not possible to determine at the outset whether the case was a desperate panic reaction or a rational suicide. Dr Krüger, however, was of the opinion that anyone who had lost everything in the economic crisis and had independently taken stock of his life should neither be prevented from ending it, nor be placed on an equal footing with a madman and locked up for the rest of his days.

'Where would we be if a man were no longer permitted to go down the route of a rational suicide but instead was forced to live the miserable life of a beggar?' This was Krüger over lunch one day in the canteen. 'Everyone must have the right to decide their own fate.'

'Yes,' said Richard, 'but how can we know whether the deed was done after mature consideration? And what's to lose if, after a failed suicide attempt, someone has the opportunity to think about whether there might be other solutions?'

'Like Ahlers, who has turned into a dribbling idiot because his wife didn't have the decency to let him die?'

'Oh yes, if only he'd had the decency to carry on and face life instead of taking refuge in death and leaving his family alone with all those debts, it would never have happened,' bit back Richard. 'Family men who end it because they've lost all their money are irresponsible and cowardly. A decent man in that position doesn't put a bullet in his head but tries his hardest to find other ways of supporting his family.'

'And in suicide cases the life insurance companies won't pay out,' said Dr Morgenstern. 'Otherwise, I could perhaps understand it as the final loving and caring thing to do.'

'And how on earth does it help the Ahlers when the head of their family is an idiot living permanently in an asylum?' Krüger was still enraged. 'Is he supposed to take his idiocy to the fair and appear in the freak show to earn something? He will now cost the nation huge sums of money year after year, and all because a completely senseless operation has preserved the ruin that his life has become.'

'So who are you blaming now? The wife? The surgeon? Or Ahlers himself, for being a bad shot when he put that pistol to his temple?' Richard replied angrily. 'Fortunately, cases like Ahlers' are rare exceptions. How about looking at Joachim Kleinfeld? His case is the exact opposite of Ahlers'.'

Kleinfeld was another who had lost everything in the crash and then tried to hang himself. His twelve-year-old son had found him in the attic and cut him down just in time. Because he wouldn't talk about his suicidal thoughts, he had been placed in the secure unit. Here Richard had taken particular care of him and in just a few weeks had helped the man get back the courage to face life and his family responsibilities.

'Are you going to keep on bringing up Kleinfeld?'

'No,' said Richard. 'I can also bring up Anton Müller, Bernhard Hartwein and Justus Bergstedt. That gives us a ratio of 4:1. Four men who managed to find their way back into life because we didn't just let them die. And that's how I measure what I do. It would, of course, have been better for Ahler if he'd died instead of living as he does now, but it would have been even better if we'd really been able to save him. And that was attempted. Hindsight is a wonderful thing.'

'Are you saying that because the surgeon who saved him is your friend, or do you truly believe it?'

Richard stopped short at this. How did Krüger know who'd operated on Ahlers and that the surgeon was his friend?

'You seem to have gone into Ahlers' case very thoroughly, considering the man's not your patient.'

'I didn't have to. You find out more than you might think just by reading the relevant professional journals, my dear colleague. It would seem you don't read any case descriptions, is that right? Otherwise, the publication by Professor Wehmeyer and Dr Ellerweg on successfully operating on an attempted suicide case would definitely not have escaped you. And Dr Ellerweg is a good friend of yours, isn't he?'

'You certainly seem very interested in my private life, given that you know the names of my friends.'

Krüger grinned. 'It's a passion of mine. I like to know who I'm dealing with.'

'Then I've got one more detail for you, my dear colleague. I am not only a friend of Fritz Ellerweg's but also a friend of his dachsie, Rudi. Do you need more information? Rudi's twelve weeks old, a German longhair with a good pedigree.'

'Very witty, I'm sure,' Krüger said, pushing aside his empty plate. 'I have things to do and don't have time for your facetious remarks.' With that, he got up and left.

Chapter 16

The economic crisis affected Richard's personal and professional life, as it did the whole nation. On 27 March 1930, the country saw the collapse of Chancellor Müller's great coalition of Social Democrats, the Centre Party, the German Democrats and the German People's Party.

Richard was deeply concerned when Paul von Hindenburg, President of the Republic, decided to appoint Heinrich Brüning, leader of the Centre Party, as Chancellor. Brüning proceeded to form a minority government without the Social Democrats.

Opinion in the family was divided. Richard, his father and Paula were sceptical, while Dr Engelhardt maintained that Hindenburg knew exactly what he was doing and that they should have faith in him. He felt that in the end it was all about forming a bloc in opposition to the communists.

'I'd rather see a bloc against the Nazis,' commented Richard.

'My dear boy, you've perhaps seen too many SDP election posters,' was Dr Engelhardt's reaction. 'The biggest danger is of Germany having a red revolution and ending up living under the Russians.'

'And you think the Nazis would be a better option? When I hear the way they rant against the Jews, I get so worried about all our Jewish friends and colleagues.'

'Oh, they're all talk; it's all about finding a scapegoat. It's won't be as bad as you think.'

'Leonie sees it rather differently,' countered Paula, 'and, by the way, so does her father. He's already thinking about picking up with old contacts in Switzerland in case the situation in Germany gets any worse.'

'Isaak was always an old pessimist.' Dr Engelhardt made a dismissive gesture, adding, 'Just wait a while and it'll come out all right in the end.'

Richard was ready to disagree, but Paula gently placed her hand on his arm and shook her head. There was no point getting into an argument with her father when there was nothing any of them could do about it anyway.

It was now summer 1930 and Paula completed her doctorate. She set about preparing for her final medical examination, which she was due to take on 10 September, later in the year. She passed with ease, although her personal triumph in becoming a qualified woman doctor at last was diluted by the political situation during those few days, when everyone was talking about the new parliamentary election to be held on 14 September.

The economic crisis had given the National Socialist Workers' Party, the NSDAP, an unforeseen boost, and the party's supporters, all dressed in their brown shirts, paraded through the streets in the run-up to the election, engaging in increasingly frequent and bloody skirmishes with the communists. Even inside their own flat, Paula and Richard once heard shots and shouting outside.

'This is even worse than during the war!' exclaimed Richard as he made for the window to see what was going on.

Paula held him back. 'Don't, there could be stray bullets!' And sure enough, soon afterwards they heard a window shatter one floor below.

Richard contacted the police. 'How have these idiots got hold of firearms?' He and Paula had taken refuge in their bathroom, which had no windows. 'I tell you, I'd like to stick a round of ammunition up their backsides.'

Paula couldn't help but laugh, in spite of the tension. 'Who'd have thought we'd be hiding from stray bullets in our very own bathroom?' She looked at Richard, her eyes betraying her love for him. 'We live in exciting times, eh?'

'I'd much rather live in boring times,' retorted Richard. 'But we must always make the best of a bad situation, mustn't we?' With that, he drew Paula closer and kissed her.

It was half an hour before the police arrived and the shouting and shooting stopped, putting an end to their ordeal.

When Richard related the incident to Fritz he was not surprised.

'In the last couple of months I've had eleven cases of bullet wounds, always on night duty. Eleven! You'd think there was a war on. And they're not all Nazis or communists – ordinary criminals are using weapons too. They have no scruples whatsoever and don't give a damn about getting locked up. And as for the number of people using knives, I won't even start on that.'

Richard nodded gloomily. Everybody knew that crime rates had gone sky-high since the start of the economic crisis. Many lacked the bare necessities, respectable women chose prostitution over starvation and the tally of burglaries and thefts kept on growing. The police were completely overstretched and the governing parties remained silent. The communists aspired to a republic modelled on that of the Soviets and campaigned for the dispossession of the wealthy in order to break the inequity in society, something which left people in Richard's circle feeling deeply troubled. The Nazis, on the other hand, promised to create more jobs, safeguard private property and oppose any such Soviet-style conditions. They said that the nation should stand as one unit, with nobody worse off and everybody better off. The Social Democrats couldn't offer any compelling answers to the urgent questions of the day, and were reduced simply to fighting against the increasing influence of the NSDAP. Although Richard was a convinced Social Democrat, he was furious that the party's election campaign had revolved exclusively around preventing any further growth of Nazism instead of coming up with new ideas to motivate the people to a renewed sense of vigour.

The radio started to broadcast Adolf Hitler speeches more frequently. 'National Socialism is fighting to take the German worker out of the hands of swindlers,' proclaimed Hitler in a big speech at the Berlin Sportpalast. 'What we promise is not material improvement for one class and one class alone, but growth in strength of the entire nation, for only this can lead to freedom and power for the whole people.' The rejoicing that broke out defied all description.

'Do you really want to listen to that rubbish?' asked Richard when he saw Paula sitting by the radio in the kitchen.

'Yes, I do. I'm still waiting for him to explain how he's going to do it.' She poured herself a cup of real coffee, which was a luxury she refused to give up.

'You'll be waiting a long time, then,' observed Richard, helping himself to coffee too. 'And the people are not interested in that in any case. Krüger said today that the other parties have had a chance and haven't seized it. Why shouldn't Hitler have the chance to show what he can do?'

'Krüger's nothing to go by.'

'No, but yesterday even Kurt Hansen supported him. He reckons we need law and order on our streets again. I didn't go along with that, told him people can hardly be expected to get involved in shoot-outs with the communists, but that didn't convince anyone. Quite the opposite – everybody else thought that the current chaos was down to the established parties and that it was high time for a new broom. Even Dr Morgenstern said nothing, and he's a Jew. He should know better than anyone what the Nazis think of people like him. I just don't understand it.'

'Maybe my father's right after all,' said Paula. 'The Nazis do a lot of bragging, but perhaps it's not such a bad idea to get a bit of fresh air into parliament. And the SPD has had the majority for so long. If they want to stay in power, they really need to give the people some hope.'

'Do you know what the problem is? We need characters in politics. Ebert's dead, Stresemann's dead, and there's nobody left to take on the NSDAP demagogue. We've got a cabinet full of puppets.'

◆ ◆ ◆

Despite this, the SDP went on to get the most votes in the election. But Hitler's NSDAP election campaign had had an impact and they swept into the Reichstag in October 1930 as the second biggest party. The following night saw numerous clashes with uniformed Nazis in Berlin, their victims predominantly Jewish.

All of this left Leonie extremely uneasy, and she feared Hamburg would start to see attacks on Jewish people as well.

Paula saw it a bit differently. 'I'm just afraid everyone's going to have bullets flying around their heads, whether or not they're Jewish. Didn't I tell you about what happened right outside our house last month? We had to hide in the bathroom.'

'Yes, you did, but that's not what I mean. There are also specifically targeted hostilities against Jews, and it's my belief that's a result of the Nazis' success. Have you found somewhere to do your compulsory spell in surgery?'

'Yes, but unpaid and only because Fritz found me a place in his department. At the moment male graduates take preference. I'm starting on 1 November. What about you?'

'Well, of the male graduates, it's the non-Jewish ones who take preference. So as a Jewish woman around here I'm basically the equivalent of a pariah in India. I've applied to lots of Hamburg hospitals but because of my gender and my religion I get nothing but rejections. Even for unpaid roles. Even the Israeli hospital rejected me, and that's because all the current Jewish doctors are flocking there and men, of course, take precedence there as well.' Leonie's frustration was clear. 'So then I asked Fritz, and he put in a word for me, but I can't start until 1 May, when you finish, and I don't want to wait that long. So my father's managed to find me a post at a small Jewish hospital in Göttingen.'

'When are you starting?'

'On 1 November, like you. So we've still got time to do a few nice things together.'

'And do you know where you want to work when you come back from Göttingen? Still at the Rothenburgsort Children's?'

Leonie nodded. 'Yes, and the head there is Jewish so I don't need to worry. What about you?'

'All rejections up to now. It's mostly because I'm a married woman and my husband has a secure job.' She let out a sigh. 'Men get priority everywhere, supposedly because they have families to feed – even the bachelors. I was once asked if Richard was one of the army of unemployed. I said he wasn't, then was told firmly that I had no right to take a job away from another man and that I'd do better to concentrate on my innate abilities and have children. I could have scratched his eyes out for saying that.'

'Do ask Dr Stamm. He's a great admirer of your father and women get far more recognition in paediatrics than in psychiatry.'

'I'll think about it.'

'Don't think for too long. Some man will snatch the job from right under your nose. And anyway, I'd love to work with you.'

Paula nodded. In one way she'd have loved to have been as pragmatic as Leonie, but at the same time she felt angry that her job search was being hampered by the two millstones of her gender and her marital status.

That evening she told Richard about the advice Leonie had offered and found him suspiciously enthusiastic. She was puzzled because Richard had always so unreservedly supported her every professional concern, including her desire to become a psychiatrist, so she dug a bit deeper.

'I hate to say it,' he began, 'but I'm afraid you won't get a position in psychiatry.'

'Why on earth not? You said yourself there'd be two vacancies in the spring.'

'Yes, there will be. And I've asked Dr Sierau about them because by then you'll have done your compulsory period in surgery. He declined because you're my wife.'

'On what grounds? He doesn't even know me.'

'No, but he doesn't want a married couple working at the hospital, not if they're both doctors. If you were a nurse, it might be easier.'

'But why? I don't understand.'

'Well, I didn't either, so I probed a bit. And basically, he assumes we'll soon have children and that you'll then give up work, so he'd rather put a man in the post, someone who'll be there long-term. He also thinks that a married couple could make the planning rota too complicated. Nothing could persuade him otherwise. So, you've got two options: either you choose Hamburg, where the only possibility is the children's hospital, or you choose psychiatry and have to look for a post in another city, which would mean we could see each other only on the weekends when we're not on duty, and I don't want that. I want to live with you and have children together.'

'That's what I want too. But it's so unfair. Why do women always have to carry the burden? Why's it always about taking second place?'

Richard put his arms around her. 'Give me fifteen years, then I'll be in charge and I'll change everything.'

'You're a nutcase,' she said lovingly.

'But a nutcase who makes an effort. I'd do anything to help you do what you want but I'm really up against it here. And I don't want you to leave our city to go running after a dream that's perhaps not worth it. Working in psychiatry in a closed institution is no picnic. Just yesterday one of our patients went completely off the rails, smashed up one of the tables in the dining room and had to be forcibly restrained. And we've had another patient for ages who smears himself with his own excrement, so on both hygiene and safety grounds we have to keep him in the closed bath most of the time. You've achieved so much, Paula – you're a qualified doctor, and you've done your PhD. We've already got two psychiatrists in the family. Perhaps it would be a good thing if you went in for paediatrics. We both want children one day in any case, and it goes well with that.'

With Richard's arms around her, Paula felt her disappointment and anger melting away. He had tried everything to support her, but these were very difficult times. She should actually be grateful for any post as a doctor. Even Richard had had to lower his original expectations and face the long drive over to Langenhorn every day.

'Well, all right, then,' she said with a sigh. 'I'll bow to reason. Two psychiatrists in the family is plenty.'

Chapter 17

In May 1931 Paula took up her post as junior doctor in Rothenburgsort Children's Hospital. Her short cycle ride to work meant she saw the many signs of increasing poverty in that part of the city at first hand. More and more little shops were being forced to close down; she noticed how it would start with a banner in the window advertising big reductions. A week later a different sign would announce CLEARANCE SALE. One more week and the shelves would be empty and the proprietor would be seen, hammer in hand, boarding up the windows. The number of boarded-up shops grew by the day. Occasionally, there'd be notice of a new trading address a couple of streets away, but more often than not the small shopkeeper's living had been wiped out. And the people looked more down at heel than a couple of years earlier: the adults' clothing was shabby and threadbare; the children were often barefoot. As soon as darkness fell, robbery was a growing hazard. Paula had no fears for herself, as it was now May and she set off on her bike in the light and came back before sunset. But ever since a neighbour had been set upon and robbed at dusk only two streets away from their flat, Richard had insisted that when it started to get dark earlier he would take her to work by car and pick her up again in the evening. While Paula appreciated being so well cared for, she nonetheless hoped that the situation would have eased by the time autumn came. She valued the freedom of setting off in the morning a whole hour after Richard had left and then getting back an hour before him. This meant she had time to check that their daily help had done everything asked of her and to Paula's exacting standards.

She soon started to enjoy the work at the children's hospital much more than she'd expected. The working atmosphere was relaxed, and as Leonie had started there at the same time, the two friends shared an office. Rothenburgsort Children's Hospital was considered one of the most modern in Europe and, thanks to its many financial supporters, it suffered less than other hospitals in the economic crisis.

This wasn't the case at the Langenhorn asylum; Richard had told her of drastic cutbacks there. Those working on the land still got normal rations, but inmates in the secure unit received the absolute minimum, only enough for them not to starve. Langenhorn had the benefit of its own food production surplus and so even had to provide for patients from other institutions for a short time, largely because those patients were considered of greater economic value than the mentally ill. This made Richard's work a lot more difficult because the nagging hunger left his patients nervy and agitated, and this in turn caused outbursts of aggression on an almost daily basis. Once, Richard came home with his shirt ripped after he had tried to separate a pair of fighting patients. When he related these incidents to Paula in the evenings, she often caught herself feeling relieved that she'd listened to him and was now working with children. Yes, some could shout, scratch, stamp and bite, but they soon calmed down again once the medical procedure they didn't like was over.

Paula's area of responsibility included treating child diphtheria cases. Inoculation had been available for a couple of years but the disease was still widespread. Without treatment requiring an antitoxin serum prepared using equine blood, diphtheria usually resulted in death. During her first few days of work, Paula found herself repeatedly thinking of her mother, who had died of the disease when Paula had still been a little girl. As there'd been no inoculation in those days, she hadn't been allowed to enter her mother's sickroom.

Now, when she was treating the children, whether painting their throats, administering injections or tending to the terrible skin lesions that were sometimes a complication of the condition, she wondered over and over how much her mother had suffered in her final days. Had her neck been so swollen that she could hardly breathe? Or had her heart simply given up the fight, as had just happened with little Peter Melchior, apparently well on the way to recovery, only to die quite unexpectedly? She knew it was futile to dwell on these things but found it hard to banish these thoughts.

For Paula, diphtheria became a bogeyman. The sickness appeared in so many different guises, causing not only the agony of suffocation but also sudden heart failure and severe paralysis, and she wondered why health officials didn't place greater value on getting every child inoculated. She acknowledged that the jab didn't give full protection because three of her little charges had fallen sick in spite of having been inoculated, but at least for them the symptoms were not as severe.

'It's always a matter of education and money,' said Dr Stamm when Paula spoke to him about it. 'As you can see, there are children here from all levels of society, but those from working-class homes are clearly in the majority. The families often don't know about the usefulness and value of inoculation, and although most working families are part of the health insurance system, they only go to the doctor once their own methods have failed. If a child suddenly develops a sore throat and painful swallowing, most mothers try to clear it up with hot poultices or camomile tea first. Few of them seem to realise that it could be anything fatal like diphtheria, and by the time they have an accurate diagnosis most of the children in the household, and the majority of the adults, are all infected.'

'Why don't we set more store on education and prevention being provided by the midwife at birth? Or by health visitors?'

'Now that really would be a blessing, but so far there haven't been the necessary means,' Dr Stamm said with a sigh of regret. 'The law on public health does need urgent reform, but I fear that our politicians have other things on their minds at the moment.'

Soon after this conversation, Paula was approached by Sister Elfriede, an enthusiastic young nurse with a mass of freckles and strawberry blonde hair who Paula had always found to be exceptionally hardworking and caring in the way she dealt with the children.

'You're absolutely right, Doctor,' said Sister Elfriede. 'Healthcare in this country is a disgrace, but there is a solution. If you want, I can tell you a bit about it.'

'Please do, Sister Elfriede.'

'I've been a member of People's Welfare for a few weeks now. We're not registered as an association yet, but we're working on it. The aim is to provide healthcare support to struggling families and lone mothers. This is not only about educating and providing information but also about caring for infants and offering balanced nutrition for children. We concentrate our efforts on those otherwise shunned by society. We rely on voluntary donations, but our organisation is growing all the time.' Sister Elfriede reached into her uniform pocket for a leaflet. 'If you're interested in becoming a member, here's all you need to know,' she said, handing it to Paula. 'You can keep this one – I've got plenty of others. I've been involved in Workers' Welfare for a long time, but its structures are as old as the hills and the people in charge care only about their own advancement. There are no new ideas there, no new blood. That's why I was so inspired by the aims of People's Welfare.' She gave a cheeky wink. 'I've already recruited eleven new members here.'

'Thank you,' Paula said, putting the leaflet in the pocket of her white coat. 'That sounds like a tremendous opportunity to put help where it's needed.'

'At last, someone's had a good idea,' commented Leonie later when Paula showed her the leaflet. 'I notice it's been set up by a private foundation in Berlin and I think it's time to engage with more of these, instead of pinning our hopes on political parties.'

'The minimum monthly contribution is only fifty pfennig,' said Paula. 'I think it's my duty as a doctor to go for five marks a month.'

'So you're going to join?'

'Yes.'

'Good, me too. And I'll persuade my father. The money's bound to be put to good use. I particularly like what they do for lone mothers.'

'Is that in case you're ever looking for a handsome beast to sire your children so you don't have to marry?' Paula teased.

'Don't be daft,' Leonie said with a laugh. 'No, I think it's time people stopped looking down on women with illegitimate children. Nobody speaks ill of a man with illegitimate children all over the place, quite the opposite in fact – he's seen as a bit of a lad. But the women are always seen as tramps. They're the ones who need the support after falling foul of one of those lousy lechers. And children can't be blamed for the way their parents have behaved.'

'You're right on everything except one point. Men like that are not seen in a good light. You should hear Richard on the subject.'

'Does he believe in castrating them?' Leonie grinned.

'No, not quite. But he might have thrown around words like "sterilisation" when he's been ranting about it.'

'I can just imagine him saying that,' said Leonie. 'It's a shame not all men are like Richard.'

When Paula showed the leaflet to her husband that evening, he was equally enthusiastic and suggested they jointly donate ten marks a month. Like Leonie, he thought it a good sign that this was run by a private body with charitable status and no political aim.

◆ ◆ ◆

The overall economic position remained bad and the number of people out of work kept on rising. Even Richard's father's carpentry business hit a slack period as commissions slowed. Most customers were restricting themselves to repairs only and hardly anyone was ordering a whole new piece of furniture. There was enough work not to have to get rid of any staff, but for the first time in years Hans-Kurt Hellmer couldn't afford to take on any apprentices.

On the streets there was yet more criminality, and burglary was an increasing problem. There were repeated break-ins at the workshop, so Richard's father got himself two guard dogs, who slept in there overnight. The break-ins suddenly stopped.

As the days grew shorter and the nights drew in, Richard stuck to his word and drove Paula to the children's hospital in the morning before heading off to Langenhorn; he would then pick her up again at the end of the day. Leonie loved teasing Paula about this, but every time he offered her a lift she was very glad to accept.

At Christmas, Richard and Paula were invited, as usual, to his parents' to share in the family's roast goose. Paula wasn't feeling that well, but she kept quiet about it as she didn't want to spoil the visit home for Richard. She told herself it was probably the two exhausting night shifts she'd done in the week before Christmas.

Richard's mother had prepared and stuffed the goose, and while everyone else enthused about the appetising smells coming from the oven, Paula just felt nauseous.

Richard's father was in a particularly jovial mood. 'We always have a proper goose here, but I'm not so sure about the neighbours. Maybe they've poached a couple of swans off the Alster!'

Everyone burst out laughing at the thought, but Paula knew she couldn't hang on any longer and rushed to the toilet to be sick. She'd hoped she would feel better after that but her stomach carried on rebelling until she was bringing up nothing more than bile.

Richard had followed her and knocked on the door to the lavatory. 'Everything all right?'

'Yes, just feel a bit sick. Do go back to the table; I'll be right there.' But she found herself retching again, even though there was nothing left in her stomach.

Richard waited outside the door until she emerged. He was the picture of concern, and Paula wondered whether he'd been going through all the serious illnesses that nausea might indicate and whether he would now examine her for other symptoms.

'It's all fine,' she said, trying to reassure him. 'You don't need to look so worried.'

'Yes, but you're working on the isolation ward, and anything can happen there.'

Margit, who'd been helping their mother in the kitchen, caught the last few words.

'That's just typical of my smart-alec doctor brother,' she said with a smirk. 'You don't think of the most obvious thing! And as the big expert on birth control, you couldn't possibly admit it!'

Richard whipped around to face her. 'What are you on about?'

Paula stood there, working out when she'd had her last period. 'I think Margit might be right,' she said at last.

'And about time too!' commented Margit. 'You've been married for three years!'

She went off, leaving the two of them together.

'Do you really think that's it?'

Paula nodded. 'I think I even know when. Do you remember that evening at the little wine bar? And when—'

'Yes, yes, I remember.' He cut in and then lowered his voice. 'Don't go into that here. Margit's eavesdropping knows no limits.'

'Heard that!' shouted Margit from the living room.

'*Quod erat demonstrandum,*' sighed Richard. He put his arms around his wife. 'I predict we'll be washing nappies next summer instead of heading to the coast.'

'We could always find a resort with a laundry!' Paula said, twinkling at him, and somehow the nausea disappeared, leaving her feeling only excitement for the future.

Chapter 18

Paula continued working at the children's hospital in spite of her pregnancy, something which irritated colleagues, who felt that, as a married woman with a husband earning enough money to keep her in what was then deemed as 'the appropriate manner', she should have been at home. Even Dr Stamm had asked her whether, given her condition, she wanted to carry on working with seriously ill children. He added that any maternal infection could eventually have a serious impact on the unborn child. Paula assured him that she wanted to have a full year of professional practice at the hospital to look back on and would work until the end of May, seeing as her due date wasn't until August.

Dr Stamm agreed, but from then on Paula was no longer responsible for the isolation ward.

◆ ◆ ◆

In spite of the economic problems that continued to dominate at national level, the early months of 1932 went well for Richard and Paula. Her pregnancy ran smoothly and Richard was officially awarded his status as a consultant in psychiatry. Then, when Dr Morgenstern retired in April 1932, Richard and Dr Krüger found themselves in competition for the post, and to Richard's delight, he won.

'You see,' he said to Paula on the evening after his success, 'I'm well on the road to keeping my promise to you. This is the next step towards becoming lead consultant, and by the time I get there, our child will be much older and you'll be able to find your dream job.'

'Will you just stop and let me say how incredibly proud I am of you?'

'Absolutely – that's just what I want to hear. So?'

'I am incredibly proud of you, Mr Consultant.'

As Richard held Paula close and gently stroked her rounded belly, he noticed an open envelope on the sideboard.

'Who's writing to us from Berlin?'

'Oh, I'd forgotten all about that.' She broke away from his embrace and picked up the letter. 'You remember People's Welfare? The charity we give ten marks a month to?'

Richard nodded.

'They've written to say they are now a registered association under new trustees. They've already sent us new membership cards and we don't need to do anything else. Here, see for yourself.'

She took the two membership cards out of the envelope.

Richard took the bright red pass with his name on it.

The Gothic lettering at the top proclaimed *N.S. Volkswohlfahrt* – National Socialist People's Welfare. Beneath that was Richard's name, his date of birth and his address. Further down were two boxes waiting to be filled in, one headed: NSDAP Membership Number, the other headed: NSDAP Entry Date. The card was stamped with the swastika used by the NSDAP.

'So the NSDAP has taken over People's Welfare?'

Paula nodded. 'I'm not sure what we should do. I assume they expect us to continue to support it, no matter who the trustees are.'

'You're right, that's exactly what they expect. But we signed up with them precisely because they weren't answerable to any party-political thinking; otherwise, we would just have donated to Workers' Welfare. This makes a nonsense of the fundamental principle.'

'My fundamental principle is to support struggling families so they can get health care and good information about how to control infectious diseases like diphtheria,' Paula shot back.

'What's Leonie saying about it? Has she been sent a membership card like this?'

'I don't know. I only found the envelope when I got home.'

'Perhaps you should ask her.' Richard gestured towards the telephone. 'I can't imagine Leonie keeping any membership that's suggestive of joining the NSDAP. They have a nerve, leaving a space here where you're supposed to write in your party membership number.'

'No need to get so worked up about it. I'm not mad on the idea either, but I ask myself whether it's right to discount them simply because one doesn't agree with every item on their list of objectives.'

'Not every item?' Richard snorted with rage. 'Which particular item do you agree with the Nazis about?'

'OK, then, the idea of People's Welfare!'

'What else?' Richard said, probing further and clearly furious. 'What else, precisely, do you agree with the Nazis about?'

'What's the matter with you, Richard?'

'I only want to know what you think. Do you also believe that we need safe streets again and that we need more jobs to stop the people suffering? That our people must be great again and need a voice on the world stage?'

'Yes, I do,' replied Paula angrily, 'but that doesn't make me a Nazi. Of course I'd like to be able to walk the streets alone at night again. Of course I'd like to see the back of this economic crisis, people finding work again and all those little ghost shops reopened and full of life. Who doesn't want all that? Or perhaps you don't?'

'I don't want anything with the swastika on it in my home!' Richard shouted. 'And I will not pay into an organisation that supports the NSDAP.'

'And exactly why are you shouting at me?'

'Because you're seriously considering staying in this Nazi organisation!'

'Yes, I'm "considering" it, Richard. It's not a crime to consider something, it just demonstrates a bit of intelligence! Starting to bellow whenever you see a swastika is just primitive. You'll be beating your chest like a gorilla next!'

'You know what? Fine.' Richard's voice had dropped, but his anger hadn't. 'You just carry on considering it. I'm off for a stroll around the jungle so that your deliberations are not interrupted by my primitive behaviour.' He picked up his coat and left.

Paula took some deep breaths. In many ways, she shared his opinion, but she was angry that he wasn't prepared to break down the issues a bit first. Did they really have to give up everything that as far as Richard was concerned had the wrong political leaning?

She phoned Leonie to see what she thought about it.

'Oh, they've sent you a new card straight away, have they?' Leonie sounded amazed. 'My father and I have just been sent a letter, that's all, saying that the old People's Welfare has been dissolved following new trustees taking over and that all existing memberships are terminated.'

'Didn't they say anything more than that?' Paula was puzzled.

'No, but I think my father's first name is a bigger giveaway than our surname. Do you really think that an organisation like the NSDAP wants a Dr Isaak Hirschthal on its books? Anyway, the feeling is mutual. If the Nazis have appropriated People's Welfare, that's no place for me.'

'Nor for us. I'm going straight to the typewriter to confirm our resignation. Leonie, thank you.'

When Richard came back a couple of hours later, he reeked of beer.

'Nice that you're back. Were you drinking alone, or did you meet up with Fritz?'

Richard looked at her guardedly. 'So what's the outcome of your deliberations?'

'This. See if you could put your signature to it.' She handed him the letter she'd just typed.

Richard read it.

> Sir,
> We joined People's Welfare in May 1931 because we welcomed the idea of an independent, universal welfare organisation supported by donation and separate from politically motivated welfare movements. With the party-political takeover of People's Welfare by the NSDAP, we believe our independent interests are no longer sufficiently represented and for this reason are informing you of our withdrawal. Enclosed are the cancelled membership cards.
>
> Yours, etc.
>
> Dr Richard Hellmer and Dr Paula Hellmer (née Engelhardt)

The two membership cards were torn in half.

'I apologise for flying off the handle like that,' said Richard rather meekly after he had read the letter.

'Don't worry about it,' said Paula, putting her arms around his neck. 'I just reminded myself that expectant fathers can be moody too.'

He managed a laugh. 'You're a cheeky one today!'

'I'm allowed to be. In fact, it's the basic right of all pregnant women to be cheeky.' But she became serious again as she told him about her phone call with Leonie. 'Do you think they're deliberately filtering out Jews?' she asked him.

'Yes, that's exactly what I think. I just wonder where it's all going to end. I'm dreading the elections in the summer.'

'Do you really think it could get any worse? Surely we've hit rock bottom and will start to see signs of new hope and peace to warm people's hearts. I'd like our baby to be born into a world at peace.'

'We'll do that for him, whatever else is going on,' Richard promised her. And Paula knew he meant it.

Chapter 19

Richard's new position meant his work as consultant shifted into a new direction. Of course, he continued to be devoted to his patients and always tried to establish a rapport with even the most obstinate of individuals, but most of his time was now taken up with the preparation of expert statements.

This was usually related to the continuity of invalidity pension payments. Wartime veterans whose mental health had been damaged as a result of their experiences in combat had to demonstrate at regular intervals that they still fulfilled the conditions for receipt of their pension. During the course of this work, Richard had noticed how a new system of patient appraisal was gradually coming into use among psychiatrists, a system based on the beliefs of Professor Alfred Hoche of Freiburg. Very few expert witnesses dared ever to contradict the famous and respected academic, something which infuriated Richard, particularly as each time he heard the name he couldn't help thinking of 'approving the destruction of life unworthy of life'. In Hoche's opinion, a war pension should be granted only to those whose mental illness could be directly related to a brain injury suffered in the war. All other psychological illnesses were not seen by the Freiburg professor as causally related to wartime trauma; rather, they were caused by a weak psychological disposition and any connection to military experience in the field was purely coincidental. In evidence he cited many men who had withstood similar experiences without lasting damage. Therefore, he stated, due to their inferior constitution, they could not be equated with true disabled war veterans and had no entitlement to the state services provided for those other veterans.

Each time Richard found this argument in an expert statement, he would channel his professional passion into the most skilful counterargument he could muster. It wasn't long before he had earned a reputation for developing hard-nosed, caustic points of opposition that were used in many controversial cases.

One day in June 1932 he found himself working on the case of one of their long-term patients who had lived for many years in one of the open houses and was able to carry out simple jobs on the land. The man had literally been buried alive in the trenches after a grenade went off and was the only one of his group to survive. He had endured hours buried among his comrades' shredded remains before he was found. While buried he had developed some of the symptoms of schizophrenia, hearing the voices of God and the Devil and believing himself chosen by a higher power for special deeds.

At first people blamed it on the shock, but his behaviour became increasingly erratic and he was eventually diagnosed as schizophrenic. Sometimes he lost all control and thought he was being buried alive again and needed to escape. At these times he would start screaming and was prone to attack anyone who stood in his way. The tragedy was that the man had a wife and two daughters. At the time of his experience in the trenches, the younger child had been a babe in arms and the elder one had just turned three. Given the severity of her husband's illness and the demands of her young family, his wife had struggled to cope and her only possible course of action had been to have him admitted to special residential accommodation. His health meant that he could no longer provide for his family, so the invalidity pension was their sole source of income. But now a notification had come from his pension office claiming that a new appraisal of his case based on the examination of records had shown there was no connection between his mental illness and his traumatic wartime experiences. Not only were his pension payments to be stopped but the six months' already received had to be repaid.

When the man's wife, weeping and in despair, had appeared in Richard's office, he had promised her he would do everything in his power to help with her claim.

He was working on his statement, pondering his choice of words for his final assessment, when his telephone rang.

'Hellmer here.'

'And here!' It was Paula's voice. 'I just had to phone you. Have you got a minute?'

'Of course. But what's up?'

'I went to Dr Torgau this morning, and he said there's no doubt.' She paused for dramatic effect. 'We're having twins. He could feel two little heads!'

Richard took a sharp intake of breath. 'Twins? Are you serious?'

'I am! I wouldn't joke about something like this.' She gave a laugh of delight. 'Now we've just got to wait and see if they get in the right position for the birth, but Dr Torgau is confident that everything will be all right.'

'What if they don't turn?' As soon as he'd asked the question, he kicked himself, because he didn't want to worry Paula. But the very word 'twins' reminded him of all the stories of difficult births and risks to the mother. Of infants dismembered inside their mother, of emergency Caesareans and complications ending in death . . . he tried to shake off all such thoughts, but the images persisted.

'Of course they'll turn properly!' said Paula happily, her buoyant mood clear from her voice. She didn't seem worried at all, although she also seemed to have read his thoughts. 'And if they don't, we can rely on Finkenau. After all, they've got a modern operating theatre, and a

Caesarean using a Pfannenstiel incision carries no greater risk than a spontaneous delivery.'

'I don't know whether to be happy or concerned,' Richard admitted. 'A Caesarean always carries a risk.'

'Complication rates at Finkenau are below five per cent at the moment.'

'Did you know all that before, or have you just asked today?'

'I did a lot of research on this for my doctorate because post-partum infection rates were significantly lower for mothers who'd had a Caesarean. I was even present in the operating theatre when twins were delivered by section. Richard, it's straightforward. The babies came into the world in about fifteen minutes. What took the time was the stitching afterwards – the uterus, abdominal fascia and the skin. That took the doctors around half an hour. So if you include setting up and giving the anaesthetic, you can assume one hour at most for a Caesarean. And since people have opted for the Pfannenstiel method, the mother is not left with a huge scar. I was very impressed when I saw this young mother's scar after seven days. Only a thin red line, almost hidden by the fold in her belly.'

'I see.'

'Come on, you should be celebrating our efficient family planning. Why have two pregnancies with double the risk when you can achieve the same outcome in nine months?' She laughed that carefree, happy laugh again.

'I don't know what to say,' he confessed.

'That's unusual for you! Please don't worry, Richard. It'll be all right, I promise.'

'Yes.'

'You don't sound convinced. Listen, I've bought cinema tickets to celebrate. They're showing *No Money Needed* at the Capitol. Heinz Rühmann and Hans Moser. It starts at eight. Make sure you're home in time.'

'Whatever my lady says!'
'I can't wait to see you.'
'Same here.'

Once he'd hung up, it took him a while to concentrate on his work again. Paula's confidence helped him banish the horrific images of complications during the birth, and he resolved to look forward to the twins with the same unreserved joy he'd sensed in her. Then he turned his attention to the expert-opinion statement once more, as the words for the final assessment had now come to him:

> Even if another influence on the patient's mental health condition cannot be fully ruled out, the effects of wartime damage presented in this case are irrefutable. As a result of a grenade attack, the patient was buried alive amid the largely mutilated corpses of his fellow soldiers and had to wait hours for help while oxygen levels ran increasingly low. In addition to suffering severe physical injury, he also suffered psychological damage of at least equal severity, for he remained in fear of his life over a number of hours with no possibility of being able to save himself. To equate this individual's state of mortal fear with the more customary mortal fear experienced by men in the trenches, in the way the first expert statement has done, is inadmissible because fighting soldiers in the trenches retain at least the prospect of self-defence and control over their actions, whereas a man buried alive is robbed of all bodily and mental means of defending himself and is restricted in all possible movement. The man who is buried alive has nothing left but to struggle for every breath until rescue arrives, and has not even the smallest possibility of taking

control of his situation in the way that soldiers in a trench are still able to do. Further demonstration of the inappropriacy of comparing the two situations is the fact that the patient had previously been deployed to the Front for a period of eighteen months without any lasting change in his mental state. Compare this with cases of wartime neuroses, where patients struggle with significant symptoms even without the trauma of 'live burial', and, in the case of this patient, this speaks of a particularly strong mental constitution. It can therefore be deduced without a doubt that it is uniquely and specifically the experience of being buried alive, something which goes far beyond what any human being can endure, that became an essential influence in the onset of the illness. Even under the purely hypothetical admission that there could have been a hereditary disposition to schizophrenia, the onset of illness lies in direct correlation with the trauma of being buried alive. It remains a matter of speculation as to whether the onset of illness would have come about if the patient had not experienced trauma of this type.

Six weeks later he heard that the pension office had accepted the argument presented in the expert statement and would continue to pay the invalidity pension.

Chapter 20

During the night of 8 August 1932, Paula went into labour. When Richard drove her to Finkenau the waters had already broken and the first baby's head was pressing down hard in her pelvis. The cervix, however, had dilated very little and took the whole day to open further. Richard waited in vain at his desk for the call to say he was now a father. Kurt Hansen tried to distract him, but all Richard could think about were the possible complications. He knew this was because he felt so out of control and helpless and tried to take his mind off his worries, but neither patient care nor paperwork helped.

At five he packed up and drove over to Finkenau. He arrived around half past and heard that his wife was still in the delivery room. The nurse he spoke to was brisk in response to his questions. 'It's all taking its course. Honestly, you men are always so impatient!'

'It depends on what you think is impatient. My wife's been here for eighteen hours already.'

'Yes, and that's how it is with twins: they need time. Now go and have a coffee or a walk and let us get on with our work.'

'And how's my wife?'

'Well, what do *you* think? Having a baby's no fun. You certainly ask some stupid questions.' And she walked off.

For a while Richard wandered up and down the empty corridor, but nobody brought him any information on Paula's progress. In the foyer there was a public telephone, and not knowing what else to do, he called Fritz.

'Shall I come over and keep you company?'

'Would you really?'

'Of course – what do you think? Now calm down and tell yourself everything's OK, because if anything was wrong with Paula or the babies, they'd have told you by now. They certainly called me about Doro, even though I was in the operating theatre at the time.'

'Paula called you,' Richard remembered.

'Yes, because she happened to be there. I'm sure that Brandes would have phoned me himself otherwise. Even if it was just because he wanted a nice specimen for his collection.'

That sent a shiver through Richard. He usually admired Fritz for the way he'd started to talk openly about his son but today it stirred up his worries.

'I'll wait for you in the foyer. Thank you for offering to come.'

Another twenty minutes passed with still no news and nobody bothering to acknowledge his presence. Finally, Fritz appeared, carrying a briefcase.

'Brought some provisions,' he said, winking at Richard. 'If this lot are ignoring you, then we don't need to worry about our behaviour either.' He produced two bottles of beer from his briefcase and handed one to Richard.

'So we're just going to sit here and drink beer out of the bottle?'

'If it bothers you that much, I'll see if I can get some glasses. We wouldn't want to lower our standards!'

In spite of his anxiety, Richard couldn't help but laugh when Fritz really did come back with a water glass for each of them. They sat down together on the huge wooden bench in the foyer and Fritz poured each of them a beer. As they were about to chink glasses, the grumpy nurse reappeared.

'Typical man. Your wife is having the most difficult time of her life and you sit here drinking beer. This is a hospital!'

'See? Works every time,' said Fritz. 'A drop of alcohol anywhere in a hospital and a raging nurse comes running. Pleased to see you. Sister Mathilde, it's a long time since we last stood at the same operating table.'

'Dr Ellerweg! I might have guessed.' She put her hands on her hips, but instead of the torrent of anger that Richard was expecting, she laughed and Fritz joined in.

Richard looked from one to the other in some confusion.

'Sister Mathilde and I are old acquaintances,' Fritz explained. 'If I said we were old friends, she'd bite my head off for being disrespectful.'

'Not just for that either.' Sister Mathilde wagged her finger at Fritz in mock anger. It was obvious she liked Fritz.

'And how's my wife?'

'Come on, Sister Mathilde, spit it out. You can see my friend's practically dying with worry here and I can only keep him alive with liquid refreshment for so long.' Fritz pointed at Richard's glass.

'I've come to tell you that everything is all right. Congratulations, Dr Hellmer, you have two healthy babies – a girl and a boy. And as you might expect, your daughter was a very good girl and arrived quickly, but your rascal of a son took his time and had to be delivered by forceps. Just typical of a man.'

'And my wife?'

'She's done very well. At the moment she's still in the delivery room as she needed stitching afterwards. But I can show you the babies through the window of the newborn ward. Provided you leave the beer here!'

'Can't throw it away!' said Fritz. 'To your twins!' They chinked glasses this time and drained them.

'Men!' Sister Mathilde shook her head as she turned to lead the way to the ward, but there was rather more warmth in her voice now that Fritz was here.

'She's OK, really,' whispered Fritz. 'Bark's worse than her bite. She was our theatre sister up to about a year ago and I always really liked working with her, but when she didn't get the promotion she wanted, she moved here to Finkenau and I was sorry to see her go.'

At last they arrived at the ward and Richard could see his children, even though there was a pane of glass between them to protect the newborns from visitors' germs. His daughter was bigger, her bright blue eyes already taking in everything, her head covered in downy fair hair. His son looked more delicate and had Richard's dark hair. The mark of the forceps still showed on his temples and, unlike his sister, he blinked only once, as if tired, then fell asleep in the arms of his nurse.

'Congratulations again on two little smashers!' Fritz said, clapping Richard warmly on the shoulder. 'The little lad looks a bit battered but that'll sort itself out.'

'I know.' As he gazed at his two healthy offspring, Richard's worries started to melt away and slowly, very slowly, a tremendous joy grew in his heart.

'Have you thought about names?'

'What do you think? We'd chosen a boy's name as well as a girl's back when we didn't know it was to be twins. Paula wanted Emilia for a girl and Georg for a boy, after my dear departed brother.'

'And what if it had been two boys or two girls? Would it have been Georg and Emil, or Emilia and Georgina?' Fritz grinned and got a playful dig from Richard.

'We've got exactly what we need for these two.' As he stood there with Fritz, he felt almost dizzy with happiness. He wanted to shout for joy.

'What shall we do now? Another beer?'

'I want to see Paula first.'

Fritz glanced up at the clock. 'It's getting on for eight. I don't think they'll allow visits now.'

'Then see if you can charm Sister Mathilde again. I'm not leaving till I've seen Paula.'

Fritz's sweet talk did the trick and the new father was permitted a short visit to his wife.

'I'm so proud of you,' said Richard. 'And I couldn't even grab you a bunch of flowers on the way.'

'Not to worry, the fruit takes up all the space,' Paula said, smiling up at him. She looked pale, exhausted and yet also indescribably happy and relieved. 'Aren't they wonderful?'

'Yes, they are,' replied Richard, sitting down on the edge of the bed and taking her hands in his.

'You see, everything went just fine. But to be honest, if I'd known how long it was going to go on for, I'd have had a Caesarean. Anaesthetic, wake up in an hour and the babies are there.'

'And I couldn't do anything to help, my darling. Only wait.'

'I hear you actually drank beer with Fritz, or so Sister Mathilde told me. She was not amused! Told me I should clip your wings a bit!'

'Sister Mathilde is a horrible sneak. And she didn't even tell you why I was drinking!'

'Dearest Richard, there's no need to justify a thing. I can imagine what it was like. You phoned Fritz, all worried, and he brought moral support in the form of beer.'

'Exactly.'

'Fritz is a good friend. I'd love him to be Georg's godfather.'

'Good idea.' He kissed her on the forehead. 'I love you, Paula.'

'Perhaps you could leave me now. I'm so exhausted.'

'Then have a really good sleep to recover, my darling.'

Fritz was waiting for him at the door.

'OK? Shall we go for another drink?'

'Definitely,' said Richard. Unlike Paula, he felt so lively and cheerful that he couldn't think of anything worse than spending the rest of the evening alone in the flat. Life was too good for that!

PART TWO

The Third Reich 1933–1945

Chapter 21

In the elections on 31 July 1932, the NSDAP emerged the strongest party, with 37.3 per cent of the vote. On 6 November, there were further elections and once again the Nazis got the most votes: 33.1 per cent.

Richard always followed political developments with great interest, but the birth of his twins just a few days after the July elections meant that his attention was largely taken up by his young family. Emilia was thriving, already responding to her mother's voice with little babbling noises. Georg was quite different, a placid child showing only a fraction of his sister's alertness. Richard's father went so far as to praise what he called the baby boy's nerves of steel when, unlike his twin, he didn't flinch when the two guard dogs started barking right next to him. But this merely stirred Richard's vague feeling that something wasn't right. Paula tried to reassure him that it was normal for boys to develop less quickly than girls, that it was just more noticeable when you had one of each. Richard wanted so much to believe this and was only too willing to take the good-natured mockery of the family for being overanxious, but it did nothing to allay his fears.

On 30 January 1933, Adolf Hitler became Chancellor. Richard and Paula sat in the kitchen together and listened to the radio as it broadcast the NSDAP victory celebrations. Cheering crowds accompanied speeches by Adolf Hitler and his head of propaganda, Joseph Goebbels.

Even though the children were asleep in the nursery, the noise woke Emilia and she started to cry. Paula went through to see to her and brought her to join them in the kitchen.

'Turn the radio down a bit, would you, Richard? I'm afraid she doesn't know what the new Chancellor's speeches are about.'

'And what about Georg?'

'He's sleeping like an angel, quite oblivious to everything.' She cradled Emilia in her arms to calm her. 'Your father would definitely be praising his nerves of steel again now!'

Richard nodded thoughtfully. 'And what if it's nothing to do with nerves of steel?' he said after a while. 'Have you ever wondered whether he can hear properly?'

Paula stopped rocking Emilia and looked at Richard in amazement. 'What on earth makes you think that? As his mother, I'd have noticed. He reacts to me whenever I pick him up and talk to him, in just the same way that Emilia does.'

'He reacts to you when you pick him up. And you talk to him as you do it, of course, but are you sure he can really hear you? He's never startled by loud noises, is he?'

'Not every child is immediately startled like that. Richard, he's quite normal, just a bit quieter than Emilia. Boys need a bit longer – you can see that from the way Emilia can already turn herself from her back to her front but Georg can't.'

'Have you ever noticed him showing a typical startle response?' Richard wouldn't let it drop.

'No,' she conceded after some thought.

'And do you consider that normal?'

Paula chewed her lower lip. 'It doesn't mean anything, Richard. He's still so little.'

In spite of her defensive remarks, Richard saw his own worries reflected in her.

'I'm going to check something,' Richard said, standing up and going to the nursery. Paula followed him, Emilia in her arms.

Georg was still asleep.

'Georg!' Richard called his name. No reaction. He leaned closer and shouted out his son's name again. The child slept on.

'What do you think of that?' he asked Paula.

'He's a good sleeper and knows it's you by your voice so he's not scared. I consider that to be completely normal. All the more so when I think how difficult it can be to wake you! Like father, like son.'

'All right, then. Something different.' Richard went into the bedroom, got their huge alarm clock and set it. A deafening ring quickly followed and Emilia started to cry. Georg slumbered on, quite undisturbed.

'What do you think now? That's enough to wake anybody.'

Paula had gone pale. 'I don't know . . . but if it's true, why hasn't it occurred to me before? I should have noticed.'

Richard saw guilt in Paula's eyes and held her close. 'I didn't notice either,' he consoled her.

'Yes, but I'm the one with him all day. I was pleased that he's so calm and put everything else down to the fact that boys develop more slowly. I should have paid him more attention.'

Just then Georg stirred and made a lovely gurgling sound. Richard let go of Paula and picked up his son.

'Now then, little one? Can you hear what Papa's saying?'

Georg chuckled in response.

'So did he hear that?' Paula asked hesitantly. She put Emilia, now calm again, back in her cradle and looked carefully at her son.

'I don't know. Let's get the little bell, then we can see if he reacts if you ring it behind his head.'

Paula went to fetch the bell while Richard continued to hold Georg and watched him carefully. Now that Georg was awake, he was looking all around, his eyes wide and attentive. But when his mother rang the little bell behind his head, he showed no reaction. It was only when Paula held the toy in front of his face and rang it again that he looked and tried to get hold of it.

'So did he hear that, or is he just responding to what he sees?' Paula's anxiety was now obvious.

Richard placed Georg back in his cradle and picked up Emilia. 'Now let's try it with her,' he said.

Paula rang the bell behind her daughter. Emilia turned her head towards the sound.

Paula's and Richard's eyes met as Emilia tried to touch the bell.

'So it's true,' said Paula, shocked. 'Georg can't hear.'

Richard nodded. 'But at least we know and can do something about it.'

'What are we supposed to do about it if he's deaf? There's no treatment.'

'No,' Richard acknowledged, 'but we can learn how to live with it. Perhaps he's simply hard of hearing – we don't know yet. And if he really is profoundly deaf, then . . . we'll teach him the special sign language for deaf mutes.' He took a deep breath and carried on cradling his daughter.

'We'll have to learn it ourselves first.'

'Then that's what we'll do,' said Richard with determination. 'Worse things happen. Fritz and Dorothea would have had a better time if all Gottlieb had suffered from was deafness.'

Richard noticed Paula discreetly wiping away a tear and felt that telltale pricking of the eyes, but wouldn't give in to it. He would not despair simply because his son couldn't hear. He would rise to the challenge. Whether Georg was deaf or not, this would not change his love for his son or his desire to give him the best possible start in life.

'I'll take Georg to Dr Stamm tomorrow and he can check him again,' said Paula. 'If he confirms what we suspect, then I'll start to investigate where we can learn this sign language for deaf mutes.'

'Good,' said Richard. 'But I don't like this term "deaf mute". We both know he can bellow just as well as any little human being! And we'll put everything into making sure he learns to speak properly so that people who can't do sign language will be able to understand him. There are plenty of deaf people who can lip-read too. If he learns all that, well, he'll be able to live almost like anyone else.'

Paula was thinking. 'Could it be because of the birth? You know, the forceps? He had the marks on his little head for a whole week afterwards.'

'I don't know,' said Richard. 'But is that important? It is how it is. We can't change anything. We can only feel hope for the future. He'll always have things harder than Emilia, but he'll battle through because we'll both do everything possible for him.'

'Do you know, Richard, that's exactly what I love you for the most. You're never defeated and, whatever happens, you always manage to bring out the good things, but you don't lose sight of the difficulties.'

'Paula, we've got two wonderful children. Nothing in the world's going to change that.'

Chapter 22

The next day Paula set off to consult Dr Stamm. Her old boss had known the twins since they were born, and Paula valued his experience as a paediatrician. He smiled indulgently when she related what they had done and why.

'At that age you can't be absolutely certain,' he said. 'And sometimes an infant doesn't respond in the way expected and that can be due to tiredness or sheer lack of interest. After all, little Georg is doing well.'

'If it had only been the business of the bell or Richard's voice by his cradle, I wouldn't have thought anything of it either. But that jangling alarm clock – that really should have woken him up. And now I'm asking myself if it's a direct result of his birth.'

'My dear Frau Hellmer, I have never known a case of forceps delivery causing deafness. But let me examine the little fellow.'

First of all, he expertly inspected Georg's acoustic canals, something which the baby tolerated with remarkable calm.

'Nothing noteworthy there,' he remarked.

Then he checked Georg's hearing ability in much the same way Paula and Richard had done the previous evening. The result was exactly the same. Georg showed no reaction to sounds beyond his field of vision.

Dr Stamm frowned. 'It's far too early for a definitive diagnosis. With most children it first becomes noticeable at the age of two or three if they haven't started talking. I've rarely met parents who observe their children as closely as you and your husband, Frau Hellmer. It's very unusual to entertain doubts like this in such a young baby.'

'But what do you advise? Even though it's too soon for a definitive diagnosis, what are we supposed to do? Richard thinks we should learn the special sign language for deaf mutes so that Georg can use it to communicate with the outside world.'

'Dear Frau Hellmer, you have two options. Either you wait and see how he develops and hope that he suffers only from being hard of hearing, something which can improve over a few months. Or you assume the worst and as a result seize opportunities denied to other, less vigilant parents. Most children born deaf are of average intelligence and possess the anatomical requirements for speech, but because they can't hear, they can't grasp how language and speech function, and this is why most remain dumb. However, there is some good research going on at the Institute of Phonetics in Hamburg. I'd advise you to get in touch with Alfred Schär. He teaches at the deaf and dumb school in Bürgerweide and has also made a name for himself in the field of experimental phonetics. I'll give you the address.'

'Thank you so much!'

Dr Stamm handed her a note of Schär's home address and that of the deaf and dumb school. 'I'm very keen to hear how Georg develops, so please do keep me informed, Frau Hellmer.'

'Of course, Dr Stamm, sir.' Paula placed Georg back in the twin pram alongside his sister, took her leave of the doctor and set off for the deaf and dumb school in Bürgerweide.

As she stepped outside flakes of snow danced towards her, so she paused to put up the hood on the pram as well as her own umbrella. A thick layer of snow had covered the pavement over the last hour, making it difficult to push the pram to the tram stop. Fortunately, a young man came to her rescue when the tram arrived and helped her get the pram on board, which required considerable skill, given its width.

From the outside, the deaf and dumb school at Bürgerweide didn't look different from any other school. When Paula got there, the children were enjoying break and she heard them in the playground, just as high-spirited and boisterous as any other youngsters letting off steam. This sense of normality spurred her on as she hunted for the school secretary and asked if she might see Alfred Schär.

She was lucky. He was there, and he had time to see her.

'It's about my son,' she said, once in the staffroom and seated opposite Schär. It was a bright and friendly room, the window ledges covered with houseplants and cacti, and the walls with framed pictures, probably the product of the school's art classes.

'Dr Stamm recommended I come to you after our appointment this morning with Georg.' She indicated her son in the pram. 'His twin sister has a clean bill of health but, with Georg, there's a strong suspicion he may be deaf.'

'How old is he?'

'They'll be six months on 9 February.'

'That young? And you've observed deafness? Is there a family history?'

'No, everyone in the family's always enjoyed complete health.' She summarised the examination carried out by Dr Stamm while Herr Schär listened attentively.

'I've never come across a case of parents noticing deafness this early,' he conceded.

'That's why Dr Stamm felt we should take this opportunity to get the best possible support for Georg, given that we already know about his condition. We want so much for him to grow up feeling normal, but on the other hand we really don't know anything about dealing with children who are deaf or hard of hearing. My husband thinks we should learn the sign language for deaf mutes.'

'That's very much in dispute at the moment,' explained Schär. 'Some experts believe it's better to get the children used to spoken language and lip-reading only. For the hard of hearing, I share that view, but profound deafness is a very different matter. You have to remember that sign language is not simply a question of translating spoken language into gestures, but an independent language with completely different grammar. We have a few pupils here with deaf-mute parents, and they've grown up with sign language alone and now show severe grammatical shortcomings when writing anything in their mother tongue. There are two different worlds, Frau Hellmer, and in the end people have to decide whether to choose the world of the well or the world of the deaf mute.'

'And what if people want to live in both?'

'Then they have to learn sign language and teach it to their children too. Be warned, though, it's a protracted process and as time-consuming as learning a foreign language.'

'Could you recommend someone to teach us privately? We'd pay well for it.'

Schär nodded. 'I think I know someone suitable. Katharina Felber is a young teacher here at the school and has a very unusual background. She herself enjoys complete health but has a deaf-mute mother, so she learned sign language as a child but at the same time normal voice speech. She lives in both worlds.'

'She sounds perfect!'

'If you'd wait just one moment, I'll see if Fräulein Felber is free. She's just been on playground duty.' Schär got up and left the room. He was soon back and brought with him a young woman not long out of school herself. She had long dark hair drawn up into a bun and wore a simple blue dress with a white lace collar, which was just a little too long to be fashionable.

'Frau Hellmer, this is Fräulein Felber.'

Paula shook hands with the young woman. 'I'm very pleased to meet you. Has Herr Schär already told you why I'm here?'

'You and your husband would like to learn sign language.'

'That's right. I'll need to speak to my husband about timings. When would it suit you during the week?'

'I can fit in with you, Frau Hellmer.'

'Thank you! I'll phone you as soon as I've discussed it with him. Do you have a telephone?'

'No, we don't – my mother's unable to use one. But you can definitely reach me through the school secretary's office.' Her voice was very timid.

'Then I'll get in touch here as soon as I've talked to my husband about it.'

Richard was very impressed when he heard that evening what Paula had already done and was interested not only in sign language but also in the experimental phonetics that Paula had mentioned in passing.

'What's that actually about?' he asked, but Paula had to confess she hadn't asked much about that side of things.

'Maybe you should ask Herr Schär more about it yourself, Richard. He came across very well – an expert, but so humane too. I think the two of you would get on really well.'

'That's a good idea. I'll see if I can reach him by phone in the morning.'

'What day shall I say to Fräulein Felber, then?'

'Tuesdays.'

'Tuesdays? That was quick!'

'Anything I don't get through on Monday is out of the way by then. On a Tuesday I can finish work promptly and do everything else later in the week!'

He said this with such a twinkle in his eye that Paula marvelled at how swiftly they'd both come to terms with a situation that was truly tragic and which no one knew about apart from her father and Richard's family. At the same time she refused to see Georg's deafness as a terrible stroke of fate. It had seemed that way at first, but today she'd realised how many children like him led a normal life, albeit at a specially equipped school. For a moment she even glimpsed the benefits that can come from such a challenge because it would open her eyes to a completely new world, but she knew she couldn't say that to anyone other than Richard. Neither her father nor her parents-in-law were remotely capable of seeing it that way. Of course, they would all support Georg, but their pity and sympathy would always be paramount, so it was up to her and Richard to smooth the way ahead for Georg without pity, but with all the love and care that parents can bring.

Chapter 23

The next few weeks were full of highs and lows for Richard. He tried to be strong and optimistic, and he had largely managed to allay the fears of his parents and father-in-law as he told them about all the possibilities for helping Georg develop. His mother, however, remained devastated by the news.

'But he'll never be able to use a telephone or listen to the radio,' she'd said. 'He'll be cut off from the world.'

'That's nonsense!' her husband said, wanting to be positive. 'He can read the paper and write letters! Not many people have a telephone, in any case.'

'Well, if those Ritters next door have already got one, you can bet that everyone else will too by the time Georg grows up.'

'Then that's how it is. At least he'll be able to enjoy a soak in the bath without that wretched bell disturbing him the whole time. There's always a bright side.'

'Hans-Kurt – you're incorrigible!'

'I just hate moaning. The boy'll make his own way in life. Deaf or not.'

This made Richard smile and reminded him how similar he was to his father.

The regular contact with Alfred Schär also helped him. In the early days of their burgeoning friendship, they had talked predominantly about speech acquisition. Schär had emphasised that it was perfectly possible for the deaf to master speech, but it was difficult for the hearing to understand them. He explained how their speech was unclear because they had no sense of how the words should sound. They could only try to imitate lip movement and create the same sounds in the larynx and pharynx.

'It's hard for them to adopt the right breathing technique too,' explained Schär during their first telephone conversation. 'Phonetics is a complex process, although those of us who can hear don't realise it as we have been using it since childhood. We hear what we are saying and can modify it to sound right, something that a profoundly deaf child can't do. They rely constantly on the response of their immediate environment. And we can see how important hearing is in the formation of speech when we look at someone with age-related hearing loss.'

'But they go on speaking quite normally?' suggested Richard.

'Yes, but noticeably louder. Because they themselves no longer hear so well, they speak at a volume that enables them to hear their own voice, but do that without realising it's happening.'

'That's true,' Richard acknowledged. 'I've often noticed that but didn't think about the link.'

'Yes, that's because there are so many things we don't ever consider, precisely because they're obvious to us, which can cause quite a bit of confusion. It's such an effort for hearing people to follow what a deaf person is saying that they'd rather have it all translated for them by someone else.'

'But can the speech be understood?'

'Better in some than in others. As far as your son is concerned, I have high hopes because he is still an infant. Always demand the best of him and never allow him to get away with less than that, even if he fights against it. He'll thank you for it later because most people think that someone who can't speak clearly is backward. This impression is often reinforced by the fact that those who have grown up with only sign language know only that form of grammar and it's quite different from that of our language. If you read a letter written by one of these people, you'll find it full of muddled and incomplete sentences. This is particularly unfortunate if writing a formal letter to one of the authorities.' Schär laughed bitterly. 'You can imagine how difficult it is for these people to be taken seriously.'

'I certainly can.' Richard recalled his experience of writing expert statements for the invalidity pension office.

Over the next few weeks the contact between him and Schär was strengthened by their shared political views as well as their common interest in helping deaf children.

During this period he and Paula started their private tuition in sign language with Fräulein Felber. During the first few weeks, Katharina Felber taught them the basic signs and gestures and dispelled their reserve in expressing themselves not only with their hands but also through mime and posture. After each lesson, Richard would feel as if he had been talking all evening, although not a single word had been said.

When he described this feeling to Paula, she confided that she felt the same. 'That accounts for what Herr Schär said about it really being a language in itself,' she said. 'We spent the whole evening talking, but not with our mouths. And yet the brain recognises it as speech and communicates to us the feeling that this was a real conversation with words. I'm finding it fascinating.'

'And tiring. My mother will say, "Oh, poor Georg, he's not going to be able to talk when the light's off."'

Paula laughed at the imitation of his mother's voice. 'Yes, but when the light's off, people have lots of other ways of making themselves understood,' she said with her most impish smile.

Tenderly, he took her face in his hands. 'Do you ever have doubts, Paula? You always come across as so strong and completely at ease with this.'

'So do you.'

He let out a sigh. 'Yes, because we have no choice. But there are times when I want to shout and scream and let go of all the self-control and rant on and on about how unfair it is that Georg will never be able to hear.'

'So why don't you?'

He sighed again. 'Because it wouldn't change anything and wouldn't make me feel any better.'

'It might sound strange but I never feel the need to do that. Somehow, it's become quite normal for me that Georg is as he is. He'll never play the piano or listen to the radio, or as your mother put it, make a telephone call. But he'll be able to drive a car, go off with you to do photography and learn how to develop the pictures; he'll also be able to run, swim, do gymnastics, and will have a highly developed sense of sight with which he can enjoy his surroundings. Isn't that enough?'

'Of course, of course,' said Richard quietly. 'And that's why I don't yell out all my despair. I don't have any right to do that – all the more so when I think of Fritz and Dorothea, who pour out all their love on the dachsie.'

'And they're happy, you know, so don't forget that.'

'Yes,' he acknowledged, 'though I reckon Fritz would be even happier if Dorothea could eventually get over her fear of another pregnancy. He'd hoped that seeing ours would give her a nudge in that direction, but Georg's deafness seems to have had the opposite effect on her.'

'Maybe that'll change when she realises that it doesn't matter and that baby Georg will grow into a happy little boy.'

'Let's hope so. I'd love that for Fritz.'

Chapter 24

In the first few months after the change of government, Richard's thoughts revolved largely around his son, so he didn't immediately notice the insidious changes that were taking place at the asylum. He first caught on at the weekly consultants' meeting, when the senior consultant announced that their colleague Dr Jakob Goldner, who'd been in charge of the open country houses, had left the hospital at short notice and that the widely respected Dr Krüger would take over the post.

'Where's Dr Goldner gone to?' asked Richard. He'd always liked Dr Goldner and he hoped that he'd now fulfilled his dream of getting a more senior role in another mental hospital.

'I don't know.' The way the senior consultant spoke made it clear that he wanted no further questions, and that got Richard thinking. When a colleague moved on, there was never usually any secrecy over their new position.

'Right, that concludes this item on the agenda. Let's move to the next. A new law has been passed this month, and it will have an impact on our work. It's the Law for the Prevention of Progeny with Hereditary Diseases, and it allows for the sterilisation of people with hereditary diseases.'

This news was greeted with applause. Even Richard joined in, as he had never understood why people should be prevented from having themselves sterilised if they were carriers of a hereditary disease. It had long been permitted in most other European countries and in the USA. Only in Germany had the Church vehemently opposed it. Richard vividly recalled the arguments put forward by several bishops in which they lamented the promotion of immorality through allowing those with hereditary diseases to indulge in unrestrained fornication without fear of pregnancy. The draft bill had been tabled by the previous government and Richard had to admire the efficiency of the new government in getting it ratified in the Reichstag.

'I've brought you the relevant extract.' The senior consultant passed around copies of the document, still smelling strongly of alcohol from the duplicator.

> Law for the Prevention of Progeny with Hereditary Diseases
>
> 14 July 1933
>
> The Government of the German Reich has passed and hereby announces the following law:
>
> § 1
>
> Those with hereditary disease may by surgical intervention be rendered infertile (sterilised) if, in accordance with medical research, there is a high probability that their progeny will suffer from severe hereditary physical or mental defects.
>
> In accordance with the purposes of this law, hereditary disease includes those who suffer from the following:

innate feeble-mindedness

schizophrenia

circular insanity (manic depression)

hereditary epilepsy

Huntington's chorea

hereditary blindness

hereditary deafness

hereditary severe physical deformity

Furthermore, those suffering from severe alcoholism may also be rendered sterile.

§ 2

The request is to come from the person who wishes to be rendered sterile. Should this person be incapacitated in law, or incapacitated due to feeble-mindedness, or under the age of eighteen, then a legal representative is authorised to make the request. That person additionally requires authorisation by the court-appointed guardian. Where an adult has a personal carer, then the carer's agreement is required.

Certification from a German Reich qualified doctor is to be appended to the request to confirm that the process and consequences of sterilisation have been explained to the person concerned.

The request can be withdrawn.

§ 3

An authorised doctor can also request the sterilisation of inmates in a hospital, mental asylum or nursing home, as can the head of a penal institution.

This law comes into effect on 1 January 1934

Berlin, 14 July 1933

Chancellor of the Reich,

Adolf Hitler

Minister for the Interior,

Wilhelm Frick

Ministry of Justice,

Dr Franz Gürtner

Richard read it once, then a second time, and eventually spoke. 'I notice that schizophrenia is cited here as a hereditary disease. Has there been some new academic research? To my knowledge, no hereditary element has ever been proven, although there can be a higher incidence in some families. The same applies to manic depression.'

'Herr Hellmer, you can safely assume that the specialists involved in drafting the new law have had as their source the most recent academic research. Our job is not to question the law after the event but to follow it. Simultaneous to the release of this text came the call for a number of asylum heads to examine inmates in relation to the application of section three.' The senior consultant paused briefly. 'Gentlemen, in the coming weeks you will receive the necessary registration forms, which must be carefully filled out with regard to each and every one of our inmates. Concentrate on those patients who are easier to treat and expect an early discharge – these have preferential status for sterilisation.'

'And if they refuse?'

'If they have a legal advocate, their decision will hold good. Should there be no advocate, then it is our job to persuade the patient of the advantages of sterilisation.'

'And if they won't be persuaded?' Richard persevered.

'We'll discuss that if it arises. Any other questions?'

Dr Harms raised his hand. 'What's the definition of severe alcoholism?'

'We don't have to deal with that. It relates purely to inmates of institutions for drinkers.'

There were no further questions and so the senior consultant declared the meeting closed.

Dr Harms caught Richard at the door. 'You asked about Dr Goldner earlier on. Do you really not know?'

'What do you mean?'

'He's a Jew.'

'So?' asked Richard.

'Quite a few state hospitals and asylums have been under pressure from on high to distance themselves from all Jewish doctors. Dr Goldner isn't the only one. An old student chum of mine, a consultant in general medicine, has just been discharged as well, but he was lucky and got a job at the Israeli Hospital instead.'

'And on what basis are Jewish doctors being dismissed?'

'For being Jewish.'

'But that's ridiculous.'

'Go and look at *Mein Kampf* – you won't believe some of our new Chancellor's ideas.'

'I have no intention of giving these people any additional support by buying his book.'

'You don't need to. The library here has a number of copies in stock. I know because I borrowed one of them. I'd be interested to hear what you think of it because at the moment you seem to be the only other person here, apart from me, not letting himself be infected by this insanity. Have you been in Dr Kleinschmidt's office of late?'

'No.'

'He's decorated it all with party symbols, including a huge framed motto in Gothic script, reading: "National Comrades! Remember you're a German. Heil Hitler!" He even expects his patients to say it when they greet him. Bizarre, don't you think?'

'Dr Kleinschmidt? You can't be serious!'

'Just go to his office.' Dr Harms shook his head. 'I wish you a pleasant day, my dear colleague.'

Early in the afternoon Richard went over to the institution's library to borrow a copy of *Mein Kampf*. He had no trouble finding one as the library seemed to have a dozen copies on the shelves.

Back in his office, he started to leaf through, looking for specific references. '*What is being neglected on all sides in this matter has to be made up for by the people's state. It must place race at the heart of everyday life . . .*

The people's state must make a declaration of infertility regarding anything of sickly appearance or hereditarily burdened, and thus additionally burdensome, and to assert this in practice.'

Speechless, Richard slammed the book shut. And to think he'd got worked up over the writings of Alfred Hoche and Karl Binding.

◆ ◆ ◆

When he got home that evening, he found Paula in the kitchen trying to console a tearful Leonie over a cup of coffee.

'What's happened?' Richard had never seen Leonie look so distraught.

Paula replied on her behalf. 'They've dismissed a number of Jewish doctors at the children's hospital. Even Dr Stamm. Nobody's thought about what a good doctor he is and how much he's done for the place. They've just dismissed him because he's a Jew. Leonie too.'

Richard sat down at the table with them and poured himself a coffee. 'What are you going to do now?' he asked Leonie.

'I'll help my father in his practice. There's not much else I can do.' Leonie sighed miserably. 'There are rumours going around that Jewish doctors will soon no longer be approved to use the national health insurance scheme.'

'But they can't do that,' raged Paula. 'That would mean the end for many practices and for health care itself.'

'I don't think our government is going to care about that,' commented Richard, 'not after what I've experienced today.' He told them about the consultants' meeting and his conversation with Harms.

'And what will you do if you have to fill out these forms?' Paula asked him.

'I can't decide,' he confessed. 'On the one hand, I think that sterilisation would be a blessing for some of our patients. But I don't like the way the voluntary aspect seems to have been taken away from certain people, while in the original version of the law it was voluntary for everyone. This is not about patient welfare or avoiding the burden of unwanted parenthood. Now it's all about the absurd ideas of a totally uneducated, unenlightened and obsessed politician like Hitler. Then there's all the nonsense he's written in his book! I just can't believe it. But it appears to be our new bible – how else could you explain the library at work having a dozen copies in stock?'

'So what will you do?' Paula asked him again.

'I have no idea.' Richard looked weary. 'You both know what a passionate advocate of birth control I am. In certain cases sterilisation is actually indicated, and if this law were approaching the issue with caution and care, it wouldn't be such a bad thing, but the radical nature of it disgusts me. Why do so many patients have to be assessed and registered? It makes no sense at all. It would be enough simply to have a conversation with them shortly before their discharge to make sure they know about the opportunities for sterilisation.'

'I don't envy you that job,' said Leonie. 'I'd almost prefer dismissal to doing that.'

'You can't be serious!'

'No,' conceded Leonie, 'not completely, but I'm trying to look on the bright side.' She let out a huge sigh. 'Maybe my father's idea of emigrating to Switzerland isn't so crazy when I think about what's happened here in just the last six months.'

'Try not to get too down about it,' said Paula. 'It can't get any worse, surely.'

Richard raised his eyebrows at that. 'No? And what if Leonie's father loses access to the health insurance scheme?'

'Don't say that! Do you really think the Medical Council would allow respected colleagues to be treated like that? I know they have no influence over state hospitals but surely eligibility for the scheme can't suddenly be declared invalid.'

'Why on earth not?' Richard persisted.

'Oh, stop it. I don't want always to fear the worst, like you do.'

'Nor do I,' said Leonie. 'And if we're desperate, there's always Switzerland.' She managed a smile in spite of her despondent state.

Richard said nothing more, but his sense of unease was growing.

Chapter 25

When Richard found the initial pile of registration forms on his desk and saw that one of the first patients he had to assess was Herbert, he felt as though he'd been punched in the belly. This wasn't because of the case itself – he accepted that Herbert would never be able to support a family. His shock and disappointment owed more to the fact that dear, naive Herbert still dreamt of leading a normal life in spite of his perpetual failure to get transferred to an open country house. Richard also knew that Herbert could never be talked into agreeing to sterilisation, but then he started to wonder why Herbert of all people should even be considered, because he never left the secure unit and had no contact with women.

He reflected for some time as to how he might best complete the form in order to protect Herbert's dignity and integrity. Eventually, he put a cross beside the statement that sterilisation was not required, and gave as the reason the unlikelihood of such a seriously ill patient ever being released, given his repeated failures to be transferred to an open house and therefore being at no risk of fathering a child.

Next he addressed the forms relating to births of the 'feeble-minded'. This included Julius, the older Downs' syndrome patient who tended to the cows. Why sterilise Julius? Most men with his condition were in any case infertile and Julius had never shown any particular interest in women. Again he marked the statement that sterilisation was not indicated and gave some thought as to how he could best justify this. The simplest would be to state that Julius was infertile, although such an assertion would mean he was breaking the rules of medical conduct, as he would be quite deliberately falsifying an official document. Under certain circumstances this could cost him his job. He took a deep breath and put Julius's form on the pile for resubmission.

The next case was comparatively straightforward. The subject was a mentally deficient, or 'feeble-minded', man, already father to one illegitimate child, who had inherited his father's hydrocephalus and was so deficient that he couldn't even benefit from attending a special school. In this case sterilisation would be a blessing for the patient and for the women who for some inexplicable reason allowed him into their beds. Richard marked the statement that sterilisation was indicated on medical grounds provided that the patient was in agreement with the explanation given him.

By evening Richard had worked through the first half of his cases and continued to avoid the pile of resubmissions – a very different approach to that of his colleague Krüger, who he encountered with his own stack of forms tucked under his arm as he made his way over to the secretariat.

'Oh, did you get caught up in an emergency?' he asked Richard, giving his small batch of papers a hard look. 'How can a hard-working expert like you have done so few in a day?'

'In my view, the wording of the questions is highly complex and has far-reaching implications.'

'Is it now?' Krüger said with a smile. 'It's very simple, actually. Can you imagine any one of our inmates in the role of father?'

'No,' Richard conceded.

'There you are, then. Why take so much trouble? It's a waste of time for specialists to have to give thought to this, but on the other hand, sterilisation costs money and is not necessary for those who are already infertile. The way I consider a case is whether reproduction could occur.'

'Aha,' observed Richard.

'And how do you go about it?'

'I scrutinise whether sterilisation is necessary in each individual case. In my estimation, it's not necessary for patients whose discharge will be in the distant future because they have no contact with women. And as you yourself have said, a sterilisation operation is expensive. We should consider the indications very carefully.'

Krüger muttered something under his breath, while Richard suddenly realised that he had hit upon the crucial solution in getting around any blanket compulsory sterilisation for his patients. It was all about cost – an unbeatable argument both before and since the economic crisis.

As soon as he returned to his desk, Richard phoned Fritz. He was lucky to find his friend in the office and not stuck in the operating theatre, as was more usually the case when he tried to contact him.

'Richard, what a pleasant distraction!' Fritz greeted his friend effusively. 'And perfect timing – I've got some excellent news!'

'Tell me!'

'Dorothea is pregnant. We found out yesterday and she's so excited about the baby.'

'That's fantastic! I hope Rudi won't be jealous!'

Fritz laughed. 'Never – he's as pleased as we are! Isn't it magnificent news, though? So fingers crossed that everything goes OK and we have a lovely healthy baby.'

'When's it due?'

'That's the only thing that's bothering Dorothea,' Fritz conceded. 'End of January – same as Gottlieb. But that doesn't mean anything. We're just quietly looking forward to it all.'

'I'm really pleased for you both. How about a celebratory beer?'

'I might run late today; I've still got two operations to go. But tomorrow's fine, so I'll take you up on that! Now, what can I do for you?'

'Have you heard about this new Law for the Prevention of Progeny with Hereditary Diseases?'

'Only in passing. Something about sterilisation being permitted as a matter of course.'

'Have you ever carried one out?'

'That's been prohibited for years, so why are you asking me?'

'So you've never carried out a male sterilisation procedure?'

'I have.'

'Even though it's prohibited?'

'It was last year, when I was at a conference in London. I got to know an English doctor – nice chap. Max Cooper had been very keen on my research publications on operative care for bullet wounds to the skull. I seem to have become rather well known in British medical circles as a result.' He chuckled with pleasure at this. 'Maxwell is a consultant neurologist and showed me his operating theatre. There happened to be a sterilisation scheduled for that day and because it's so rare here in Germany I took up his offer of lending him a hand.'

'Can you give me an idea of what a sterilisation procedure like that costs?'

'No idea. Why do you want to know?'

Richard explained.

'That's bad,' Fritz agreed. 'You know how much I love surgery, but we should avoid unnecessary operations like the plague. You only need to tot up the hourly cost of the surgeon, theatre nurse, anaesthetist, then add on the equipment, so I'd say around thirty marks for the operation alone. Then, with post-operative care, you're probably looking at fifty marks, and that's without complications.'

Richard gave a low whistle. 'A tidy sum – half the monthly wage of an ordinary worker. I can see how to work that into my argument. Thanks, Fritz. Shall we meet at The Green Man tomorrow? Six o'clock?'

'I'll be there,' Fritz promised.

◆ ◆ ◆

After a consultants' meeting a fortnight later, Dr Harms praised the argument Richard had put forward regarding the costs incurred by serial sterilisation without critical analysis of need. 'Did you see Krüger's face?'

Richard smiled. 'When obvious resistance is useless, then we have to fall back on our own resources. Your advice about looking at *Mein Kampf* was worth its weight in gold. It's only by seeing what's behind their thinking that you can come up with an effective countermeasure.'

This was only one small triumph, but Richard relished it, because over the next few months it allowed him to stay true to his moral ideals in spite of the difficult times in which they lived.

Chapter 26

One sunny Friday afternoon in May 1934, Richard was at his desk as usual, signing letters and going through files, but his mind wasn't fully on his work. He had the next day off and was already looking forward to spending the weekend at Travemünde with Paula and the children. Fritz also had the weekend off and planned to join them, together with Dorothea, their daughter, Henriette, now four months, as well as their dachsie, Rudi, who was adored by Richard and Paula's twins. Emilia could already say a few words and had learned quite a few sign language gestures, as had Georg. Fräulein Felber continued to come to their home every Tuesday to teach Richard and Paula. In addition, Paula had become good friends with Fräulein Felber's deaf and dumb mother and often went to see her with the children to perfect her knowledge of sign language. Richard was quite relaxed about the fact that his wife had long surpassed him in that regard.

As he sat thinking about the Baltic coast, there was a knock on his door. 'Come in!'

It was Dr Krüger. 'This case landed on my desk, but I think you'd better review it as it's concerning your expert statement of two years back.' He placed a brown folder on Richard's desk. The name on the front was Johannes Mönicke. Richard remembered the case straight away: it was the man who had developed schizophrenia after being buried alive in the trenches.

'Thank you,' said Richard. 'I'll take care of that.'

He expected Krüger to leave, but the man stayed where he was, in front of his desk.

'Was there something else?'

'I'd be very interested to know what you think of the argument put forward by this expert statement in which Dr Brockmann no longer sees this patient as meeting the eligibility criteria for continuing to draw the invalidity pension.'

'I shall tell you as soon as I have read the statement. Anything else?'

'No, not at all. May I wish you a pleasant afternoon and an enjoyable weekend, sir?'

'And the same to you.'

The name Dr Marius Brockmann didn't mean anything to him. But no sooner had Krüger left the office than Richard picked up the file. Krüger's smugness had made him fear the worst:

> My colleague Dr Hellmer argues in his preliminary statement that the patient has a particularly strong psychological constitution in comparison with others suffering wartime trauma because prior to his burial alive he had been deployed to the Front without demonstrating any distinctive mental condition. Taking this fact into consideration, it cannot be concluded from a medical point of view precisely why the experience of being buried alive, without any innate disposition to the condition, should have led to the onset of schizophrenia. On the other hand, the patient was twenty-five years old at the time, the peak age for the early manifestation of this hereditary illness. Even under more desirable conditions the onset of this illness could have been expected at precisely this time. Scientific literature finds no reference to a hereditary illness being brought

on by war trauma. This would be medically impossible because the genes are determined at conception. The argument put forward by the writer of the preliminary statement suffers from a lack of specialist analysis of the given facts, using instead an embellished writing style to try to arouse sympathy, something more suited to light romantic fiction.

Being buried alive is, of course, a traumatic event, but there are numerous examples in scientific literature which show that a man who is hereditarily sound and of pure blood can withstand this without damage. Where, however, inferior stock comes into play, then the sick genome will always prevail. From a human standpoint, it is understandable that Dr Hellmer has let himself be ruled by sympathy in writing this statement, but such sentiment should never take priority in the preparation of expert statements.

An expert who allows his feelings to dominate has failed in his profession. With regard to the proven hereditary nature of the illness in this patient, as well as his previously recognised strong mental state, the onset of schizophrenia can be explained uniquely by the fact that the patient had reached the age at which the sick gene prevails. The connection with being buried alive is of a merely temporal nature. The preconditions for further payment of the invalidity pension are therefore not met.

'Arrogant idiot!' hissed Richard to himself. He took a few deep breaths. He could usually easily spot weak arguments in statements of this kind. But this one didn't read like an expert statement. More like a pamphlet in the style of Hitler's *Mein Kampf*.

While he mulled over how to respond, a thought came to him. If schizophrenia was considered hereditary, then there had to be a transparent line to follow in Mönicke's family. However, if Mönicke was the only sufferer, there would be the opportunity to question the diagnosis and in its place put forward an organically conditioned psychosis with parallels to schizophrenia.

Mönicke's wife had no telephone so Richard wrote her a letter asking her to let him have a statement on any mental anomalies in her husband's family. He then placed the folder on the pile of resubmissions and resolved not to let this case spoil the weekend he'd been looking forward to so much.

◆ ◆ ◆

The drive to Travemünde was enjoyed by all, even though Paula complained loudly about Richard and Fritz repeatedly overtaking each other on the empty country road.

'Slow down! You boys always want see whose car goes faster.'

'What the heck! Fritz knows it's ours. He only wants to show me how well his car accelerates! We're saving ourselves for the real contest, when the motorway to Lübeck's ready.'

'Which motorway's that, then?'

'I read about it in the paper a few days ago. Work's due to start in May 1937 and the second section between Lübeck and Travemünde should come in 1938. If you really put your foot down, you could do Hamburg to Travemünde in an hour and a half.'

'So that's what you're both practising for,' Paula said with a sigh. 'I'd still rather you didn't drive like this! It's not as if Fritz urgently needs any new patients.'

Richard laughed, but relented and moderated his driving to a more sedate pace.

They had booked rooms at the Emperor Hotel, along with two beach chairs, which Fritz and Richard immediately surrounded with a suitably grand wall of sand. Meanwhile, Paula collected shells with the twins while Dorothea was busy with Henriette and Rudi. They'd smuggled their little dog on to the beach in a basket and put a towel over him whenever the beach supervisor hove into view.

The sea was still very cold, but the twins splashed happily at the water's edge. Anyone looking at Emilia and Georg would never have guessed that the little boy was deaf as he shrieked with delight just as much as she did, although he couldn't use words in the way she had started to.

Baby Henriette lay content on a woollen rug with Rudi obligingly acting as a pillow of sorts. Richard had brought along his camera and took around twelve photos of their group, especially the children and the dog.

◆ ◆ ◆

'Times are not nearly as bad as we feared,' confided Fritz as he and Richard lingered over a beer in the hotel bar that evening.

'Apart from public hospitals dismissing all our Jewish colleagues and my patients having to battle even more repressive treatment than before, things couldn't be better,' retorted Richard, barely able to conceal his bitterness.

'Of course, yes, I'm really sorry about Leonie,' said Fritz quietly. 'Is she still working with her father?'

Richard nodded. 'Yes, and he's been allowed to keep his access to the health insurance system because of his status as a war veteran. Dr Stamm's only allowed to treat private patients now.'

'That's absurd.' Fritz said, taking a gulp of his beer. 'Although one thing you have to hand to the Nazis: there is order on the streets now. I haven't had a single gunshot case in the last six months.'

'There is that at least,' said Richard, a harshly ironic edge to his voice. 'All you need to add to the list now is stable prices, a fall in unemployment and Germany having the fastest recovery in Europe from the economic crisis.'

'Yes, that's really something. But as for the other things . . . if they overdo this business with the Jews and the sick, they'll get taught a lesson at the next elections.'

'For God's sake, Fritz, haven't you realised that the SPD and many other parties were banned last year? And then there's this new Law Against the Founding of New Parties.'

Fritz stared at Richard in amazement. 'I didn't know that. I don't really follow politics, like you do. So if there are no other parties, why bother to vote at all?'

'I'm wondering how more than why. A ballot paper with just NSDAP on it? And they can win with a single vote in their favour?'

'That would be grotesque!'

'As grotesque as dismissing Jewish doctors, as replacing our black, red and gold flag with the black, white and red German Empire one with a swastika stuck on it, and then there's this laughable "Heil Hitler" business being used as the national form of greeting.'

Fritz laughed.

'And you're laughing?' Richard flushed with anger.

'No, I was thinking of something else. A colleague of mine was telling me the German greeting is ideal for pub-goers. Say "Three litres" as fast as you can.'

'*Dreilitter.*'

'And if you raise your right arm at the same time, it starts to sound the same as "Heil Hitler". So if people don't want to do the German greeting, they just say how much beer they want.'

Now Richard saw the funny side. 'Takes a bit to understand it.'

'Yes, but you mustn't go muddling it up and say, "Three pints," by mistake. Doesn't work then. I'm having another. What about you?'

◆ ◆ ◆

Four days later Richard was in his office when Frau Mönicke's reply arrived. She wrote that she knew nothing of any mental illness in her husband's family, but that his grandmother had hanged herself in the attic years ago.

Richard sighed. For most expert opinions, one suicide would be a clear indicator of long-standing mental illness in the family. He'd have to think of something else. But what? His mind was a blank.

Eventually, he wrote:

> Whether or not one agrees with the general view that schizophrenia is hereditary – something for which there is no adequate evidence, only the power of a decision made in law – there is at the present time no verified way of determining its onset in advance. Furthermore, the influence of environmental factors and the traumatic experiences at the time of the onset cannot be ruled out. The assumption made by Dr Brockmann that schizophrenia, independent from any trauma, developed in the patient's twenty-sixth year, is unreliable because it deals with only a statistical average of the first manifestation. In our asylum alone, original cases have been observed between the ages of eighteen and forty-seven. Even if one assumes a genetic predisposition, it remains speculative as to when the illness would have manifested itself in favourable conditions. Taking into consideration the

fact that first manifestations are regularly seen well into the fifth decade of life, in more favourable conditions the patient would have expected fifteen to twenty years of good health during which he would have been able to support his family. Because his war trauma took this opportunity away from him, it seems only fair that the state undertake to provide an invalidity pension for a deserving war veteran and national comrade.

Six weeks later he heard that the payment of the invalidity pension to the family had definitively ceased. The pension authority went along with his expert statement only insofar as saying the wife need not pay back monies already received, because one could not rule out with any certainty that the schizophrenia had been prematurely triggered by trauma.

Chapter 27

Hamburg, January 1936

'You can't mean this! Leonie, please think it over again, both of you!' Paula was on the telephone and very upset.

'Paula, I'm so sorry, but we've been thinking about little else for ages, I promise you. But Papa has decided and I'm going with him. There's nothing for us here now.'

Paula gasped. On the one hand, she completely understood Leonie's logic. The Law for the Protection of German Blood and German Honour had now been in place for a few months and was a kick in the teeth for all Jewish citizens. Marriage between Jews and Aryans had immediately become an offence, as had sexual intercourse outside marriage, described as 'racial defilement' and punishable by imprisonment. On top of this, Leonie's father had now lost his access to the health insurance system and therefore the majority of his patient base. Yet Paula kept hoping that things would change. She didn't want to lose her closest friend.

Leonie carried on, 'My father's got friends in Switzerland. They're desperate for doctors. He could open a really successful practice there and I could work in a hospital. And I won't be halfway to prison if I make my own choice about who I want to be with.' Leonie gave a bitter laugh. 'Paula, there's no other solution. We're ready to close up our home here and leave behind everything we can't take with us.'

Paula went cold. She just couldn't believe what was happening. 'And when are you leaving?'

'Early March. But don't worry, we'll see each other lots before then.'

Paula swallowed hard and changed the subject before she slipped into even greater despair. 'You're due to come over again soon in any case. The day before yesterday, Georg said a whole sentence and it was completely intelligible. Well, intelligible to us.'

'That's wonderful. I'm so thrilled for you. Who'd have thought he'd make such good progress!'

'He benefits a lot from having a twin who can hear and who practises every day with him. Dr Stamm was saying that in different times he'd have written a paper on Georg's positive development and the opportunities created for deaf children by early intervention, but given the times we live in, this would only harm Georg and we shouldn't in any way push ourselves forward and attract attention. The longer we can conceal his deafness, the better.'

'But there's no inherited deafness in Georg's case.'

'That doesn't interest the Hereditary Health Court. They demand proof of no hereditary factors. And if you can't prove it, you're sterilised – it's arranged, and that's it. Did you know the government now arranges marriages between those who've been sterilised so they can remain among their own kind and not marry anyone who wants children?'

Leonie was speechless.

'That's why we don't want Georg to be noticed by the Gesundheitspolizei – that's what they're calling these so-called enforcers of "racial hygiene". It'll be hard in two years' time when he starts school because he can't follow the lessons in normal school, which is why we've been sending him to Bürgerweide. Richard asked a trusted colleague to produce a statement for Georg, saying that he has no hereditary condition and that only the circumstances of his birth caused his hearing loss.'

'I thought you weren't completely sure about that.'

'You're right. We're not. But it's not about the truth, it's about protecting Georg.'

'Have you two ever thought of leaving the country like us?'

'No. This is our home.'

'That's how my father and I used to feel. But as time goes on, that home's being destroyed for us.'

'I don't think you can compare our situations, Leonie. Richard knows how to protect Georg. Apart from our boy's condition, we have no other major problems to deal with. Life's pretty good if you fall within the Führer's approved racist definitions. And anyway, who knows, maybe the Olympics will change things in the summer. With the whole world coming to Germany for that, they'll have to ease off those restrictive laws at some point.'

Leonie sighed. 'Paula, much as I value your optimism, I can't see it as you do. To be honest, I feel as though everything that's ever meant anything is collapsing around my ears.'

This gave Paula pause, as what Leonie had said could just as easily have come from Richard's lips.

◆ ◆ ◆

At the Langenhorn asylum Richard had long been accustomed to writing expert statements in a certain style. He continued to use his argument in favour of saving money by being more careful about indicating sterilisation and was seen as a respected colleague. But his regular contact with Alfred Schär meant he knew how hard it was for the deaf and dumb. Schär was frequently asked to interpret at Hereditary Health trials, and what he had to tell was shocking. Even if someone was demonstrably the first deaf mute in the family, this was no guarantee of their safety. There was an accumulation of expert opinion which assumed a new mutation and pronounced in favour of sterilisation. While it had originally been Richard asking Alfred Schär for advice, now it was Schär who had to turn to Richard with complex questions, in the hope that Richard might find a loophole with which to influence the opinion of the court expert.

Once Richard recognised that logical debate was not what this was about, he let slip during a phone conversation with Schär that he was protecting his son by means of a falsified medical certificate, according to which Georg had hearing difficulties due only to birth trauma and that there was no indication whatsoever of anything hereditary.

Schär listened attentively and invited Richard to come to his home in Hamburg's Volksdorf district in order to discuss the matter in more detail. Richard had already been there twice with Paula on social occasions, but when he asked if he might bring her this time, Schär said no.

'I'd like you to come here alone this time. And park your car a couple of streets away.'

'That all sounds rather furtive!' Richard tried to cover up his uncertainty with a gentle laugh.

'Some things are better discussed in person than over the phone. I'll see you at eight.'

With this Schär put down the telephone, and Richard rang Paula to let her know he'd be home late. She seemed unconcerned by this, and as he could hear the children making a noise in the background he didn't want to keep her, much as he'd have loved to hear what she thought about Schär's odd behaviour.

◆ ◆ ◆

At eight o'clock sharp he rang the doorbell. As requested, he'd parked his car a couple of streets away, though he still didn't understand why.

Schär opened the door. 'Quickly, come in, please.'

'Why? Are the Gestapo after you?' Richard joked, but he paused when he saw Schär's expression. 'What's wrong?'

'My neighbours are rabid Nazis. In the last six months or so they've reported me because I let out two rooms to a Jewish family. And old Dellbrück opposite has started noting down my visitors' registration plates. I'm on the blacklist around here.' He let out a bitter chuckle. 'The Gestapo have already called me in once in the last year to caution me.'

'What for? It isn't forbidden to rent to Jews.'

'Not yet,' said Schär, 'but it's not exactly encouraged. Especially if you were on the Volksdorf municipal council until 1932, as I was, as a member of the SPD.'

As they talked, Schär led him through into the living room, where two men were already seated. One looked very young, twenty at most; the other was around Richard's age.

'Klaus Weber and Matthias Olderog.' Schär introduced them both to Richard. 'ISK comrades.'

The men got to their feet and shook hands with Richard.

'ISK?' he asked. 'Is that the International Socialist Action Group?'

Schär nodded. 'In a country where all political parties are banned, it's our job to preserve the values of liberty and to fight for a society free from exploitation.'

Richard cleared his throat. 'I'm honoured that you have so much faith in me . . . but I've really no interest in joining a forbidden organisation.'

'You don't need to join anything at all.' Matthias Olderog was quick to appease. 'But your knowledge and professional competence could help us.'

'How's that?'

'The same way you've helped your son,' explained Schär. 'We need respected experts to provide medical certificates that rule out hereditary illnesses or permanent damage. Without them, the people affected are simply being handed to this repressive regime on a plate.'

Richard swallowed hard. 'And what illnesses are we talking about here? I'm a psychiatrist. I can't produce a certificate for a deaf mute. It was hard enough finding someone to take on the risk for my son.'

'It's predominantly comrades who are suffering from shell shock,' said Olderog. 'Can you see yourself helping men like them?'

Richard suddenly saw his brother before him, reduced to terror and helplessness by the slightest sound, unable to eat or drink, existing only in his own world. It brought back to Richard how powerless he himself had felt when their bad decision had put his brother in an asylum where he had been subjected to such merciless treatment that it had killed him. He swallowed hard again.

'How far can I actually help, though? If the invalidity pension is suspended, there's little I can do; the current legal position doesn't leave much room for manoeuvre for any expert opinion. And even if one does support it, the pension authority is pretty much always opposed.'

'It's only about confirming the full recovery of the individuals concerned, especially if they haven't been in receipt of the invalidity pension for a long time. Would you do that?'

'Yes, I can see that working. But I don't fully understand why that's so important.'

'We fear that what we're seeing now is just the beginning,' explained Schär. 'Who knows where all this fanaticism about race and soundness of health is leading? The only people who are safe are those who are completely inconspicuous.'

'Another problem is that most people are not aware of how dangerous the new legislation is,' added Olderog. 'Anyone who's healthy and of pure blood in line with the new law, and who isn't interested in politics, will see only the sunny side and be bewitched by the cult of the Führer. But the more people cheer without really seeing, the further the Nazis will go. And we want to protect our comrades and all those considered weak and worthless by the regime. Just like you with your son. We have the same aim.'

'I'll help you,' said Richard, 'but I don't want my name to be associated with the ISK. Precisely because I must protect my family and not put them at risk.'

'That goes without saying,' promised Schär. 'You'll be at your most useful to us if nobody knows that we're working together. That's why I asked you to park your car a couple of streets away. If anyone asks, this meeting never happened.' He held out his hand in farewell. While his handshake was firm and confident, Richard's response was hesitant at first. His heart told him he was doing the right thing, but a warning had sounded in his head. He was on a tightrope here and needed to be very careful.

Chapter 28

The task turned out to be far easier than Richard had expected. The men concerned contacted him by telephone, and he would quite openly ask them to come during his consulting hours. For a year now his work had required him to call in outpatients himself and personally assess them. Nobody was going to notice a couple of favourable statements here and there, especially as they had no impact on expenditure.

He had agonised about confiding in Paula, but didn't want to worry her, especially as she had been so low since Leonie had left for Switzerland. In the end, he kept to his resolution never to have secrets from his wife.

To his amazement, Paula showed no concern and was actually very proud of him for doing it.

'There'd be far less suffering if we had more doctors like you. And what's the worst that can happen? Someone could say you've made one wrong assessment and your reputation gets a bit of a dent? Doctors are allowed to make mistakes; it's not forbidden, and nobody will say you've done it on purpose. I only wish I could do more myself.'

'You're already doing so much by being there for our children,' replied Richard. 'Without you, Georg would never have made the progress he has.' This wasn't just a compliment but the truth. Paula practised with Georg for several hours a day. He was learning how to do phonetic voice exercises while placing his fingers close to the larynx so he could feel the vocal cords vibrate, something which happened only when the sound was correctly produced. And so strong was the bond between the twins that his sister was almost always at his side, even though she could have chosen to play instead. Emilia took care to correct her brother if his speech wasn't clear enough and had even invented her own sign to tell him so. The desire not to fall behind his sister spurred Georg on more than any of his parents' pleas and exhortations. However, it was a daily struggle and there were often tears of frustration when Georg didn't want to carry on because it was so tiring for him and he wanted to rely on signing instead. Paula was always mindful of Alfred Schär's advice to insist on the best from her son, although it hurt sometimes to demand so much of him. And so she practised patiently with him while trying to maintain a balance between strictness and kindness, sometimes pushing herself to the limit. But all of that was forgotten when Georg's speech continued to improve and he could successfully sound out new and difficult words. He made good progress with lip-reading too. Paula practised with him, talking to him without signing so that he could read it only by watching her lips, then he had to repeat it back to her using sign language. What she had to watch out for was his sister standing behind her and secretly showing him the signs. The first time she caught Emilia doing this, both the children had burst out laughing and couldn't see anything wrong in what they were doing.

'Emilia, you're not helping Georg by doing that.' Paula managed to sound reproving while concealing her own amusement.

In August the twins were excited to be looking after Rudi, the dachshund, for a few days while Fritz and his family went to Berlin to enjoy the Olympic Games, something they wouldn't have missed for anything. For Georg, any time spent with Rudi was a big incentive to improve his speech because the dachsie was really stubborn. He did what he was told only if the instructions sounded completely familiar to him; otherwise, he would just stand there, wagging his tail and gazing up at him with that trusting dachshund face.

The evening before Fritz was due to collect him, Georg asked his father a question with the most perfect pronunciation. 'Papa, can we have a dog too?'

Richard was sure Georg had been practising this sentence with his sister for ages. The children had worked out a long time ago that if Georg spoke clearly and well, there were always rewards. But Richard wasn't to be persuaded on this one. 'You're both too young for that. Maybe when you start school.'

They were bitterly disappointed, and Richard was sure he hadn't heard the last of this one.

Fritz came to collect Rudi the following evening, bursting with excitement. 'The games were magnificent! The whole city was decked out with the flags of every country you could think of. Not just pennants but huge banners – five metres long, I'd say. For people with no stadium tickets, there were loudspeakers all over the place, broadcasting announcements direct from the inside. And then there were these things called television suites where you could go and watch it all on a television set.'

'Television?' Richard looked puzzled. He hadn't heard this word before and imagined a room full of huge binoculars trained on the Olympic arena.

'Haven't you seen the newsreel about it?' asked Fritz.

Richard shook his head. 'We haven't been to the cinema for a while.'

'It's a wooden chest, bigger than an orange box.' Fritz demonstrated the size with his hands and Richard couldn't help but smile. His old friend never used to be one for gestures, but now that sign language was part of normal life in Richard's family, Fritz was unconsciously adapting his own style. 'At the front there's a pane of glass called a screen. I spent so long getting the technician to explain it all to me that Dorothea got fed up waiting and Henriette started grizzling.' Fritz chuckled as he remembered the scene. 'When you switch it on, you see moving pictures on the screen. It's similar to the cinema, but the difference is that these pictures are created within the box and then transmitted on to the screen. The film recordings from the Olympic Stadium were broadcast in the same way, using radio waves, so that you could be in a television suite and still see what was happening inside the arena. OK, these recordings weren't as clear as cinema newsreel and you could often make out only shadowy figures, but I was really impressed by the technical side. Just imagine if everyone had a box like that at home – it would be better than the radio. You hear it but have the pictures as well. It would be an absolute blessing for your boy. It's a shame nobody's thinking of mass production yet, but it's all too pricey at the moment.'

'That's a relief for the cinemas, I imagine,' observed Richard.

'That's true, yes, but there's no comparison with the big screen. Television can transmit only black-and-white pictures. The German Film Academy ought to be bringing more colour films into our cinemas.'

'So did you actually see any sporting events or just enjoy the technical novelties?'

'Of course we did! We saw that miracle of a runner, Jesse Owens, in the hundred-metre final and long jump. He pushed our Luz Long into second place in the long jump and Long congratulated him warmly. Near us there was a Nazi in uniform making comments about how any German national comrade should be ashamed of embracing a Negro. I couldn't help but tell him that this was in keeping with the traditional spirit of the Olympics. Most of the crowd thought Long's gesture was the right thing to do and cheered Owens for his achievements – the man won four gold medals, after all. I pointed this out to my neighbour and he told me it was no great surprise because Negroes are natural runners. Then he started talking about Darwin and claimed that it's genetically determined that only the fastest Negroes escaped being eaten by lions and could then reproduce. When I asked him if his knowledge of Africa came exclusively from those Tarzan films with Johnny Weissmüller, the conversation came to an abrupt end.' Fritz laughed and Richard joined in.

'Then we saw Karl Hein's Olympic record in the hammer. And we were there when the women's four by one hundred relay team were in line for a new world record but lost the baton in the final and got disqualified. You should have heard the crowd – like an earthquake! But the television made such an impression on me. It's technology that matters. However fast you can run, horses have always been faster, and since the motor car, well, any old tortoise can outpace an Olympic champion.'

'Sounds as though you had fun.'

'Certainly did.' Fritz was beaming with delight. 'And even though we'd gone to Berlin for the games, we made time to go to the Egyptian Museum as well and saw the bust of Nefertiti. But you'll never guess who we ran into there.' His grin broadened. 'Maxwell Cooper, of all people, along with his wife and daughter.'

'Maxwell Cooper?' The name didn't ring any bells with Richard.

'My English colleague – the one from London I meet up with at conferences. The one who showed me the surgical procedure for sterilisation.'

'Yes, I remember now.'

'Anyway, there we were, standing in front of Nefertiti, and we couldn't believe our eyes. It was so funny. Everyone else was still at the stadium, so we had the place pretty much to ourselves. All the Coopers are mad on Ancient Egypt – they learned hieroglyphics even as children. Maxwell's brother is curator at the British Museum in London and, last time I was there, he showed me some of the rooms where they do restoration work that aren't usually open to the public. As a side interest, Maxwell researches causes of death in mummies. It's fascinating. Dorothea was a bit bored by it all as she doesn't speak much English and Maxwell and his wife speak no German at all, but that didn't stop Helen giving our little Henriette a hug and telling me to bring Dorothea and the little one with me next time I'm in London for a conference. But nothing will come of that for a while, not now Dorothea's pregnant again.'

'You're having another baby?' Richard was surprised and delighted.

'We certainly are. The baby's due end of January, early February.'

'Just like before. At least I know when the mating season is for you two.'

'Very funny!' Fritz laughed and gave him a playful punch.

◆ ◆ ◆

On 8 February 1937 Fritz and Dorothea became parents to a healthy boy they named Harald, known by everyone as Harri.

Three days later Richard was at his desk reviewing an expert statement when the phone rang.

'Hellmer here.'

'This is Matthias Olderog. Are you alone?' He sounded hunted.

'Yes.' Olderog's tone unsettled Richard. 'What's wrong?'

'I wanted to warn you. Alfred Schär was arrested yesterday. There's been a countrywide operation against the ISK.'

Richard swallowed hard. 'What's he accused of?'

'I don't know. He was summoned for questioning at the Gestapo headquarters at Stadthausbrücke and then taken straight into custody.'

'Is there anything I can do?'

'No, I just wanted to inform you. If you get a summons from the Gestapo, just say you know Alfred only in his role as a deaf-mute teacher.'

Richard felt his hands go cold. There'd been rumours of torture in Gestapo prisons, but that had always seemed so far removed from himself and his own life. And yet now here was someone he viewed as a friend in the clutches of the Gestapo. At the same time he realised it wasn't just Schär he was worried about. What would happen if he was summoned too? If he was arrested? What would happen to Paula and the children?

'Am I on their list?' He struggled to keep his voice steady. 'How much danger is there?'

At the other end of the line Olderog's breathing was uneven. 'Klaus and I won't say a word. I can't imagine that Alfred will give anything away and you're not a member of the ISK in any case. But I'm very worried about Alfred. The Gestapo are known for their brutality.'

'So is there nothing we can do?'

'Nothing, other than sit tight and wait until the danger has passed. I have to go now.'

Once Olderog had hung up, Richard rang to inform Paula.

She said nothing for a long time and he was afraid they'd lost the connection.

Eventually, she spoke. 'Don't worry. You've done nothing illegal. You've just done your job. And I don't believe Alfred Schär would name you. You're not important in this. Stay calm and wait.'

Over the next couple of days Richard gave a start every time the phone rang, but there was no call from the Gestapo and his life continued as normal.

On the third day after Schär's arrest, Olderog rang again. 'I've got bad news.'

His voice was subdued and Richard felt his stomach tense. Had Schär given him away? Were the Gestapo after him? Was Olderog warning him to disappear? And if he was, how could he, when he had a wife and children?

What Olderog said next shocked him out of his panic.

'Alfred is dead.'

'Dead?' Richard couldn't take it in. 'How . . . how can he be dead?'

'They say he hanged himself in custody.' Olderog's voice cracked. 'But I don't believe that. My fear is that they've overdone the interrogation and are covering it up as suicide.'

Richard took some deep breaths.

Dead . . . Alfred Schär was dead.

However often he repeated this to himself, his mind just couldn't take it in.

'But he was determined to the last and didn't betray anyone.' Olderog's voice trembled with emotion. 'That should be some consolation to us.'

Didn't betray anyone . . . dead . . . determined . . . Richard couldn't concentrate.

'I simply can't believe it – it's a tragedy.' He wanted to say something but nothing felt right. 'My thanks to you, Herr Olderog. Do you know how Alfred's wife is?'

'No. I'm avoiding contact with her at the moment in case she's being watched by the Gestapo, and you should do likewise. Just live your life as before, Dr Hellmer. That's the best thing to do.' With that, he rang off.

Live life as before? What did Olderog envisage? And yet alongside his horror, Richard sensed something else making its presence felt and was ashamed of it: relief. Schär had not given him away, and now he was dead there was no fear of betrayal. When the full scope of this thought sank in, he wondered whether Schär had hanged himself as final proof that he was loyal and had not betrayed comrades. Richard secretly hoped this was the case, because he wanted to remember Schär as a man who had taken his life to protect others, not as a man beaten to death by the Gestapo.

Chapter 29

A few months after Schär's death, Richard was confident in his belief that any danger of his being in the Gestapo's sights had been banished once and for all. He had followed Olderog's advice and tried not to draw attention to himself, even though he still got calls from people wanting medical certificates. It was risky, but he turned no one away. He understood their desperation too well and Paula was right behind him. Around the same time his colleague, Krüger, joined the NSDAP and regularly deputised for the lead consultant. Richard wasn't too bothered as Krüger rarely came to the secure unit and the number of times he deputised as either senior or lead consultant could be counted on one hand.

But then one morning in September Paula phoned Richard at work. She sounded agitated. 'You've got a letter here from the Hamburg police headquarters at Stadthausbrücke.'

Richard froze. That was the Gestapo headquarters. 'Open it and read it out, would you?'

He heard her opening the envelope.

> Dear Dr Hellmer, *she read*. You are hereby required to attend the police headquarters at Stadthausbrücke 8, Department II, Room 12, for questioning on Monday 27 September 1937 at 11 a.m. sharp.

It concluded with 'Heil Hitler' and the name of the Hauptkommissar, Chief Inspector Gustav Liedecke.

Richard's throat tightened. Department II meant the political police. Had someone linked him to Schär?

'You've nothing to blame yourself for.' Paula did her best to calm him. 'You've nothing to feel guilty about.'

'I know.' But his mind was racing. What if someone had talked? Mentioned him in relation to favourable expert statements or denounced him in some other way? All of a sudden he found himself thinking enviously of Leonie and her father's wise decision to move to Switzerland. She wrote to Paula on a regular basis. Did the Gestapo know about the letters? That his wife was in contact with Jews who had left the country? But that wasn't against the law. The fear that had gripped him after Schär's arrest came back now with a vengeance. Schär had been summoned like this and never came back. That had been his second summons, though, and he had been a known member of the ISK. His first summons had just been a warning. Perhaps it would be the same for him.

◆ ◆ ◆

On the morning of 27 September, he bade his family a longer goodbye than usual, trying to imprint their expressions, their faces, their movements, everything about them, into his memory in case he never saw them again.

The police headquarters was an imposing three-storey, eighteenth-century baroque building that from the outside gave no hint of the dark secrets within. As Richard made his way through the entrance hall, he considered how best to conduct himself. Anything the Gestapo thought they knew about him could only have come from informants. Perhaps it was time to dispense with his old aversion to the so-called

German greeting and take the wind out of the Hauptkommissar's sails at the outset.

Room twelve was on the first floor. He looked at his watch. Seven minutes to eleven. Should he wait or knock straight away? He took three deep breaths and knocked.

'Come in.'

Richard opened the door, raised his right arm and said, 'Heil Hitler. My name is Dr Hellmer. You wanted to see me?'

The official was sitting behind an enormous oak desk, but when Richard hailed him so promptly with the German greeting, he felt obliged to get to his feet and return the gesture. Richard noticed that there was an open newspaper beneath some files on the desk, as if the other man had tried hurriedly to hide it when he'd knocked.

'You're rather early,' observed the Kommissar.

'We Germans are like that. Always punctual. Do tell me how I can be of assistance to you, Herr Kriminalkommissar.'

Uncertainty flickered across the official's face. Few summoned would ever enter the room so full of self-confidence. Richard decided to carry on in the same vein. He wouldn't see himself as the accused but as a respected doctor who took it in his stride to be questioned from time to time as an expert witness.

'Do sit down,' said Liedecke, gesturing at the chair on the other side of his desk. 'Now, this is purely a routine matter.'

'I had assumed so, Herr Kriminalkommissar. But like any decent German national comrade, I am ready at any time to stand shoulder to shoulder with the police to give advice and support. What can I do for you?' He leaned back in his chair in a relaxed fashion, noting how irritated this seemed to make Liedecke. And the more irritated the man became, the more confident Richard felt. He took in the room, noting the obligatory Hitler portrait hanging on the wall behind the desk, with a map of Hamburg to the left of it, while a few cacti decorated the window ledge.

'It's been passed on to us that you knew Alfred Schär.'

'Schär? Oh, yes, that's right, the deaf-mute teacher. He was recommended to me as a phonetics expert. That was . . . wait a moment, let me see – February 1933, soon after the seizure of power.'

'Why did you need a phonetics expert?'

'It's like this . . .' Richard hesitated a moment. 'I don't know how much you know about me, so I'll go back a little. On 9 August 1932 my wife gave birth to our twins. My daughter was born quickly and is a completely healthy little girl. For the birth, however, my son was a transverse presentation, which meant my wife's labour lasted for hours and in the end he was helped out with forceps. Sadly, this resulted in severe injury, but the extent of it became apparent only after several months. Since then he's been very hard of hearing and so of course we wanted to get him the best possible support so that he could learn to speak properly in spite of this tragic birth defect.'

Liedecke cleared his throat. 'I'm sorry. I had been informed that your son was born deaf mute.'

Richard's heart skipped a beat but he quickly reverted to his role. 'Really? Then you need to subject your informant to some tough questioning because he seems to have provided you with incorrect information. My son's speech is quite intelligible. Being very hard of hearing, he has to be able to see the face of whoever is talking to him in order to understand absolutely everything, but he is not a deaf mute.'

Liedecke didn't pursue this and changed the subject. 'I have also been informed that you are a doctor at Langenhorn asylum and that you forbid your patients from using the German greeting.'

Richard gave a start. Who had told the Gestapo about that? And why? He pulled himself together.

'Herr Kriminalkommissar, I'm amazed. The German greeting is for pure-blooded German national comrades born in good health. This is why the use of the German greeting is prohibited in the Rhineland during the carnival season, because it would be robbed of its dignity if used by any drunken Tom, Dick or Harry. I assume you know about this?' He left a dramatic pause to see what effect his words were having on Liedecke. He'd got this information from Fritz, who had in turn got the story from his cousin down in Cologne.

'Yes, but . . .'

'Now,' said Richard, cutting across him, 'you'll understand how odd it would sound to me, a psychiatrist, to be greeted with "Heil Hitler" by people who have no idea of the significance of this splendid word "Heil" and its association with noble German cultural anthems but know it only in relation to the "healing" of illnesses. You can imagine how I would feel as a psychiatrist if my patients were to enter the room demanding that I heal our leader.' He'd got so carried away by his own argument that he suddenly wondered if he'd overdone it. But a swift glance at Liedecke's face reassured him. The man was clearly not a hard nut, more a pleasant official who was gradually letting himself be won over by Richard's eloquent performance, reinforcing Richard's suspicion that some evil-intentioned colleague had informed on him and the Gestapo were going into the case only as a matter of routine and had no concrete evidence against him.

'If you would like me to, then I shall of course in future ask my patients to use the German greeting,' said Richard in a more conciliatory manner. 'That being the case, I'd like you to give me written authority that this is in line with the law and that it renders my patients equal to all national comrades born with good health. I wouldn't want to lay myself open to attack through any perceived disregard of our German greeting. I respect the Führer far too much for that. Do you have any further questions?'

'No, none. Many thanks, Dr Hellmer, sir.' Liedecke stood up. Before he could hold out his hand, Richard raised his right arm, clicked his heels and said, 'Heil Hitler.' Liedecke swiftly collected himself and returned the greeting.

Once Richard was outside the door, he calmed himself with some deep breaths. His acting had been second-rate, he thought to himself, but how fortunate that this official had fallen for it. Then he found himself wondering why he'd really been summoned – Liedecke hadn't said a word. Richard couldn't shake off the idea that Krüger was behind it. Krüger, who liked to know so much about his colleagues and had rebuked him only a few weeks ago for not having his patients say 'Heil Hitler'. And did Krüger know about Schär? He couldn't say with any certainty, and the concern lingered. He decided, however, to be much more careful from now on, when it came to his own safety and that of his family.

Chapter 30

'You should stop coming here, my dear Frau Hellmer. You know it puts us both more than halfway to prison,' Dr Stamm reminded her.

Paula noticed how much he had aged in the last few months.

'Who could possibly stop me, sentimental woman that I am, from visiting my old boss from time to time and bringing my children along?' She gave him a comforting smile. Dr Stamm was still her own children's doctor, in spite of the fact that he was no longer allowed to treat Aryan patients. Paula still relied on his advice and was able to get any of his recommended prescriptions made up for them by Fritz's father, a registered general doctor working in private practice.

'My work as a doctor comes to an end on 1 October in any case.' Dr Stamm sighed. 'A letter came yesterday saying that any certificate of appointment held by a Jewish doctor will lapse by 30 September. But provided we're not dispossessed, we can survive.'

Paula didn't know what to say. When she thought about it, though, and given everything that had been happening, she wasn't so surprised. For the first time, she felt happy that Leonie and her father had gone to Switzerland when they did.

'Have you ever thought of leaving our country?'

'An old tree shouldn't be uprooted. I've been a patriot all my life and have put my heart and soul into my work as a doctor. First, they take away my fatherland and in the end my profession. But I'll get by somehow.'

'I'll carry on visiting you,' Paula promised.

'Only if it doesn't put you at risk, Frau Hellmer; otherwise, I could never forgive myself.'

'And I could never forgive myself if I didn't stand by the people who mean something to me. And you're one of them, whether you like it or not.'

Was she imagining it or were there tears in the elderly doctor's eyes?

That evening she told Richard the sad news. He took it in without a word.

'Haven't you got anything to say about it?' she asked him.

'I don't know what to say any more. Sometimes, I envy Fritz. He at least tries to enjoy the brighter side of the new Germany. He told me that in September they're going on a cruise with the KdF, that Strength through Joy organisation. They've booked a cabin on the *Wilhelm Gustloff*.'

'The children will love it. Why haven't we been on any KdF cruises?'

'I don't care for that kind of group activity, you know, when they're all promoting "Strength through Joy".' He made a face. 'I'd rather have a couple of days in Haffkrug or Travemünde. Besides which, I have no desire to spend my holiday having to watch everything I say and playing at being the staunch national comrade.'

Paula sighed. Since Richard had been called before the Gestapo the previous year, he had changed. Even though he'd very deftly slipped the noose and had never heard from them again, he'd lost part of his natural optimism. In the meantime, he had found out for sure that it was Krüger who'd informed on him because Dr Harms had told him of a conversation he'd overheard between Krüger and Kleinschmidt. The pair had been greatly amused to note how amenable Hellmer had become since their call to the Gestapo and the resulting summons.

Previously, Richard had approached his work with real passion, always inspired by his desire to help people and make everything better. But ever since the supposedly deserving party comrade Dr Krüger had taken over the lead consultant role and become Richard's superior, things had changed. Resources intended for the good of the people were no longer to be squandered on 'inferior beings' and it was hard for him to get anything at all for his patients. In the past, Richard had always been able to rely on Dr Harms, but he had handed in his notice and started a new post in Brandenburg following a vehement disagreement with Krüger a few weeks previously.

All this gnawed away at Richard and since Harms' resignation he had seriously been considering applying to the asylum at Lüneberg, simply to escape the poisonous atmosphere at Langenhorn. Sadly, there wasn't a suitable school there for Georg, so Richard gritted his teeth and hoped for better times ahead.

In August it was time for the twins to start school. Emilia joined the reception class at the local school in Rothenburgsort, only a short walk from home, while Paula took Georg to the deaf and dumb school in Bürgerweide, accompanying him herself in the early weeks until she felt sure he could do the tram journey alone.

For the twins it was a major adjustment to be separated from each other for several hours a day and to make new friends. Georg was disappointed that his best friend, Horst, had started school with Emilia and not with him, but after a few days at the new school, he managed to put these concerns aside because for the first time in his life he was with children of his own age who couldn't hear either. It was a new experience for him to be understood immediately whenever he used sign language without first having to explain that he couldn't hear. On top of that, he soon became a favourite of the teaching staff because his speech was so good and he was often used as an example for the others. At first, Georg enjoyed being in this position but he soon realised that there were disadvantages, as he suffered the jealousy and aggression of those who couldn't speak and who begrudged him his special place.

Richard felt a strong empathy with his son during this period in their lives because it so much reminded him of his time at university. As the academically gifted son of a carpenter, he had found there were plenty of students from wealthy homes who held his social class against him. At the same time he always remembered what Schär had once said to Paula – that deaf people have to make a choice and decide whether to belong to the world of the hearing or to the world of the deaf mute. So he encouraged his son not to be put off by jealous children, telling him he was better than them in every respect.

'But what do I do if they beat me up?' asked Georg one evening. 'Willi has threatened to give me a thrashing.'

'When he starts to do that, you've got to punch him as hard as you can, right on the nose.'

'Richard, shouldn't you be advising him to go to his teacher?' Paula sounded reproachful.

'He's tried that already, but it doesn't help if Willi's lying in wait for him on the way to school, and you can't be there with him all the time. So if someone goes for you, Georg, you hit them back, hard as you can.' Richard took a cushion off the sofa and held it up in front of him. 'Now, show me how hard you can thump it.'

Georg punched the cushion with his fist.

'Not hard enough! You want to thump him, not stroke him. Have another go!'

Georg laughed and did it again.

By now Emilia had joined them. 'Can I do it too?'

'Good, yes, off you go!'

Emilia punched the cushion.

'That's a good punch, Emilia. You could be a boxer.'

'Or thrash Willi if he does anything to Georg.' Emilia giggled.

Paula intervened. 'Richard, do you really think violence is a solution?'

'No, but I believe in self-defence. Come on, Georg. Have another go!'

When Willi threatened Georg again the following day, Georg addressed him in sign language. 'OK then, you get first go, but I'm ready. And I'm warning you, I did boxing with my dad yesterday.'

Willi hesitated and Georg noticed how his own fear vanished.

'What's up?' Georg asked. 'Are you scared? It's just as well; otherwise, I'd be showing you how a real boxer does it.' He raised his fists and Willi stepped back.

'I'm not going to talk to you any more, you stupid swot,' signed Willi, and walked off. That day he started to spread the rumour that Georg's dad was a real boxer and was teaching his son how to do it.

When Georg related all this to his father, Richard laughed but said it wasn't right to make too much of a fool of Willi and that he'd better let everyone know the truth.

'If a young hooligan like Willi is scared of you, that's a good thing, Georg. Any deterrent that helps avoid a fight is always better than actually having the fight.'

'So is telling a lie allowed?' piped up Emilia, listening intently next to her brother.

'If by telling a lie you can prevent someone from doing something bad, then that's all right, yes. Telling lies is only bad if you do it deliberately to harm other people or to disadvantage others who don't deserve it.'

In the background came Paula's voice. 'You seem to have a rather casual approach to the truth!'

'Yes,' he said without hesitation. 'But in times like this, it's vital.' Paula picked up the hidden message but Emilia and Georg just laughed, unaware of the full implications of their father's remark.

Chapter 31

Friday 1 September 1939

'So glad you could come, colleague Hellmer. Please do take a seat.' Krüger indicated the chair in front of his desk. Richard paused before doing so. Krüger's warm welcome made him wary.

'Your assessment skills are well known to me, and this is why you're just the right man for a new assignment.'

'What's it about?'

'It's about registration of our patients in the context of the economic plan. You, with your wide-ranging competence in preparing expert statements, are ideally suited to the job.'

Krüger's arrogant smile confirmed what Richard suspected. A thankless, burdensome task to be delegated to the most unpopular colleague. In some ways, it made him angry but he could also see that it might be another chance to avoid reprisals against his patients.

'What exactly is this registration?'

'The state would like a survey that registers all the mentally ill and feeble-minded who have lived in the asylum for more than five years, or who are no longer employable, or who can be considered only for the simplest of tasks. Your job is to complete a registration form for every single patient, giving the individual's capacity for productivity.'

Richard immediately wondered whether this new set of expert statements had something to do with the food stamps and petrol coupons that had come in for the first time on Monday, all stamped with today's date. A week ago Paula had got hold of as many provisions as she could lay her hands on, while he himself had filled up the car, as well as two spare petrol cans. Far worse than the fuel shortage, though, was the growing threat of war. Were rations going to be reduced even further for the sick and unproductive if war came?

He put these worrying thoughts out of his mind and asked a question instead. 'And what are the consequences for patients of this classification exercise?'

'You needn't trouble yourself with that. That's the job of the state.'

Before Richard could respond, there was a loud knock on the door. It was Krüger's secretary, Frau Handeloh.

'Dr Krüger, sir, you must switch on your wireless!' she cried.

Krüger was clearly irritated at the intrusion, but as it was so out of character for his normally restrained secretary, he immediately did as she asked. Richard glanced at his watch. Ten fifteen.

> 'Overnight Poland has for the first time opened fire on our own territory using regular soldiers.' Hitler's voice rasped through the ether. 'Since 5.45 fire has been returned. From now on any bomb will be repaid with a bomb. He who fights with poison will receive poison gas in return. He who does not abide by the rules of humane warfare should expect the same from us. I will wage war in the same way against anyone, and for however long is required, in order to guarantee the security of the empire and of its rights.'

'We're at war!' Frau Handeloh sounded very agitated. 'But everyone said it wouldn't come to this!'

'You're surprised?' Richard was amazed at how calm he felt. Instead of leaping to his feet and screaming out his frustration and hatred of the government, he felt like a detached observer. 'So why did you think petrol coupons were handed out on Monday?'

'All the more important now that we get on with our duties,' said Krüger, casting a warning look in Richard's direction. 'The resources of our people must be fairly distributed in these difficult times. You understand, I hope, how much depends on your future work, colleague Hellmer?'

Richard nodded. 'I understand perfectly and will carry out this work with the utmost conscientiousness.'

Krüger gave a pompous little nod of the head that Richard knew meant he could now leave the room. He rang Paula without delay.

'Have you just heard the radio?'

'Yes, Frau Walter next door rang our bell to tell me to listen. I can't believe it, Richard. I know we've feared it, but did we really believe it could happen? Do you think it'll stay as a conflict with Poland? Or . . . or will the English get involved now?'

'I have no idea, but it doesn't look good. Krüger has just told me that from now on I have to assess all our patients for their "capacity for productivity". The government's providing registration forms and I'm expected to separate out those who can no longer do any productive work or who've been at the asylum for more than five years.'

'Why?'

'My guess is to curtail food rations. Krüger was very cagey about it.'

'What'll you do?'

'Follow my conscience. Krüger wants to humiliate me with this tedious work but what he doesn't realise is that it gives me a degree of power. I'll have to wait and see what these forms look like, then I'll know how much room for manoeuvre there is. By the way, it would be an idea if you could get out today and buy everything you can find that doesn't need food stamps or petrol coupons. We don't know what the supply situation's going to be in the next few weeks.'

'Yes, Frau Walter was saying the same. I'll go now, before the children get home from school.'

Richard finished work early that day to go and fill up the car again. There was already a long queue for the pump. When it was his turn, the attendant first asked for his coupon.

He handed it over and waited while the man filled the tank for him. One tank lasted him a week but had just cost him a whole month's ration.

'This old girl's in good nick,' said the attendant, taking a look at the vehicle. 'Adler Standard 6. You don't see many of those now. What's the year – 1928?'

'Actually, it's 1927,' said Richard. 'It never lets me down. Even took me over the Alps.'

'My brother-in-law would give you good money for a car like that.'

'Thanks, but I'm totally dependent on it,' he said, before paying the man and driving home.

That evening he phoned Fritz.

'How are you getting on with the petrol rationing?' he asked.

'I take the tram to work and save the fuel for the weekends. Dorothea thinks I should sell the car but it's ten years old, and if rationing goes on, I'll never get rid of it and won't have any fuel either. What about you?'

'I can't do without it. You know how bad the tram connections are out to Langenhorn. It'd add an hour to the day every morning and then again in the evening.'

'But will your ration let you go on driving there every day?'

'No, I'll get through it in just a week,' replied Richard.

'I could let you have my winter coupon,' suggested Fritz straight away. 'Doro and I don't go away at the weekends at that time of year.'

'Would you really do that?'

'Gives me a good reason to hang on to the car! I'll say to Doro, *No car, no coupon.*' He chuckled.

'So you're definitely not going to sell it?'

'No, because who knows when I could ever afford another one! Maybe I'm being pessimistic. Maybe this nightmare will be over in a couple of weeks.'

'That's what everyone said in 1914.' Richard's voice had a bitter edge to it.

At first, Fritz said nothing, but Richard sensed that his friend had something he wanted to say. Finally, Fritz said, 'Let's not look on the dark side, Richard. Come round for a beer tomorrow – at least that's not rationed – and then I can give you the coupon and one of my spare cans. I'll ask around a bit to see if anyone else wants to sell coupons. That'll keep you going for a while, won't it?'

'Now that's a real friend,' said Richard, laughing. 'Sharing his last drop of fuel!'

'Hey, at least we won't need to share our last shirt – the army will be providing them soon enough.'

'Fritz, you don't seriously think people in our position will be called up?'

'Well, I don't know the situation for psychiatrists but we surgeons are in demand. Professor Wehmeyer said only this morning that he's expecting the call-up for military doctors to start at any moment. I won't be volunteering, of course, but lots of my younger colleagues see it differently and think it's a way of advancing their careers. Ah well, as long as there are enough volunteers, nobody'll think of calling us up. Let's leave it like this – you're coming round for a beer tomorrow and we'll drink to this war being over by Christmas, not like back in 1914.'

'If drinking to it helped, I'd cheerfully become an alcoholic.'

'Watch out there! Didn't you tell me alcoholics have to be sterilised?'

'I can take the risk. My family's complete.'

Fritz cleared his throat.

'Hey, Fritz, are you telling me Dorothea's expecting again?'

'What on earth makes you think that? No, our family was complete when Harald came along.' He laughed. 'I'd risk being an alcoholic and drinking to peace, but shaky hands aren't too good in the operating theatre!'

'See you tomorrow.'

'And a toast to peace,' said Fritz firmly. 'Looking forward to it.' Then he put down the receiver.

Chapter 32

Early in October, Richard made a start on the first batch of forms. It was tedious work, hard grind too, but he got a new typewriter for it. This was because at the top of these new forms, heavily underlined and festooned with exclamation marks, was the instruction that forms were to be typed, not handwritten.

Next to personal details was a space headed 'race'. Richard shook his head in disbelief when he read the options he had to choose from: 'Of German blood, or related, Jew, Jewish mixed-blood Grade 1 or 11, Negro or Negro mixed-blood.' Good thing he had no Indians or Chinese among his patients, he thought with a bitter irony. He couldn't have classified them at all.

In addition to this, he had to give information about whether a patient received regular visitors, whether the patient was a war veteran or a twin and whether there were any mentally ill blood relatives. Then came all the questions about diagnosis, symptoms, treatment, the course of the illness and any criminal offences. At the end, the patient's occupation and degree of productivity had to be compared with the average performance of a healthy individual for the same work.

So this was the loophole he needed. The standards for comparison with the average person were not specified. It was for the expert witness himself to make his own estimate.

Richard first set to work on the files for those patients based in the open country houses. They all worked in agriculture, so he compared their capacity for work with that of the average agricultural worker. He gave eighty per cent to those he knew were barely capable and pondered what plausible reasons he could find to disguise the true extent of their condition.

His secure-unit patients, however, presented him with greater problems, particularly when he saw Herbert's file in front of him. Herbert, his old patient, the first one he'd worked with so intensively and who, through his repeated failures, had demonstrated to Richard that he simply could not cope outside the secure unit. He had now known the man for ten years and an almost affectionate relationship had developed between them in spite of their being worlds apart. Richard had worked his way up from being a young and inexperienced junior doctor to a consultant and a recognised writer of expert statements, while Herbert had simply grown older. He was as charming as ever and had managed to improve his concentration, which meant that he could now work for a few hours on simple tasks, such as making paper bags, but despite spending a long time thinking about how he could, at least on paper, make the capability of this severely ill patient look better, Richard finally had to acknowledge that there just wasn't a way. Fifty per cent was perhaps plausible, but he would be hard pushed even to justify that. Anything higher just would not wash.

It seemed, though, at least for now, that the completion of the forms had no particular consequences, and when rations for the secure unit were barely reduced, Richard felt he could breathe more easily. The supply situation in Germany remained stable, although petrol rationing became a constant problem for most drivers. Thanks to Fritz, Richard had enough fuel to carry on going to work by car. That wasn't entirely due to Fritz's personal generosity but owed a great deal to the black-market contacts that he had been cultivating. Black-market petrol coupons were expensive and illegal, but Fritz took the view that it didn't matter whose car was filled up as long as the coupons were genuine. When Richard asked him how he'd managed to get these contacts, Fritz explained how three weeks back he'd started working Saturday afternoons as a prison doctor in Fuhlsbüttel. 'The previous prison doctor decided to join up and they couldn't fill the vacancy. It was circulated among us as a fee-paying role, so I went for it. The money's good and it reduces the likelihood of my getting called up if I'm holding down two important jobs. Besides, you get to meet some rather interesting people with even more interesting connections!' He grinned.

On 3 September, Great Britain and France did indeed declare war, but this made no appreciable difference to daily life. In October, Hitler announced that the Polish campaign had concluded successfully. The German military now turned its attention to the Western Front and France. Richard's nephews were called for scrutiny and the two eldest were conscripted. This was a blow for Richard's father as Karl had only just become a master craftsman and was set to take over his grandfather's business. In addition, the outbreak of another war stirred old memories.

'The last war took my elder son from me,' said Richard's father sadly. 'I don't want this one to take my two eldest grandsons.'

Richard tried hard to reassure his parents, his sister and her husband, Holger, but the very words 'French campaign' filled the four of them with such horror that even he could not lift their spirits. The last war had broken his brother, but Richard had always believed that Holger had somehow weathered the whole experience, mentally at least, and had even come to terms with the loss of part of his leg. Margit, however, now told him a different story of how Holger had regularly suffered nightmares since his two sons had been called up, just as he had in the first few years after his own war. Sometimes, she told Richard sadly, Holger seemed to be in another world and she would have to call his name several times before he came to again. This caused Richard grave concern as he recognised these symptoms from other severely traumatised men and yet Holger's experiences lay twenty years in the past. Could it be that the anxiety over his sons had brought back the mental trauma they all believed he had overcome?

While Richard stayed strong on the outside for the sake of his family and continued to do everything he could for Holger and Margit, it was Paula who kept him afloat. She kept saying they couldn't compare this war with the last one and was firm about Richard still taking her to the cinema and watching the positive newsreel reports. The German army was on the advance, was victorious; this was not trench warfare like the last time. In his heart Richard knew these newsreels were nothing more than clever propaganda but he was only too willing to be taken in as it gave him the strength to give moral support to Holger and Margit. Karl and Jürgen would come unscathed through the war and be home soon. That was all that mattered.

◆ ◆ ◆

At Christmas, Karl and Jürgen came home on leave. As the lads recounted their adventures, there were moments when the war lost its horror. Their stories sounded more like wild escapades and seemed entirely different to the terrors experienced by their father, Holger, and uncle Georg.

'If it carries on like this, it'll be springtime in Paris for us,' said Karl, full of confidence as he tucked into the Christmas roast.

'We'll send you a postcard of the Eiffel Tower!' added Jürgen with the same smile he'd had when he'd been the little rascal at Richard and Paula's engagement party, secretly pilfering biscuits from the celebration table with his brothers and little sister. Richard's heart ached at the memory. Had that really been twelve years ago?

After the Christmas meal, Richard took a photograph of the whole family, Karl and Jürgen in uniform in the middle – two young men, full of the joy of life, their military duty hopefully soon a thing of the past because their grandfather needed them in the workshop.

By the time Richard developed the photograph in his makeshift dark room at home a couple of days later, his nephews were already on their way back to the Front.

'That's turned out well,' said Paula, when she saw the photograph hung up to dry.

'Yes.'

'Something wrong?'

'I've been thinking about Georg such a lot recently. He had the same bravado as those two at the beginning of the war, and this photo reminds me of the one my father took before he left. It was the whole family with Georg, so proud to be wearing the Kaiser's uniform. He left here a proud young man with his whole life ahead of him and came back a wreck. But Karl and Jürgen have no recollection of that – after all, they weren't born until 1917 and 1919.' He paused. 'Have you noticed Holger's and Margit's eyes? Have you seen the worry in them?'

'Yes, I know exactly what you mean. All parents are worrying about their sons, and Holger knows better than anyone what war means.'

'I worry too. On days like this, I wish I was a believer. Believers can at least pray.'

Paula looked up at him, her gentle hands on his shoulders. 'Whatever happens, Richard, we'll get through it together. The whole family.'

◆ ◆ ◆

It was a hard winter. Richard was fearful for his nephews, although the field post from the two of them was always bursting with confidence and entertaining anecdotes. He wondered whether these letters were genuine or whether they were simply to reassure the folks back home. Either way, they had the desired effect. Holger regained his old resolve and Margit told Richard the nightmares had stopped. Life carried on as usual for a while, in spite of the food stamps and petrol coupons. Meanwhile, the Reich clothing ration card was introduced, restricting the purchase of new clothes through a points system. Every German had one hundred points for one year and these were deducted according to purchases made. A pair of stockings worked out at four points, a pullover put a twenty-five-point dent in your card, and at the beginning of February Paula's new suit cost her no less than forty-five in one go.

Richard teased her. 'Oh well, you can still afford thirteen pairs of stockings and one sock for the rest of the year.'

'You shouldn't be so stingy with your own points! Do get yourself a couple of new shirts,' retorted Paula as she looked at herself in the bedroom mirror in the new suit. 'Your clothes are starting to look so threadbare.'

On the previous day, Richard had intervened in a violent struggle between patients and the seam of his shirt had been ripped in the process, although Paula had been able to mend it for him.

'Oh, they're not that bad and, anyway, yesterday's incident was only the second like that since I started there.' He deliberately played it down, although he was sure that incidents like this would increase as the change he had feared for some time had now come into force: the reduction in food rations for all inmates who couldn't make a productive contribution. The atmosphere became increasingly tense, as it had during the economic crisis, and there were more and more outbursts of aggression in the secure unit. While Richard had come out of it with a torn shirt, Kurt Hansen had ended up with a nasty bite on his forearm.

By March, Richard was more relieved than usual to feel the gradual arrival of spring as the temperature finally moved above freezing and the snow melted.

On the last Friday of March 1940, Richard arrived at work earlier than usual as the streets were clear of snow and very few cars were on the road due to the scarcity of petrol. It was still dark as he drew up in front of the secure unit and saw a large black bus in his parking spot. Richard parked next to it and went into the building.

Kurt was already there, looking out for him. 'Did you know about the transfer?' He sounded upset.

'What transfer?' Richard was alarmed.

'All secure-unit patients are being taken to an institution in Brandenburg. That bus was outside here really early and we were ordered to pack everybody's things.'

'This is all news to me. Who gave the order?'

'Dr Krüger came here yesterday after you'd left and made the announcement. But he didn't say the bus was coming today. He said something about a transfer in the next few days. I thought we'd have a bit of time to work out what was going on. Krüger said there's going to be some restructuring – some of the country houses are to be set aside for children, and our own asylum inmates will be transferred to the secure unit. Our good Dr Krüger seems to be extending his expertise to include the children's department at Langenhorn.'

'As far as I know, he's good friends with Dr Bayer, the senior consultant at the children's hospital in Rothenburgsort,' said Richard. 'My wife used to work there and is still in touch with an old colleague. I don't know any more than that.'

'Dr Hellmer, why must we go away?' Herbert had seen Richard and Kurt talking outside Richard's office and made straight for them. The uncertainty in his eyes was obvious and Richard wanted to reassure him, as he would do with a child.

'I presume it's because there's better food in the country. Here in the city provisions are really not so good now because of the war.' He didn't know whether there was any truth in what he said, but he wasn't going to let Herbert see his own uncertainty. And, anyway, his theory was quite logical. Why else would all the patients be moved to Brandenburg?

'Kurt, tell me something,' said Richard, turning to his senior nurse while Herbert still stood anxiously next to them, shifting his weight from one foot to the other. 'Isn't Brandenburg where Dr Harms went?'

Kurt Hansen nodded.

'You see?' Richard said to Herbert. 'You know someone there already. You always got on well with Dr Harms, didn't you?'

Herbert's face lit up. 'Yes, he's a nice man. Maybe there are cows there too.'

'And no pubs to lead you into temptation,' added Richard with a smile.

'But I don't do that any more,' replied Herbert sincerely, with an innocent expression. Kurt Hansen rolled his eyes while Richard patted Herbert on the shoulder in farewell. 'Perhaps there'll be new opportunities for you there. I wish you the very best.'

'Thank you, Dr Hellmer.' For the last time he gave Richard his trusting smile, then set about gathering up his bags before climbing on to the secure bus, which also contained a number of men in uniform.

An hour later, Richard and Kurt Hansen walked together through the empty building where they had worked together for almost eleven years.

'It feels somehow dead,' said Hansen. 'Like a grave.'

'Yes. I feel like someone's walking over mine this very minute. When are the new residents arriving?'

'No idea. I hope Dr Krüger will give us due warning this time.'

'Maybe you could ask him. You know he has no time for me,' said Richard.

'What makes you think he's got any time for me? He never saw our patients as human beings. To him they were only ever unpleasant cost factors, and every act of aggression here simply confirmed his opinion.' Lost in thought, Kurt ran his finger over the fading bite mark on his forearm.

'Perhaps Brandenburg really will be better for our patients,' commented Richard. 'After all, Dr Harms went there to get away from Krüger's views, and he always shared ours.'

'Let's hope so. I'd be really glad for Herbert and all the others if they could have a new start there,' added Hansen, his mind still preoccupied.

Richard waited throughout the morning to hear whether the residents from elsewhere in the asylum would be moving into the secure unit, or whether Dr Krüger was about to divulge something different. His telephone rang.

'Richard, it's me, Margit!' His sister's voice was thick with emotion. 'A letter's come for Holger – Jürgen fell on 21 March.'

'My God, my God!' shouted Richard. 'Oh, Margit, I'll come straight away. How has Holger taken the news?'

'He's with Papa and both the journeymen on the way to our woodland to get new timber; they're not due back until this evening. He doesn't know yet. What on earth do I say to him?' She broke down in tears.

'Nothing, Margit. I'll talk to him. I'll drive straight to where they are.'

'But can you really just leave work like that?'

'No question. All my patients have been taken to Brandenburg and the others aren't coming for a couple of hours. I'll ring Paula and she'll come and keep you company while I let Papa and Holger know.'

'Thank you, thank you, Richard.'

'Margit, there's nothing to thank me for – you're my sister. I'm here for you whatever happens.'

He hung up, then phoned Paula to tell her what had happened. She was as horrified as he was and promised to take care of poor Margit. Then he went to find Kurt Hansen.

'I have to leave straight away, Kurt. If anyone's asking for me, you can tell them my nephew has been killed. I must go to support my sister.'

Hansen was white-faced. 'Which nephew is it? Oh, Richard, I'm so very sorry.'

Richard blinked back the tears. 'The younger one, Jürgen. He would have been twenty-one next month.'

'This is terrible for you all. Please tell your sister and her whole family that I'll pray for them to stay strong.'

'Thank you, Kurt.'

The roads were even emptier now and Richard reached the family's woodland plot just outside Hamburg faster than he'd expected. His father and brother-in-law were hard at work, checking the quality of the trees they'd felled that day, while the two young journeymen loaded the timber that had passed muster on to the truck. But as soon as they saw Richard's car, they stopped what they were doing.

His father walked over, smiling. 'What brings you over here at this time of day?' His smile froze the moment he saw the look on Richard's face. 'What's happened?'

'Margit phoned me.' Then Richard turned to Holger. 'Holger, a letter came for you this morning.'

'What kind of letter?'

Richard saw his brother-in-law start to tremble. It was clear he already feared the worst.

'Jürgen has fallen.'

Holger looked stunned. Richard's father cried out, 'No – please, no!' The two lads, horrified, let go of the logs they were about to heave on to the vehicle and blurted out condolences. Holger couldn't take it in. His eyes couldn't leave Richard's face.

'And Karl?' His voice was shaking.

'We've heard nothing from Karl.'

'Jürgen, Jürgen,' whispered Holger. 'He was always so careful, so cautious. How could it happen?'

'I don't know,' Richard replied, carefully assessing his brother-in-law. Was he really as composed as he appeared, or would he break down? Given what Margit had told him of late, he feared the latter.

'And we've heard nothing from Karl?' Holger asked again.

'I'm sure he's not been harmed,' said Richard, although he felt no certainty about this. It was the second time this morning he'd had to make things look more positive than they were. 'He's bound to write to you both soon with what actually happened.'

Holger said nothing, but his hands were trembling violently now and reminded Richard uncomfortably of his brother, Georg.

'Can I drive you home, Holger? Papa, Ernst and Hannes will take care of everything here.'

'Yes, my son,' said Richard's father, resting his hand consolingly on Holger's shoulder. 'Let Richard take you home. Margit needs you.'

Holger nodded without a word and let himself be helped into Richard's car. The journey passed in silence. Holger was deep in thought and Richard thought it best to leave him be. As soon as they arrived, Holger and Margit fell into each other's arms. No words came. Just as they let one another go, Lottchen came in from school, saw her parents in distress and ran to them. Holger held his daughter close and wept silently.

And in that silence, Richard, not a religious man, found himself praying fervently for Karl's safe return.

Chapter 33

That there could be no burial in Ohlsdorf Cemetery was especially hard for Holger and Margit to bear. Jürgen had been laid to rest in some military cemetery between Belgium and France. He was to have no gravestone, just a plain wooden cross, like the hundreds already in place and the thousands more Richard feared would follow. He no longer believed the weekly newsreel.

In the meantime, he had found out how Jürgen had died and what this meant for Karl.

His two nephews, with a few other soldiers, had become separated from their company and fallen straight into an ambush. The ever-vigilant Jürgen was one of the first to spot it. Karl would have run straight into it, had Jürgen not pulled him down at the last minute, fatally wounded by a ricocheting bullet as he did so. His comrades returned fire while Karl gave his brother first aid, even managing to get him to the nearest field-dressing station but there was nothing the doctor could do. The bullet had lodged deep in Jürgen's heart and the pericardium had filled with blood, leaving no room for the vital organ to beat. The attempt at emergency surgery, which had a questionable outcome in any case, had come too late. Since then Karl had suffered unbearable guilt because Jürgen had been shot while trying to protect him. He couldn't bring himself to tell his parents of his guilt and his failure to save Jürgen but his inner torment drove him to confide in his Uncle Richard by letter.

In reply, Richard wrote:

> Dear Karl
> I feel the deepest of sympathy for you and share with you the loss of your brother. But you bear no guilt for Jürgen's death. Your brother acted instinctively to protect you, as you did for him when you risked your life by crossing the lines to get him to the nearest field hospital. If anyone is guilty, then it's the man who fired that bullet. Or those who gave the order to open fire. Guilt also lies with whoever forced you to leave your family to occupy France. There are many people who are guilty of Jürgen's death, but you are not one of them. You are free of all guilt because you were a fine and loyal brother. Jürgen loved you as much as you did him. He gave his life to save yours and you should honour his memory and commemorate him with love and a sense of solidarity, while you live the life that he saved and enjoy it in all its beauty.
> If you poison your life with self-accusation and tear yourself apart inside, then your brother's sacrifice will have been in vain because he won't have saved your life, he'll only have saved your body. You know that Jürgen would want you to come back safely and somehow to find your old joy in life again. Be honest, Karl; that's what you'd have wanted Jürgen to do if it had happened the other way around. You wouldn't have wanted him constantly to punish himself about it or to weigh himself down with self-reproach.

I know these words sound hollow and empty while you're still mourning, but once the initial pain has passed, read these words again and let them help you. I empathise with how you feel because I have experienced the same helplessness and guilt at being the survivor, although in very different circumstances. This was when your Uncle Georg died; I know you barely remember him. I persuaded our father, your grandfather, to take Georg to a mental hospital. I genuinely believed it would help him but instead he died a terrible death there. If anyone carried the guilt for that, it was me, because I was the one who sent my dear brother to a place where unscrupulous doctors subjected him to horrific treatment that tortured him to death. That was when I decided to be a psychiatrist so that this could never happen again. Never again.

It brings nothing to keep on asking what would have happened if . . . It is as it is – we can't turn back time, but we can give thought to what we can do differently, and better, in the future. I can't tell you which path to take in dealing with your loss. I got back my joy in life once I'd worked out what gave my life meaning. Once I'd explained to your grandfather that I wouldn't be taking over the workshop but wanted to study medicine instead, he immediately understood and did nothing to stand in my way.

From the bottom of my heart I want you too to find something that gives your life meaning, no matter what it is. It's not that you *may* find happiness again, it's your duty to do so. Our dead brothers have long absolved us of guilt because they know we've done everything in our power for them. The fact that it wasn't enough to protect them is tragic, and we have to live with that loss. We mustn't poison the life and memory of each of our brothers but must instead show ourselves worthy of their love and forgiveness. This is why I chose to call my own son Georg. Think of a way of keeping Jürgen in your life and remember him with warmth and love.

Your Uncle Richard

Ten days after Richard had sent this letter, Margit told him that Karl had at last written and told them how Jürgen had died.

'I know,' was all Richard said in response. He too had just received a letter from Karl.

Dear Uncle Richard

Thank you for your letter, which has given me so much valuable insight and understanding. I'm going to follow your advice in every way. And when we get to Paris, I'm going to do what Jürgen and I always planned. That's to climb up the Eiffel Tower, send you all a postcard and then at last come home, where I know more than enough woodwork awaits me in the workshop, and then I plan to lead a normal life.

Your nephew, Karl

When he showed Karl's letter to Paula, she said, 'Karl's lucky to have not just a good uncle but a good psychiatrist too. He will cope.'

'Yes, I'm sure he will. But I'm still concerned. As long as this damned war goes on, no one can be sure of coming out alive.'

'But it looks all right at the moment. Our troops are edging across France without any static warfare.'

'Sounds like the newsreel I don't set any store by.'

'So what do you set store by? What do you hold on to to get through it all?'

'You, my dearest Paula. You're worth more to me than any newsreel.' He gave her a loving kiss on the cheek.

◆ ◆ ◆

A lot had changed in the asylum at Langenhorn. The secure unit was no longer that and the new patients had the right to leave the building and work on the land. There were difficulties only when aggressive new arrivals came. One of the two observation rooms was set aside for new admissions, while the other was used by peaceful former residents of the open country houses. But it was getting overcrowded: there were now eighteen beds in each room instead of the previous twelve, and even one of the day rooms had been converted into a dormitory. On top of that, Richard was still required to complete the registration forms assessing patients' productivity. These were then dispatched to an address in Berlin: Tiergartenstrasse 4.

One sunny morning in April, just four weeks after Herbert and the other patients had been transferred to Brandenburg, Richard's telephone rang.

'Dr Hellmer speaking.'

'Hellmer, it's Harms here. Are you alone there in the office?'

'Dr Harms, this is a surprise!' Richard's voice came joyfully down the line. 'Yes, I'm on my own here. Have our patients settled with you all right? How's our old friend Herbert?'

Dr Harms cleared his throat before speaking. 'Listen, this is strictly confidential and nobody must know, but I can't go along with what's happening and you have to know what's going on here.'

'What on earth do you mean?'

'Am I right in thinking that you're still completing those registration forms about productivity?'

'Yes.'

'They're using the information to separate out the lives considered unworthy of life. Every patient deemed economically unproductive is being murdered.'

There was a sharp intake of breath from Richard. 'Did I hear you right? Patients are being murdered? Who by?'

'I know it sounds impossible, and I don't think anyone other than you will believe me, but this is the truth. All our former patients from the secure unit are now dead. A few days after their arrival, they were bundled into sealed, airtight lorries that were driven into the forest and had carbon monoxide pumped into them until everyone was dead.'

Richard froze. Had Harms gone crazy, or had he developed a strange version of black humour?

'This . . . this has to be some kind of joke, surely. Why would doctors tolerate something like that and risk a jail sentence for being an accessory to murder? What would they get out of it? And why are you telephoning me and not the police if you're witness to something like this?'

'I know how it must sound, Dr Hellmer, but this is the truth.' Harms spoke very firmly. 'This is why I have handed in my notice, but because I am in the know they don't want to let me go, so I've had to come up with something to get myself out. So I've volunteered to go to the Front as a doctor. I'd rather that than take part in mass murder here. You don't believe me? The orders are coming right from the very top. From Hitler himself. They call it mercy killing and it's subject to the utmost secrecy. It's the extermination of life unworthy of life, just like Professor Hoche described in his book in the twenties. This lot are taking it really seriously. First the sterilisation programme, then the killing of all those no longer deemed fit for work. In Tiergartenstrasse in Berlin there are doctors whose only task is to assess the registration forms and separate out all those who are no longer productive – they're the ones that get sent to Brandenburg. Apparently, there are other institutions doing their share of the killing, but I don't know exactly. It's difficult enough to piece together what's going on here, right under my nose. If it ever came out that I've told you, we'd both be put straight into one of these new concentration camps – you know, where the government locks up and maltreats all its political opponents, along with anyone else it doesn't like, for the purposes of re-education.'

Richard's belly knotted and ached. He found himself thinking about Alfred Schär's terrible end.

'But you have to know what your classifications mean for the sick,' Harms went on. 'Herbert was one of the first to be gassed. They told him the lorry was going to the cows and that's why he got on so willingly. Later on, all the corpses were burned and the relatives sent a bit of ash. The only opportunity I had to hint at something here not being right was the death certificate. We were instructed to think up some plausible causes of death and were supposed to vary the dates of death so that nobody would wonder why all the Hamburg patients had died on the same day. For Herbert, I wrote "burst appendix".'

'He had no appendix,' said Richard. His voice was dull; he felt dazed, as though moving in a thick fog, and everything Harms was telling him sounded like cheap horror fiction. Herbert . . . Of all the patients in the secure unit, Richard had been the most fond of Herbert. He had sincerely wished him a future life worth living, but all he'd done was send him to his death . . .

No, he told himself, before the guilt could overwhelm him, *I didn't send him to his death. I was duped, like Herbert was. The guilt lies with those who organised this.*

'That's precisely why I chose this as cause of death.' Richard realised Dr Harms was still talking to him. 'Ask his next of kin, Dr Hellmer. Ask if they've received an urn showing his date of death as 4 April 1940 and a message of sympathy saying that he died of a burst appendix. Then you'll know I'm telling you the truth.'

Richard tried to swallow. The full implications of what Dr Harms was telling him had not yet sunk in.

'Can I phone you if I still have questions?' he asked, unable to think of anything else.

'Yes, I'm working here until 15 May, but after that I'll be at the Front.' Dr Harms gave him his telephone number. 'And we need to see how we can spread this information to as many hospitals as possible without being exposed ourselves. As I said, this is all taking place in extreme secrecy and the kind of deliberate error that I have built in will be weeded out. But the world has to know about this. There is mass murder going on here, in front of our very eyes, of the weakest and the most helpless.'

'But why are the other doctors going along with it?' asked Richard. 'Why aren't they doing what you're doing?'

'Do you think for one minute Krüger would do what I'm doing? And there are hundreds of Krügers in white coats.' With these words, Harms hung up. The registration form he had last been working on caught Richard's eye. Eighty per cent productivity. He'd embellished it to that level. He screwed up the form and completed a fresh one. This time he gave the patient the rating of a healthy individual. And that's precisely what he would do from now on. Krüger didn't check the forms in any case, and Berlin was a long way away.

After all, a bit of impudence had got him through that earlier business with the Gestapo.

Chapter 34

The phone call from Dr Harms had thrown Richard into far greater confusion than he'd cared to admit. The story was monstrous, absurd and hardly credible. On the other hand, its treachery made it a perfect fit with the system: first the sterilisations, then the reduction in rations, finally culminating in extermination by carbon monoxide poisoning...

Ordinary people had to resort to the black market for their petrol coupons, or stop driving altogether, but in Brandenburg a vehicle dispatched you to your death. And that was probably not the only place.

That evening he told Paula what had happened. Her initial reaction was similar to his, one of disbelief, just like her father, who went so far as to suggest that Harms was simply crazed.

Yet when Richard phoned Herbert's parents to extend his condolences on the loss of their son at Brandenburg, they confirmed what Harms had told him. Herbert's father was furious at the cause of death being described as a burst appendix, as Herbert had had his appendix removed as a child. For a moment, Richard wondered whether he should tell him the truth, but he shied away from that. Even his father-in-law hadn't wanted to believe it, and in any case, what were Herbert's elderly parents supposed to do about it? So he simply said something about how there must have been a mix-up and maybe they should ask the hospital exactly why their son had died and left it at that.

He told Fritz about it, and his friend was as incredulous as the others.

'This can't be right,' he said over and over. 'This is barbaric! What on earth are they doing this for?'

'It's purely economic. The sick who are unfit for work are seen as a drain on the state. Even sterilisation's more expensive than killing them.'

'But . . . but if this is what's happening, we must make it public!'

'Yes, but it's happening by stealth, really secretly – precisely because it is unimaginable. Do you know what'll happen if we make this public? They'll simply declare us insane, lock us up, and then treat us to a trip in the mobile gas chamber or make us disappear, like they did with Alfred Schär.'

Fritz was pale, struggling to find words. 'That means there are murderers in our government.' Richard nodded. 'What are you going to do, Richard?'

'I have no scruples about putting false information on the forms. From now on, all my patients are going to be as capable of work as the healthy.'

'And what if that gets out?'

'I'll take the risk, particularly as it's so small. Krüger has no interest in my expert statements and the forms are sent off to Berlin, along with forms from all the German asylums and clinics for nervous diseases. How on earth are they going to check up on individual cases from Hamburg?'

Richard kept his word. Henceforth, every one of his patients was recorded as being in a position to carry out work of economic value. He also tried to discharge new additions as swiftly as possible so that they weren't even registered in the first place. On top of that, he'd asked his father to take on Manfred and Rolf, twenty-one-year-old Downs' syndrome twins, as helpers in the family business and to give them accommodation in the workshop itself. This was because in a later telephone conversation with Dr Harms he had discovered that identical twins, regardless of their productivity certification, were not immediately gassed but sent off elsewhere for alleged scientific experiments to take place.

Manfred and Rolf couldn't do the full range of jobs, but they could at least sweep up the workshop, run errands and look after the guard dogs. They were both always cheerful and made huge efforts to do everything well. At first Richard's mother had been uneasy and was worried it could be dangerous taking in asylum residents, but once she got to know them and learned more about the background to Richard's desire to help, she even managed to persuade Margit to let them have Jürgen's old room.

'I can't understand why their own parents are not doing all this for them,' commented Margit later. 'How can they take the risk of these terrible things happening to their sons? They might be feeble-minded, but they're likeable enough and know how to work if you give them the right things to do.'

'I agree with you, Margit, but that's why I asked Papa to take them on. Their mother died when they were born and their father put them in residential care very early on, but they're only allowed to stay there until they're twenty-one. That's how they came to the asylum, but I saw straight away that they wouldn't be safe there for long.'

'They'll be safe with us,' promised Margit. 'I've spoken to Holger. We could take on another one like these two, if it helps to save a life.'

'Really? I do know someone.'

And that's how Johannes Mönicke, the schizophrenic who had been buried alive during the previous war and had consistently favourable reports from Richard, also got a position at the Hellmer joinery workshop and so vanished from the files at Langenhorn.

Come the end of April, every member of the population received a gas mask. They came in all sizes, even for infants. Emilia and Georg were intrigued and tried them on, complaining about the strong smell of rubber.

'There now, that's why car tyres are rationed. They need the rubber for the gas masks,' said Richard drily.

'Do you really think the British will launch gas grenades at us?' asked Paula, for once disconcerted.

'Yes, and cluster bombs, firebombs, no expense spared. That's if our flak guns don't shoot them down first,' commented Richard. 'Haven't you seen the towers for the anti-aircraft guns being put up all over the place?'

'I have, actually,' said Paula. 'And this morning someone came here from the local authority wanting to check our cellar for its suitability as an air-raid shelter. They're going to put in a couple of extra beams over the next few days and want us to clear out our stuff to make space for bunk beds.'

'Have we got much stuff down there?'

'The old pram, both the cradles and the changing chest, and then the tinned food.'

'I'll phone my father and ask him to have his staff clear the cellar there. Could be they'll know someone with a use for the cradles and the changing chest.'

Paula sighed. 'I hope we're never in the position of having to use this cellar, and definitely not with these gas masks.'

◆ ◆ ◆

A fortnight later, deafening sirens woke Richard in the middle of the night. He looked at the clock: just past midnight. Paula was already awake, sitting bolt upright in bed.

'Air-raid warning! Paula, get the children ready!'

Paula was out of bed and dressed in a trice. Richard was ready quickly too and hurried to the children's bedroom, where he simply got Emilia and Georg into their dressing gowns and gathered up their clothes.

'Papa, are they going to throw bombs at us now?' asked Emilia.

'They'll try, but the flak guns will shoot them down first. You've nothing to worry about.'

'And why are we going down to the cellar?'

'Just in case someone drops a bomb before the flak man can shoot it down. It's just to make sure. Anyway, you've been wanting to try out those beds for ages.'

'That's right,' said Emilia. Then she signed to her brother, 'You're lucky you can't hear the noise of the sirens. It really hurts my ears.'

Paula came in with a suitcase. 'Let's put the children's clothes in here. There's still space.' As she held out the open case, Richard saw that all their photo albums were already safely packed, together with birth certificates, professional certificates and reports.

'We can replace clothes and furniture any time,' said Paula, 'but I don't want to be running around trying to replace papers like these!'

'Well done!' said Richard proudly. 'Maybe we should just leave everything in there from now on, ready for the off.'

They made haste down to the cellar and on the staircase bumped into their neighbours, some in nightclothes, others fully dressed, also on their way to the shelter.

'Oh dear Lord, are they going to blow this house to pieces?' wailed old Frau Walter.

'Don't worry, Frau Walter,' piped up Emilia. 'Our flak man will shoot the bombers down first, isn't that right, Papa?'

'Yes, our anti-aircraft rockets will get there first,' confirmed Richard. 'This is just a precautionary measure.'

Emilia and Georg had always wanted to have the top bunks, but once they were actually in the darkness of the cellar, lit only by a few paraffin lamps, Emilia asked her father if she could stay close to him in the bottom bunk and Georg asked to be with his mother.

'Of course, poppet,' said Richard to his daughter, smiling a little to himself that she was wanting to take refuge with him while Georg had opted for his mother. Sigmund Freud would have definitely put all this down to an Oedipus complex.

In the distance they heard the sinister low-level hum of aircraft, interrupted by the flak rockets, and now and again individual strikes. At the moment it all sounded a long way off.

'Right, it's not directly overhead,' confirmed Richard, while Emilia snuggled closer into him. 'Go to sleep, little one. I'll keep a look-out and make sure that nothing happens.'

'I'm not at all tired,' she said.

'We could look at some old photos!' suggested Paula brightly, taking one of the albums out of the suitcase. So she and Georg sat on Richard and Emilia's bunk and the lamp seemed brighter.

'Shall we look at the photos of Italy?' As she spoke, she put everything into sign language for Georg.

Georg nodded and Emilia said, 'Ooh, yes! I'd like to see the ones of the Colosseum and hear those stories about the Christians getting thrown to the lions.'

'So you want scary stories, do you?' asked Richard with a smile.

'Yes!'

'All right, then. But we must tell the stories really quietly so as not to disturb other people.' To any observer, they presented an unusual scene, a family of four conversing through signs and gestures, the only sounds a laugh or a whimper. Richard was relieved to see how concentrating on the stories helped Emilia to forget about the disturbing background noise of bombs and flak fire, while Georg had, for the first time in his life, a distinct advantage in not hearing anything.

The all-clear sounded around three in the morning and all residents went back to their flats.

'That wasn't so bad,' announced Emilia as they went back upstairs. 'Our flak man was really careful.'

'You're right there,' said Richard. 'He was.'

Next morning, however, he heard that overnight the British had dropped over four hundred incendiaries and eighty high explosives on Altona, St Pauli, the port and on Harburg. Houses and barns had gone up in flames, thirty-four people had died and seventy-two were injured. This was 18 May 1940 and Richard realised this war could not be compared with the earlier one. He feared it would be far worse.

And yet, by contrast with the previous war, the German army remained on the advance. Paris fell in June 1940 and everyone celebrated. Adolf Hitler was now seen as the greatest military leader of all time and there was talk of a blitzkrieg. The disgrace of Versailles had been wiped out.

Karl sent a postcard from Paris and a photo which showed him up the Eiffel Tower with his comrades, all of them in uniform. His smile came across as genuine, and Richard felt relieved that his nephew seemed to have conquered those feelings of guilt. He hoped Karl would soon be home, but nobody, and nothing, for that matter, was any safer in Hamburg. There were new concerns about enemy attacks against civilians.

And so it was that early in July a British fighter aircraft came out of the clouds without warning and dropped four high explosives directly on Steilshooper Strasse, where children were at play. Eleven children, four women and two men were killed. The newspapers condemned this as a cowardly act of aggression and Fritz told Richard how he'd tended to two of the victims on his operating table. A seven-year-old had slipped away as he treated her and he'd managed to save a boy of eleven, although both his legs had been blown off in the attack.

'What kind of people are these, bombing children?' Fritz raged after the event. 'Yes, OK, we're at war, but why can't they just bomb the port, the wharf and places like that, not just come in from nowhere and hit kids out playing with their friends? It's barbaric; it's abnormal.'

'I know,' said Richard. 'It's worse for the children in any case. Not just that they can't sleep undisturbed at night, but there are even daytime raids now. Paula worries every time Georg goes to and from school on the tram.' He let out a huge sigh. 'How are Henriette and Harri with the nights in the air-raid shelter?'

'Relatively good, to be honest. Rudi's more scared than anyone, really. He creeps into a corner with his tail between his legs and whimpers fit to break our hearts! Henriette and Harri stroke him and calm him, and that helps them both forget to be frightened. And of course I always tell them our flak rockets will shoot down all the bombers before they get anywhere near our house.'

Richard gave him a look of sympathy. 'You know, if Hitler was clever, he'd negotiate a peace treaty now that he's taken Paris, then he could go down in history as some great military leader and we'd get a decent night's sleep at last.'

'Unfortunately, great military leaders are so full of themselves that they go on and on until they fall off their mighty pedestals! Just look at Julius Caesar and Napoleon,' said Fritz.

'Yes,' said Richard quietly. 'I fear this is only the beginning.'

Chapter 35

February 1941

Humans are creatures of habit, as Richard liked to say, and by now it had become routine to seek safety in the air-raid shelter at least twice a week. Losses were still being contained and at least no one had had to use their gas mask yet. People adapted. On every staircase, and in pretty much every flat, there was now a bucket of sand or a pail of water to put out the incendiaries. If the air-raid warning had lasted more than three hours overnight, then the children had leave to go to school two hours later than normal.

Repair squads proved dependable. Even a hit on a power station would be put right in under two hours.

The war had changed Hamburg. No white pleasure boats steamed across the Alster now, as a timber structure had been put in place across the water to mislead enemy aircraft and remove any point of orientation.

Fritz frequently brought horrific tales from the operating theatre, where he would be in the middle of surgery when the sirens went and have no option but to carry on with the operation throughout the raid. The majority of patients in Hamburg's hospitals could not in any case be taken down to the air-raid shelters, due to lack of facilities. Their only hope was that the anti-aircraft rockets would do their work while they lay helpless in their beds.

The asylum at Langenhorn, however, remained relatively safe as it was too far out to be of any interest to enemy bombers, so life there went on in its usual way, until one morning in February 1941 when Richard got a call from Fritz.

'I've got bad news,' said his friend. 'I'll start with the less dangerous part. The black-market trader I've been getting all your petrol coupons from has been rumbled.'

'Shit,' muttered Richard. 'I hope he hasn't got a customer list that'll drop us both in it.'

'Don't worry, there's nothing to implicate us. But that's not the only thing. I can't even go on giving you my own coupons because I've got to sell the car. My call-up papers came this morning.'

'What?' Richard couldn't believe what he was hearing.

'My call-up papers.' Fritz practically had to spell it out for him.

'But you're the senior consultant and Professor Wehmeyer's deputy! They can't just conscript you like that!'

'Yes, they can. And it's to serve as director of a medical battalion for the German Africa Corps in Tripoli. My research into operating on bullet wounds to the skull and on multiple abdominal traumata, the work I published with Professor Wehmeyer, is what's led to this disaster. The top brass must have thought, *Oh well, the Prof's too old for the Front, we'll leave him in Hamburg,* so my hard-won skills are sending me off to serve the fatherland alongside its other battling sons.' His laugh was bitter. 'And there was I, idiotically believing that if I did the best work possible that I'd be indispensable to the home front and not get conscripted.'

'When are you reporting for duty?'

'On 1 March. As if all I'd been waiting for was to sacrifice myself for the Führer, the people and the fatherland.'

'Fritz, I am truly sorry.'

'Maybe you made the better decision, going for psychiatry, but surgery's my whole life now.'

'Shall we have a beer together this evening? While you're still here in town?'

'You bet, then I can bellyache to you in person about it all.' Fritz chuckled quietly in spite of the sombre mood.

Moments after Richard had put the phone down there was a knock on the door. It was Krüger's secretary, Frau Handeloh.

'Dr Hellmer, Dr Krüger wishes to speak to you immediately. Your telephone line has been engaged, so he asked me to come and fetch you.'

'What's wrong?'

'A supervisory commission from Berlin is here and there are a few queries about your statements.'

'What kind of supervisory commission?' asked Richard, getting to his feet and preparing to follow Frau Handeloh.

'From Tiergartenstrasse in Berlin, the place we send all the statements to.'

Tiergartenstrasse! The place where life-and-death decisions were made on the basis of those patient registration forms. Richard's face burned. Was this a routine visit, or had they noticed that for the last nine months every single patient at Langenhorn had demonstrated the same productivity as a healthy person? If they'd looked at the forms carefully, they'd have seen straight away that everything had been embellished. Would it be a case of insubordination or incompetence? And what would happen to him now?

He followed Frau Handeloh down the corridor, his mind rapidly working through ways in which he could outmanoeuvre them if what he suspected was true, but nothing seemed appropriate. He couldn't play the staunch but stupid Nazi as he had before, because Krüger was going to be there too. And Krüger had had it in for him for a long time now. Whichever way you looked at it, if they examined his statements alongside the original files, he'd had it.

Dr Krüger's impatience was evident as soon as Richard entered his office. With him were two men in civilian clothes, files open in front of them on the desk.

'Ah, here at last!' he snapped. 'These gentlemen are from Berlin and have questions to ask.'

'Good morning,' said Richard. 'How can I be of assistance to you gentlemen?'

'Good morning.' Although they both returned his greeting, they didn't do the usual 'Heil Hitler'. Was that a good sign? Richard wasn't sure.

'I'm Dr Nissen,' said one, acting as spokesman for the pair of them, 'and this is my colleague, Dr Clausner. The Ministry for the Interior has asked us to come here and look into your patients' files.'

'You've come all the way from Berlin to look into our patients' files? What have we done to deserve this honour?' asked Richard.

Krüger threw him a scathing look.

'It has come to our attention that the efficacy of treatment here is well above the average. For nine months now every one of your patients has received a productivity assessment comparable to the average healthy worker. This has sparked our curiosity.'

'I see.' Richard's throat tightened. He tried to conceal his disquiet.

'Our colleague Dr Krüger has told us that you are responsible for the registration and classification of all inmates.'

'That's right.' Richard folded his hands behind his back so that nobody could see them shaking.

'It is remarkable that most of your classifications do not seem to match with the files themselves,' Dr Nissen went on. 'We have sampled eleven at random. And in nine of these the productivity assessment is falsely positive. What do you have to say?'

Richard tried to clear his throat. 'I've filled out so many registration forms that it's perfectly possible that one or two errors have crept in.'

'One or two errors?' Dr Nissen studied him with raised eyebrows. 'In this sampling your error rate is more than eighty per cent. That would suggest an error in your methodology, don't you think?'

Richard remained silent.

'You have nothing to say?'

Richard's mind was feverishly working on how to get around this. The truth would send him straight to prison.

'I was expected to determine precise percentages regarding patients' capacity for productivity in comparison with that of a healthy man. In the end, I'm a doctor, not a farmer. If you look at agriculture, you'll understand that work of economic value is in fact being done, work that contributes to nourishing the patients here and indeed those in other institutions, particularly those with children's wards.'

'And this is why you certificated every single mentally ill patient here with one hundred per cent capacity, in spite of the fact that this applies to only twenty per cent of the patients at the very most?'

'I see the work and the contribution that the sick make when performing tasks for the hospital. I have no figures to draw a comparison with the typical average agricultural worker. From the outset, it has been incumbent on the expert witness to define the terms of the capacity for productivity. I have completed the forms to the best of my knowledge and conscience.'

'But you ought to have recognised the variable quality of your patients' work and taken the trouble to show some gradation,' Nissen said, flaring up at him. 'Any idiot could have done that!'

'Excuse me, I'm a doctor, not an idiot.' Richard let this slip almost involuntarily.

'Is that so?' snarled Nissen. 'It looks as though it's the other way around with you.' Then he turned to Dr Krüger. 'It seems to me we have here either a case of crass stupidity or of calculated insubordination.'

'I'm afraid I have to assume the insubordination,' said Krüger. 'Dr Hellmer has been an outstandingly reliable provider of expert statements for some time. I would not otherwise have given him this responsibility.'

Richard was seized by an idea so bold it was almost reckless. He now had nothing to lose. Krüger had already stabbed him in the back. It was time to take Krüger into the abyss along with him.

'So I'm your sacrificial pawn, although you yourself informed me that those of our patients on the first wave of registration forms were gassed in Brandenburg, and because of this you asked me to fill out all future forms differently in order to save the others from this same fate?'

Krüger stared at him, aghast, and bellowed, 'That's an out-and-out lie!'

'Gentlemen,' said Richard, addressing the two visitors, 'if you look carefully at the files, you will see that my incorrect entries started nine months ago and that all those prior to that were correct. I had orders from Dr Krüger to carry on. I'd have kept that to myself if my colleague had at least showed the decency not to charge me with insubordination over something that he himself ordered.'

'Hellmer, you are summarily dismissed!' roared Krüger. 'This is grotesque!' He turned to look at the two visiting doctors. 'Gentlemen, I deny all knowledge of this monstrous impertinence.'

Nissen nodded. 'It's not for us to be thinking about disciplinary measures here. Dr Krüger, if you are minded to start a procedure for insubordination, you are at liberty to do so, of course. I would, however, advise against it because a procedure of this type would merely draw unnecessary attention to the deed. I think that the dismissal of the guilty party on the grounds of gross misconduct and the reworking of the registration forms would be the most elegant solution to the problem. Do we understand one another?'

Then he turned to Richard. 'As for you, Dr Hellmer, in such times as these it would be a waste for a doctor like you, someone who pays so much attention to his patients' capacity for productivity, to stand in court for insubordination. To my mind, you will be of far greater service to our people at the Front. I shall today inform the conscription office of your immediate availability. And you can get on your knees to thank God that I am in such a lenient mood. That is all. You may go.'

Richard was stunned, which made him slow to take in what had just happened. Not only had he been dismissed from his post and would now be conscripted, but his patients would all now be reassessed. He felt some relief that he had already removed the twins, Manfred and Rolf, as well as Johannes Mönicke, from Krüger's sphere of influence. But was that any compensation? Had he been too arrogant when he'd thrown caution to the winds and basically declared every patient as fit for work? Would it have been better to sacrifice a few in order to save the lives of others?

Without a word, he left Krüger's office and went to gather up his belongings.

While he was still packing things away, there was a knock on his door. It was Kurt Hansen.

'Is it true what I've heard? You've been summarily dismissed?'

'Yes.'

'But why?'

'Because I've behaved like a doctor and not an idiot. Take care of yourself, Kurt, and look after our patients. They desperately need you, even more than ever.'

◆ ◆ ◆

And that is how it came to be not Fritz but Richard who needed to pour his heart out over a beer that evening.

'That's dreadful,' said Fritz. 'Looks like I did choose the right specialism after all.'

'Certainly the way things are, yes.' Richard took a large mouthful of beer. Paula had been horrified when he'd told her what had happened.

Losing his job was one thing, but to have conscription looming, well, that was quite another.

'What if they put you in a punishment battalion?' she'd asked him, her face and voice full of worry. Richard had just shrugged his shoulders. He'd run fresh out of ideas to get him out of this.

But Fritz had a brainwave. 'Head them off before the marching orders even arrive,' he said. 'Sign up of your own volition for the medical battalion that I've been assigned to. I'll write out a formal recommendation, saying that I need you there. We'll do it first thing in the morning, before that idiot in Berlin has time to act. That means you'll already be committed, out of sight and out of mind. And on top of that they won't be afraid of their mercy-killing scheme coming to light because you'll be tucked away in North Africa.'

'And we can go through it shoulder to shoulder, like we always have. Do you know what? That doesn't sound so bad.' Richard turned to the barman. 'Two more beers here, please.'

'Exactly,' said Fritz. 'Shoulder to shoulder. I'll ask Professor Wehmeyer for a statement in support as well, saying that you can be deployed as both a surgeon and psychiatrist at the Front, and that this makes you of significant importance in the war effort. I'm sure there'd be no further questions asked.'

'Except by Krüger, perhaps. I've already caused him a fair bit of trouble. I'm afraid he'll never forgive me.'

'Are you dependent on the forgiveness of an idiot who stabbed you in the back and sacked you?'

'No, absolutely not.'

The barman brought over their beers.

'To life!' said Fritz. 'And may we always find a way, even in the darkest of times, of seeing the light at the end of the tunnel!'

'To life!' repeated Richard.

They clinked glasses and, in spite of all his concerns, Richard felt some comfort. He was not alone.

Chapter 36

Paula tried to make Richard's last few days in Hamburg as pleasant as she could and not let her worry affect him, but he knew her too well not to sense her inner anguish at the prospect of this separation.

'You won't have any money worries,' he reminded her. 'The army may not pay so well as the hospital, but it's better than dole money any day!'

'Don't you dare tell me you won't need clothing ration cards any more and that we have to look on the bright side!' She was watching him try on his uniform in front of the bedroom mirror. And although she'd rather never have seen him in uniform in the first place, she had to admit he looked tremendous. The grey jacket, with its silver-blue lapels and epaulettes bearing the classic symbol of his profession, the golden staff of Asclepius, was so dignified and showed off his handsome physique. The elegant peaked cap and highly polished black boots completed the picture of a well-turned-out officer. Thanks to Fritz's intervention and outstanding references from Professor Wehmeyer, Richard had immediately been assigned to a junior doctor post rather than an auxiliary role, and this gave him the rank of lieutenant.

'I'll only be in the medical service,' he said, hoping to lessen Paula's fears. 'We carry a weapon purely for self-defence.'

'I know all that. Have you got a photograph for your ID card?'

'No, they need one in uniform. I was thinking we could all go to the photographer tomorrow and have a couple of family pictures done at the same time.'

'Family photos with you in uniform?' Paula frowned. 'Not that I'm superstitious, but it hasn't exactly brought your family any joy to have a farewell photo of someone in uniform, has it?'

'We've got to break the bad spell some time!' said Richard airily. 'Nothing'll happen to me, anyway. Fritz thinks we'll be in the main military hospital in Tripoli and that's miles from the front line. It's probably much quieter than Hamburg in an air raid.' He paused. 'I'm far more worried about leaving you alone with the children at such a terrible time.'

'We'll manage. What matters is that you watch out for yourself and come back to us safely. I don't ever want a letter like the one Margit and Holger received.'

'As a matter of principle, I have no intention whatsoever of dying for the sake of the Führer, the people and the fatherland. I promise you, I'd far rather survive as a coward than die as a hero.'

He drew her close.

'You'll never be a coward, Richard,' she said, sinking into the comfort of his embrace. 'If you were a coward, you'd have joined the party long ago and outdone even the likes of Krüger in bootlicking for self-advancement. But you've always stayed true to yourself and tried to do the best for your patients. You are the bravest man I know.'

The doorbell rang.

'That'll be Emilia,' said Paula, breaking away from Richard and going to open their front door.

Shortly afterwards, Emilia came rushing into the bedroom, her school satchel still on her back.

'Daddy, I've brought you something!' she shouted boisterously as she took off the satchel.

'Really? What can it be?'

'Ooh, is that your uniform? You look really smart, Papa!'

Paula came back in, just in time to see Richard smiling broadly at his daughter's compliments and enthusiasm.

'Thank you, poppet. And what have you brought me?'

She undid her satchel and took out a pot of greasy cream. 'This! Look! Because it's much hotter in Africa than here and you mustn't get sunburn!'

Laughing with delight, he took the pot and then wrapped his arms around his little daughter. 'Thank you so much, darling! You're just wonderful – you think of everything! What on earth would I do without you?'

'Are you staying in Africa long?'

'I don't know yet.'

'And will you fight against the English when you're there and stop them dropping these bombs on our heads?'

'No, I won't be fighting anyone. I'll be working in a hospital with Uncle Fritz, treating our sick and wounded soldiers.'

'Can I try on your new cap, Papa?'

'Of course, darling.' He took it off and handed it to her. She put it on and looked at herself in the mirror. The peak almost covered her eyes, and with her long fair plaits hanging around her shoulders, it made for a comical contrast.

'Suits you perfectly,' said Richard, whereupon Emilia tried to salute him.

'Pity I won't get a cap like that when I join the League of German Girls next year.'

The sirens started.

'Air raid!' exclaimed Paula. 'And Georg isn't back yet, but the tram's due any minute.'

'Get yourself and Emilia down to the cellar straight away – I'm off to the tram stop for Georg.' He grabbed back his cap and put it on.

Leaving the house in uniform still felt alien to him, but there was no time to change.

While Paula and Emilia hurried down to the cellar with the suitcase full of their precious photo albums and documents, Richard ran to the tram stop. The few people still out were moving fast towards their own shelters and most people were already somewhere safe. Richard found himself wondering what the tram driver would most likely do. Would he wait at the next stop so that everyone could find somewhere to take cover or simply carry on with his schedule? Fritz would definitely still be in the operating theatre, ignoring the threat from overhead in order to finish the operation.

In the distance, he saw the tram coming and heaved a sigh of relief. When it stopped, most of the passengers got out fast and rushed away. Georg was confused and had to look twice before recognising his father in uniform.

'Quick! Air-raid warning!' Richard signed to Georg. The little boy nodded and ran straight up to him. Richard seized him by the hand and they set off for home.

Almost immediately, Richard heard the roar of enemy bombers. He paused and looked skywards. This was the first time he'd been outside in an air raid. Georg followed his gaze. The bombers were still very high, probably aiming for the port area. Soon afterwards, he heard anti-aircraft rockets and they saw an aircraft going into a spin, coming down and exploding on the far side of the Elbe. Richard flinched but at the same time was so fascinated by what they were witnessing that he forgot to keep running. Georg, spared the horrific background noises, was spellbound. The lad stared fixedly up at the sky and pointed towards a tiny white blotch that seemed slowly to float down to earth.

'That's the pilot,' Richard signed for Georg. 'He jumped out just in time with his parachute. As soon as he lands, our people will capture him and he'll be a prisoner of war until it's over.'

Several more planes tumbled from the sky, and the flashes continued for a while before the enemy turned back and the sirens sounded the all-clear. Georg was still transfixed by the sight of columns of smoke now rising from the port.

'We've been lucky again, haven't we?' said Richard to his son. Georg nodded, beaming from ear to ear.

'Weren't you frightened?'

'No,' signed Georg in reply, 'because I was with you, Papa.'

Richard's spirits fell. He'd have given anything not to be forced to leave Paula and the children alone with all this.

◆ ◆ ◆

Next morning it was time for the photography session to secure Richard's ID photo as well as some family shots. While the photographer was busying himself in the back room with the final photos, the bell at the shop door announced the arrival of a new customer.

It was none other than Fritz, also in uniform, along with his family and Rudi, the adorable dachshund.

'I had a feeling we'd see you all here!' he said, as Rudi, tail wagging, ran straight over to Georg and Emilia.

'So even a captain in the medical corps needs an ID photo in full regalia, eh?' commented Richard with a smile.

'He certainly does,' confirmed Fritz. 'But while we're all here, shall we have one of us all together? We haven't got any like that.'

'That's true.' Richard was ready to agree, but at the same time he couldn't help thinking of Paula's superstition. Did it really bring bad luck to photograph the family group with one in uniform, ready to leave for the Front? He'd always refused to believe it but suddenly it didn't seem so absurd. This time, though, there was one big difference, he told himself. His brother, Georg, as well as Jürgen and Karl, had been called up as ordinary soldiers. He and Fritz were medical officers. They wouldn't be fighting. And yes, he'd love a photo of all of them together. As he was always the photographer, he was usually missing from the many photos they had of Fritz and his family and Paula with the twins.

Four-year-old Harri picked Rudi up, then they lined up in two rows, both sets of parents at the back, the four children with the dog in front.

'We'll need four prints, please,' said Fritz. 'One for each of us to have with us at the Front, and one for each family to have at home.'

The photographer nodded, pleased to have such good business.

'May I make a fifth print for my window display? Family photos with an officer in uniform are so popular.'

Fritz and Richard glanced at one another briefly and read each other's thoughts.

'No, I'm afraid not,' replied Fritz. 'It's very much a private matter.'

'That's a shame,' said the photographer.

'But you're welcome to photograph our dachsie and put him in the window!' said Fritz with his most mischievous laugh. 'He's very photogenic.'

In response the photographer merely handed Richard his collection number and got on with the ID picture for Fritz.

Chapter 37

Once Richard had departed for Tripoli with Fritz on 1 March 1941, the gap in Paula's life was hard to bear. She had to stop herself from writing him a long letter even on the first day. The worst time was when the children were at school. Of course, Richard had always been out at the hospital at that time of day, but she knew he'd be back in the evening and that he and the children would fill the flat with life. She had the mornings to herself for housework and making sure that everything was done, but since the air raids had intensified she found herself constantly worrying if the children were not home. As a distraction, she and Fritz's wife spoke often on the telephone. Dorothea felt the same and there came a point when both women confessed to missing their jobs.

'It wasn't a problem when Fritz was here,' Dorothea explained. 'He used to talk about operations so much that I felt as if I was still working there and knew what all my old colleagues were up to. Now I feel twice as cut off. I take care of the housework and the children, but that isn't enough.'

Paula sighed. 'Same here.'

'Maybe we could make ourselves useful somewhere for a couple of hours a week – you know, just on a voluntary basis,' Dorothea suggested. 'Then nothing at home would be neglected but we could still do something meaningful outside the four walls.'

'Good idea,' said Paula enthusiastically. 'Any ideas where?'

'I'll ask around.' Dorothea's doorbell rang and Rudi started barking. 'There's Henriette! I'll have to go. I'll get in touch once I've found out more.'

'Thank you so much. Bye, Doro.'

One bright spot on the horizon, at least. The second bright spot came only one hour later when the post arrived. Here was the first, longed-for letter from Richard. In spite of the privilege of the army postal service, it had still taken ten days to reach her.

My darling Paula, it started, and her heart beat faster. They might have been married for over twelve years, but whenever he called her that she felt like a love-struck teenager.

> We've arrived in Tripoli safely. The railway journey to Italy passed without incident and, being medical officers, we were lucky and had our own compartment. In Brindisi we boarded the ship to Tripoli. It was unfortunate that we got there in the dark so I had no opportunity to take photographs. The sea was rough and lots of people were seasick. Fritz and I escaped unscathed, but we decided to spend all the time below deck once we realised that being out in the open meant the risk of slipping over on the vomit left by those who didn't quite make it to the railings in time.
>
> Tripoli's a wonderful city, a blend of Middle Eastern charm, the culture of Ancient Rome and Italian flair. Did you know that a third of Tripoli's inhabitants are Italian? You could almost think yourself in Europe. In the twenties the Italians built a beautiful cathedral, the Santa Maria degli Angeli. I'm enclosing a photo so you can get an idea of how Italian it is here. You'd hardly think there was a war on. Just as Fritz promised, we're in the main military hospital

and our job is to take in all the field hospital patients and either get them fit for further duty or send them back home for full convalescence. The main military hospital is very well equipped. We've got two operating theatres, an X-ray department, dentistry and a pharmacy. Fritz has officially allocated me to surgical work because there's no psychiatric ward, but every unit has three mad-nurses and our three are something special. There's Walter, the highest ranking – when he found out I'd originally been a psychiatrist, he commented that no decent German uses foreign words and that the word for me is 'mad-doctor'. I countered this by saying that the only person who'd say 'mad-doctor' is someone who doesn't know how to pronounce 'psychiatrist' and that this is a diagnostic tool for measuring a colleague's intelligence. Walter looked at me in some irritation while the other two, Bert and Wolfgang, burst out laughing and said they would show me around. To my surprise, Walter joined in the laughter and gave me a knowing slap on the back. Since then he hasn't once referred to a mad-doctor in my presence and enjoys the joke of no longer referring to his own profession as mad-nursing but as psychiatric nursing. He's really gone up in my estimation now. Walter is also a rarity when it comes to getting anything organised. He's one of those people who can get hold of the most extraordinary things. So, for example, he knows a cobbler who can make you bespoke shoes without coupons and at a good price. Fritz and I are going to pay him a visit – after all, we have to take whatever opportunities come our way. If it turns out that he can make ladies' and children's shoes without doing an actual fitting, I'll tell you next time I write what measurements he'd need and then on my first home leave, although I've no idea when that might be yet, I'll bring you all new shoes! And do tell Emilia from me that I haven't needed the cream yet because here in March it hardly gets above twenty degrees. Besides, we're in the military hospital all day, and because there's more surgical work here than psychiatric, I'm often indoors with Fritz in his theatre. It's lucky that he more than makes up for my lack of experience in the field, so sometimes I hold the clamp to assist him and so far nobody's realised that the last time I operated was as long ago as 1929.

There are a lot of cases of diarrhoea so the most I prescribe at the moment is charcoal tablets. I'm pleased to say that Fritz and I have escaped all that so far. Fritz thinks it's because Walter provides us with beer every evening and this cleanses the gut. Whether that's medically correct, well, I very much doubt it. I think it's far more to do with the fact that we only ever use boiled water. Still, it's a good excuse for a beer. When we sit on the terrace outside the military hospital in the evening, both of us enjoying a beer as we watch the sun set behind the palms, you could almost believe we were on holiday.

Tell the children I love them and give them big hugs from me.

With all my love,
Richard

Paula's heart ached as she read the letter, all the more so when she'd studied his pin-sharp black-and-white image of the cathedral against the city backdrop. She remembered vividly how he'd spent a couple of years deliberating over whether he should indulge in the expensive Leica III, which professionals used, or whether he should choose the cheaper, earlier model. Once he'd forced himself into a decision, he'd been like a little boy with his new camera. Nothing escaped his viewfinder. His first home leave would see him turning up with not just a bag bursting with new shoes but also three new photo albums boasting everything worth seeing in Tripoli. This was some consolation to her as it meant she could share something of his experience.

She read the letter several times over before setting it down and writing an equally long and affectionate letter in return, even though she didn't have anything special to relate other than little anecdotes about her everyday life with the children. But that was exactly what he longed to hear about and she was only too happy to recount as much as she could. Then she stowed his letter away safely in the suitcase with their family albums and documents. From now on, that would be as important a memory as every single photo in the albums.

◆ ◆ ◆

A couple of days later, Dorothea got back in touch.

'I've found a way of us doing some voluntary work without it coming under People's Welfare.' She said this first and foremost as she knew how low an opinion Paula had of that organisation ever since it had become a purely National Socialist set-up. 'At Finkenau there are now even more lone first-time mothers because their husbands are fighting at the Front. Not all of them want a mother's help from the NSV. Sister Mathilde suggested putting us in touch with these women and we could then help them if they need support with newborns or have questions.'

Paula was pleased. She still had warm memories of the young mothers she had worked with at the women's hospital when she'd been doing her PhD thesis. 'When can we start?'

'We could go to Finkenau tomorrow if you like to introduce ourselves to two young mothers and their babies.'

'Let's do that! I'm really looking forward to it!'

'I'll leave Harri and Rudi with my mother and then we won't be restricted. By the way, I've had a letter from Fritz at last!'

'And what does it say?'

'He's working on a new approach to amputation. It'll decrease the safe distance from healthy tissue so that in certain cases he won't have to amputate as high on the thigh, but lower down at the knee joint. He even sent me all sorts of detailed drawings and descriptions of the dermatoplasty he'll use to create a weight-bearing stump for a new prosthetic limb.' Dorothea laughed. 'That's Fritz all over. His work is his life and he likes being married to an old theatre nurse who understands what he's on about! And I must admit I'd rather be taken seriously like that than have him write me soppy love letters.'

'We're so lucky with our two, aren't we? They see us as equal partners they can share everything with,' said Paula with warmth.

'I know. That's why I miss Fritz so much.'

Chapter 38

'You people really are something else!' Richard didn't know whether to be pleased or embarrassed. The medics' common room had been decorated with a huge banner, proclaiming:

AFRICA, 23 JULY 1941
DR HELLMER'S 40TH BIRTHDAY

Various bits of furniture had been pushed together to create one long banqueting table on which stood a magnificent cake, the number 40 beautifully marked out in frosting.

Walter was the first to congratulate Richard. 'Many happy returns, Doctor, sir.' Other colleagues came over to do the same, but Fritz was nowhere to be seen. This surprised Richard as he was sure that Fritz was behind everything.

Just as he was wondering where his friend could be, the man himself appeared, together with the two musicians from their regiment, Fieten and Max, both of whom also worked as hospital porters. Fritz had also brought Richard's camera from the room they shared.

'Many happy returns, Richard, my dear chap!' Fritz said, shaking him by the hand. 'You didn't really think we'd let your fortieth birthday pass unnoticed, did you? Especially as you're spending it so far from home!'

'I hoped you would, to be honest.' Richard looked awkward.

'Never! And now time for the birthday boy's serenade – Fieten, Max, ready? We need everyone to join in!'

As the two musicians struck up the well-known melody of 'Happy Birthday' and eleven male voices chimed in, some less tuneful than others, everyone felt the emotion of the occasion.

After the choral offering, Fritz got the men organised for a souvenir photo. 'Now everyone stand behind the long table, please, and hold up the banner, birthday boy in the middle. The folks back home will want a picture, won't they?'

'You've got to be in it too, Fritz!'

'OK, but who's going to take the picture?'

'My camera has a self-timer,' Richard explained. 'All we need is something steady and at the right height for it to stand on.'

'We can manage that!' said Walter. 'Let's use one of the little tables and put a chair on top of it.'

Although this reduced the impressive length of the banqueting table, it meant the camera was at the right height and in exactly the right spot. Richard set the self-timer then dashed to his position in the middle, between Walter and Fritz and in front of the banner they were all holding up. Then they cut the cake.

'Delicious!' said Richard. 'Who made it?'

'Our mess sergeant's a mate of mine,' explained Walter with a grin. 'We all put aside a bit of flour from our own rations too.'

Richard was touched. He knew the current supply situation was tight. People didn't speak of it, but everyone had difficulty getting enough food at the moment. Which was why, to try to secure deliveries from Italy, the chief of staff had planned a major offensive to capture Tobruk and its large harbour.

'Any news from home?' asked Fritz.

'Nothing. The army post seems to be as slow as our supply ships at the moment.'

'Not to worry, there's still time today. Maybe there'll be a convoy this afternoon. And I've already lined up something you'll like for this evening.'

'Really? What's that, then?'

'A touch of the Middle East in an Italian colony in Africa!' Fritz said with a grin. 'Bring your camera. It'll be worth it.' That was all he would tell him.

When the little party ended early in the afternoon, there were still three operations scheduled. The advantage of working in the main military hospital was that the life-saving emergency work always had to be done out in the field units near the front line, which meant that the patients arrived at the main hospital in a stable condition and so surgery was always done to a timetable. Infected wounds continued to cause problems, however, and often made amputation inevitable. Working in conjunction with a consultant in general medicine, Dr Buchwald, Fritz tried to combat this through early intervention with antibiotics, first using sulphonamides to fight the infection and only then carrying out any surgery, so as to minimise the necessity for amputation. Sadly, many of the men arrived in such a weakened state that the infection could not be contained even with the use of antibiotics.

Two out of today's three cases had ended in amputation.

'I've heard that the British have a new antibiotic called penicillin,' said Fritz as he carefully stitched the skin flap over the stump of his patient's amputation at the knee. 'Trouble is, it's very expensive and hard to make. There was a really interesting lecture about it at that last conference I went to in London in '37. If they've found a way of producing it in quantity by now, they'll have a huge advantage over us when it comes to dealing with the wounded.'

'So why aren't our chemists working on it?' asked Richard.

'Dr Buchwald reckons it's best to rely on our mass production of sulphonamides because penicillin hasn't really proved itself yet. And producing it on an industrial scale isn't possible at this stage, so it wouldn't really contribute much to the war effort at the moment.' Fritz let out a sigh of regret. 'Do you know what I hate most about this war, apart from the obvious stuff like the death and destruction? It's not being able to exchange ideas with colleagues in other countries for the benefit of all our patients. You know I'd like to see the Royal Air Force shot out of the sky, but the few times I was in London for work I met such good people and we always had really productive discussions.'

Darkness had fallen by the time they left the operating theatre and Fritz decided this was the right moment for the surprise. 'I've got leave of absence for us both till seven in the morning,' he told Richard. 'Get spruced up and bring your camera!'

They headed for a bar with more than a hint of Middle Eastern and Italian influences, where the main draw was belly dancers in their exotic and revealing costumes.

Guests sat at tables or lounged on couches, enjoying the traditional hookah.

'Shall we try a pipe?' suggested Fritz.

Richard wasn't keen. He'd never had a taste either for cigars or cigarettes, whereas Fritz enjoyed the occasional cigar.

'I'll just watch, I think,' said Richard after a bit of hesitation, 'then you can tell me if I'm missing anything.'

'Then your job is to get a couple of nice photos of the dancers. I'll take care of all the tips.'

Fritz certainly hadn't exaggerated the delights of live belly dancing. They'd only ever seen anything like this in moving pictures, so to experience it now with authentic local music and two professional dancers was something very different. The girls' costumes were a mass of sequins and reminded Richard of the new two-piece swimsuits that had become fashionable of late. Paula had got herself one during the summer just before the start of the war. She'd gone for emerald green, and with her bare midriff and long blonde hair falling loose, had looked for all the world like a mysterious sea goddess in Richard's eyes.

One of the girls wiggled her way over to the two friends on their couches and gave them quite a close-up of her swaying hips, while other men cheered on in the background. But Richard treated this as all just part of the show and didn't consider that the dancer was doing this especially for his benefit. She realised she wasn't having quite the desired effect on Richard so turned to Fritz, who reacted in the same way as his friend and seemed to prefer another drag on the hookah. Richard detected a look of disappointment on her face as she moved away.

The lighting hadn't been good enough for any photography during the dancing so when the girls came over at the end for a bit more attention and the usual tip, they were surprised to find that Richard still wanted nothing more than a few pictures. He noticed how their stage smiles turned into genuine laughter as he asked them to adopt a few dance poses for him to photograph, something they were more than happy to do. When Richard explained in a mixture of German and Latin, the latter due to its closeness to Italian, that he wanted to show the pictures back home to his wife and children, the women looked so puzzled that Fritz couldn't help but laugh.

'I suppose most men wouldn't even tell their families they'd been anywhere like this,' remarked Fritz.

'What about you?' asked Richard.

'Me? I'd just like a couple of prints to show Doro and the children. I'm a decent family man like you, my friend.'

They lingered a while in the bar and watched the next act, a turbaned man juggling with flaming torches. While Richard stuck to his usual beer, Fritz was already on his third pipe of the evening.

'And how was the hookah?' Richard asked him as they made their way back to their quarters, long after midnight.

'I feel pretty sick, to be honest. That stuff's really gone to my head.'

'You can't go wrong with a good German beer,' Richard said with a grin. 'Shall I fetch you a sick bowl?'

'Don't you dare! It's not that bad!'

◆ ◆ ◆

The following day, the long-awaited supply convoy rolled in, bringing post as well as the urgently needed food supplies.

There was a parcel for Richard. In it was a new, beautifully framed photograph of Paula and the twins, and a copy of Stefan Zweig's biography of Marie Antoinette, covered in a deliberately inconspicuous dust jacket. As he unwrapped the book, he broke into a broad smile. Paula had always loved buying him Stefan Zweig because she knew how much he admired the man's writing. He wondered how on earth she'd got hold of a copy. Since the Nazis had outlawed Zweig and publicly burned his books, it hadn't been possible to find them anywhere. She had probably found it at her favourite antiquarian bookshop, where the owner would keep special books under the counter for particular customers. A wave of love and affection flooded him with warmth. Not only had his wife sent him something good to read, she'd also chosen a symbol of rebellion against the dictatorship under which they lived. As well as the gifts, there were letters from his children and a very long one from Paula.

> My dearest Richard
> Not a day goes by without us missing you, although the children are very brave and don't want to let it show. Your birthday will be especially hard for us and we hope that our good wishes arrive in time. Summer has truly come, and even though it's not as hot here as it must be for you in Africa, we're enjoying warm weather that makes me long for those spontaneous trips we used to make to the Baltic coast. Yes, I know I could go there alone with the children but I thought it better to store the car at your father's place in the garage. With the constant air raids I wouldn't feel easy driving out to the seaside resorts. So instead of that we're spending

the summer at Moorfleet at your parents' allotment. The children love it here and can splash around in that little tributary of the Elbe. Georg is thrilled because his friend Horst is out here too, spending the summer at his grandmother's. The two are inseparable and Emilia felt a bit shut out at first, mostly because the boys love the *Winnetou* books by Karl May and play at cowboys and Indians the whole time. Horst likes to be the cowboy Old Shatterhand and Georg is his native friend Winnetou. Horst thinks that's the right way round because Winnetou is silent and Old Shatterhand does all the talking. Emilia didn't want to be Nscho-tschi because she dies. Fortunately, your father loves reading Karl May and came up with the perfect solution. He suggested to Emilia she should be Kolma Puschi from the *Old Surehand* books – the woman who lives and fights like a man. Horst and Georg couldn't argue with that! It looks as though the original adventures will need a rewrite as the boys are now both in thrall to their leader, Kolma Puschi!

Alongside all these light-hearted things, there is one that's really serious, Richard. A health worker from the NSV turned up here at the allotments and inquired where she would find Georg. She asked the other children whether he was simply hard of hearing or completely deaf and knew he went to the deaf and dumb school. Luckily, the first child she spoke to happened to be Horst and she didn't know how much he hates it when someone he doesn't know asks him questions. So he told her that Georg understands him perfectly well when they talk together. And when she asked Horst if he understood Georg equally well, he said, 'Well, I can understand you, can't I? What a funny question.'

This was when I happened to walk by and so I asked the woman what she wanted. She explained that she'd been informed that Georg was deaf mute by heredity and that this is why she needed to look into his case. I asked who had told her this but she replied she wasn't allowed to tell me. I explained to her as pleasantly as I could that Georg had been made hard of hearing due to complications at birth but that his twin sister was in perfect health, something which argues against any hereditary cause. Then I made a big point of telling her that I'm a trained doctor and not in need of her help and that there are plenty of other people in far greater need of medical support. She went away then but I can't put it out of my mind and when I spoke to some of the other parents from Georg's school, I found out that a lot of the older children have been called for sterilisation.

But the worst thing is what has happened to Martin Wessel. He was only fifteen, lost his case at the Hereditary Health Court and was subjected to forced sterilisation but died during the operation. Apparently, he had a previously undetected heart condition and couldn't tolerate the anaesthetic. His parents are trying to get some financial compensation, even if only to pay for a decent burial, but it's not looking good for them.

When I hear stories like this, I want to scream and shout and weep all at the same time, but I do what you do. I bite my tongue because shouting and crying will change nothing. All I can do is protect our twins and try and give them a decent childhood, in spite of the raids every night. And there really are good moments. One of our neighbours here has a small canoe and he regularly lets the children use it. Georg and Horst play at being forest Indians like in *The Deerslayer* and spend ages paddling along the little channels here. Emilia prefers to stay in her favourite role, living and fighting like a man, which in no way lessens her enjoyment of these excursions.

When the sirens go off at night, we feel really safe here because we're so far from the edge of the city and any industry, so we're not a target. Ever since Georg saw that air raid with you in the street, he looks out of the cabin windows at night to see the bombers coming, and Emilia does the same. They find it exciting to watch the anti-aircraft rockets lighting up and shooting down the enemy.

Thank goodness they're still too little to be involved as flak helpers, but I sense they'd both volunteer for it if they were old enough. When I said something about it being dangerous work, Emilia said she'd rather do something than sit here waiting for bombs to fall on her head. She sounded so like her father. Richard, she's so similar to you that I sometimes think she's the boy. Georg has more the reserved nature of a little girl. Yes, I know what you're thinking – that he couldn't possibly have inherited his reticent personality from his mother! Yes, I would also rather take action and do something, not just wait for something else to happen. But the only thing I can do, apart from looking after my children, is help the young first-time mothers whose men are all fighting at the Front. It was Dorothea's idea. It's doing her good to feel like a professional nurse again because she misses talking to Fritz so much, just like I do you.

I hope you soon have home leave. We are all longing to see you and love you so much,
Paula

Paula's letter left Richard uneasy. Family news always filled him with joy and affection, but now he was concerned about this visit from the health worker. Immediately, he suspected Krüger of having a hand in this. Nobody else would be minded to query Georg's medical certification. Paula had clearly fended off the immediate danger, but Richard feared that Krüger's desire for vengeance could drive him to hound his family long-term, all because Richard had dared to accuse him in front of the supervisory commission. He had assumed that Krüger would be satisfied with ruining his career and sending him to the Front. It hadn't occurred to him that he would stop at nothing, including reporting on his young son. But then a man who could happily send the sick to their deaths was lacking in any moral scruples.

As Richard turned all this over in his mind, he found himself questioning the way his military colleagues hoped for the 'final victory'. He loved his home and his fatherland but victory would put a regime that he deeply despised and which had become a threat to him and his family permanently into power. On the other hand, he didn't want to live through another dispiriting period like after the last war. Whichever way he looked at it, he could see he would emerge from this war a loser, regardless of how it ended.

Chapter 39

'You know how much I appreciate your visits, my dear Frau Hellmer, but you need to be careful. Walls have ears here, and eyes as well.' Dr Stamm gave a weary sigh. 'Our Aryan neighbours are constantly watching to see who comes here and waste no time in informing on visitors.'

'That may be so,' said Paula, 'but I'm not letting that frighten me away. The Nuremberg Laws don't forbid Aryans from paying a call on a Jew. And it's certainly nothing more than a friendly visit. And I certainly didn't know those laws prohibited anyone from bringing a home-made cake along.' With that she placed her basket on the table and lifted out an apple cake.

'Oh, you shouldn't have,' protested Dr Stamm, but Paula could see how genuinely touched he was.

'Oh, but I had to! Our neighbours at the allotments have showered us with apples and they've got to be put to good use, haven't they?' She tried to lift his mood, but with little success. It was as if oppression and despair had infiltrated every corner of his home.

'Thank you so much,' said Dr Stamm. 'Perhaps it is a fitting farewell gift to be able to enjoy the last fruits of summer in a cake.'

'Farewell gift?' Paula was puzzled. 'Have you decided to leave Germany after all?'

'We non-Aryans no longer decide anything for ourselves. No, I have not decided to do so, but in October we have to report for resettlement.'

'Resettlement?' Paula stared at him. 'And where are you supposed to go for resettlement?'

The elderly doctor shrugged. 'I don't know. Somewhere in the new eastern regions. We've already been given a list of what we're allowed to take with us. It's not much. One suitcase per person and a limited amount of cash.'

Paula gasped. 'And your flat? What will happen to your flat, your furniture and everything?'

'Presumably some kind of enforced contribution to the German war effort or the NSDAP.'

Paula was lost for words. Everything in her heart cried out that this couldn't be so, that it was unjust, that this couldn't be happening in a civilised country like Germany, and yet at the same time she knew she was deceiving herself to think this way.

'I have never told you why my husband's at the Front,' she said. 'He was dismissed from his post because he had uncovered something monstrous and tried to fight against it.'

'What did he uncover?' Seeing the old gentleman's weary eyes spark with interest, Paula told him of Richard's battle, everything from the forced sterilisation plans to the transfer of his patients and their deliberate murder.

'I had always believed we were a civilised nation,' Paula concluded, 'and I'd like to go on seeing us that way, but whatever we ourselves may believe, the present government's nothing more than a gang of murderers and sadists who attract more like them. Before Hitler came to power, Richard was a respected psychiatrist and a valued expert witness and the man who dismissed him would never have become a leading consultant, given his negative attitude towards the sick. But he wormed his way into the senior post on the heels of a Jewish colleague who had been discharged, become a party member and Richard's superior. After Richard was dismissed, it was only with the support of his closest friend and a renowned professor of surgery that he got to be a medical officer in Africa. He'd probably otherwise have ended up as an auxiliary in a punishment battalion on the Eastern Front.' She swallowed hard. 'Is there no chance of you avoiding this deportation, Dr Stamm?'

He looked at her with his kind but tired eyes, placed his right hand comfortingly on her shoulder and said, 'Oh yes there is, my dear, there is a way, and we'll do it when the time is right.'

Although there was sadness in his voice, he sounded so serene that Paula returned home feeling calm and comforted.

◆ ◆ ◆

Two weeks later she heard that Dr Stamm had died. The exact circumstances of his death were not clear. Gossip from some of their neighbours suggested that he and his wife had killed themselves because of the threatened deportation. Others claimed the old doctor had suffered a stroke and died of a brain haemorrhage after his wife had been struck down by pneumonia. Whoever Paula asked, no one could tell her with any certainty what had happened and her fear grew that he had taken his own life in order to escape the worst. But what was the worst? Being resettled and uprooted? Or the suspicion that Jewish citizens were about to meet the same fate as the sick? The very thought sent a shudder down Paula's spine, and she wished Richard were there to listen to her fears. She didn't want to entrust her suspicions to the military postal service.

All this made October 1941 the darkest month of Paula's life.

◆ ◆ ◆

Fritz came home on leave at Christmas, bringing Richard's presents for Paula and the children with him, including the promised shoes.

Fritz clearly felt terrible that Richard was spending Christmas at the Front and not coming back on home leave before January.

'We couldn't both be away at the same time.' He looked embarrassed as he explained it to Paula. 'I wanted Richard to toss a coin for it but he insisted I travel back to the children for Christmas. He said it was because my intervention had got him in the medical corps in the first place, and that Henriette and Harri are much younger than Georg and Emilia. That's why he'll be here on 4 January, when I'm back at the Front.'

'Fritz, you don't need to justify anything! Richard's done the right thing, regardless of how much you've helped him. Your children are younger than ours and need their papa home at times like this. At least it was peacetime when the twins were little.'

'But they were only seven for the first wartime Christmas,' Fritz reminded her.

'That was before the bombing started, and we still had a normal family life. I hope you all have a wonderful Christmas! I know we will too, because we're so excited about Richard coming back in January.'

'Paula, you're marvellous. And now I have to do exactly what Richard instructed me to! He told me to give you a big hug from him.' He put his arms around her.

She hugged him tightly in return, enjoying the sense of security she'd had to do without for so long. 'And you're a wonderful friend, Fritz. The best in the world.'

'Now you're embarrassing me again.'

'That's the price you pay for bringing Christmas gifts!' she said smiling, then let him go.

◆ ◆ ◆

With the prospect of Richard's much-anticipated home leave, Paula and her children managed to enjoy Christmas in spite of the painful gap in their lives. Paula's father spent Christmas Eve with them, bringing gifts for the children. For Georg there was a toy rifle, studded with silver nails like the weapon used by his favourite Apache character, Winnetou, and he was beside himself with delight. For Emilia there was the Karl May trilogy, *Satan and Ischariot*.

'These were always my favourites, Emilia,' explained her grandfather. 'The first book's set in America, then in the second one Winnetou comes to Dresden to set off for the Middle East with his white blood brother, Old Shatterhand. Then in the third book, they're back in America.'

Emilia was agog. 'Winnetou was here? In Germany?'

'Yes, and the Middle East too, among the Arabs. I think in the book they even go to places your father is seeing. They have lots of exciting adventures.'

'Papa sent us a photo of real belly dancers,' said Emilia. 'Have you ever seen anything like that?'

'No, but now you're making me curious!'

And so, after the traditional Christmas Eve exchange of gifts, the little family spent the evening going through the many photos that Richard had managed to enclose in nearly every letter.

Paula always marvelled at how Richard's pictures managed to give the impression of a research trip and not a tour of duty. As well as the belly dancers, there were landscapes with palm trees, sunsets, locals in exotic robes and even one of a Bedouin with his camels.

'Well, well, it wouldn't surprise me if your papa sent us a photo of Hadschi Halef Omar's grandchildren. You remember all those adventures in the Middle East that I've told you from Karl May's other books, about the faithful Muslim and his friend, the German explorer Kara Ben Nemsi?' said Paula's father with a smile when Georg excitedly showed him the one with the camels. Then he said to his daughter, 'He could have done far worse, you know. From what my patients tell me about the Eastern Front, it's appalling and has little or nothing to do with all that propaganda in the weekly newsreels.'

Paula nodded. 'Yes, you're right. And I'm so grateful to Fritz for getting Richard into his battalion.'

◆ ◆ ◆

The fourth of January 1942 fell on a Sunday. The thaw had started, the sky was grey, and it looked like rain. For the first time in months, Paula and the children collected their car from her father-in-law's garage, and set off to meet Richard at the railway station.

Men in uniform were everywhere, some saying goodbye to their families, others being joyfully welcomed home. Paula spotted only three men wearing civvies, and they were a ripe old age. It also struck her that hardly any of the train and platform staff were men. Women were clearly in the majority among the civilian population that thronged the station and staffed the railway. She couldn't help but think back to the late 1920s and how tough it had been for her to secure any professional post, all because she was a married woman. She'd even heard how other married women, whether childless or with older families, had been encouraged by the National Socialist Women's League to take up their previous professions once more, or had been drafted into semi-skilled work previously done by men. Paula saw this not as liberation but as a slap in the face. Women were nothing more than the silent reserve. While the men were at war, they were being trusted to keep the country going, but once it was over they would be squeezed back into subservient roles and ousted from any positions of responsibility. She thought of Leonie – this attitude was precisely what Leonie had been so critical of and had actually stopped her from wanting to marry. Since the war had started, their exchange of letters had dwindled. Post from abroad was viewed with suspicion, even if posted in neutral Switzerland. At least Leonie had got out at the right time and escaped the horror. Paula didn't like to think what might have happened to her friend if she hadn't emigrated in 1936. Now she had a good job as a paediatrician in a hospital in Berne, while her father was in general practice with a Swiss colleague. They had a good living and could sleep at night, safe in the knowledge that their peace wouldn't be shattered by air raids.

The barely intelligible public address system announced the arrival of Richard's train on platform eight.

'That's Papa's train,' Emilia signed to Georg, who was already hopping from one foot to the other in his excitement.

Puffing and steaming, the train pulled alongside the huge concourse, its brakes screeching so loudly that Emilia covered her ears, while Georg couldn't take his eyes off the engine. When the train stopped, what seemed to be hundreds of men in grey uniform poured out of the carriages and flooded on to the platform. Paula wondered how she would ever find Richard in this mass of uniforms, while Emilia clambered up on a bench for a better view.

'Emilia, don't put your mucky shoes on the bench – the next person to sit there will get filthy!'

Emilia promptly shifted to the arm, trying to keep her balance as her eyes took in the whole platform while she shouted, 'Papa! Papa! We're here!' A lot of men turned in her direction, thinking they were being called, but quickly saw it wasn't for them.

The platform gradually emptied and Emilia was still shouting out.

'Emilia, get down now,' said Paula.

'But where's Papa?'

'Knowing him, he decided to let everyone get off first so as not to have to push his way through the crowds.'

And there were indeed still some men disembarking, mostly officers from the rear coaches. Paula took a closer look.

'There he is – at the front of that group!' she called out. Then she shouted even more loudly than Emilia, 'Richard – we're here!'

Emilia joined in, waving furiously. 'Papa! Here we are!'

The combination of both voices must have carried over the background noise, and Richard turned towards them, saw his family and broke into a run. Paula and the twins did the same. Emilia and Georg reached him first. Richard let go of his case and wrapped his arms right around the twins.

'Look how you've both grown! It's been such a long time!'

Then he turned to Paula and held her close. 'I've missed you so much!' he whispered, then kissed her with all the passion he'd stored up over their ten-month separation, blissfully disregarding their surroundings. Paula felt so happy in his love, in his firm embrace, in the feeling that she could let herself go and not bear the burden of responsibility alone, even if only for seven days. Seven days. One week after ten months apart. She was grateful for every single minute.

When they eventually let go of one another, she took a closer look at him. Had he changed? His eyes still had that old gleam, the one that signalled the unshakeable optimism that had carried him through so many tough times.

She linked her arm through his and, slowly, they walked to the car.

'Would you like to drive?' asked Paula.

'Oh no, I'll enjoy being chauffeured by you,' he said, putting his case in the boot and holding the door open for the children to clamber aboard. Then he took his seat beside her in the front. Only then did he take off his cap.

'Greying at the temples, eh?' she commented, giving him a sidelong glance.

'That's right.' He ran his hand over his hair. 'Shall I get the boot polish to it?' he said with a grin.

'Don't you dare! I love you just as you are. Don't change a thing and, anyway, you'd ruin the pillowcases.'

Emilia giggled from the back and Paula saw in the rear-view mirror how she was signing the conversation for Georg.

'Or we could just get black bed linen,' came Richard's retort. 'Hey, maybe we should try that. Get away from the old hospital white.'

'Black bed linen? Is there such a thing?'

'Oh yes, very popular in certain circles. There are even sheets of red silk – only hearsay, of course. Never been in such establishments myself.'

'I didn't think so; otherwise, you'd have sent us photos!' said Paula.

Richard burst out laughing and Paula joined in. The children laughed with them, innocently unaware of all the deliberate ambiguities.

Richard's parents and his sister had prepared an enormous spread to welcome him back, particularly as Karl also had home leave and had come back from France just one day before Richard.

'I've been really lucky,' his nephew told him. 'I made myself indispensable to the occupying troops at the right time and so didn't get sent off to the Eastern Front. It's really not a bad life in France.'

'So you're in charge, are you?' Richard loved teasing his nephew.

'Not exactly. I've ended up in military admin, nice little desk job – got a friend to thank for that,' Karl said with a grin. 'I got him out of a real mess and he did me a favour in return.'

'A real mess? Sounds like a good story there!' Richard was eager for more.

'It's more for men's ears.' Karl glanced at the children and shot Richard a conspiratorial look.

'And how's life in Africa?' Richard's father cut in to change the subject. 'The newsreel only tells us about all the victories for the Africa Corps. Sounds like a lot of heroic yarns to me.'

'To be honest, I don't play a part in any heroic deeds,' replied Richard. 'We've been working pretty comfortably in the main military hospital in Tripoli, but I think that could change this year. There's a push towards Tobruk, and that'd put Tripoli not far from the front line. I'll be fine as long as we carry on being deployed where we are, and I just hope I'll be spared the field hospital.'

'How's it different? The main one from the field hospital?' asked Margit.

'In the main military hospital, you're miles away from the fighting and work in relative safety. It's more like a normal hospital with various specialist departments. The other kind of hospital, the field unit, is located out of enemy reach but is mostly busy with emergency surgery and the badly wounded with a view either to getting them back to operational fitness as soon as possible, or sending them on to the main military hospital for further recovery. It's really hard work.

'When Fritz was on home leave, we had a surgeon in from the field hospital to cover for him. I haven't got enough surgical experience to fully deputise for him, you see. If the operation's not complicated, I can do it, but Fritz is a real wizard when it comes to finding solutions in complicated cases. He's developed two new surgical methods and has passed these on to Professor Wehmeyer for the next research paper. I reckon Fritz will be heading for a professorship himself after the war.' Richard smiled gently.

'But I digress,' he went on. 'The stand-in surgeon from the field hospital said working with us was like a holiday, with everything done according to a timetable and Tripoli being such a pleasant place. There are hardly any air attacks and, if there are, well, it's all dealt with through aerial combat. The Brits fly over, our people take off to meet them, and then it's fighter pilot against fighter pilot.'

'That'll be like Hans-Joachim Marseille, then,' butted in Karl. 'All the newsreels are full of him as the big hero. Have you come across him?'

'No, we have virtually no contact at all with fighter pilots. They live in their own world. And any fighter pilot who doesn't get out in time when he's shot at – well, he doesn't come to us in the hospital. He ends up in the heroes' graveyard.'

An awkward silence fell around the table.

'Don't let's deceive ourselves,' said Richard. 'No matter what the weekly propaganda tells you, men are fighting and dying at the front.

Daring deeds come at a price. I'm very glad I'm only in the third row and have never had to act the hero.'

'Don't do yourself down, Richard,' said Paula. 'It was your heroic work that got you sent to the front in the first place.'

'My failure, you mean, surely?'

The bitterness in his voice took her breath away.

'You didn't fail.'

'I did. Because I took it too far. I wanted to save everyone and in the end saved no one.'

'That's not true, Richard,' piped up Margit. 'Just think of Manfred and Rolf, the twins here. Or Johannes Mönicke. You saved all of them. Johannes has turned out so well. He's living with his family again and comes here to work just like any of our other journeymen. OK, he's not quite as productive as someone who's fully fit, but it's amazing how being included here at the joinery has helped him get back a sense of normality. And his wife is so happy about everything.'

Richard didn't say anything, although it was clear how Margit's words had moved him.

◆ ◆ ◆

Once Richard and Paula were back in their own flat that evening, he showed the children how to develop a film and let them enjoy seeing how the images slowly came to life in their makeshift darkroom. And so in their own bathroom they saw photos of the crossing from Africa back to Italy, brilliant blue skies and an enemy destroyer on the horizon at a safe distance, the Italian coast, the main station at Rome where they had changed trains, and then some landscapes he'd taken from the moving train.

Eventually, he got the children to bed and sat with them until they fell asleep, while Paula sorted out which of his clothes needed to be taken for laundering by their daily help the next day.

She'd just finished the job when Richard came out of the children's bedroom.

'Are they asleep?' she asked him.

'Like little dormice,' he said, pulling her towards him. 'I hope we don't hear the sirens tonight. I've wanted you for so long.'

'And me you,' she said, smiling at him. 'We've got some catching up to do.'

He swept her off her feet suddenly, like a bride being carried across the threshold. 'Then let's get started before some idiotic Tommy interrupts us with his bombs.'

Chapter 40

Richard's home leave was over much too fast. When Paula drove him back to the railway station with the children the following Sunday, she wondered where the time had gone.

'I hope it won't be so long this time before we're together again,' she whispered to him. 'I don't know how I'm going to stand it without you.'

'Remember we're not alone. You've got the whole family around you, and I've got Fritz, at least.' Before she had a chance to reply, he drew her close and embraced her with the same passion as when he first came home.

'Take good care of yourself and the children.' Then he hugged Georg and Emilia and got on the train.

The twins stood on the platform, waving until the train was out of sight.

'Mama, do you think we're going to win the war this year, and then Papa can come home again?' asked Emilia.

'I don't know.' It struck Paula for the first time how everyone around her, including the children, constantly spoke of victory. They would win the war and then it would be over. Even if they were right, what would happen then? Her mind went back to the conversations she and Richard had had in the privacy of their bedroom, undisturbed, with no one to overhear them. 'However the war ends, we'll be the losers,' he'd said. 'If we win, just think how that would strengthen Hitler – he'd be so powerful, he'd be out of control, and I don't know how I'd keep silent about the injustices going on here. And if we lose, well, it'll be even worse than the last time.'

'What makes you think that?'

'Because this time the war's raging all around us here at home,' he explained. 'Every single bomb that hits our city and kills innocent civilians stirs up more hatred and makes people even more defiant. The desire for vengeance and retribution will drive even youngsters to man the flak guns. You only have to listen to Emilia. Looking at it from where she stands, she's quite right. She needs to feel angry so she can take action and not be suffocated by the fear. And the whole population needs that too. The war fires everyone up, and the worse it gets, the worse the mutual hatred, and the end can only come when the enemy is wiped out. And that's either them or us.'

The bitterness in Richard's voice shocked her. 'Richard, tell me what you really saw at the Front.'

'Nothing worse than I've seen here. In fact, I think the children have something even worse to struggle with, and that's the loss of faith in having any safety in bed at night.'

'Emilia and Georg have faith in our flak guns.'

'Yes, that's true, but only until the first house in our road is destroyed, and with it the myth of our all-conquering army that protects us from every evil.' He took a deep breath. 'And there's nothing, absolutely nothing, we can do about it. Whatever the outcome, we lose. I've often wondered what would have happened to me if my falsified registration forms had been found in a different era. With no war going on. With no Front for an insubordinate doctor to be sent to. Maybe I'd have ended up like Alfred Schär. I don't know how I'll live with the injustice if the Nazis achieve their final victory and Hitler's ideology reigns everywhere. And I'm fearful that we won't be able to protect Georg for ever.'

'We'll always protect our children, Richard. We'll find ways, no matter what happens.' She snuggled in close, sensing how her presence gave him some reassurance.

◆ ◆ ◆

After Richard's departure, Paula felt empty. It was even worse than after the first time because she now knew the difference between the reports in his letters where he tried to paint a positive picture for her and the children and his real thinking. Yes, he was still intrinsically optimistic but his confidence had taken a severe beating. And she feared that being apart from his family again could cause him to lose it completely.

With the arrival of May, the days grew warmer and so Paula spent weekends and school holidays at her parents-in-law's allotment garden. The children loved the simple, natural life there but what Paula treasured even more was their relative safety from the air raids.

At the end of May came the traditional Whitsun holiday, and they spent it outdoors with their neighbours. There were barbecues and Georg and his friend Horst enjoyed bathing in the little tributary of the Elbe, while Emilia told them they were crazy to swim in such cold water.

'Red Indians know no pain,' announced Horst. 'And it's not surprising that Kolma Puschi stays away from the water, 'cos if she put on a swimsuit, everyone would know she isn't really a man at all.'

'And she's a chilly mortal anyway,' said Georg, his words beautifully clear. Whenever he was with Horst, he made huge efforts with his enunciation and his friend always made sure Georg could see his lips. He'd also learned some of the gestures that Georg recognised so well.

'What on earth's a "chilly mortal"?' asked Emilia.

'It's what Uncle Erich always says,' retorted Horst. 'It's what you are. The water's fine.'

'No, it isn't, silly! I bet you'll both have colds tomorrow.'

'Oh no, we won't!' Horst shot back. 'We're tough nuts – we can put up with anything!'

That night Georg said he had a sore throat.

'Told you,' said Emilia. 'Winnetou isn't such a tough nut after all, and I'm sure Old Shatterhand has got it too.'

By morning, Georg had a high temperature. Paula was horrified when she looked inside his mouth at his throat. The white coating was an unmistakable sign of diphtheria. Emilia had no symptoms at all.

'You've spent the last few days with Horst, haven't you?'

Georg nodded.

'Then I must go and see him.' Paula pulled on her cardigan and went off to knock at Horst's grandmother's cabin on her allotment.

'Good morning. I've just come to ask how Horst is today.'

'The boy caught a terrible cold somewhere yesterday; a bad sore throat too. I've made him some camomile tea. Is Georg sick too?'

Paula came straight to the point. 'Yes, but this is no ordinary cold. It looks like diphtheria.'

Horst's grandma was puzzled. 'But they all had their inoculation. It can't be.'

'I'd still like to examine him. Inoculation doesn't always give full protection.'

Horst was as poorly as Georg. One look inside his throat confirmed her suspicions.

'It's diphtheria,' Paula said to his grandmother. 'We must take both of them to the children's hospital at Rothenburgsort straight away.'

So Georg and Horst didn't get to spend those early summer days in their paradise at the allotments, but on Paula's old ward at the children's hospital. She felt a trace of wistfulness for her old life when she arrived but was anxious for the lads too. Although she knew the illness would be a little less severe due to the boys' previous inoculations, she was painfully aware that a period of unpleasant treatment and a mass of injections lay ahead for them both.

'At least you're not on your own here,' she said as she prepared to leave them. 'You two friends will see it through together, I know.'

'Like Papa and Uncle Fritz in Africa,' Georg replied, taking the greatest of care how he enunciated every word. Paula had drummed it into him that at the hospital he was to use spoken language only. Georg had no idea why this mattered so much, but he'd made a promise to his mother and Paula was sure he'd do it for Horst's sake too.

As Paula left the ward, she caught Horst saying to Georg, 'We'll escape before anyone ties us to the stake!' and she couldn't help but smile, in spite of the gravity of their condition. She felt sorry for Emilia, as the boys were her best and only playmates. She wondered if this might change in August, when the twins would turn ten. This meant the two boys would have to join the Hitler Youth junior wing and Emilia the League of German Girls. Richard loathed the Hitler Youth, as did Paula, but membership of both was compulsory and there was no way of avoiding it. Paula hoped that at least the company of other girls for once would be good for Emilia and that she'd have fun at the outdoor camps and make friends. It was Georg she was worried about. The deaf and dumb were routinely excluded from the Hitler Youth and it was doubtful whether Georg would be accepted as hard of hearing and not deaf. What would happen if someone uncovered his secret?

Paula composed herself. They weren't there yet. What mattered now was to get both boys better.

During the week following Whitsun, the sirens went almost every night. Paula and Emilia would hurry down to the cellar, but their thoughts were always with Georg and Horst. The seriously ill and infectious couldn't ever be taken down to the hospital air-raid shelter. She hoped the boys would help one another through it. Fortunately, another letter from Richard had recently arrived to divert her mind from these worries.

My dearest Paula

I don't know when this will reach you, but we've now left Tripoli and are in a field hospital outside Tobruk. The work here is so different from the civilised, leisurely existence we had in Tripoli, but we're still a good way from the Front. As ever, Fritz is our best surgeon, and for the first time I don't feel like a useless hanger-on because we've got a lot of distressed and traumatised men here. Up to now they've been on the receiving end of the tough old 'cruel to be kind' approach that's supposed to get them back on duty. It took me a while to persuade people to let me do things my way, but when they actually saw it working I got my own allocated area and am now responsible for getting our men back to strength mentally.

    Calming people who are utterly terrified and lashing out in all directions is no easy matter. In many cases only an intravenous dose of Evipan works. I hit on the idea when I was dealing with a man we just couldn't bring under control and we were afraid he would beat some of us to a pulp. I thought that whatever helps administer an anaesthetic effect must surely help here too. The result was astounding. He fell asleep straight away, and when he woke up, his nerves had settled completely. It was as if he'd woken from a nightmare with a bad head and now felt ashamed of his previous behaviour. This worked the same way a second time. Since then I've used varying doses of Evipan, depending on how badly the patient is suffering. I know this can't be a long-term treatment because there's a risk of addiction, as with morphine. But when it comes to breaking the vicious cycle of panic, anxiety, panic and making the patient somehow receptive again, this is ideal. I have even observed how a lower dosage can facilitate the use of suggestion to restore the inner equilibrium.

I'd never have thought I could make myself more useful as a psychiatrist at the Front than at the main military hospital. I haven't yet seen any cases of shell shock here and that's probably because we're not forced to crawl through the trenches in constant fear of gas attacks and being buried alive. No, the dangers here go by the name of bombs, grenades, tanks and gunfire. And then, of course, there's the constant worry about our loved ones at home, where we can't protect them.

Don't be concerned about me – nobody attacks a field hospital. As soon as we're in Tobruk, I'll send you photos.

With my love
Richard

Nobody attacks a field hospital. How dearly Paula wanted to believe that – and that nobody would bomb a children's hospital either. But three days after Richard's letter came, her worst fears were realised. This time the aircraft struck by daylight and specifically bombarded residential areas. Three homes went up in flames only one street away, but far worse for Paula was the gigantic column of fire rising from the direction of the children's hospital. The news spread in no time. The hospital had received a direct hit.

Fear gripped Paula. As soon as the all-clear sounded, she told Emilia to hurry to Aunt Margit's house while she herself got out her bike and set off for the children's hospital.

The fire brigade were already there. Apart from the fire itself, she saw little damage.

'Where are the children?' she cried. 'My son's here!'

'Ask over there,' replied the fireman, pointing towards the hospital gardens, where a group of nurses tried to calm anxious parents.

'Frau Doctor Hellmer!'

Paula turned towards the voice. 'Sister Elfriede?'

'You'll be here for Georg. Nothing to worry about – they're all safe. After the first attack we evacuated all the children to a number of shelters. There were a couple of minor injuries from flying glass. The children's hospital has taken over some of the old pavilions at Langenhorn asylum, so we're moving the children there.'

At first she felt only relief that the children were safe, but then Paula registered fully what Sister Elfriede had said. 'Langenhorn? Under Dr Krüger?'

'Yes, but the treatment will be as it is here. Some of our staff are being allocated to Langenhorn while the hospital is repaired.'

'Are you going too?'

Sister Elfriede nodded.

'Then please keep an eye on Georg. My husband and Dr Krüger clashed over a number of matters and I'm afraid that could interfere with Georg's treatment.'

'I'm sure Dr Krüger doesn't have time to wage a vendetta against an innocent child.'

'I pray you're right. But please take great care of him in any case. If anything strikes you as odd, please phone me immediately.'

'Of course.' Sister Elfriede took a notebook and pencil from her uniform pocket to write down Paula's number.

'Do you know where Georg and Horst are now?'

'They're probably already on the way to Langenhorn. You can visit tomorrow afternoon.'

'Thank you, Sister Elfriede.'

◆ ◆ ◆

Georg and Horst had got through the bombardment without physical injuries, even though the glass wall separating the beds from the office had shattered into a thousand pieces, depositing fragments all over the bedspreads. Not so lucky was Dieter, the five-year-old in the bed next to Horst. He hadn't noticed the cuts to his face and burst into tears as soon as Horst pointed them out. Perhaps the worst thing had been the nurses' obvious panic as they frantically pulled the children from their beds and hurried them in nightclothes and slippers to shelters nearby, when, as a rule, they were not allowed even to get out of bed. During air raids they normally stayed put, secure in the knowledge that the flak rockets would protect them and that hospitals were never attacked.

'I'd never have thought our flak would let all this through,' said Horst to Georg as they waited it out in the air-raid shelter.

'Must have been too many planes,' Georg reasoned. 'They just couldn't hit everything.'

'Blasted Tommies,' cursed Horst. 'Now they're bombing hospitals, and that's not allowed. It's forbidden – my grandma told me.'

'I want to shoot them all down,' said Georg, 'but we can't be flak auxiliaries till we're fourteen.'

'The war'll be over by then.'

At Langenhorn they had adjacent beds, like before.

'Didn't your papa used to treat the lunatics here?' asked Horst.

Georg nodded.

'And d'you think there're still lunatics here?'

Georg shrugged.

'Shall we go and find some?' suggested Horst. 'I've never seen a real lunatic before. Have you?'

'No. And we're supposed to stay in bed,' said Georg firmly.

'Hey, come on – let's see if we can find the lunatics.' Horst got out of bed, gingerly at first, and peeped through the door of the observation room. 'The coast is clear – nobody there. Come on!'

Georg's weakened state made him hesitate at first, but he didn't want to be left behind so he followed Horst. The door leading to the garden was open but nobody was outside. 'No lunatics here at all,' he said.

'Maybe they've been sent to the Front as well?' Horst wondered.

'Lunatics can't be soldiers,' retorted Georg.

'So why's your father at the Front if there are no lunatics there?'

'He does operations there, and if anyone new goes mad, then he does the treatment.'

'And do many go mad there?'

'Don't know.'

'What are you two doing here?' A nurse had spotted them in the garden. 'You're supposed to stay in bed until you're better!'

'We, er, we were looking for the toilet,' fibbed Horst.

'You're not allowed to get up yet at all, and if you must go, young man, you ring the bell, if you don't mind!'

'Yes, but I can't always do it in the bedpan. I wanted a proper toilet.'

'And you thought you'd find one in the garden?'

'We went the wrong way,' said Horst. 'It's quite confusing here. And anyway, we thought there were lunatics here.'

'Lunatics?'

'Yes, there always used to be. His father gave them treatment 'cos he's a psy— . . . psych— . . . mad-doctor.' Horst gestured towards Georg.

'Something wrong, Nurse Susanne?' A tall man in a white coat came towards them.

'I think these two wanted to see some lunatics.'

'Lunatics?' The doctor raised his eyebrows in surprise. 'You wanted to see real lunatics?' He gave Horst a hard look, then Georg.

'Will you show us some?' asked Horst.

'There are no lunatics here, just two naughty boys.'

'Dr Krüger, what shall I do with the pair of them?' asked the nurse.

'Send them both to bed.'

But Horst didn't let it drop. 'Georg's papa used to look after the lunatics here.'

'Georg?' Krüger repeated the name, then stared at Georg once more. 'Tell me, boy, is your full name Georg Hellmer?'

Georg had no difficulty lip-reading the doctor's words and was aware of something malicious in the man's eyes, something he didn't like.

'Yes.'

'Take this one back to his bed, nurse. I'm going to have a little chat with Georg.'

Chapter 41

Georg felt very unsure as he followed Dr Krüger into the examination room of the ward. There was a couch, a weighing machine, a white medicine cupboard – which reminded Georg of the kitchen cupboard at home, except that was oak – a writing desk and two chairs. Not one single picture decorated the sterile white walls, not even one of Hitler. The only wall decoration was a height scale for measuring the patients.

His father had never told him much about his work and, unlike Emilia, he had never been able to listen in on any of his parents' conversations. But he remembered all too well his mother's concern as she repeatedly impressed upon him that he was never to tell anyone that he was completely deaf. Why this was such a problem he really didn't know, as he had never felt in any way rejected for his deafness. Yet this Dr Krüger scared him in a way he couldn't explain.

The doctor sat down at his desk and gestured at the chair in front of it.

'So you're Dr Hellmer's son,' said Krüger. Georg was glad the man was facing him as this meant he could lip-read without any trouble. It was bad when people turned away without realising but carried on talking.

'Yes,' said Georg, concentrating on the best possible enunciation.

'Where is your father now?'

'In Africa.'

'The Africa Corps. Interesting. He's been lucky there too.' There was that nasty smile again. 'You speak astonishingly well.'

Georg said nothing.

'For a child born deaf.'

Georg still said nothing. An icy chill ran down his spine.

'Your father used to try and tell me you were only hard of hearing.'

'I am hard of hearing,' confirmed Georg. 'That's why I need to see people's lips.'

'You have a twin sister, is that so?'

'Yes.'

'Can she hear normally?'

'Yes.'

Krüger folded his hands and rested his chin on them, partly covering his lips.

'Definitely . . . deaf . . . liar.' Georg made out these three words.

Krüger lowered his hands.

'Nothing to say?'

'I didn't fully understand you then,' retorted Georg. 'I didn't see your lips. I heard only the words "definitely", "deaf" and "liar".'

'You're a remarkable boy, Georg. As gifted a liar as your father. I intend to examine you more thoroughly over the next few days. This seems to me to be a very interesting case of hereditary deafness.'

'How can anyone inherit deafness?' asked Georg, looking puzzled. 'You only inherit things from dead people. When someone deaf dies, they can't leave it to anyone. And I've never inherited anything from anyone.'

For a moment or two Krüger seemed nonplussed. 'You're very quick-witted for a nine-year-old. Just like your father, which is not necessarily a good thing.' He stood up. 'I'll take you back to the observation room.'

'What on earth did he want with you?' asked Horst as soon as his friend came back.

'He asked me about my father and kept wanting me to say I was deaf, but Mama told me nobody here is to know that so I told him I'm just hard of hearing.'

'I won't say anything,' promised Horst. 'There's something strange about that doctor.'

'Yes, very strange. I don't think he likes my father and so he doesn't like me either. He said he wanted to examine me some more.'

'That sounds uncomfortable.'

'Yes,' said Georg, fighting back the fear.

◆ ◆ ◆

The next day Paula came to visit her son and heard about his encounter with Krüger. Georg's fear was apparent and her own anxiety became almost overwhelming. She tried not to let him see she felt the same, however, and promised that nothing would happen to him.

'I'll talk to the doctor. He's an old colleague of your father's. He'll listen to me, and there'll be no unnecessary examinations, I promise,' she said, although she wasn't sure how far she could really keep that promise.

After she'd spent as long as possible with Georg, she sought out Krüger's office. His secretary tried in vain to keep her out. She was no match for an anxious mother.

Dr Krüger took it all very calmly. 'Frau Doctor Hellmer, I'm delighted to meet you.' His courtesy was exaggerated. 'Please do have a seat. What did you want to discuss with me?'

Paula accepted the seat offered and sat down on the other side of his desk. 'My son has told me you are planning to examine him further. As his mother, I'd like to know what this is about.'

'It's about treating his condition.'

'The diphtheria is already receiving suitable treatment. I know what I'm saying here as I worked as a doctor on the infection ward of the children's hospital for a whole year.'

'Yes, I know, Frau Doctor Hellmer.'

'Oh yes, I forgot – my husband told me how much pleasure you take in finding out about your colleagues' private lives.' Paula couldn't conceal her bitterness.

Krüger noticed the anger in her voice. 'Do you really think that's the right way to speak to me, Frau Doctor Hellmer? After all, you want something from me, don't you?'

'You're right,' conceded Paula. 'I want to appeal to you as a professional. I know that you and my husband had serious differences, but Georg is an innocent child. He doesn't deserve to be drawn into this conflict.' She paused for breath. 'Besides, doesn't it give you enough satisfaction to know that my husband has been at the Front for the last fifteen months and in that whole time has spent only seven days with his family?'

Krüger smiled at her in the most arrogant way. 'Is that so?' he said. 'Your husband can consider himself lucky that we wanted to avoid any scandal and did nothing more than discharge him. He can cause less havoc at the Front than here.'

'He only ever wanted to help people.'

'He was guilty of deliberate insubordination and went against express instructions. There is no excuse for wilful falsification of an expert statement.'

Paula managed to swallow her rebuke on the tip of her tongue. She knew that if she annoyed Krüger any further there could be fatal consequences, and not only for Georg.

'My husband bears the consequences of what he did,' she said, 'and that's for him alone to bear, Herr Doctor Krüger. Don't drag my son into your conflict with my husband.'

'Don't worry, Frau Doctor Hellmer.' There was that superior smile again. 'I'm only doing my duty, and that includes comprehensive examination and treatment of all my patients. To all appearances, your son is deaf, although he speaks remarkably well for a child born deaf.'

'My son was not born deaf! His hearing ability was severely impaired by a complication during the birth.' Paula was vehement.

'If your son really is only hard of hearing, then there may be ways in which his hearing ability can be improved. But if he is deaf, then it is our duty to report it in accordance with regulations. I'm sure you know that in cases of hereditary deafness we must take appropriate action.'

'His twin sister is perfectly healthy. He does not present any hereditary disease. We have documents which provide evidence of the difficult circumstances of his birth. He was born after his sister and had first to be turned in the womb and then delivered by forceps. I had an eighteen-hour labour.'

'Oh, but Frau Doctor Hellmer, we both know forceps delivery can't cause hearing loss.'

'His twin sister has perfectly normal hearing,' repeated Paula. 'It is out of the question that this is a hereditary condition.'

'Well, perhaps it is a hereditary condition that only female relatives carry without developing it themselves. Have you any brothers or sisters, Frau Doctor Hellmer?'

'I don't know what that has to do with you.'

'If you have no healthy male siblings, it is perfectly possible that deafness has been passed on, undiscovered for generations, by the women in your family and has now manifested itself for the first time in your son. All of this is worth looking into. It is possible that your daughter will also be subject to the Law for the Prevention of Progeny with Hereditary Diseases.'

'You can't be serious!' cried out Paula.

'I am perfectly serious, Frau Doctor Hellmer.' His face was cold and without expression. 'I serve Germany and the German people – something your husband will probably never understand.'

'My husband is serving Germany out there, where he's needed. He saves lives no matter where he is. How many lives have you saved, Herr Doctor Krüger?'

'By rooting out and destroying hereditary disease, we are saving the entire racial corpus of the people. And now you will have to excuse me, as I still have a lot to do. If your son's documentation fits with the truth, you will have nothing to fear. However, if my suspicion is confirmed and hereditary deafness is diagnosed, then the health police will be dealing with your daughter as well.' He got to his feet. 'I wish you a pleasant day, Frau Doctor Hellmer.'

Chapter 42

The conversation with Krüger left Paula stunned. In her desperation, she decided not to go straight home but to call on her father for help and advice.

Frau Koch opened the door to her. Her own flat had been bombed a few weeks earlier, so Dr Engelhardt was now letting out Paula's old room to her.

'What on earth has happened? Come in, come in, Frau Hellmer – you look quite devastated.'

'Well, yes, something devastating has happened all right.'

'Richard . . .?'

'No, no, don't worry, nobody's died,' Paula quickly said to reassure her, then went to find her father in their front room to tell him everything.

Dr Engelhardt was visibly shaken. He thought hard for a few moments before speaking. 'Would it help if I confirm to him that your mother's brother had normal hearing? There was no hereditary deafness on your mother's side.'

'I know that, Papa. I fear that you can confirm as much as you want but Krüger won't accept it. And because Uncle Bruno fell in the last war, Krüger will say you're biased. He'll have as little faith in what you say as he did in anything Richard said.'

A tear rolled down her cheek. 'I don't know what to do, Papa. It's so obvious that Krüger wants to take his revenge on Richard through our children, but I can't just take Georg out of hospital in his condition. Yes, I could treat him at home, but Krüger will have the Gesundheitspolizei on my back because Georg is still infectious.'

'Unless he can be discharged in the usual way.'

'But he's only been in hospital for three weeks. We both know that with this kind of infection it's four weeks of strict bed rest. He's still on an antitoxin and only people with up-to-date inoculations are allowed on the infection ward. No doctor in his right mind would discharge him early.'

'So we've got to ride it out for a week.'

'Yes, a whole week at the mercy of that brute. A week when it would be so easy for Krüger to see through our hard-of-hearing story. And who knows whether even then he'll let Georg come home. He might put him straight on the sterilisation list.'

'Nothing can happen that quickly, Paula. He has to get parental consent and you can find ways of stalling. Even if it comes to anything more, carrying out a sterilisation procedure on a child who has only just recovered from diphtheria would carry a significant risk. On top of that, Paula, he's only nine. You could play for time by giving official agreement but only when he's fourteen.'

'That's assuming a rational conversation with Krüger. With him it's not about applying the law but maliciously getting his own back on Richard. This is a man who has sent dozens of sick people to their deaths. If anything gets in his way, he'll simply quote the section of the law that says the head of an institution makes the decisions regarding sterilisations.'

Now the tears really flowed. Her father put his arms around her and held her close. They didn't speak and Paula's tears soon soaked the front of her father's shirt.

'Perhaps he needs some other problems to take his mind off Georg,' said her father eventually, breaking the silence.

Paula raised her head. 'What do you mean, Papa?'

'Hard times can drive any of us to a few dirty tricks. You know how Krüger denounced Richard to the Gestapo.'

'I'll never, ever forget that. I was so frightened for Richard.'

'Now we need to think something up, some malicious accusation, and then report him to the Gestapo anonymously. By the time he gets all that sorted out, Georg will be back home, safely discharged.'

'Papa, that's . . .'

'Evil, underhand and unlike me?' he said, smiling at her.

'No, I wanted to say that's ingenious!' She laughed. 'But it is, of course, also evil, underhand and unlike you in normal circumstances.'

'So we're agreed! All we need now is some credible accusation that'll get Krüger into real trouble.'

'That's tricky. He's such a pillar of the party.'

'That doesn't mean anything. We could hang something on him about homosexual activity, along the lines of what happened to Ernst Röhm. That's enough to ruin any Nazi.'

'Papa, I admire your imaginative powers, but isn't that a teeny bit far-fetched?'

'Why do you say that? Is he married?'

'No idea,' admitted Paula. 'I must confess I don't know anything about his private life.'

'That makes it more difficult.'

They both thought hard.

Paula had an idea. 'How about the black market? We could say he's secretly selling hospital supplies on the black market and so hospital medicines are falling into the hands of enemies of the state.'

'That would keep him tied up for a week while they check stocks of all the medical supplies. Unless someone's already been helping themselves, of course. Have you still got someone there you could trust to "relocate" something so that it takes a while to find it?'

'No, but we don't really need all that. Just a whiff of scandal like that around him will give him a bad week.'

'Good, so tomorrow I'll deliver an anonymous report on him to the Gestapo. Meanwhile, you can visit Georg every day and make sure he's discharged as soon as he's allowed.'

◆ ◆ ◆

Visits to the children's ward were normally only permitted on Wednesdays and Sundays, but because Paula had worked on the infection ward and still knew a few of the staff, she was allowed to see Georg outside visiting hours. She brought a tiny bag of toffees for him and Horst but advised them to hide the sweets from the nurses. Then she explained to Georg that he must continue to try and conceal his deafness from Krüger.

'If he wants to examine you, Georg, you must cry and tell him you've got a sore throat and a bad headache,' she told him. 'Don't cooperate with him, just whine and grizzle as much as you can. For a sick child, that's not a strange thing to do. Be quietly naughty – that's allowed!'

'Can I be naughty as well?' asked Horst.

'Yes, but don't take it too far! Just do it enough to stop Krüger doing anything straight away, so that he has to leave it all for the time being. He mustn't see that it's pretend. That's very important!'

'Mama, what'll happen if he realises I'm deaf?'

Paula hesitated. How was she going to explain the Law for the Prevention of Progeny with Hereditary Diseases to a nine-year-old?

'Dr Krüger believes that people who can't hear will have children who can't hear either, and he wants to wipe out deafness. He would carry out an operation to stop you ever being a father.'

'But Fräulein Felber's mother is deaf and Fräulein Felber can hear perfectly.'

'Exactly, and Dr Krüger is an idiot, but that doesn't stop him having the power to do these things and to push through his horrible opinions. And this is not only to do with you – he will make out that Emilia would pass on deafness to her children.'

'But Emilia can hear perfectly too.'

'As I said, Dr Krüger is an idiot – but a dangerous, scary idiot,' Paula said with a sigh.

'A real villain,' said Horst.

'Yes, a real villain, and a powerful villain at that. But you two can outfox him if you're really cunning and clever. Do everything to stop him being able to examine Georg. You only need to prevent it for one week and then everything will be all right.'

After his mother had gone, Georg spent a long time thinking about what she had said. He'd never thought about having his own children once he was a grown-up. And he certainly hadn't thought about whether they'd be able to hear or not. His deafness had never really been so important. Of course, it was often hard not to hear everything that was going on, but it had some advantages too, like not hearing all the air raids that Emilia and Horst had to endure. Why couldn't this stupid doctor leave him in peace?

Krüger didn't make an appearance until the ward round on the following day, when, one by one, he had a look at every child, a gaggle of nurses and young medics trailing in his wake. He didn't spend long on Horst but when he came to Georg's bed he pulled up a chair and sat down.

'How are you?' he asked Georg, looking him straight in the eye.

'I've got a sore throat and a headache,' replied Georg, mindful of his mother's warning. 'And I feel sick.'

'So, you're feeling sick. Are you going to vomit?'

'No.'

'Good. I've brought you something.' From the pocket of his white coat he took a small bell. 'I'd like to establish how severely hard of hearing you are. Sister Elfriede will ring the bell behind your back and you must tell me when you hear it.'

'I feel sick,' said Georg again. 'I've got a headache.'

'Sister Elfriede, you can start.'

'I feel so sick,' groaned Georg.

'Pull yourself together! Tell me when you hear the bell.'

Georg noticed how Horst leaned forward very slightly. A barely perceptible wink.

'It rang,' he said. *Do your worst*, he thought to himself.

Krüger registered surprise. 'Correct.'

'I feel so sick. Can't we stop now?'

'No, again.'

Just then, Georg noticed Horst sticking his finger down his throat and vomiting copiously all over Krüger's back.

'Ugh!' roared Krüger, shooting out of his chair. 'Why didn't you ask for the bowl?' He stripped off his soiled white coat and let it drop to the floor.

'I feel so sick too,' groaned Horst.

The sight of the vomit combined with its smell made Georg's own tummy rebel. Almost immediately, he vomited all over his bed.

Krüger was almost beside himself now. 'Sister Elfriede, clear up this mess. And I need a fresh coat.' He left the room.

Georg noticed the ghost of a smile flit across Sister Elfriede's face as she stripped off his bedding and took it to the laundry bin.

'That was really disgusting,' said Georg.

'Yes, I had to force it,' admitted Horst. 'But hard times serve to make us stronger is what my grandma always says.' He rummaged inside the drawer of his bedside chest for the toffees they'd stowed away and fished out two.

'To take away the vile taste,' he said to Georg, handing him one and putting the other in his own mouth.

The following night there was another air-raid warning. Georg realised this when he saw Horst creep right down under the bedclothes, and this meant, of course, that he couldn't see him to talk. He guessed a lot of the children were whimpering, some crying out in fear as memories of the bombing of Rothenburgsort flooded back. The nurses dashed frantically between the rows of beds, threatening 'jabs' for those who couldn't be quiet. This was the most shocking sight of all – trusted adults showing their own fear. Cracks began to appear in Georg's safe world, and in his faith that grown-ups could always protect it. He longed for his mother and sister.

When Paula came to visit the following day she heard from Sister Elfriede how Georg and Horst had thwarted all Krüger's attempts at examination.

'I think the boys were quite right,' said Elfriede. 'Dr Krüger homed in on Georg straight away. We must make sure he's discharged as soon as possible. His test results are very good now, and I've already spoken to Dr Braun about him. He feels we could let him go as early as Thursday, as long as you can personally nurse him once he's home.'

Paula was so relieved. 'Thank you, Sister Elfriede!' Dr Braun was one of her previous colleagues from her year at the children's hospital. He was a kindly, rather retiring man, never one to push himself forward, dedicated to the welfare of his little patients. 'I just hope Krüger will leave the boy in peace now.'

'I hear he has a few other problems at the moment. Did you know he's suspected of sequestering medical supplies to sell on the black market?'

'Good heavens! That's monstrous!'

'He claims it's all malicious slander, of course, but that doesn't alter the fact that he's now got to account for every single item of stock. He's been freed from all other duties to get it done and Dr Braun is now in charge of the infection ward instead.'

'But do you think it's true? Has Krüger really been selling to the black market?'

'Who knows? The man's obsessed with his own career, always plays his cards close to his chest, so I think he'd do anything for personal gain.'

Paula's anxiety eased just a little. Once more, evil had passed her by. She decided, however, not to let Georg spend his convalescence at home in their flat. They would sit it out at his grandparents' allotment again. She assumed that Krüger would never suspect where they were so, hopefully, he wouldn't be able to set the Gesundheitspolizei on them. All she had to do now was wait for Thursday, so she occupied her time with packing for herself and the children and preparing for Georg's return. She decided to write an absence note for Emilia, saying she wasn't well and would be off school until the start of the summer holidays. Emilia was delighted.

'Will Horst be out soon too?' she asked.

'A couple of days later, I think.'

'Maybe he could get fully well at his grandma's! Mama, could you talk to her about it?'

'No, Horst is going to be at his parents' flat first of all. That's the best thing for any sick child. To be honest, I wouldn't be taking Georg to the allotment in normal circumstances.'

'Why not?'

'Because he's still in a weak state and needs lots of nursing and we have no proper bathroom there. But I don't want anyone to know where we are. It wouldn't occur to anyone that we'd take a seriously ill child straight from hospital to stay at the allotment gardens.'

Emilia looked puzzled, but Paula was so tired after the worry of the last few weeks that she didn't have the mental energy to explain it to her.

'It would be lovely if you could help me with the packing. Georg will explain everything to you when he's back.'

◆ ◆ ◆

On Thursday Georg was discharged, as promised.

'It's still a bit too soon,' Dr Braun cautioned her kindly. 'But you're one of us and you know what needs doing for him. I've got medicine here for him until Monday, and then you'll need a fresh prescription.' He handed her the little paper bag and Georg's discharge papers.

'Thank you so much, Dr Braun. You can't imagine how grateful I am.'

'I think I probably can. To be honest, not all of us are behind what Dr Krüger represents, although very few have the courage to protest. I know what happened to your husband and I admire his courage. I'd have been too frightened of the consequences to do the same.'

'You're doing all you can. Nobody can expect more than that.'

With that, Paula took Georg to the car. His legs were still wobbly, but he was so pleased his allotment garden life could continue.

That night there was heavy bombing again, and Paula was relieved she didn't have to bundle the children down into the cellar, as she would have had to if they'd been at home. As usual, Georg and Emilia watched from the small window as the anti-aircraft searchlights latched on to so many aircraft. But a lot of bombs hit their target and soon there was a different kind of light – the glow of fires burning.

'There're more planes all the time!' exclaimed Emilia. 'They're like giant insects! We need a huge fly swatter to bring down three at a time!'

Paula said nothing. She too was looking out of the window but with unease, not fascination. The fiercest fires were blazing exactly in the location of their flat.

The next day her unease turned into sickening certainty. A bomb had hit their block and destroyed it. All residents, thinking themselves safe in the cellar, were now dead. Paula shuddered as she realised that she and the children owed their lives to the malicious Dr Krüger . . .

Chapter 43

Tobruk was a disappointment and its capture had cost effort and lives. Although Richard had his own dedicated psychiatric work, the surgeons still needed his help. In the days leading up to the fall of Tobruk, Fritz constantly pushed himself and often worked fourteen hours at a stretch.

'You can't go on driving yourself so hard,' Richard kept warning his friend. Fritz would brush all this off. 'What's a couple of hours of lost sleep if you can save a life?'

'Yes, but if you collapse you won't be helping anyone at all.'

'Don't worry, that won't happen. When Tobruk falls to us, everything'll go back to normal.'

Fritz had rather hoped that Tobruk would be on the scale of Tripoli, but as they entered the city they realised that wasn't the case. It was simply a little port bordered by a handful of houses, with even fewer small shops, empty of all stock, and some abandoned storage sheds. Not even Walter, with his magnificent talent for organisation, could make anything of this. They had no choice but to wait for the supply ships to come from Italy.

The supply convoy arrived a couple of days later. At last there was enough to eat, even some beer, and the long-awaited military post.

While Fritz opened his to find a new photo of his wife and children with their beloved Rudi, Richard was struck by the Göttingen postmark on his letter from Paula. What on earth was she doing there? He ripped open the envelope.

My dearest Richard

I don't know whether you ever got my last letter? We haven't heard from you for a long time. I don't want to bore you with the same information, but in case my last note never arrived, you need to know we were bombed out at the end of June. We were fortunate because we were at your parents' allotment, but all our old neighbours were in the cellar at home and were killed in the raid. It's an absolute tragedy. You'd never recognise our street now. Our block has been completely destroyed and the nearby buildings look somehow like the rotting teeth of a giant and are all at risk of collapse.

Soon after Whitsun, Georg was in hospital with diphtheria, the hospital got bombed and all the children were moved to Langenhorn. Georg caught Krüger's attention and I've done everything possible to keep him out of the man's clutches. I'll tell you about it properly when we're together again.

After we were bombed out, I thought long and hard about what to do. I could have moved in with your parents or my father, but Krüger was threatening us with the health police, the Gesundheitspolizei. My father still has connections from his time in Göttingen and so was able to contact Professor Ewald. As a result, I'm now working as a doctor at the Göttingen-Rosdorf asylum. We're very lucky to have found lodgings with a nice widowed lady whose son is at the Front. It's near my work and we rent two rooms from her. Frau

Heiroth is so kind to the children, especially when I'm out. There's no special school for Georg, unfortunately, but I've made enquiries and have found him a private tutor who comes here three times a week. On top of that, he gets to do the same exercises as Emilia as she brings them home from school. I've also managed to get him excused from the Hitler Youth by using the documentation attesting to his impaired hearing being a result of birth trauma.

Emilia's been going to the League of German Girls for three weeks now. I haven't told her any of our misgivings, as she should be able to take part in summer camps with other girls without any preconceived ideas. She's so obviously having fun and has already asked me if she can go on their spring trip to a youth camp. I'm letting her do all this because she needs the change of scene and I don't want us to become conspicuous. The girls play various sports, sing together, learn how to do roll call and salute the flag, and even do cross-country activities like the boys. Emilia thinks this is all wonderful and has already made friends among the girls. She's got a lot of pluck as well as being bright. And it does no harm that they learn a bit about housekeeping and cooking too. Sometimes I find myself looking back at how Fritz used to enjoy the bright side of this new Germany in the days before the war because he could do nothing about the dark side of it. That's how Emilia is. She should be free to enjoy anything that bears some semblance to a happy childhood.

You'd like what I'm doing for Professor Ewald. We treat patients very much in line with your own thinking and are dealing with the kind of problems that preoccupied you too. I'll tell you more when you're back on home leave.

I'm wondering if your organisational genius, Walter, knows where he can get his hands on some decent civilian clothing. Grab some if you can! Because we were living at the allotment at the time of the bombing, we had most of our clothes here with us, but we couldn't salvage any of yours. It pains me to think how all our books are gone for ever and how we'll never replace some of them, like the Stefan Zweig. Still, we're all alive. And I hope our optimism will carry us through the dark days ahead, because good can come from bad if we really believe it. Here in Göttingen there are hardly any air raids.

I hope you're all right. Please do send news soon.

Your loving Paula

Fritz noticed how quiet Richard had gone. 'Bad news?'

'Mixed. The last letter seems to have got lost in the post. Paula's moved to Göttingen with the children. Our flat's been bombed.'

'Your flat?' said Fritz in horror.

'That's right. Paula had gone down to the allotment gardens with the twins. All our neighbours are dead. She says I wouldn't recognise our street now.'

'God, I'm so sorry.'

'But that's not what matters. At least they're all safe. They're alive. What's the news from Doro?'

'Just the usual. She hasn't said anything about Paula or your flat. In fact, she never writes about the bombing. I thought there was less of it. She's probably trying not to worry me.'

Richard looked bleak. Being on the other side of the world while loved ones were at the mercy of British and American bombing was unbearable.

Chapter 44

The new life in Göttingen and her daily work in psychiatry came as a relief to Paula and at least now she had no need to worry for Georg's safety, although it was a matter of some regret to her that he only had private tuition at home and wouldn't find new friends the way Emilia had.

Professor Ewald and Paula's father had been students together and held similar views concerning euthanasia. Paula knew from her father she could trust Professor Ewald, so she told him about Richard's attempt to protect and save patients – and about his failure.

'That's the crux of the matter. If we overdo things and try to save everyone, we end up saving nobody because the supervisory commission in Berlin is on our backs. We have to make the decisions – that's what we've done here from very early on. We've been able to save two thirds of our patients from death, but I regret to say there have been some we couldn't do anything for.'

'So a third have lost their lives?' Paula was shaken.

The professor nodded. 'In asylums with really staunch Nazis at work only about a fifth of patients survive, if that's any consolation to you. My sources tell me they've stopped using gas in some large asylums and instead they create a category called something like "the unproductive sick" and leave them to starve or give them an injection of Luminal.'

Paula stared at him, her eyes wide, as she took this in. 'That's horrific! How can any doctor allow this? And we really can't do anything?'

'We can. We can't override the system, as you know. But what we can do is give individual attention to each and every patient and bring as many as possible to safety. That's where I need you, Frau Doctor Hellmer. Do what your husband did, but don't repeat his errors. We can't claim full productive capability for everyone – that gets noticed – but we can intervene sooner. It's not only about the registration forms. It's also about discharging patients early so they can go back to their families or find jobs in workshops whose owners put humanity above profit. Your father told me how your father-in-law saved three lives this way.'

'That's right.'

'That's how to do it. At the moment a mental hospital is one of the most dangerous places in Germany for anyone who is sick. Whatever the bombs don't get rid of, our own people do. Make yourself known to the families and encourage them to take their loved ones home. Frau Doctor Hellmer, you are a highly gifted and insightful doctor. Use these gifts to persuade the healthy to help the sick.'

So that's how Paula came to carry on with Richard's work, but in Göttingen. She had always known that he'd carried a heavy burden but only now did she fully appreciate what it meant to hold a life in your hands. Over and over again she told herself she wasn't the judge, she hadn't decided that these were the people to die, but at the same time she knew what would befall those she couldn't protect. For a moment she envied Richard, as he hadn't allowed himself to get involved in a selection process but had instead simply refused to participate by declaring all patients economically productive. Unlike Richard, she now knew she wouldn't be in a position to save anyone if she refused to make a selection.

What gave her the most satisfaction was to visit a patient's relatives and persuade them of the wisdom of their loved one coming back home. In most cases, the families were grateful for her candour and for the warning, but not all. Otto Krahl's father was a case in point. Otto was a young man of only twenty-one. He suffered from spastic paralysis and had never learned to talk. He was able to laugh and show emotion but had to be cared for like a baby. His mother had always looked after him at home, but with her death a few weeks before Paula's visit, Otto's father had decided to place his severely disabled son in the asylum.

He gave Paula a warm welcome to his home, even offering her the luxury of an ersatz coffee as she took a seat in the old-style German living room. It reminded her a lot of her father's front room. Framed photographs of rather severe-looking men and women hung on the walls. There was one of a young woman holding a baby.

'My wife with Otto soon after he was born,' explained Herr Krahl when he saw Paula studying it. 'He was still well at that stage. A few weeks later he caught meningitis.' The man took a deep breath. 'All the doctors said Otto wouldn't survive, but my wife was like a lioness fighting for her young. You wouldn't believe how often I've felt it would have been better if she'd lost that fight.'

Paula listened in silence.

Herr Krahl continued talking. 'You might think I'm being completely heartless, but Otto was our firstborn. If he'd died, we'd have mourned him, of course, but we might have gone on to have another child, a healthy one. But my Hannelore put all her energy into caring for the child, even though it was clear from the start that he'd stay a baby for ever. She refused to let him go into care. He was her purpose in life. She didn't want any more children and I, well, I stood by her because a decent man doesn't leave his wife and a handicapped child, but it wasn't a life. Everything revolved around Otto, and caring for him left Hannelore completely drained. She became terribly thin. I suspected she was giving Otto most of her food ration, although he didn't need much as he didn't move about. She gradually faded, and died of pneumonia six weeks ago. She'd lost all resistance.' He paused to compose himself. 'And you'd like me to bring Otto back home, Frau

Doctor Hellmer? How can that work? I'm expected to work ten hours a day in an industry that's essential to the war effort – that's why I haven't been sent to the Front. And on top of that, I haven't got the will to have him near me. After all, he sent my wife to her death.'

'I've told you what it would mean for your son to stay in the asylum.'

Herr Krahl nodded. 'Yes, I know. What am I supposed to say? Perhaps that's not such a bad thing. Perhaps death is a blessing for someone who's never been a son to me, only a burden, and who lost any purpose in life with the death of his mother. We should break free of all the sentimentality that drove my wife to her grave. Otto should have died twenty years ago instead of being a parasite taking up the place that the healthy children who were never born would have had.' He wiped away a tear.

'Herr Krahl, thank you for talking to me.' Paula stood up. 'I hope you'll never regret your decision.'

'I know I won't. But I have always regretted letting my wife keep him at home. I should have put him away twenty years ago. That would have spared us all.'

Paula was lost for words. Part of her was shocked at Herr Krahl's cold-hearted approach to his son's certain death and yet she found she could understand why. If he had ever felt any love for this child, it had been eaten away by years of worry and privation, and by the destructive effect on his marriage. She wondered whether those who believed in letting the sick and disabled die had experienced something similar but in different, distant surroundings. How else could people bring themselves to take the lives of those entrusted to them?

◆ ◆ ◆

When she got back to the hospital, she sat down with Otto Krahl's form. She completed it according to the rules. Capacity for productivity compared with a healthy individual . . . zero per cent. She took the form out of the typewriter and signed it. This was a life she couldn't save, but it could save two others from transportation because she would have met her quota. As she sat there thinking this through, she felt the tears flow, and one dropped straight on her signature, making the ink run. She nearly did a fresh one but decided not to. The murderers weren't interested in whether her signature was legible or smudged by tears.

Chapter 45

The war pressed ahead without let-up and in autumn 1942 Richard and Fritz were deployed to a field hospital at El Alamein. Fritz's brilliance as a surgeon and Richard's effective treatment of the mentally shattered, together with his noticeably improved surgical skills, had, in the eyes of their superiors, made them the perfect team for El Alamein.

'I've always wanted to see Egypt, but not like this!' commented Fritz. 'Oh well, at least we can get a beer here.' They were sitting on the steps of the only solid building in the place, now the hospital, drinking their beer straight from the bottle. Over the last few days it had become a bit quieter on the front line, but they'd had a spate of emergency operations to perform after an attack by fighter aircraft. Although their own fighter squadron had scrambled and shot down a couple of enemy planes, medical help had come too late for seven German soldiers, and four others were so badly wounded they had to be swiftly operated on.

'I'd love to see that famous museum in Cairo – you know,' said Fritz to Richard, 'the one with all the treasures of Tutankhamun and the mummies of the pharaohs. Then there's the Valley of the Kings. When I told the children about it, they were really excited and wanted to come straight over to see it all.' He gave a wistful smile.

'Yes, I'd like to see all that. Especially those old Egyptian burial caves with the wall paintings. Or the Pyramids. You went to the British

Museum when you were in London, didn't you? Did they allow photography there?'

'Don't know, to be honest, as I didn't have a camera anyway. But I did buy a book with pictures of all the exhibits and really detailed descriptions.' Fritz sighed. 'Sometimes I wonder what Maxwell's doing now, whether he's still in London in his favourite operating theatre, or whether he's at the Front as well. It scares me just to think about it. We last met up in London in May '39, with both of our families.'

'Oh, I remember, yes – we were looking after Rudi for you!'

Fritz nodded, lost in thought. 'Isn't life mad? Seems as though, yesterday, he and I were good friends and colleagues, swapping ideas, and now we're all throwing bombs and shooting each other down. And why? Can you tell me? You were always interested in politics. Why are we fighting this bloody war? What was the reason again?'

'No idea,' said Richard, taking a slug of beer. 'Something about *Lebensraum* in Eastern Europe.'

'So why are we sitting here in Africa?'

'Because the world's gone mad, as you have so eloquently put it.'

'Aha, this is where the doctors are! Caught you both lounging around!' Walter came dashing energetically up the steps towards them. 'Come and look at this.'

'What – an emergency?' asked Fritz.

'No, no emergency, just a nice change! There are a couple of Bedouins over here selling all sorts of fancy stuff, and there's something for the gentlemen too!'

'A cold beer? This stuff's too warm,' commented Richard.

Fritz laughed and Walter rolled his eyes suggestively. 'No beer, but a couple of luscious lovelies worth looking at.'

'Hey, you know we're decent married men!' replied Fritz. 'Luscious lovelies don't do anything for us, but the rest sounds worth a look. Richard, shall we?'

'Let me get my camera.'

'Same old Richard! Anyway, how d'you manage to get new film and developer out here in the desert?'

'I've got stuff left over from when we were in Tripoli.'

'I remember him buying a whole crate of it in Tripoli,' added Walter. 'It would have lasted the war photographer a whole year, but Richard zips through it in a couple of months.'

Richard grinned and went off to fetch his stuff. When he returned, they followed Walter to where the Bedouins had set up their camp.

'Isn't anyone wondering whether they're British spies?' asked Richard.

'What on earth is there for them to spy on? The British aerial reconnaissance fellows have known for a long time what's here, and our own security forces have questioned everybody in the area.' Walter pointed at the army jeeps parked not so far from the camp. 'Our lads need a bit of variety. Good for morale.'

But the Bedouin camp had little of the exoticism usually shown in films about the Middle East – no colourful tents with huge interiors littered with silken cushions fit for a sultan, just small, gloomy canvas shelters, outside which sat a few scruffy, undernourished camels. The Bedouins themselves were dressed in grey-brown gowns and their women, hanging around outside the tents, were of indeterminate age, somewhere between thirty and fifty, with bad teeth and weather-beaten faces.

'Please tell me our men won't be that desperate,' whispered Fritz to Richard. 'They're not exactly luscious lovelies.'

'They've made some nice stuff, though. Look,' Richard said, pointing to a stall full of carved scarabs and gods from Egyptian mythology. Fritz picked out a wooden scarab the size of a man's fist, turned it over and showed Richard the hieroglyphics on its underside.

'This is a really good reproduction of a heart scarab,' he said.

He asked the trader how much he wanted for it and got immersed in a protracted haggling process in a mixture of German, English and

Arabic while Richard browsed his way around the other goods. He noticed a boy of around twelve squatting behind the traders' tents carving out more figures. Richard went over.

'Do you make all the figures?' he asked.

The lad indicated that he spoke no German but a little English.

Richard switched to English and asked him what he used as models for his work.

'Picture in caves, many picture,' he said.

'Caves? What caves?' asked Richard.

'Dead people there. No far, no far.'

The boy looked around all the time, as if to be sure no one was watching or listening, then pulled out a battered old scarab and passed it to Richard. 'Look, is from dead people in caves.'

Richard took the object from him and gave it a good hard look. It came across as genuine, but Richard knew the local traders had a knack for producing convincing fakes and the probability that the boy was spinning a yarn was high. He replaced the scarab among the carvings still to be worked on.

'You think not real? Can say where found. I got good map. Me and uncle know all about caves.' His uncle was still haggling with Fritz.

'What kind of map?' Richard's interest had been sparked now.

'Wait.' The boy vanished inside one of the tents and came back with a piece of parchment. It was well worn, stained, tattered and some of the symbols were faded, but Richard knew his own map of the area well enough to be sure that this carefully drawn document was accurate.

Meanwhile, Fritz had bought the heart scarab and a statue of Anubis. 'Have you bought anything?'

'Not yet, but this boy doing the carvings reckons the originals of all their merchandise here come from a burial cave nearby. He wants to sell me the map.'

'Map good!' The boy nodded eagerly. 'Secret grave, pictures on walls. You buy map?'

'How much do you want for it?'

'Hang on there, Richard. You don't believe all this nonsense, surely? These desert shopkeepers will tell you anything to earn a bit of money.'

'Tell me about this old winged scarab.' Richard gestured towards the battered object sitting on a rug in front of the boy.

Fritz picked it up and examined it. 'I'd say he buried it somewhere for about six months to make it look old and valuable.'

'You may be right, but I'd really like to know where these burial caves are.' Richard turned back to the boy. 'So, what do you want for the map?'

'Five marks.'

'Five marks?' Richard was amazed. 'I'll give you twenty pfennig.'

'Old map. Only one map of grave. Five marks.'

'He knows plenty about German money,' said Fritz drily. 'You can drink yourself silly for five marks.' Then he took a good look at the map himself. 'What's your name, my lad?'

'Hassan.'

'Right, Hassan. Before my friend here gives you his hard-earned cash for a fake, show me what your map's good for. Where's our camp?'

Hassan immediately showed them not only the exact location of the camp but also quite deliberately pointed to a symbol in the no man's land between the German and British front lines where the burial cave was allegedly to be found.

'It wouldn't surprise me if our young friend also does business with the Brits,' commented Fritz. 'He knows the area well, whatever he's up to.'

'D'you think there could be something in it?' asked Richard. 'After all, the biggest archaeological finds came about with the help of grave robbers, didn't they?'

Fritz shrugged. 'I really don't know. There might be. Buy the map if it'll make you happy!'

Richard negotiated the boy down to one mark and then asked him if he would agree to a photo. Hassan agreed with a big smile so Richard photographed him at his carving and promised Fritz a print for his children.

'And what do you think, Fritz? Shall we take a look there tomorrow?'

'You can't seriously believe we'd get leave of absence for that, surely! A nice trip into no man's land to look for a secret burial site?' He shook his head.

'We wouldn't have to say what we wanted the leave for,' retorted Richard. 'We'll only be away a couple of hours – they can all think we're enjoying the desert flowers or something! Anyway, it's very quiet at the Front just now. We can afford the time for a bit of an excursion.'

'So am I supposed to risk my reputation for this?' said Fritz good-naturedly. 'OK then, I'll sort out the leave of absence, but we'll have to walk for a good hour to get there, so get yourself a compass and some rations.'

'And a torch and my camera. Goes without saying.'

'Do you know, this is the craziest thing we've ever done?'

'In what way? I consider it to be absolutely normal. When in Egypt, the typical cultured German will visit ancient burial sites. What would be crazy is not to do it.'

'You know we could get into real trouble for this, don't you?'

'Fritz, be honest. Is there anything I've done of late that *hasn't* got me into real trouble? And if we're caught out, what's the big problem? We'll talk our way out of it, say we went the wrong way or pretend we'd had a drink or got sunstroke. They're hardly going to put their two best doctors in front of the firing squad or on punishment duty. They need us too much here.'

'You're right there,' acknowledged Fritz. 'But I'm warning you, if there's nothing there, you owe me a couple of beers!'

Chapter 46

'I'm starting to feel like that Karl May explorer Kara Ben Nemsi, but without the horse,' grumbled Fritz, wiping the sweat from his face. 'D'you really think this thing exists?'

'Well, the map shows quite clearly the pile of five stones marking the entrance to the cavern.'

'I think this was a bad idea. Wouldn't it be better to go back before we run into the English or get spotted by an enemy plane?'

'We've come this far, so let's keep going for another ten minutes or so, then turn back if we still haven't found anything.'

Fritz was ready to disagree when Richard saw the pile of stones, easily recognisable between some gnarled tree stumps and a patch of dried-out grass.

'See that?'

'You're right! At least the boy wasn't making it up.'

They walked towards it with caution, keeping an eye on the surrounding terrain. Nobody was in sight.

'Are we some way from the British lines?' asked Richard. Fritz looked at the map. 'I'd say about as far from theirs as we are from ours.'

Richard was right by the pile of stones now.

'There's an opening here; it leads downwards!' he called out to Fritz, then took off his kitbag, which had food, water, torches and his camera inside, got down flat on his belly and shone his torch inside.

'Anything to see?' asked Fritz, crouching down beside him.

'It doesn't drop down very deep and then it goes level. There really does seem to be some sort of shaft.'

'What if there are snakes down there? Something poisonous? Or perhaps the place is cursed, like the tomb of Tutankhamun.'

'If that's the case, then Hassan wouldn't have come back so cheerful, surely?'

'OK, agreed, but there still might be snakes and scorpions.'

'Fritz, I never knew you were such a coward!'

'Hey, a bit less of that, please! One of us has to show some common sense, now you've got the explorer bug.'

'I'm going to climb down.' Richard got the extra torch out of his kitbag, handed it to Fritz and reached for his camera.

'And what am I supposed to do if you get bitten by a snake?'

'You'll think of something. You're a surgeon, aren't you?'

The opening was very narrow and Richard eased himself forward on all fours. He gave a start when a little creature darted across his hand, but it was only a lizard, nothing to fear. Composing himself, he continued to make his way, and after about three metres the gallery widened out and led into a small chamber roughly four metres square in size. He stood upright and gasped when he caught sight of the many wall paintings showing Egyptian gods.

'Fritz, this is unbelievable – come and see! It's all true, what the boy told us.'

Fritz was soon at his side. He'd brought the kitbag with him and cleared away all trace of their presence from the entrance. 'Just in case a reconnaissance aircraft comes by,' he said.

They flashed their torches around the chamber.

'Hey, there's the sarcophagus.' Fritz pointed towards a huge, sand-coloured stone receptacle, its cover broken in two on the ground. The inner sarcophagus itself lay empty. 'Plundered – I might have known.'

'D'you think we're the first Europeans ever to come here?' asked Richard.

'I should think so. Who on earth would ever pay for an excavation here? The whole area's so inhospitable.'

He shone his torch on the wall paintings. 'Look at that! Wonderful. That's the Opening of the Mouth ceremony, and here you can see Anubis leading the dead towards the throne of Osiris. It's not as impressive as the photos you see of the Valley of the Kings, but it's—' He suddenly stopped talking. 'Did you hear that?'

'Hear what?' asked Richard.

Fritz drew his pistol from its holster. 'Torch off!'

Richard did as he was told, then heard the same as Fritz. From above them came men's voices, speaking English!

Instinctively, he too reached for his gun, the first time since his military training. He'd never thought an army doctor would need to use a weapon. Had someone been watching them? Had someone followed them all the way here? Richard's heart pounded. Under the cover of darkness, Fritz pushed his friend back behind the sarcophagus so they had at least some cover.

'Over here, Arthur!' shouted someone in English as a new beam lit up the chamber. 'There really is an old tomb here! It's quite remarkable!'

They heard scratching and scraping, as though a second man was now also crawling along the gallery.

'Hey, look! Is that a German kitbag?'

Fritz shot up from behind the sarcophagus. 'Hands up!' He gave the order in English.

Richard was on his feet too and trained his pistol and his torch on the two British soldiers, who were stunned to find themselves confronted by a pair of German officers. Slowly, they raised their hands.

'We're from the medical service,' said one of them. 'We're not in a fighting unit.'

Fritz looked more closely at the man opposite him. 'Maxwell? Maxwell Cooper?'

'Yes,' came the hesitant reply. Richard saw how the Brit was trying to see their faces in the glare of the torches. 'Do we know each other?'

'It's me, Fritz Ellerweg.'

'Fritz? Good Lord! You really do get everywhere!'

'Listen, this is really awkward for all four of us. But tell me honestly, how many more of you are lurking outside?'

'None,' said Maxwell, earning a kick on the shin from his companion.

'None?' said Fritz. 'Do you give me your word?'

'I do.'

'Good. Then can we talk as the old friends we are? Put away our guns? Or do you insist on war?'

'I rather think this place looks a bit like Switzerland,' said Maxwell, 'and medical officers don't wage war.'

'Agreed,' Fritz said, lowering his gun.

But Richard kept his gun where it was, pointing straight at the two Englishmen. He reverted to German with Fritz, saying to his friend, 'Can't you at least tell them to take off their gun belts?'

'Maxwell's a good friend of mine. He wouldn't lie to me.'

'And the other one? Looks really sinister. I wouldn't trust him an inch.'

'Keep it that way,' the second man snarled in German. 'I can't stand you damned Krauts.'

'See? We'll have to watch that one.'

'Stop all that, Arthur,' hissed Maxwell.

'Don't tell me to trust a German,' said Arthur icily, and in English this time.

'The position you're in, you have no choice,' said Richard. He spoke in English so as not to exclude Maxwell from the dialogue. 'I am the one with the gun. It is for me to decide whether I trust you.'

Maxwell tried to smooth things over. 'Listen, my colleague's home was bombed in the latest air raid over London. It was sheer luck that his wife wasn't home. She'd never have survived it.'

This only stoked up Richard's anger. 'Oh, so does he think he's the only one? My own home was razed to the ground by British bombers, and our neighbours met a miserable end in the basement where they'd gone for shelter. It was luck too that my wife and children weren't at home. But the difference between the two of us is that I know how to distinguish between the Royal Air Force and an innocent party.' He gave Arthur a long, hard look, the camera hanging around the Englishman's neck catching his eye and prompting his next remark. 'Anyway, you can't despise all Germans if you go around with a Leica II on show. Or is that a battle trophy?'

'I didn't say that I despise all Germans,' retorted Arthur. 'I said I didn't trust any!'

'You don't have to do that,' said Richard. 'It's enough if you give me your word not to shoot if I put my gun down. Even if it's naive and stupid of me to trust an embittered Brit.'

Arthur hesitated. 'You have my word,' he said with a nod.

'Well, at last,' said Richard, stowing away his pistol. Fritz and Maxwell both sighed with relief.

'So what on earth are you both really doing here?' asked Maxwell.

'Yesterday we bought a map from a Bedouin boy that shows the route to an undiscovered tomb,' explained Fritz. 'We thought we'd have a look, seeing as it's quieter at the Front at the moment.'

'A map? Is it like this?' Maxwell reached into his uniform jacket pocket, pulled out a folded parchment and slowly opened it out. Richard and Fritz stared at the map.

'That little trickster!' hissed Fritz as Richard got their own map out of his kitbag.

'Here's mine.' He showed it to the two Englishmen. 'Identical. Right down to the well-thumbed edges. Seems to be a flourishing Bedouin business model.'

Maxwell burst out laughing. 'I bought mine over a week ago, but it was only today it felt safe enough for a jaunt into no man's land. We thought, *Oh well, the enemy's quiet, nobody'll notice if we're out for a while.*'

'Our logic too!' Fritz grinned. 'Isn't it nice of the enemy to give us a bit of peace so we can indulge our cultural interests?'

'Nobody would believe us! Have you been here for long?' asked Maxwell.

'No, we got here just before you. May I introduce my closest friend, Dr Richard Hellmer? We met during our first semester as young students.'

Richard and Maxwell shook hands.

'And this is Dr Arthur Grifford,' said Maxwell, presenting his companion. 'We haven't known each other as long as you two, but long enough to have been on a few mad trips!' He laughed.

Arthur Grifford didn't look too pleased about the friendly introduction and accepted Fritz's outstretched hand only after some hesitation.

'I knew those Bedouins had a deal with the enemy,' he muttered to himself.

'I wouldn't call it a deal. They just sell both sides their rubbish!' observed Richard.

Arthur ignored him so as to avoid shaking hands with yet another German.

Meanwhile, Fritz was enthusiastically shining his torch on the wall behind the sarcophagus. 'Maxwell, you're the hieroglyph expert. What does all this say?'

'Hang on, it looks really interesting.' Maxwell went over to him and started explaining the significance of the various images.

Arthur clapped his hand to his forehead in frustration.

'Headache?' asked Richard, keeping a sharp eye on him still.

Arthur's tone was icy again. 'We've got other problems at the moment, more than hieroglyphs.'

'You're right there,' conceded Richard. 'Getting any decent photographs in this light is a real challenge. Well, for you, that is. I've got a Leica III, you see.' He held out his camera for Arthur to see. 'This one doesn't need such a long exposure time, and I've got a good flash. Sometimes it's worth investing in the latest technology instead of making do with a cheaper, older model!'

'Show-off!'

Richard laughed. He trained his camera on the painted walls and took a number of shots. Although Arthur had obviously decided to treat the Germans with utter disdain, Richard noticed how interested he was in the finer details of the camera, although he was too proud to ask him any questions.

Meanwhile, Fritz and Maxwell seemed to have completely forgotten there was a war on. They were exchanging news about their families, showing one another the photographs they always carried with them.

'Harri's really grown!' exclaimed Maxwell.

'And is that lovely young woman really little Sarah? She'll be married before you know where you are, and then it'll be Grandpa Maxwell!'

Arthur made very obvious coughing noises.

'Frog in your throat?' Richard's quip didn't raise a smile. He thought for a moment, then decided it was time for some straight talking. 'Listen, I can understand why the war makes you detest every German but, presumably, you didn't always feel like that. You speak German, you use a German camera, and your colleague here is good friends with a German.' He nodded towards Fritz and Maxwell, deep in conversation about new methods in surgery. Maxwell was listening attentively while Fritz explained how skin grafts he had carried out during the amputation process could guarantee better results in any later use of prosthetics.

'You surgeons are a breed apart,' said Arthur.

'I'm not a surgeon, actually.'

'Really? So what are you?'

'I'm a psychiatrist.'

Arthur gave a low whistle. 'You could do with sorting out Hitler then.'

'I'm a psychiatrist, not a miracle-worker.'

Arthur hesitated before carrying on. 'You won't lose your rag if I say a few bad things about your wonderful leader then?'

'He is not my wonderful leader. I didn't vote for him.'

'That doesn't tell me anything. You're all always cheering him.'

'You have absolutely no idea what's been happening on the ground in Germany over the last ten years or so.'

Arthur fell silent.

'So what's your specialism?' Richard expected a touchy reply and so was surprised when Arthur simply said general medicine.

'I had no desire to go to the Front,' said Arthur, 'but once we'd been bombed out at home, it seemed like a good solution. My wife's a nurse and reported for duty at the field hospital at the same time. I reckon we're the only couple both to enter the medical corps. It's not how we planned our future together, to be quite honest. But there's no point in having a family now, and who knows how long this war will drag on.'

'Didn't your wife want to come and see the tomb as well?'

'We didn't tell anyone what we were planning. They'd all have said we were insane. I didn't even tell Lisa.'

Neither spoke for a while. Fritz and Maxwell had moved on to the effectiveness of antibiotics.

'Did you sign up of your own accord?' Arthur asked Richard.

'Long story. It's almost as incredible as us meeting here in this tomb.'

'Will you tell me?'

Richard could hear that Arthur's icy tone had vanished. Had he managed to penetrate the Englishman's armour? Or maybe he was making the best of the situation because he knew Maxwell and Fritz would carry on talking for a while yet.

'OK, why not? You're welcome to pass it on to your press scribblers, but leave my name out of it if you want to spare my family. I can't possibly broadcast this in Germany – it could literally be fatal, but the world must know.'

'I'm intrigued. Go on!'

So Richard told him about the Law for the Prevention of Progeny with Inherited Diseases, about how, as a psychiatrist, it was his job to write expert statements assessing patients' productivity, about the killing of those considered unworthy of life. Arthur's face registered increasing disbelief as he listened.

'In the end it all came out that I'd deliberately falsified registration forms in order to save my patients. I was dismissed without notice and escaped a punishment battalion only by signing up of my own volition for the medical battalion.'

'It's absolutely unbelievable.'

'It's absolutely true.' Richard struggled to hide his bitterness.

'No, don't misunderstand me, I wasn't questioning what you say. It's just that I'm lost for words.'

'I've been lost for words for a long time,' said Richard. 'At the moment, my wife's trying to do her bit. She's a doctor, trying to spare as many of the sick and handicapped as she can, but it's a struggle.'

Fritz gave Richard a nudge. 'I wouldn't like to break up your new friendship, you two, but I fear it's time for us to get moving.'

'Have you taken any pictures?' Maxwell asked Arthur.

'No, my camera can't cope with the light down here.'

Richard grinned. 'When the war's over, I'll send you a couple of prints. It's definitely paid off, getting a Leica III.'

'Show-off!' said Arthur again. This time it was said in a spirit of fun.

'As we were the first to arrive, it's probably best if we're the first ones to leave,' Fritz suggested, 'and you two had better wait until we're out of sight.'

'What do we do if your or our people are running around outside?' Maxwell wondered.

'OK, if any of them catch us together, just play it depending on whose side it is. If they're Brits, you say that we're your prisoners, and if they're ours, then you're our prisoners.'

'But are medical officers allowed to take one another prisoner?' asked Richard.

'I don't think anyone's ever expected anything like this to crop up, to be honest.'

'Then we need to make sure we don't establish a precedent!' Maxwell smiled, then said his farewells to Fritz, enthusiastically sending his warm regards to Dorothea and the children.

'If someone had told me when I got up this morning that I'd be telling a German it had been a pleasure to meet them, I'd never have believed it,' said Arthur, 'but that is the case. Perhaps we'll even meet up after the war.'

'Never say never,' replied Richard, shaking hands with Arthur, then they all made their way out of the burial chamber as planned and back to their own lines, unscathed and undiscovered.

'I owe you two beers,' said Fritz when they were safely back in their quarters. 'That trip to the tomb was a really good idea. The whole world has gone mad, but at least some things stay the same. Maxwell told me about a few really interesting medical developments and I explained rotation flap surgery to him.'

'That was the long-overdue conference you've been wanting to attend!' Richard said, laughing.

'And all set against the backdrop of ancient history and high culture too! Can't wait to see those photos.'

Chapter 47

In her efforts to spare as many patients as possible from transfer to the death camps, Paula turned next to the Church. She had fully expected most parish leaders to be responsive to her concerns, but in fact came up against highly varied degrees of willingness to help. Three of the pastors she approached were immediately ready to pitch in with practical support, but many others were evasive and one rejected her outright, warning her not to go around spreading such stories. It was only then that she realised that this pastor's front room boasted a Hitler portrait. So even their spiritual leaders were not immune to signing up to the NSDAP. She resolved to be more careful next time.

But she was even more taken aback when a well-known member of the NSDAP offered to employ four of her patients on light duties in his own painting and decorating business.

He explained his decision to her. 'Look, I've never been particularly interested in politics and only joined the party in 1938 because I couldn't have kept my business going otherwise. I could see that party members were getting all the work contracts. But that's never meant that I condone what's going on here. Pastor Weinheim knows that and that's why he mentioned you to me. When times are tough, we have to find ways and means of getting things done.'

Paula nodded. Even Professor Ewald had become a member of the NSDAP and thus of the NS medical association. From the outset, however, this had never stopped him from speaking out against euthanasia, even though nobody in authority listened and he himself had had to find a way of saving as many of his own patients as he could.

And what was the right way? Taking direct action against the system could lead to your own death. Alfred Schär was just one example. Then there was Richard's way, where he'd refused to comply but failed. All that remained was to walk the tightrope between adapting and resisting. She couldn't save everyone, whatever she did. It was similar to triage on the battlefield, when doctors had to decide who to treat on the spot and who was already beyond help. Paula wished Richard was there with her, or her father at least. She'd have given anything to pick up the phone, but her landlady didn't have such a thing and the only one at the hospital was in the ward office, where her colleagues could hear every word. What brought her some comfort was the first letter from Leonie for three months.

> My dear Paula
> Your last letter took all of six weeks to get here and has brought such distressing news. Everything I hear from Germany is so sad and depressing. Thank God you all escaped the bombing of your home. I may be far away, but I can't tell you how much I feel for you and the children. I hope very much that Göttingen keeps you all safe from the bombs. Richard and Fritz are often in my thoughts too, and I hope they'll return unharmed from this war.
>
> Everything continues to go well for us here. We're distanced from the conflict, although there are huge numbers of refugees seeking a new home in Switzerland – they are overwhelmingly Jewish. What we hear is so terrible, with rumours of ghettos, of camps in the east, but nobody knows exactly what's

going on. I've volunteered to help care for the many children coming in as refugees. Many have lost their parents and many more were sent off to make the journey alone. We've heard that high-ranking Nazis are pocketing bribes and the money serves only to take the children to initial safety. Think how desperate these people must be that they're sending their children off alone to another country. My father is always so glad we left when we did, when all routes were still open to us. Any worries of mine are insignificant compared with yours. I've had to do battle at work to survive in this male world of hospital doctors, but I've coped. A few weeks ago I became the first ever female senior consultant in this place.

As well as that, I adopted a little girl two months ago. Her name's Arlette, she's three years old, comes from France and was in a camp for Jews to be deported to Poland. Her parents died from typhus – the conditions there must have been appalling. Arlette was among a group of children saved by members of the French Resistance and brought here to us in Switzerland. At first, she was deeply disturbed, sat in silence in the corner, wouldn't eat or speak. My heart went out to her. I knew immediately that I wanted to look after this child with the huge, sad eyes and give her something of what she's so painfully lost. Sometimes I ask myself whether, amid all the horror, there really is a higher power guiding us and whether it's always been meant that I'd find Arlette.

She's starting to speak a little German now, and at times I can even get a little smile – so you see, I've achieved everything I wanted but in ways I'd never have dreamt possible. But our old life in Hamburg comes back to me in my dreams: our time together as young students, those wonderful hours spent by the Alster and everything that we both loved so much. If I could turn back the clock, I'd do it all again and not change a single thing.

Keep your courage up, Paula, and let's hope this dreadful war ends soon so we can see each other and you can meet Arlette. I'd like so much to see Emilia and Georg too, and how much Fritz's Henriette has grown, and, of course, meet little Harri for the first time. If you need anything, please be sure to let me know. I'll do everything I can.

Your dear friend
Leonie

Leonie's letter left Paula pensive. Her friend was successful and had an adopted daughter, albeit one with such a sad story. She hoped that Leonie's care and love would help her grow up to be contented. At the same time, she found herself wondering what kind of life her own family would have had if they too had emigrated in 1936. A life without war and bombs. A life spent worrying about the loved ones left back home. A life in which she'd have been reduced to a passive observer of all these events. No, they'd been right to stay. Unlike Leonie, they'd had the choice. Germany was their homeland and it was worth the fight not to allow all their old values to be trampled into the dust – even if that fight had to take place in silence and away from the ear of the authorities and hateful informants.

The weekly newsreels continued to report victories for the Africa Corps, but Richard's letters made things sound rather different. At the beginning of November, German troops were finally defeated at El Alamein and had to retreat to Tunis. Richard still sent home photos, as if he were on a research expedition and not in the thick of war. Among them was one of Egyptian wall paintings in what appeared to be a dark and narrow vault. He'd simply described it as a newly discovered tomb. It wouldn't have been wise to put the whole story in a letter likely to be scrutinised.

◆ ◆ ◆

At Christmas, Fritz and Richard were both granted home leave – they were now working at the main military hospital in Tunis and there were plenty of other doctors. The train to Hamburg went through Göttingen, so Fritz and Richard did most of the journey together. The train even had a fifteen-minute wait at Göttingen, so Fritz had a chance to see Paula and the children.

'I'm so sorry about your flat and the bombing,' he said to her. 'After what we've all been through together, it would have been wonderful if we could have spent Christmas together too.'

'Yes, it would have been, and I do miss Hamburg, but it would have been too risky for Georg, even if we hadn't been bombed out of house and home.'

Fritz was about to say more, but the guard had his whistle at the ready and Richard felt it was time to stop talking. 'If you don't hurry up, you really will be spending Christmas with us instead of with Doro and your two!'

'I love you all, but Doro and the children come first!' Fritz said as he climbed back on board. 'See you here in seven days, when it's back to Tunis for us, Richard!'

They stood watching the train until it disappeared from sight.

'Papa, what's Tunis like?'

'Nothing like as nice as here with you. And we used up your special cream ages ago. I'll need another pot to take back with me.'

Emilia giggled. 'But, Papa, it's nearly two years since I got you that one!'

'Wartime thrift – look, I've still got the pot!' And he pulled it out of his pocket to show her.

While Emilia revelled in the fact that her gift had been treasured for so long, Georg asked about the photos that Richard had sent them. 'Where was the tomb you described in your letter, Papa?'

'That was in Egypt. A Bedouin lad tipped us off and so Uncle Fritz and I went off to look for it, found it and took some pictures. But the sarcophagus itself had been looted and the mummy stolen. All we saw were the wall paintings.'

As they made their way to the bus stop, the children were full of questions still. Paula noticed how Richard often hesitated before replying.

Once they'd got back to Frau Heiroth's flat and Paula had introduced Richard to their landlady, she seized the first opportunity alone together to ask him what it had really been like for him over there. She was preparing herself for horrific tales of blood and death and assumed he would want to spare the children the gore, so she was surprised when he regaled her with the full story of discovering the tomb.

'I wasn't sure that Emilia would be able to keep the story to herself,' he confided. 'As a child, I don't think I could have, to be honest.' He grinned. 'And I don't want the whole world to know Fritz and I have had contact with the enemy. It would put us in a very bad light.'

'You and Fritz are impossible!' Paula said, shaking her head and laughing fondly. 'I bet it didn't even enter your heads that it might be dangerous!'

'Not really,' he admitted ruefully. 'I don't think our English colleagues thought about it either. Well, you know, you don't shoot your colleagues, do you?'

'Is that so?' said Paula drily. 'I thought being a soldier was the only profession where you'd shoot at colleagues if they work for someone else.'

Richard burst out laughing. 'That's a good one! I must tell Fritz, although he'll just say that we're doctors, not soldiers.'

'Seriously, though, Richard, be honest with me. What's it really like at the Front? The newsreels are always telling us about great victories, but you write to me about retreating. Do you believe we're winning the war?'

'I have no idea. But I do know that the magnificent victories you're being told about are mostly retreats. At El Alamein we lost hundreds of men. Fritz was working to his absolute limit. There were days when he'd stand at the operating table for fourteen hours at a stretch, and yet life slipped through our fingers so many times. And none of the vehicles cope well in the desert atmosphere. The tank division is always moaning about breakdowns and the mechanics are almost as busy as the doctors. Flesh can heal, bones can knit, but the machines have no spare parts and fuel is short. Then there are all the infectious diseases caught from contaminated drinking water. Fritz and I stick to beer when we can get it. I reckon if everything else is going like it is in Africa, then we need to be prepared to take a few whippings in the next six months.'

Christmas flew by all too fast. While they'd celebrated it in their own flat the previous year and had pictured life continuing as normal, here they were now in cramped lodgings, with their landlady feeling wretched about her son, who was fighting in Stalingrad.

Nonetheless, Richard put up a fine Christmas tree and Frau Heiroth looked out all her own decorations for it. Presents arrived from Hamburg for the grandchildren and Richard had brought them a beautifully carved set of chess pieces, the figures all from ancient Egyptian mythology.

'I think you're old enough to grasp chess now,' he explained as the twins gazed at the pieces in fascination, so between Christmas and New Year the children learned the basics of chess with great enthusiasm.

The second of January, when Richard was due to return, came all too soon. Snow was falling and the air had turned icy, and as they made ready for the long and difficult journey to the railway station Paula thought wistfully of their car, still garaged at her father-in-law's place in Hamburg.

'Well, that's the one good thing about Africa – the weather's much better,' Richard said, in an attempt to raise a few smiles as they arrived at the station.

When his train rolled in, he hugged Paula and the children one last time. Fritz was waving from the window of their compartment. Richard handed up his case, then pushed his way in through the doors, along with all the other soldiers.

'Do you think Papa will be able to stay with us for ever after next Christmas?' asked Emilia as they stood waving at the disappearing train.

'Let's hope so,' replied Paula. That was the first time she had caught herself thinking she no longer wanted to contemplate the future . . .

Chapter 48

Throughout January and February Paula's life in Göttingen became a cheerless daily grind. She continued to fight on behalf of her patients and even managed to find more employment opportunities for them within businesses willing to help out. But still the war cast its shadow over everything. At the end of January Frau Heiroth received the letter feared by every parent. Her son had fallen at Stalingrad. Paula did her utmost to console and support her landlady through this harrowing experience. Then in February they heard that the Sixth Army had been decimated at Stalingrad and any survivors had ended up as Russian prisoners of war. In spite of this dark news, Paula felt some relief that all reports from the African front continued to be positive. She couldn't begin to picture what any transfer to the Eastern Front would have meant for Richard. All reports about conditions in the prisoner-of-war camps were horrific.

With the arrival of May, the children were at last able to play outside and take regular dips in the little lake near their home. Meanwhile, news came that German troops in Tunisia had surrendered on 13 May and more than one hundred and fifty thousand German soldiers were now British prisoners of war. For Paula the expression 'Tunisgrad' reminded her too much of 'Stalingrad' and her fears for Richard's safety grew. She'd last heard from him in March.

To share her worries with someone, she phoned Dorothea in Hamburg from the hospital. She'd heard nothing from Fritz either and had already turned to the Red Cross in an attempt to establish whether her husband was among the prisoners of war.

'All they could do was feed me a few empty promises and say the situation was very unclear. It could be our letters haven't come because of so many supply ships being sunk. Maybe both our men are safe and sound somewhere.'

'Yes,' was all Paula could say. How she hated the uncertainty, but she was forced to live with it over the next few weeks, as neither she nor Dorothea received word from their husbands.

By Richard's forty-second birthday, 23 July, Paula still didn't know whether or not he was alive. How was she supposed to carry on reassuring the children when she herself was close to despair? But when she came home from work that evening Emilia greeted her with even more excitement than usual.

'Mama, there's a letter from Papa at last!' She waved the distinctive field post envelope as she ran towards her mother. 'Exactly on his birthday – it makes it seem as though he's here too!'

Paula took the envelope from her daughter and hungrily searched for clues. Richard had a new military mail number. She felt weak with relief. He hadn't ended up a prisoner of war. He was alive.

> My dearest Paula
> I haven't heard from you for a long time and fear my recent letters haven't reached you either. The final weeks in Tunis were disastrous. It was clear we would have to surrender. All the field hospitals were dismantled and made ready for travel. Fritz had arranged for us to accompany one of the last hospital ships bound for Italy. Together with all the wounded men in our care, we reached Sicily in May, only for Allied troops to

capture the island in early July. Our leaders decided the wounded should be left in the care of Italian civilian doctors, while all military medical staff were promptly shipped off to the mainland. So here we are in Rome, awaiting orders. They may send us to France. I don't know whether we'll keep this mail number or get a different one. I must admit, it's wonderful to be back in Rome. And guess what? Luigi's little shop is still there! His eldest son runs it for him these days and still has stocks of photographic film. I told him how we'd been there in September 1928, and he actually remembered something of our visit because it was the only time anybody had ever bought their entire stock of film! Just like before, the people here are very friendly and open, but there's growing unrest within the country. Many have had enough of Il Duce but will only say so off the record. I'm afraid things will soon erupt here and Mussolini won't know what's hit him. The people here are so weary of war, they're desperate for peace, but while their government goes on preaching conflict there are only two choices: victory or downfall. And most people here no longer believe in any glorious end to all this. There are, of course, always the eternal optimists who believe in miracle weapons and final victory, but anyone with a modicum of intelligence knows that after what has happened at Stalingrad and Tunis only the long-drawn-out path to the inevitable remains.

But rest assured that Fritz and I are in a safe place and enjoying Rome. As ever, I'm enclosing some photos.

With all my love
Richard

Paula studied the three photos closely. Richard and Fritz, in uniform, standing in front of the Colosseum. Luigi's shop, looking much the same as it had fifteen years ago. Then one of the Roman Forum with a comment from Richard written on the back: 'Ruins are only beautiful if they're at least two thousand years old.'

On Saturday Paula phoned Dorothea from the hospital line and told her about Richard's letter.

Dorothea's joy almost bounced down the line. 'Wonderful! That means I'll hear from Fritz soon. I'd love to be in Rome right now! What I'd give for some decent sleep and just one night without the bombing. The main thing is that our menfolk are safe. Everything else can carry on as normal in the meantime.'

Rudi started barking in the background and Paula could also hear the sound of Henriette and Harri squabbling.

'Sorry, I'll have to stop now,' said Dorothea. 'Sounds as though our own war has broken out here! Shall we talk again on Monday?'

'Yes, I'll call you as soon as I can then. Perhaps your letter will have come by then too!'

For just a moment a ray of light seemed to break through the gloom and Paula permitted herself the luxury to hope that the worst was over.

Chapter 49

Rome was paradise for Richard and Fritz after so many months in North Africa. They both worked in one of the hospitals dedicated only to military staff and could continue to do so, provided they were not deployed elsewhere. This meant that Richard could devote himself to psychiatric work again, and as they had fixed working hours, they could take time out to enjoy the Eternal City. Richard had started an Italian course every Monday and persuaded Fritz to go along with him.

'The war's got to have some use,' remarked Richard, 'even if it's just learning a new language.'

'I suppose you'll have us learning French if we get sent off to France, won't you?' Fritz still teased his rather serious friend at every opportunity.

'Let's see if there's time!' Richard said with a grin.

During their Italian class on 9 August Richard's thoughts were taken up with his children even more than usual. Today was the twins' eleventh birthday. It was the third birthday they'd had to spend without him. He hoped it would be the last time he'd be so far away on their special day.

Fritz noticed how quiet and subdued his friend was. 'Are you thinking about the children?'

Richard nodded. The class helped distract them both.

A Fight in Silence

That evening they returned to their lodgings and the latest military mail delivery. There was nothing for Richard this time, but a letter had come for Fritz.

'At last!' he shouted, but then faltered. 'This is from Professor Wehmeyer?' He was puzzled. He ripped open the envelope and read the letter in silence. Richard saw the colour drain from his face and his body start to tremble. The letter fell to the floor.

'Fritz, what is it?'

Fritz couldn't speak. His face was completely without expression. He stared straight in front of him.

'Fritz!'

Still no reply. Richard bent to pick up the letter. Fritz didn't react so Richard started reading. Still no reaction.

> My dear colleague, Herr Ellerweg
> It is extremely difficult for me to have to be the one to bring you this news. I fear, however, that nobody else here has felt able to take this on. Starting on the night of 24 July, Hamburg has experienced the worst bombing raids imaginable. British bombers pounded our beloved home city with incendiaries until 3 August, targeting our residential areas. We still don't know how many people have died. The streets are littered with charred bodies, and early estimates speak of forty thousand dead. With the greatest of sadness I have learned that your wife and two children, Henriette and Harri, all fell victim to this cowardly attack. Your father managed to save himself at first but the shock led to a major heart attack and he died two days later in our hospital. Please accept my deepest and most sincere condolences. I

always considered your wife, Dorothea, to be one of the best theatre nurses I had ever worked with. Your father was a most empathetic colleague. It breaks my heart to think of your children's happy laughter, now forever silenced. I wish I could find the words to ease the terrible pain in some way, but the tragedy that has befallen our flourishing city is too dreadful for any words.

In deepest sympathy
Your colleague, H. P. Wehmeyer

'My God, my God, Fritz, I am so very sorry.' Richard could do no more than whisper.

Fritz was still staring straight ahead, his face expressionless, but then he suddenly let out a cry of such pain and torment that Richard's blood ran cold. Before he realised what was happening Fritz had seized a bedside lamp and hurled it against the wall, where it shattered into pieces. Someone flung open the door to their shared room.

'What's going on?' This was Dr Buchwald, who shared the room next door with another colleague.

'Get away from me!' Fritz roared, seizing a chair and flinging it against the wall.

'Fritz, calm yourself. This won't help!' Richard urged his friend, but in vain. Fritz was raging like a madman.

Dr Buchwald brought Franke, his room-mate, to help Richard, who swiftly put them in the picture.

'He's just heard that his wife, children and father have all died during the latest air raids.' Richard was trying to hold Fritz.

'Oh God, how terrible.' Dr Buchwald himself had gone white.

'I need Evipan!' Richard looked straight at Dr Buchwald. 'Quickly!'

'No!' roared Fritz. 'Don't inject me!'

'Keep still, Fritz,' said Richard, using all his strength to hold his dear friend down on the floor. He feared the despair could drive him to destroy everything in the room. Dr Buchwald hurried back with the Evipan at the ready and helped his colleague hold Fritz long enough for Richard to administer the injection. It took only a few seconds for Fritz's muscles to slacken and relax. They lifted him on to the bed.

'This is strictly between us,' said Richard. 'He'll be his old self tomorrow, you have my word.'

The two colleagues nodded and left.

The effects of the Evipan lasted about an hour and then Fritz slowly came round. 'You just drugged me,' he groaned.

'That's right. You gave me no choice.'

Fritz stared at the ceiling. 'Tell me it isn't true, Richard. Tell me someone's playing some terrible joke on me.'

'You know that would be a lie,' said Richard quietly.

'Can you explain why it's always me? Why it's always my children? First Gottlieb, now Henriette and Harri. Why? And Doro, and my father . . . They've never harmed anyone. They were all completely innocent, had nothing to do with the war. Can you tell me why the Royal Air Force would deliberately target residential areas, murdering countless innocent people?'

'I can't explain any of it.' Richard felt helpless. He seized his friend by the hand. 'You've had the worst time any man could have. I beg you not to give up, Fritz. I need you. You're my closest friend. I don't want to lose you.'

'Don't worry. I'm not going to shoot myself or jump out of a window. Doro was a practising Catholic, after all. She'd have no truck with suicide.'

In the weeks following his loss Fritz was desolate and became very introverted, but Richard knew his friend was trying to fight back and finding refuge in his work. He saw how Fritz took on extra shifts and pushed himself to the limit and beyond, as he had done in Tunis and Tobruk. The difference this time was that he was doing it more for himself than for the wounded men. The more he worked, the less space there was for the pain.

Richard heard from his own father that they too had been bombed out of their home and that the workshop had been completely destroyed. At least no one had died. Margit and her family now lived at the Moorfleet allotment garden, while Richard's parents had moved in with Paula's father, whose house remained untouched.

Meanwhile, in Italy, the political unrest continued to grow. Mussolini had been toppled by his own people but Hitler had helped him suppress the rebellion and he came back to power. The Italians no longer felt themselves to be a united nation and the Germans were an occupying force who propped up Mussolini. Both Richard and Fritz noticed how the mood was shifting, how disgruntled locals now gave them and their uniforms contemptuous glances instead of the previous open and friendly reception.

The expected posting to France, to Cherbourg in fact, came at the end of November 1943.

'I'd have gone for Paris myself. What are we supposed to do in a seaside resort out of season?' Fritz had recently regained his sense of humour, but it wasn't without a cynical edge.

'Yes, the weather could be better,' said Richard in wry agreement. 'But at least this way we're getting closer to our home country.'

'What's left of it. Come on, let's look at what passes for a field hospital here and make ourselves useful.'

When Christmas came Fritz decided to forego his leave. 'I've got nowhere to go back to,' he said.

'You could come to us!'

'Thanks. I know you mean well, Richard, but it would remind me too much of what I've lost. No, I'd rather stay here.'

Richard travelled home to his family with mixed feelings that year. On the one hand, he was looking forward to seeing them, but on the other, he was extremely worried about Fritz. He knew how little joy his friend now found in life.

Chapter 50

Christmas that year was the most cheerless Paula had ever known. For the first time in their young lives, Emilia and Georg understood death. It was no longer an unknown that happened to other people. The deaths of Fritz's children had torn a huge hole in their lives, more than any other wartime death. When Jürgen had fallen early in 1940, the twins had been seven and had simply accepted it. They hadn't seen their older cousin that often and so didn't have a strong attachment to him, but they'd grown up with Henriette and Harri. On top of all this, Frau Heiroth was still in mourning for her son and constantly full of bad tidings. Paula hated this dismal atmosphere and would have preferred to move out, but accommodation was in short supply. She was relieved when Frau Heiroth announced she was planning to spend Christmas with her sister.

When Richard arrived home his mood was not a great deal better than that of their landlady. He was deeply concerned about his friend and feared that he was taking risks with his safety. He mentioned this over the Christmas meal. There was only a basic meatloaf this year, with potatoes and a bit of red cabbage.

'Will Uncle Fritz die too?' Emilia asked.

'What makes you ask that, poppet?'

'Well, if he's not paying attention to his safety, and he's stayed at the Front . . .' She hesitated. 'But you'll pay attention, won't you, Papa?'

'Always, poppet. And I always look after Uncle Fritz too.'

'What happens when someone dies?' chipped in Georg. 'Where do we go when we're dead?'

Paula was about to talk about all the souls going to heaven, but Richard got in first.

'Nobody knows,' he said.

Today of all days, why did Richard have to be so damnably honest? Couldn't he just have come up with the usual line about paradise? But there was no stopping him now.

'Life is a great mystery, you know. Medicine can do a lot, but there's one thing it can't do, and that's bring the dead back to life. If someone dies because his heart has stopped beating, we can't just bring him round again with a new heart. The spark of life has gone out and we don't know what kindled it in the first place. The Church calls it the spirit. It's like a car engine breaking down. You get a replacement engine and have it fitted and the car works again, but only with a driver at the wheel. If the driver gets out and goes off, it doesn't matter how many new engines the mechanic puts in place, the car won't go on its own.'

'So is the spirit the driver?' asked Emilia.

'Yes.'

'And it gets out when the body's broken down, instead of waiting to be repaired. So where does it go, this spirit? Does it look for a new car, like the driver does?'

'Hindus and Buddhists believe that the spirit seeks out a new body that is not yet born and is then reborn as either a human or an animal. Christians believe that the spirit goes back to God and must first go to purgatory to be cleansed of all its bad deeds. If the spirit has been particularly bad, then it has to suffer permanently in hell. I believe anything is possible. Perhaps some spirits drift into nothingness and stop existing because they've existed for long enough. Whatever it may be, we'll only find out when we die ourselves.'

'And what about ghosts?' asked Georg. 'Do you think that many spirits turn into ghosts?'

'Ghosts don't exist,' retorted Emilia.

'Well, not like in the kind of ghost stories you've perhaps heard,' Richard said, backing her up. 'But there may be some spirits that float around for a while in the place where their body died.'

'Do you think that Henriette, Harri and Aunt Dorothea are still floating around in the ruins?'

'Definitely not. If they were going to float around anywhere, it would be near Uncle Fritz, and they'd be telling him they're all right, but they've never shown up there. That's why I think they've been in a better place for a long time. In any case, no one knows which way they've gone.'

When Richard and Paula were in their bedroom much later that evening she gently admonished him. 'I hope the children won't have nightmares about that conversation. Couldn't you just have told them the usual?'

'No,' he replied without hesitation. 'I had to be perfectly honest with them and tell them what I myself believe. They're too old now for fairy tales.'

'You think Christian teaching is a fairy tale?'

'No, I see it as a parable that helps people make sense of the incomprehensible. In times like these I prefer my story about the car.'

'Richard, you're incorrigible.'

'I know. You tell me often enough!' He burst into such infectious laughter that Paula couldn't help but do the same.

Then she whispered in his ear, 'Do you know how much I love you?'

He whispered back, 'As much as I do you?'

'At least as much as that. And I just wouldn't know what to do if I were ever to lose you. Promise me you'll always come back to us unharmed, whatever happens.'

'I've promised you that right from the start, and I hereby renew my promise! Please don't worry. We're sitting tight in Cherbourg now. No Allied general would dare land in the middle of Normandy. Everything will be fine, Paula. I promise you.'

◆ ◆ ◆

The festive season, with its hint of a normal family life, ended all too soon, as it had done every year since Richard's conscription. At the start of 1944 Paula found herself once again taking care of patients and also looking for a new home tutor for Georg. Emilia had started at the local grammar school the previous autumn, and Paula didn't want Georg to fall too far behind his twin sister. She hoped that the war would soon end, whatever the outcome, and that Georg would be able to go back to specialist tuition for deaf and dumb children and prepare properly for his end-of-school *Abitur* examinations. It pained her deeply to see how marginalised his deafness had left him, in spite of his obvious intelligence.

Spring came and Richard's letters from the Front served to reassure her. There seemed to be no immediate danger and even Fritz, after everything he'd been through, seemed to be coming to terms with his terrible loss, on the outside at least.

That was until one day in June when she returned to their lodgings after work as usual only to be met by a distraught Frau Heiroth.

'Frau Doctor Hellmer, have you heard it all on the radio?'

'What's on the radio?'

'The English and the Americans have landed in Normandy! Isn't that exactly where your husband's stationed?'

Paula froze. 'Normandy's a big place. Where exactly have they landed?'

'Somewhere near Cherbourg.'

Cherbourg! Fear gripped Paula's heart.

Chapter 51

'I cannot work in these conditions!' roared Fritz as yet more plaster broke away from the ceiling and trickled on to his face. Gunfire had been thundering around them for hours, and now the explosions came nearer, making the walls shake. Fritz was tending a soldier with a gunshot wound to the upper arm and the man groaned in pain in spite of the procaine injection.

'Hasn't anyone told those idiots out there this is a field hospital?'

'D'you really think that lot care? They've already bombed a whole city full of innocent civilians to smithereens, so why would they bother about a field hospital?' Richard spoke with bitterness as he stood handing Fritz bandages. This was normally a job for the nurse, but most of them were busy preparing to evacuate all the wounded.

'You're right. Silly question,' said Fritz. Then he spoke to his patient. 'Right, all done. You were lucky the bullet went straight through without touching the bone. It'll heal well. Nurse Heidi, take this man to the transport.'

'Are we clearing out already?' asked Richard. 'I thought we were supposed to hang on here until the afternoon.'

'Can you do any decent work here? I can't.' Fritz was in no doubt. 'If we want to get out of here at all, then we should try right now. Nurse Heidi, you're acting like a headless chicken. I've already told you to take this man to the medical vehicles outside.'

'Oh God, we're all going to die!' Heidi kept shouting the same thing. She was very young, twenty at the most, by Richard's reckoning, and had probably been sent straight to the Front after completing her training. She'd arrived in Cherbourg only three weeks ago.

'You're right there,' said Fritz. 'It's just a question of when. And now, will you just do as I asked?'

Sister Heidi was still running around, quite distraught, still saying, 'We're all going to die!'

Fritz sighed and turned back to the patient he'd just finished tending. 'Go down the corridor to the back and you'll find the buses.' The man nodded and did as he was told, even though he was still wobbly on his feet.

Fritz took off his surgical apron and put on his uniform jacket and cap.

'I think Nurse Heidi's problem falls within your area of expertise, Richard. Can you do anything for her?'

Richard nodded and walked slowly towards her. The guns thundered again, there was a loud noise close by and more plaster cascaded down from the ceiling. Sister Heidi fled the treatment room in sheer panic, but not to the rear entrance and the waiting transport but to the main entrance.

Richard went after her. 'Nurse! Come back here! You're running towards enemy fire!' He caught up with her just as she reached the main entrance and grabbed hold of her. 'Come with me. Not out there.'

She stared back at him, her eyes dead. 'We're all going to die, we're all going to die!'

'Not if you come with me. Now!' Richard had started to head back to the treatment room with her when she lost all control, turned on him like a woman possessed, punched him hard in the chest and broke free.

'Fritz, quickly! Need you here!' shouted Richard as he tried to block her path towards the firing line.

'Coming!' called Fritz, still buttoning up his jacket as he ran.

Then a shell exploded, catching Richard in the belly and knocking him to the ground.

'Oh God, we're all going to die!' Nurse Heidi kept up the same lament.

'Shut your mouth, once and for all!' Fritz bellowed at her, then he knelt close to Richard. 'Damn it, Richard . . .'

'I don't think it's much,' said Richard, making light of his wound. He tried to touch the area where he'd been hit and felt something warm and wet in the place he expected only the cloth of his uniform to be. In disbelief, he gazed at the blood on his hand. 'This can't be right. There's no pain.'

'That's because you're in shock. That'll soon change.' Fritz tore away what remained of Richard's ripped jacket and shirt, took several rolls of bandage from his bag and pressed them against the wound. The pressure was uncomfortable, but there was still no pain. Was he imagining it, or were Fritz's hands really shaking?

Richard felt that time was passing more slowly than usual, and the thunder of heavy artillery and the nurse's shrieks lost all meaning. He could see and hear, but his reason told him he should be doubling up with pain. But he felt nothing, neither pain nor fear.

'Is it serious?' he asked Fritz.

'I can only tell you that once I find out what internal injuries the shrapnel's caused.' Fritz continued working on the bandaging. 'What matters now is that you don't bleed to death.'

Nurse Heidi gave another piercing shriek, causing Richard to turn and look in her direction. An American soldier had come charging into the hospital, his gun at the ready. He saw the nurse and fired. Even against the background of shelling, Richard heard her body hit the ground, lifeless.

Fritz whipped around, shouting in English, 'This is a field hospital! We are not fighting troops!' The American now aimed at Fritz.

'We surrender!' Fritz raised both his hands, still kneeling by his wounded friend. The American reloaded.

'Didn't you hear? We surrender!' Fritz was desperate, raising his hands even higher.

Richard noticed the staring eyes of this young man, probably no older than the nurse he'd just shot dead. His gaze was blank. Richard knew the boy had lost his mind. Words wouldn't touch him. He hadn't taken in the fact that Fritz was surrendering. He slowly curved his finger around the trigger. This boy really was going to shoot Fritz. Richard's right hand slid swiftly to his belt and, before he realised what he was doing, he'd drawn and fired straight into the American's face. He fell backwards, but with his final movement his index finger squeezed the trigger. The bullet missed Fritz by an inch, whisking off his cap.

'My God,' whispered Fritz, his voice trembling. 'That one was ready to shoot us even though we'd surrendered. Why?'

Richard was about to explain to Fritz that the staring eyes indicated the man had lost his mind but, before he could even begin, he felt pain so severe it took his breath away and left him gasping.

With the greatest of care, Fritz took the pistol still clamped tightly in Richard's hand. 'If I help you, can you stand up? We need to leave.' He got hold of Richard and tried to pull him to his feet. Richard did all he could to cooperate, but the pain tore through him a second time. 'Can't do it,' he gasped.

'Then I'll just carry you. It'll hurt, I'm warning you.'

Richard nodded dumbly. He couldn't even begin to imagine how this pain could possibly get any worse.

Fritz lifted him a little higher, crouched again to brace himself, then heaved his friend over his shoulder.

He was right. The pain did get worse. Richard chewed on his lip so as not to scream out loud as his own body weight pressed on the wound, while Fritz, panting with the exertion, carried him over his shoulder as he might a sack of potatoes, all the way to the rear exit, where help came at last.

'We're the last out,' grunted Fritz. 'We've already seen one Yank. We have to get out of here.'

Richard almost passed out with the pain as they loaded him into the medical transport, but he waited in vain for the blessed relief of falling fully unconscious. Fritz climbed aboard and checked the emergency dressing. The fresh patch of blood did not fill him with confidence.

'You must promise me one thing, Fritz. If I don't make it, don't tell Paula in a letter. Go and see her. Be there with her.'

'I'm not letting you die. Never.'

'It hurts like hell,' moaned Richard. 'Can't you knock me out with Evipan?'

Fritz nodded and reached inside his bag for the injection.

'I'll get you right,' he promised, easing the needle into the crook of Richard's arm. 'If I fail, I'll tell Paula myself. But that's not going to happen. I'm not going to lose you to this damned war, not after losing Doro and the kids. Never!' He pressed home the needle, and the last thing Richard saw, before everything went black and the pain went away, were the tears in his best friend's eyes.

Chapter 52

Over the last two years Göttingen had come to look more and more like a military hospital base. Surgical wards had been added to the existing psychiatric facility and were filled with wounded soldiers. Paula's responsibilities now included psychiatric counselling on these surgical wards, as the wounded so often developed psychoses or became suicidal following permanent disability.

Paula's frequent deployment to these wards meant she swiftly got an understanding of where on the Front the worst fighting was happening. Since the Allies had landed in Normandy, she had heard nothing from Richard. She tried to reassure herself with the knowledge that it was hard to maintain any communications at all in these difficult times, although the special German Reichsbahn train continued to run as before, ferrying the wounded out of France. Information was sparse, but one day she learned that one of the casualties on the ward had been wounded in Cherbourg.

'Did you happen to meet my husband there?' she asked him. 'Dr Richard Hellmer? Or his friend, Dr Fritz Ellerweg?'

'I don't know your husband, I'm afraid. But Dr Ellerweg, yes, I know him – he operated on me. It's thanks to him I still have my leg.'

'So what was it like in Cherbourg?'

'I don't want to scare you, but it was pretty horrific. We were as good as surrounded, and I'm lucky I got out in time. I've heard that the field hospital where I had my operation got heavily bombarded a couple of days after I'd left. Everyone had to be evacuated. But I only learned that second-hand, so I don't really know what happened.'

Days went by, more and more wounded arrived from the Western Front, but however many people Paula asked, nobody had news of Richard. Official reports about Cherbourg were restrained, indicating only that the men were fighting bravely.

One Saturday morning in late June, Paula was sitting writing up her patients' notes when Sister Sibylle came into her office. 'Frau Doctor Hellmer, you're asked to go immediately to the surgeon on 2B. It seems urgent.'

Paula set down her fountain pen. 'And what exactly is so urgent? Is it someone hallucinating, or just another fit of crying caused by our hardened surgeons pushing someone to the limit?'

Sister Sibylle giggled. 'I was only told that you're needed.'

Waiting for her at Ward 2B stood Dr Dührsen, a young surgeon who reminded her a little of Fritz. He was one of several who called for her only if it was really important.

'We have a very difficult case here,' he started to explain. 'The moment he arrived here, he started insisting on seeing you.'

Paula frowned and said, 'What are his symptoms?'

'That's for you to establish. Best if you take a look at him. He'll tell you.'

'He isn't behaving aggressively, is he?'

'No, don't worry, apart from the fact he persists in demanding a woman psychiatrist, he doesn't seem violent. You'll find him in the observation room, first bed by the window.' Dr Dührsen grinned and Paula wavered. Surgeons sometimes had a very odd sense of humour, especially this one.

When she walked into the observation room she noticed nothing unusual. All the men seemed calm, most were asleep, a few were reading, two were playing cards.

The man by the window pulled himself up when he saw her walk in. Paula froze in her tracks. 'Richard!' Everyone turned to look. 'Richard! You're here! You're alive!'

She rushed to his bed, put her arms around him and kissed him, oblivious to the cheering and clapping going on around them. Richard held her close and returned her kisses.

'I've been so worried about you!' she cried, once she'd let him go. 'Are you badly wounded? Is it serious?' She took a moment to sit back and look at him closely. His face was pale, there were dark rings under his eyes, and his cheeks were sunken, as if he'd lost weight.

'Everything seems better now,' he replied. 'I'm home and I'm staying.' He reached in the bedside cupboard for a sealed envelope.

'Keep this safe – Fritz gave it to me,' he whispered to her. 'There are two operative reports. One's the official one, and Dr Dührsen's got that, and one's the real one – that's what you've now got.'

Paula put the envelope out of sight in her uniform pocket. 'I don't understand . . .'

'Sit down here on the bed and I'll tell you.'

And so Richard told her how he'd been badly wounded, how they'd almost been shot by the crazed American and how Fritz had brought him to safety behind their own lines.

'But I don't really remember everything, as good old Fritz gave me a hefty dose of Evipan. By the time I came round, he'd operated on me and arranged my transport home. When he said goodbye, he told me he'd hugely exaggerated in the official report. He reckons anyone who reads it will think I've been practically disembowelled and am not fit for further service at the Front.' The trace of a tired smile played around his mouth. 'What I really had was a few bits of shrapnel in my belly and two in my liver. I was lucky it all just missed the abdominal aorta.'

'Thank God it did. When can you come home?'

'If everything carries on healing well, in a couple of days, that's all. Fritz stuffed me full of sulphonamides too, to be on the safe side. I can't tell you how sick they make me feel, but he said that's no bad thing because I mustn't eat too much until my belly's healed up.'

Paula laughed. 'That's typical of Fritz. So where is he now?'

'Don't know. The last I saw of him was when he arranged to get me to the railway station.' Richard took a deep breath. Paula could see how tiring it had been to say all this, in spite of his forced good cheer.

'Oh, something else,' he added. 'You'll need to get me some clothes from somewhere. We had to get out of there so fast that we left everything, and the uniform I had on at the time, well, it's not usable, apart from the boots.' There was another sigh. 'I couldn't even save my Leica!'

'But you're safe! That's the important thing. Nothing else matters.'

'I'm still cross about the Leica.'

'That means you're getting better.'

He gave her a smile. 'Yes, that's the end of my war at the Front. That's all that matters.'

Chapter 53

Richard made a slow but sure recovery from his war wounds. Paula was careful to secure from the chief medical officer documentation confirming that Richard was permanently unfit for service as a result of his injuries.

On the one hand, Richard could now enjoy being with his family again and sharing in the lives of his children, but on the other, he soon became all too familiar with the uncertainty suffered by Paula over the last three years. He sent a number of letters to Fritz at the Front, but got no replies. Was Fritz not receiving the letters, or had they all gone missing? Had his friend ended up as a prisoner of war? Had he fallen? No, he couldn't countenance that, but ever since he'd shot the American in self-defence it had been clear to him that neither the medical corps nor unconditional surrender could effectively protect Fritz from the worst. Gruesome images plagued Richard's mind – never the image of the soldier he'd shot in the head, only that of Fritz, kneeling helplessly on the ground, his hands up in surrender; Fritz, who'd have been shot dead if Richard hadn't fired first. And Richard had other people to worry about besides. He often thought of his family in Hamburg, and of Paula's father. His father-in-law still had a telephone that worked, but the connection was becoming more unreliable by the day so Richard decided to go to Hamburg to see the situation there for himself.

It was now the end of August, and Paula wasn't sure what to do, as Emilia and Georg wanted to accompany their father. She allowed herself to be persuaded that the trip would not be too dangerous. Since the terrible raids of the previous summer the city had been largely reduced to ruins and was no longer an attractive target for the Allied bombers. For a while now they had concentrated all their attention on hitherto undisturbed German cities, meaning that Paula had become so busy in the hospital that it was hard to take time off to go to Hamburg with the others.

'That's the price you pay for realising your dream of becoming a psychiatrist while I've been at home seeing to the children,' Richard teased her.

'When you come back I'm going to ask Professor Ewald if he can find you a post. If you're fit enough to go to Hamburg, you're fit enough to work.'

'You'll make me think you begrudge me my period of convalescence. Do you want to ask him if I could take over your job so you can be at home again?'

'Definitely not! But I do think it would do you good to have a routine again.'

'I'll ask him myself once we're back. Paula, I love you, even though you sound like a nagging washerwoman at the moment.'

'Washerwoman, that's it – that's what you've forgotten to do! You haven't collected our dry cleaning. Seeing as you're the one at home all day, you might have thought of picking that up. I'll just have to do it myself tomorrow.'

'Oh, Paula, be nice to me again. I'll do better, promise! I'll collect the laundry first thing tomorrow before I go to the station.' He pulled her gently towards him, and she nestled into him, like she used to.

'And then you'll miss your train, so no, you won't do that – I'll do it. It's OK. The main thing is that you and the children come home safely.'

'You can't get rid of us that easily!' he said, kissing her. 'We're so clingy, we'll keep coming back!'

◆ ◆ ◆

The trains were still surprisingly reliable, in spite of the damage to the infrastructure caused by the bombing raids. They found seats easily, as hardly anyone went in the direction of Hamburg these days, while all the trains coming from the other direction were packed. At Hannover, Emilia noticed a cattle truck in a siding. People were calling out for water and trying to push their hands through ventilation slits covered in barbed wire.

'Papa, why are there people in that wagon? And why's there barbed wire?'

Richard took a look out of the window with her. 'I don't know, poppet.'

'Perhaps they're prisoners of war,' said Georg sagely.

'But there are women's voices too,' Emilia explained to him. 'They're shouting in German.'

'I really don't know, poppet,' said Richard again. He tried to think of some plausible explanation but couldn't come up with anything. As far as he knew, the Nazis always shipped off their political opponents to the nearest concentration camp and the sick and feeble-minded were collected from institutions by bus.

At Hannover there was a change of crew on the train. When the woman came to check their tickets, Richard asked her outright about the cattle truck.

'I don't know what kind of people are in there,' she said, clipping their tickets. 'I just know the truck's supposed to be going to Poland.'

'Why's it got that barbed wire?' asked Emilia.

'Probably so they don't throw stuff out during the journey,' replied the conductor. 'Everyone knows how mucky the Poles are.'

'But they're asking for water in German.'

'Nobody would understand if they did it in Polish. I wish you a pleasant onward journey to Hamburg,' she said, before leaving their compartment.

'Papa, what's happening, do you think?'

Giving a light shrug of the shoulders, Richard said, 'Maybe they're Polish people who were working here and are being taken home because so much has been flattened.'

Their train arrived in Hamburg two hours later. As they crossed the Elbe they saw bombed and burnt-out buildings with only the outside walls still standing. Huge mounds of rubble made many streets impassable. Emilia and Georg stared through the train window in disbelief. The destruction was the same across the whole of the city.

'Everything's in ruins! There isn't a single house left.' Emilia was appalled.

'Grandpa Wilhelm's house is still standing,' said Richard.

'But Grandpa Hans-Kurt's workshop isn't, is it?'

'And what about our car?' asked Georg.

'The war's destroyed all that.'

As their train rolled into Hamburg main station they realised that its glass canopy had suffered too. But it was astonishing how much activity still went on in this otherwise ruined city.

'Let's see if the elevated railway's still working,' Richard said to the children. Then they heard a woman's voice calling out, 'Dr Hellmer, is it really you?'

Richard turned to find a middle-aged strawberry blonde with freckles, now a little faded by the years.

'Do we know each other?' He was puzzled at the interruption.

'Yes, but from a long way back. It's Georg I recognise.'

Richard glanced down at his son, who appeared equally baffled.

'Sister Elfriede. You used to collect your wife from the hospital by car, and Georg was in the children's hospital with diphtheria.'

Georg broke into a smile as the memory of this nurse came back to him, Richard too.

'You recruited us to the People's Welfare before the Nazis took it over.'

'That's right. A lot's happened since then.' She sighed. 'But bumping into you here today, it's a godsend.'

'Really?'

Sister Elfriede nodded. 'Can you make time tomorrow to come to Langenhorn? It's to do with Dr Krüger. There is nobody there I can trust with what I've found out, and it's too monstrous for me to keep to myself. Do come. Please.'

'When?'

'Three o'clock tomorrow, in front of the church.'

'I'll be there.'

Chapter 54

It felt strange to step inside his father-in-law's home for the first time in three years. The entrance hall with its coat cupboard looked just the same as in 1926, when he had collected Paula for the first time. The front room had hardly changed either.

'Richard, you're here! This is wonderful!' His mother was the first to greet him, hugging him as if he were still a little boy. Then it was his father's turn to rejoice in their son's arrival with an enthusiastic embrace. His father-in-law greeted him with a warm handshake and an affectionate pat on the shoulder, reserving his hugs for the grandchildren. Dear Frau Koch welcomed him with a smile, while gently scolding him for not bringing Paula with him.

'That's what it's like when the lady of the house earns all the money! Work comes first.' Richard said with a grin. 'Jokes aside, she'd have loved to come, but they can't manage without her at the hospital at the moment. So I thought I'd use a little of my convalescence period when no one is expecting anything of me to come and see you all.'

'We've been so worried about you,' his father confessed. 'Are you better yet, my boy?'

'Absolutely, Papa. With Fritz in charge, you're safe as houses. He's the best surgeon I know.'

His mother gestured him towards the table. 'Look! To celebrate, we've baked apple cake with apples from the allotment.' They all took their places around the table and Richard's mother cut the cake. 'Not too big a slice for me, thank you – just half of that one.'

'But you need to get your strength back!'

'You're right, but that's why half is enough. My belly's still recovering from all the shrapnel.'

'But it'll recover fully, won't it?'

'You bet. I'll be tucking in again by Christmas.' He beamed at his mother but then quickly changed the subject. 'It looks as though you've got everything well set up here. Do you still have the same consulting room at the end of the hallway?'

'Yes,' replied his father-in-law. 'You have to make use of whatever you've got. Paula's decision to marry into the family of a master carpenter gives us a great advantage, even though I've had to sacrifice my biggest and best living-room cupboard for your father's inventions!'

'What do you mean? It's still there.'

Wilhelm and Hans-Kurt chuckled.

'Yes, but it's not a cupboard any more.' Richard's father got up and went over to it. 'Look!' He released two hooks that were barely noticeable then pulled down the door from the top. It opened out into a large double bed.

'Books might be able to rest on a shelf, but people can't. I got hold of a slatted wooden frame to put the mattress on. The cupboard door's only there for show. You can sleep just as well in that bed as in any. This is how we're keeping our heads above water. Our workshop may have been destroyed but our ideas march on. Holger's lads can do this kind of work in the customer's home, direct to order. Our capital was always our creativity. Yes, the workshop's gone, but we still own our piece of woodland. When Karl eventually comes home from the war we'll rebuild and go for specialisation in the kind of space-saving furniture that people will need. We're already trying out kitchen benches and tables that anyone can transform into a bed in a few nifty moves.'

'That's ingenious!' Richard leapt up in excitement and went to look more closely at the bed. The linen was held down by straps so that it didn't slide off when the bed was folded back up. 'Could you make a bed like that for Paula and me?'

'Yes, but I don't know how we'd get it to Göttingen!'

'I'm not thinking of there. The war can't possibly go on for ever, and when it's over we'd like to come back to Hamburg. There's no suitable school for Georg in Göttingen.'

'So why wait until after the war? There's room for everyone here!' said Paula's father.

'With the Nazis still in power and people like Krüger acting as informants, it's still dangerous for Georg. But it might just be that fate has dealt me a card to use against Krüger.' He told them about his appointment with Sister Elfriede.

'If you need any support in sticking something on that swine of a man, I'm right with you.' His father-in-law was in no doubt. 'I know how to do it. The last time it took him weeks to shake off the suspicion that he'd been selling medicines on the black market. It was most unfortunate that he fell on his feet again and wormed his way into a senior post in the children's department at Langenhorn. I want to see that man brought down for all the suffering he's caused.'

'I'll do my best,' Richard promised.

◆ ◆ ◆

The following day at three o'clock, Sister Elfriede stood waiting for him outside the church in the grounds of Langenhorn. It had taken him an age to get there by tram, as there were problems with the network and he had to keep changing and finding alternative routes. He was amazed that any public transport was working at all in the circumstances, let alone as punctually as it was. But everything he saw from the window was painful for him and stirred memories of the old days in the late

1920s and early 1930s when he had regularly driven this route, and when the asylum at Langenhorn cared about patient welfare and people like Krüger had a rough ride.

'I'm so pleased you're here,' said Sister Elfriede. 'Let's sit inside the church, where no one will disturb us.'

Richard followed her in and sat down next to her. 'So, what's this all about?'

Sister Elfriede took something from her pinafore pocket. It was a list of names and dates of birth. 'After the bombing at Rothenburgsort and the transfer of most of the children to this place, Dr Krüger managed eventually to get himself put in charge of the children's department and, after some toing and froing, became medical director.' Sister Elfriede paused for a moment, took a deep breath, and then carried on. 'During this time, he has killed at least twenty-two children by lethal injection, dissected six of them for research purposes and sent their brains to the Neuroanatomical Institute at Eppendorf. This list gives you the names, dates of birth and file numbers of the children concerned.'

'He murdered children? And dissected them?' Richard struggled to take this in. Even Krüger couldn't have sunk to this level, surely?

'Yes, that's what he did,' said Sister Elfriede. 'It's so truly monstrous that it is hard to believe. I've already tried to get at the files in the archive, but it's difficult. The archivist is vigilant and if there's nothing to occupy her elsewhere it's impossible to take the right files without her noticing. I'd like you to distract her while I get hold of one or two files as evidence. My fear is that these documents will have disappeared by the end of the war and there'll be no proof that the children on this list really were murdered. Will you help me?'

'Definitely. Is it still Frau Unterweger in the archive? She knows me from before.'

'No. She died in the firestorm.' Sister Elfriede lowered her eyes for a moment. 'It's Frau Rating now, and she was appointed two years ago. She's very conscientious, and a dyed-in-the-wool Nazi at that.'

'Charming. I know how to deal with people like her.'

The archive was lodged in an unobtrusive little building between the pavilions that used to be open houses. The children's facility had been added during the intervening years. Richard wondered if the secure unit was the same and whether Kurt Hansen still worked there. He'd have loved to have seen his old colleague again, but the risk of running straight into one of Krüger's informants was too great.

Richard let Sister Elfriede go into the little building first, then waited a short time before knocking at the door. He heard steps approaching as if up a short flight of stairs, then the door opened.

'Yes? What can I do for you?'

'Forgive me for knocking like this, but I'm trying to find House 27C.'

'Are you sure you have the right number? There's no 27C here.'

'Isn't there? Oh, dear – nothing similar then? I've been told my son's in there. He's just turned twelve.'

'For what reason is your son in hospital?'

'Aargh . . .' Richard let out a sudden groan of pain, his hand flying to the old wound.

'Are you all right?'

'I'm so sorry,' gasped Richard, noticing that his little performance was having the desired effect. 'A shell got me a couple of months back. In Cherbourg.' He took several deep breaths. 'There, it's passing already.'

'Do you want to sit down for a moment?'

'Oh yes, please, that's most kind of you.'

She ushered him into the building and to her office, directing him to the only chair in the room.

'Shall I bring you a glass of water?'

'I don't want to put you to any trouble,' replied Richard, letting out a convincing groan.

'That's no trouble at all. Think nothing of it. One moment.' And the archivist left the room.

Richard looked around. Opposite him, the door to the basement stood open. This was where the files of deceased or simply discharged patients were stored. He wondered whether Sister Elfriede had already found what she needed.

Frau Rating came back with the glass of water.

'Thank you.' Richard sipped at it appreciatively.

'And what has your son been diagnosed with?'

'Diphtheria. I only got back to Hamburg last night. Before that I was in the field hospital at Göttingen, you see. My wife told me about Ludwig being in hospital and it not looking so good for him, so I had to come here straight away. I couldn't bear it if he died without my seeing him. In the last three years, I've only had a few days with him on home leave.' He wiped his eyes with deliberate discretion, something which didn't go unnoticed.

'I'm so sorry. If your son has diphtheria, then he'll be in the infection ward.'

They heard footsteps coming up the stairs from the basement. It was Sister Elfriede.

'Did you manage to find the files yourself?' asked Frau Rating. 'I had to look after this gentleman.'

'Yes, I've got everything. Thank you, Frau Rating.'

Frau Rating checked the numbers of the files that Sister Elfriede held quite openly and entered their details in the file loan book.

'Are you going straight back on the ward?'

'Yes.'

'Then you could take this gentleman with you, if you wouldn't mind. He says his son is being treated here for diphtheria and I know he'll need help in finding the infection ward.'

'Of course. Do come with me. I'll show you the way.'

Richard put his glass down on the desk and got up with exaggerated care. 'Many thanks. You're both too kind.'

'We must all stick together at times like this,' said Frau Rating. 'My very best wishes to you and your family.'

'Tell me how you managed to wrap her around that little finger of yours,' said Sister Elfriede once they were out of earshot.

'Tales of wounded German war heroes whose children are at death's door. That does the trick with any of our national comrades,' he said with a smile. 'So have you really got everything?'

'Yes, two files in a linen bag hidden under my pinafore. These here are the ones I was actually meant to collect. If anyone notices that the other two are missing, they'll never think it's anything to do with us.'

Sister Elfriede slid out the bag and handed it to Richard. 'Take good care of it. Maybe I can't stop anything from happening, but at least I can make sure these crimes don't go unpunished.'

'Sister Elfriede, thank you. You're very brave. I won't let you down.'

◆ ◆ ◆

Once back at his father-in-law's home, he studied the documents more closely. They were the records of a three-year-old girl with severe epilepsy and a baby boy with hydrocephaly. Both children had been murdered by injection of Luminal and then dissected. The dissection report was in Krüger's handwriting. Richard passed on the files and the list of names of the other murdered children to his father-in-law.

'Please take good care of this,' Richard said to him. 'This provides us with the evidence that Krüger's a murderer. One day, we'll hold him to account.'

PART THREE

Zero Hour

Chapter 55

On returning to Göttingen, Richard kept his word and applied for a post in psychiatry. Professor Ewald took him on immediately. It was a new experience for Richard to be working alongside his wife and for her to be his point of referral on the workings of the department. At times, he caught himself thinking of staying long-term in Göttingen because he loved the work at the asylum. Living at the home of the melancholic Frau Heiroth, however, was growing increasingly trying. She even burst into Richard and Paula's bedroom one night when she had one of her 'turns', as she liked to call them. When she refused to give them the key, Richard fitted a bolt to the inside of the door, something that led to weeks of tension. At the end of November, Frau Heiroth threatened to give them notice, so Richard and Paula made the decision for her. In December they and the twins returned to Hamburg so that Richard and Paula could take over her seventy-year-old father's practice. Professor Ewald was sorry to lose such expertise and, on Paula's departure, gave her an outstanding reference which confirmed her standing as a consultant in psychiatry.

Karl turned up unexpectedly just before Christmas, accompanied by a pregnant French girl, who he introduced to the family as his wife, Julie. She was a dainty, pretty young woman with curly brown hair and green eyes.

'When Paris fell in August, we had no choice but to disappear,' Karl explained. 'You wouldn't believe what women go through if they've had a relationship with a German. They'd never have forgiven Julie for having my child, and I couldn't possibly have left her behind.'

'So you're a deserter?' Holger was shocked. 'You know that carries the death penalty.'

'You don't need to worry about that, Papa,' Karl said with a grin. 'After all, I worked in administration and, as a good German, I know that you're nothing without your papers. So before we left I made sure I got hold of a blank military discharge form.' He fished out the document and held it out for his father to see. 'I managed to get a marriage certificate the same way, as we'd never have been given permission to tie the knot. This document shows that Julie is my wife. It's so authentic that even Hitler himself wouldn't query it.'

'And what does her family say about her going off with you like this?'

'They as good as drove me to it, to be honest,' she replied in virtually accentless German. 'They can't forgive me for falling in love with Karl and just called me a whore.'

'Julie was working with us as an interpreter,' Karl explained. 'One thing led to another. If there's one good thing to come out of this damned war, it's that Julie and I found each other.'

Still aghast, Holger stared at his son, but Richard started laughing. 'Karl, you're one of us, that's for sure! That idea with the discharge form and the marriage certificate – well done!' He gave Karl an appreciative clap on the shoulder and turned to Julie. 'Welcome to Hamburg, Julie, and to the family. My only worry is how to put you both up here.'

'If that's the only problem, there's space for Karl and Julie at the allotment,' said Holger. 'We're in the process of extending the cabin, in any case. There are plenty of bricks lying around in the rubble and we've got enough to build one more room. Julie, please don't be offended if I sounded a bit sceptical. You are, of course, most warmly welcome. I was just worried about how we'd get you any food coupons if you're living in hiding.'

'Papa, that shouldn't be too much of a problem with these papers.'

◆ ◆ ◆

Christmas was a bright spot in otherwise dark times, thanks to the family being reunited. Only the continuing absence of Fritz cast a shadow. During the next few weeks Richard made regular visits to the Red Cross offices to try to find out where his closest friend might be. But among the thousands of German soldiers who had died or landed in prisoner-of-war camps, he found no mention of Fritz.

Then, on 30 April 1945 news of Hitler's death in the battle for Berlin was broadcast on the radio. While of the highest significance in global terms, for the family, the most important news that day was that Karl and Julie now had a healthy daughter, christened Marie.

◆ ◆ ◆

British occupying forces reached Hamburg on 3 May. At first everything was chaotic and nobody was sure what was going to happen. On the first day there was a total curfew, leaving Richard's mother and Frau Koch wondering how long they could last with their limited food supplies. Fortunately, the curfew was eased the next day and thereafter had to be observed only between nine at night and six in the morning.

The British seized flats in the best areas and it was forbidden for German nationals and British soldiers to speak to one another. Anyone with a request to make of an official body had to do so in English. Anything put forward in German was simply ignored.

'They're treating us like they treat the natives in their colonies,' grumbled Paula's father. 'They see us as second-class citizens.'

'Did you expect anything different?' asked Richard. 'Just remember how they targeted residential areas in the bombing so they could kill as many of us as possible.'

'There was I, thinking things would slowly get better once the war ended,' his father-in-law said with a sigh. 'I'd hoped you'd have been able to use what you know about Krüger against him by now.'

'What makes you think that? Do you really believe the British are going to be interested in the murder of twenty-two German children when they've killed thousands with their own bombs?'

When new food coupons were handed out Richard was shocked and lost all hope that an occupying power would have any interest in crimes committed by German doctors, given its obvious lack of interest in the starving population. Rations were so small they did nothing more than delay death. His parents, Frau Koch and his father-in-law, who, as pensioners, no longer did productive work, were expected to manage on a mere nine hundred calories a day, as were children. As practising doctors, he and Paula were allocated fifteen hundred calories a day.

'How are we supposed to manage on this?' asked his mother. 'I know we can ask Margit and Holger to put something by from the allotment, but that'll never be enough. And what on earth will we do in the winter?'

'We're getting a monthly cigarette quota – sixty for all of us,' said Richard. 'I've heard from patients that you can get a loaf of bread for three cigarettes on the black market in Talstrasse.'

'Trading on the black market can put you in prison,' commented Paula. 'If you were arrested, we'd be in an even worse position than we are now.'

'I'm willing to try it,' announced Frau Koch. 'If I get caught, our little community won't lose very much because my food ration's already small. I'll do the usual fourteen days in prison, and that won't do me any harm.'

Nobody came up with any objections and so Frau Koch became an expert in black market trading. The amount she brought home each day was still not enough to live on, but it did at least help to keep starvation at bay. Holger established a link with farmers in the Vierlande district of Hamburg who worked the land not so far from the family's allotment, offering them his sons' carpentry services in exchange for food. The lads did have to watch out on their way home from these trips, as the British carried out regular checks – any excursion undertaken with the express purpose of stockpiling was forbidden. Anyone caught hoarding food not only had their supplies confiscated but was also sent to prison.

The ban on fraternisation between the British and the Germans relaxed just a few weeks later, however, largely because most of the British weren't sticking to it. There was a big difference between the ordinary soldiers and the rather pompous officers who thought they were a cut above. Survival was at the forefront of everybody's mind, but Richard still nurtured the hope that the time would soon come for him to present the evidence of child murder, particularly as Krüger still held a very senior role and Richard could imagine him holding back his patients' rations so as not to want for anything himself in such hard times.

So at the beginning of July he packed the incriminating material in his briefcase and went off to approach the British military administration.

Even though he spoke good English, the British officials who Richard first came up against could do nothing for him and sent him off to a variety of different people. Eventually, he found himself opposite a tall, lean British officer called McNeil. Richard sensed immediately that this too was going nowhere and wondered if being dispatched from one unhelpful place to the next was an example of the famous British sense of humour. He presented his case regardless.

'Are these children German nationals or children of those who have taken part in the war?' asked McNeil, who looked to Richard exactly the type of British officer to have thrashed Indian coolies with his stick.

'They are German children.' The expression on the man's face told him this was the wrong answer.

'They are not our responsibility.'

'Then please tell me who is responsible for pursuing doctors who have committed crimes against innocent children. The German police now have no authority, and the doctor guilty of these crimes is still sitting in the Langenhorn General Hospital as its medical director.'

'I'm sorry, but we're not responsible for them.'

'Do you mean that your department is not responsible for them, or do you mean that the British occupying forces have no interest in solving crimes committed by Nazi doctors if the victims aren't of the right nationality?'

McNeil gave a snort of disdain. 'How many of your countrymen do you suppose have come here in the last few weeks to ingratiate themselves with me as informants?'

'I have no intention of ingratiating myself. I want to report a crime and have the proof.' He held up his briefcase with one hand and pointed at it with the other. 'In here are the files of two of the murdered children. These files leave no doubt that these are cases of outright murder. Do you have any idea what has been happening in this place for the last twelve years? The mentally ill and disabled have been separated out and murdered. Even children. You can't sweep that under the carpet.'

A cynical smile flickered across the Englishman's face. 'Well, well, and you're the one who wants to right the wrong, Herr Doktor Hellmer?'

It was clear from the way McNeil articulated the German words *Herr Doktor* in his otherwise purely English question that he viewed the German in front of him with great disdain. 'And I'm sure you're going to tell me that you were never a member of the Nazi Party and never voted for Hitler, isn't that so? Perhaps you'll also tell me that fairy tale about how you risked your own life to save others from tyranny? Oh yes, I've met countless other informants like you in the last few weeks, all of whom want to reveal some crime or other. It's all turned out to be an excuse to curry favour with us. But that doesn't wash with me. I know exactly how to deal with your sort. First, you carry on as if you rule the world, then when you're knocked down you say it wasn't anything to do with you and come creeping in for favours. I have no interest in the information you bring and see cowardly informants like you as contemptible. Get out of my office.'

Without a word, Richard did what he was told. It was pointless. No one would ever bring these people to justice. People like Krüger would always fall on their feet. His crimes were of no interest to these new rulers. He'd suspected this for some time. It was true what his father-in-law had said soon after the occupation had started. Anyone killing innocent civilians through carpet-bombing, anyone keeping food rations so low that even small children were starving to death would not be interested in the murders of twenty-two German children. And if by some miracle they did take an interest, it would have nothing to do with compassion for the children and everything to do with keeping the moral high ground. If the German barbarians were ready to get rid of their own kind, it saved them the work. Blinded by rage, Richard charged out into the corridor and collided with another British officer.

'I beg your pardon,' he muttered without looking at the man, and hurried on. The man shouted something after him, but Richard ignored him and quickened his pace. He couldn't take any more humiliation.

Chapter 56

By the time he had spent the whole morning trying in vain to get a hearing, only to end up on the receiving end of the occupiers' disdain in the form of McNeil, Richard was in no mood to go home, where he'd have to admit his failure. Instead, he wandered aimlessly through the ruins of his city and, after about three hours of this, found himself standing on the site of the family workshop. Nothing was left, nothing. Only a huge pile of rubble. He attempted to make out familiar bits of the building in the pile, and memories of the old days crept back to him. Of his brother, Georg, teaching him how to ride a bike in the yard. Of himself and Georg feeding the horses before the family owned a modern delivery vehicle, their old Opel 'tree frog'. The horses' stalls had later been converted to make extra workshop space and a garage. Richard knew that his own car, or what was left of it, must still be in there somewhere.

As he was reminiscing he saw something protruding from the rubble, a small piece of white tin. Crouching down, he pulled at it and found himself holding a battered number plate. HH-18208. The front plate from their own car. Yet more memories came flooding back. The day he married Paula. The most magnificent present the family could have given them. Leonie had still been there then. Fritz and Dorothea, full of dreams of a happy future life together. This number plate had crossed Alpine passes, proudly carried dust thrown up by Italian roads, and now it was a part of the life he'd lost long ago, the life now visible only in the photo albums they'd saved.

Drained of all strength, he found a remnant of wall big enough to sit on. His customary optimism was at the lowest possible ebb. Whatever confidence and faith he'd had in finding justice had just been wiped out by McNeil. How was he to protect his children from starvation on these meagre rations? What would happen in the winter? Each time he'd thought things couldn't get any worse, fate had dealt him yet another blow. Each time he'd believed that life would take a turn for the better, it had immediately got worse. Fritz had already experienced that to the full, with his whole family dead and his own status now uncertain. But at least he wouldn't have to watch his children die of starvation. To die in the firestorm was horrific, but at least it was quick.

From his wallet he took the treasured old photo of him and Fritz, both in uniform, with their families, which he had carried with him like a talisman. But the curse had been fulfilled. Family photos with men in uniform bring bad luck. This time, Death had struck those left behind. Henriette and Harri looked so happy. Harri was holding Rudi, their little dachshund, and resting his cheek against the dog's fur. Next to him stood Emilia and Georg, not knowing then how it felt to be hungry . . . He felt the tears welling up and couldn't fight them back. Maybe it wasn't manly to cry, but what did that matter now? Any old sense of honour was dead. Everything he had ever believed in was dead. And if life continued in this vein, his children would soon be dead too.

Something touched his shoulder and startled him. He whipped round.

'Margit! What're you doing here?'

She sat down next to him on his bit of wall. 'I come here pretty much every day, just to look for stuff we might be able to use – that's how we got back a few of our tools. And you? What's happened?'

'Look at this. That's what's happened.' He gestured at the decimation all around them, then wiped his eyes.

'It can't be just that to upset you so much. What's really the matter?' Then she noticed the photo in his hand. 'Is it bad news about Fritz?'

'No, there's no news about him.'

'Then you must go on looking for him, Richard! Have you been to the Red Cross today to search the latest lists?'

'No. I went to see the British.'

'Why did you bother going to see those arrogant Tommies?'

He told her about his futile attempts to seek justice.

'So that's why you're so down.' Margit put her arm around him. 'But you'll bounce back. He's nothing more than a stupid, arrogant Brit with no idea what's been happening here and without even a quarter of the courage you've shown over the last twelve years. What was it you always said to Papa? The Hellmers are carved from mahogany: stable, noble and strong. We rebuilt our lives after the first war, Richard. We can do it again this time round.'

'You do realise everything's destroyed?'

'Oh well, it'll just take longer to get cleared up. But it doesn't alter the fact that we can do it.'

'Margit, where do get your strength from? You've lost so much more than I have. You've lost a son.'

'And I have four other children I need to be there for. And a granddaughter now. Life goes on, Richard. The good days will come back some time, but not on their own. We've got to work for it. Moaning and groaning never got anyone anywhere.' She let go of him and got to her feet. 'And work for it is what I'm going to do. Let's see what I can find today. So stop snivelling and go and search for Fritz. If you don't look for him, you'll never find him.'

'Thanks, Margit. I needed a pep talk.'

'That's what big sisters are there for, even when they're grandmas!' She smiled at him affectionately.

Richard put the photograph back in his wallet, then picked up the number plate and stowed it away next to the files in his briefcase.

Although he was still exhausted and hadn't eaten all day, Margit's advice gave him fresh impetus and he went off to the nearest Red Cross post. Masses of new names were on the lists pinned up on the walls there. He looked immediately for an Ellerweg but found only an Ellerwig. First name Harri. Harri? He looked at the date of birth and his heart missed a beat: 8 February 1937 – the same date of birth as Fritz's son. But Harri was dead! And why was a child on the prisoner-of-war list? Then he realised he was looking at the wrong one: this was a list of orphans looking for surviving relatives. Harri Ellerweg, who had the same date of birth as Fritz's son, was in an orphanage on Averhoffstrasse.

Chapter 57

Soon after seven that evening, Richard arrived home with Harri. Paula rushed to open the door.

'Where on earth have you been? We've been beside ourselves with worry . . .' Her voice petered out when she saw Harri holding Richard's hand.

'This little boy . . . he looks like . . . Harri?' Her hand flew to her open mouth. 'It can't be!'

'It is him, Paula – it's Harri, Fritz's son. It's a miracle, but he survived.'

Paula was lost for words and just stood there in the doorway, staring at Harri.

'Can we come in now?' asked Richard.

Paula seemed to give herself a little shake before standing back to let them through. 'Harri, is that really you? I'm so happy you're alive – you're really here!' She made as if to hug him but noticed how he shrank away from her so held back, just as she had learned during her paediatric training. 'Harri, let's bring you in properly.'

Then she turned to Richard and whispered, 'You've got a visitor. A British officer has been here for two hours and insists on seeing you. He's in the waiting room.'

'A British officer? They wouldn't usually come to a German home like this – unless of course they want to seize it!' His voice was bitter.

'But I'm sure ours isn't smart enough for them. What does he want from me?'

'He wouldn't say. Did you say or do something this morning, something that would cause a problem?'

'No, I managed to stay civil and bite my tongue. No one was interested in children having been murdered. I was told in no uncertain terms that if it's only about German children, then it's not their responsibility.'

'Oh,' was all Paula could muster by way of reply.

Richard turned back to Harri. 'Will you go with Aunt Paula now and say hello to Emilia and Georg?'

'Can't I stay with you, Uncle Richard?' Harri clung to his hand, gazing up at him beseechingly. In the boy's eyes Richard saw both a fear of abandonment and the heart-rending need for someone to cling to. He found himself wondering yet again what Harri had had to endure.

'Of course you can, Harri. Let's go and take a look at this Englishman who wants to speak to me.'

'Richard, is that wise?' asked Paula.

'Yes,' Richard responded as he went off to the waiting room, Harri at his side.

Their visitor had been reading an English newspaper but folded it away as Richard opened the door into the waiting room.

'Good evening, Richard,' he said in German. This annoyed Richard straight away. He couldn't understand why this man was using his first name, even if he did look vaguely familiar.

'Leica II and an Egyptian tomb – ring any bells?' the Englishman said, smiling broadly.

'Arthur Grifford!'

'So you do recognise me!' Arthur got up and held out his hand to Richard. 'You nearly ran me down this morning!'

Richard put his briefcase on the table and shook Arthur by the hand. 'That was you?'

'That's right!' Arthur smiled again. 'And who is this young man here?'

'This is Harri, Fritz's lad. We all thought he'd perished with his mother and sister in the bombing in '43. And then, today of all days, I happened to find him in an orphanage. It's a miracle.'

Arthur's smile vanished when he saw the expression on Harri's face and in his eyes.

'I'd rather we talked in a proper room,' said Richard, 'but our consulting room closes at seven and then gets turned into a bedroom. Eight of us live in this place – no, with Harri, that makes nine.'

'This waiting room is fine,' Arthur commented, sitting down again, 'only without the usual reading matter.'

'Yes, we had a good supplier, but that all fell apart at the end of the war.' Richard took a seat opposite their visitor, with Harri at his side, still holding tight to his hand. 'I'd appreciate it if you could make this fairly brief so I can spend time with Harri afterwards. He hasn't seen a familiar face for two years and I want just to be here for him.'

Arthur nodded. 'I quite understand.' He took a deep breath before starting to explain why he was there. 'After you'd gone charging past me this morning with a face like thunder, I asked McNeil what was going on. When he filled me in on your conversation I pointed out to him that there probably was something in your story, all the more so because as early as the end of May I'd heard of similar incidents at the children's hospital in Rothenburgsort. We're carrying out an investigation into the senior consultant there, a Dr Bayer, although it's admittedly more because he was a member of the storm troopers.'

'McNeil told me you're not responsible for German children.'

'It's not that simple. At the moment, everything here is still developing, and informants have indeed been streaming in to see McNeil. But after everything you told me back in '42 it's clear to me that you've got evidence, and that's what I'm interested in. Will you show it to me?'

Richard reached for his briefcase. The number plate lay diagonally against the files inside. He took it out, placed it on the table and then removed the files. Meanwhile, Arthur had picked up the plate and was looking at it.

'Is this part of the evidence?'

'No, it's my old number plate.'

'And why are you carrying it around in your briefcase?'

'Because I came across it today in the rubble where our old workshop used to be. Call me sentimental. Paula and I were given the car as our wedding present from the family and set off for Italy in it on the first day of our marriage.'

He handed Arthur the files, but the Englishman only said, 'Did you carry on with the photography?'

'Yes, with a box camera.'

'Still got the Leica?'

'Do you want to look at these medical files or talk about photography?'

Harri suddenly spoke up. 'Uncle Richard, have you still got pictures of Mama and Papa, and Henriette and Rudi?'

'Yes, lots. We'll have a good look at them afterwards.'

'Have a look at them together now if you like. I'll need time to read these files.'

'This isn't the right time.'

'Why not?' Arthur and Harri spoke as if with one voice.

Richard couldn't think of a good enough reason, so he picked two albums, one from 1939 and one from 1940. First of all, he showed Harri the earlier photos of their last visit together to the beach at Travemünde.

'See, there's Mama, there's Henriette with your papa, and there's Rudi, burrowing in the sand.'

Harri started to cry.

'Everything's going to be all right.' Richard put his arms around Harri again to comfort him as best he could. Arthur looked up from the files and gazed at Harri with the greatest sympathy.

'It's all my fault,' wept Harri, ''cos I didn't hold on tight to Rudi.' Then it all poured out, all the anguish of the last two years and the story of how he'd survived when his mother and sister hadn't. He told Richard how they had rushed to their air-raid shelter in the cellar on the first day of the terrible firestorm but Rudi had kept whining, refusing to go down there, and then had broken free. Harri had run after the dog, not hearing his mother beseeching him to come back, and suddenly found himself out on the street without the others. He was immediately caught in the stream of people fleeing the danger and they swept him along with them. Rudi was nowhere to be seen and the panicked crowd moved swiftly as the bombs rained down on the city and homes went up in flames. An elderly woman had seized Harri by the hand and pulled him along with her, the boy still shouting, 'Rudi! Rudi!', but then she had jumped with him into the River Elbe, where they and lots of others had clung to a boat while their world was consumed by the fire. Harri's recollections of the following days were hazy. At some point he was picked up and taken to the orphanage. He gave his name, but they heard it as Ellerwig, not Ellerweg. Harri couldn't yet read and only knew his father's first name, not his full date of birth, so his origins were deemed unknown, which was why Fritz had never found out that his son was alive.

'If I hadn't gone after Rudi, none of this would've happened,' he sobbed. 'Mama and Henriette tried to come after me, but they were forced back by the others going down into the cellar and the door got closed and then they died. All because I'd run off.'

'No, Harri,' said Richard, still holding the boy and soothing him in his arms. 'Rudi wanted to save you all. Animals have a strong instinct for danger. If Mama and Henriette had managed to follow him, they'd have been saved too. You did the right thing, and your papa will say that to you, I know. He will be so proud of you and Rudi.'

'But he's not here,' wept Harri. 'Uncle Richard, tell me the truth. Is Papa dead too?'

'No, Harri, definitely not. We're going to find your papa. I've promised you that.'

'You don't know anything about Fritz?' Arthur asked Richard very softly.

Richard shook his head. 'I last saw him a year ago, in Cherbourg.'

'You were both in Cherbourg?'

'Yes, we took advantage of everything the war had to offer,' replied Richard drily. 'You asked earlier on if I still had the Leica. No, it got lost when I was badly wounded in Cherbourg. If you've got half a dozen bits of shrapnel in your liver and belly, you don't give much thought to packing. It was Fritz who arranged for me to get home on one of the last transports for the wounded. What became of him after that, well, I still don't know, although I go through the Red Cross lists every week – like today. Although today I was really worked up and looked at the wrong list. Tell McNeil I'm grateful to him: if I hadn't been so angry about the conversation with him, I'd never have ended up looking at the list of orphans instead of the POW list. It's just amazing how good can come from bad.'

They sat in silence for a while.

Arthur eventually spoke. 'Is there anything I can do?'

'Two things, yes. Make sure these murderers in white coats stand trial for their crimes. And if you have any better sources than the Red Cross for finding out the whereabouts of German prisoners of war and their location, I'd be so grateful if you could do some digging into Fritz's case, so that Harri can have his father back at long last.'

'For sure,' promised Arthur. 'Now, I think it's time I left you two in peace. May I take these files? They're most enlightening.'

'Go ahead.'

Arthur put the files and his newspaper in his briefcase. He hesitated for a moment before reaching into his jacket pocket. 'I wanted to ask you a favour, actually. I've been trying to give up smoking. Could you possibly get rid of these for me?' He held out a packet of cigarettes to Richard.

'That shouldn't present any problems,' said Richard, taking them from him.

'Thanks,' Arthur said with a grin. 'I reckon we'll be meeting again very soon.' Then he turned to Harri. 'I'll do everything I can to find your papa. You have my word.'

Chapter 58

After Arthur had gone the family bombarded Richard with questions – how he'd found Harri, how the child had survived and what the Englishman had wanted.

'It would be so nice if you'd let me eat something first!' Richard said in an attempt to fend them all off. 'I haven't had a scrap of food, and Harri must be really hungry. But Frau Koch, look, here's something for you.' He gave her Arthur's cigarettes.

'They're real British ones!' Their old housekeeper's enthusiasm was clear for all to see. 'They sell on the black market better than German ones. How on earth did you come by those?'

'Harri's sorrowful look.'

Paula came in from the kitchen with two bowls of lentil soup. 'It's only lukewarm.' She put the soup in front of Richard and Harri. 'That's what happens when you're late home and then spend ages talking to your visitor.'

'Never mind. At least we won't burn our tongues,' Richard said with a playful grin.

'You probably do enough of that all by yourself!' she said, kissing him lightly on the cheek.

Harri savoured his soup one spoonful at a time while Richard wolfed his down and then set about answering the family's questions.

'That man was Arthur Grifford. Fritz and I met him at El Alamein in 1942.'

'You met an Englishman? In the middle of the war? Had you taken him prisoner or something?' Richard's father was baffled.

'Not really, as the Brits would say. Although I was pointing my gun at him at the time.' Richard laughed softly. 'It's a very strange story and certainly wasn't one we could tell anyone at the time.' He related the incident in the Egyptian tomb.

'This morning I had a pretty unpleasant encounter with a certain McNeil, who seems to view German children as the lowest of the low and who saw fit to throw me out of his office. I was so furious I couldn't see straight and collided with another officer on my way out. It was Arthur, but I didn't recognise him and rushed off. Well, after that, he made the effort to come and see me and is actually interested in what I had to say. He'd already heard of similar cases at the children's hospital at Rothenburgsort.'

'Does that mean these murders will be looked into at last?' asked Paula's father.

'I certainly hope so.' Richard then went on to relate how he'd found Harri.

'We must find Harri a bed,' said Richard's father, 'but the sofa will do the job for now.'

Richard nodded. 'I have complete confidence in your organisational skills, Papa!'

◆ ◆ ◆

Over the next few days Richard and Paula worked as normal in their quarters at home. Since January, when they'd started offering general practice as well, the waiting room was always full. Meanwhile, the rest of the family was fully occupied with getting hold of enough food. The schools were still closed, so Emilia and Georg spent a lot of time down at the allotment with Aunt Margit and her family. Someone had to watch over the fruit trees and vegetable beds in case of theft, and the children also enjoyed fishing in the stream where they used to go canoeing. They regularly added a fish or two to the family menu, something that made them both burst with pride. They held no licence, so this was technically poaching and therefore all the more exciting.

Harri was very withdrawn in the early days and suffered terrible nightmares. Richard hoped that Arthur would soon find out what had happened to Fritz, and continued to comb through the Red Cross lists himself. But there was no sign of him. Richard found himself wondering if he needed to adjust to the fact that Fritz might have fallen after all. He wondered how he could possibly tell Harri.

One Thursday in July the twins had been especially successful on their little fishing expedition, catching no fewer than five fat roach, each one weighing a good kilo or so. The catch was so precious that Karl personally escorted the pair of them home in case anyone ambushed and robbed them on their way back. Richard's mother and Frau Koch immediately set about gutting and baking the fish. They asked Karl to eat with them, but he had to get back to Moorfleet in time for curfew.

Just before eight the meal was ready to serve. Richard could see they'd be going to bed with full bellies tonight for the first time in months. They had all just taken their places at the table when the doorbell rang. Frau Koch started from her chair, but Richard was first on his feet.

'I'll go – you stay there, thank you, Frau Koch.' He assumed it was going to be a patient in urgent need of help before curfew. But when he opened the door he saw an unshaven, hollow-cheeked man in a tattered army uniform.

'Fritz!'

His friend gave an almost imperceptible nod. They lurched towards each other and Richard wrapped his arms around his friend, pressing him close, before calling out for Harri.

'So it's true?' whispered Fritz. 'Harri's alive?'

Only then did Richard realise that Arthur Grifford was standing behind Fritz in the corridor. But before Richard could reply, Harri had come into the hall of the flat and stopped dead when he saw the man in the torn uniform. Fritz crouched down in front of him. 'Harri?' he whispered. 'Don't you recognise me?'

Harri was stunned. There was an agonising silence. 'Papa!' He threw himself into his father's arms.

Fritz held him tight. 'You're alive,' he whispered, his voice thick with sobs. He lifted the boy up into his arms. 'Harri, I'll never leave you alone again. Never. D'you hear?'

Harri clung to his father as if he would never let go.

'I'm so very sorry for what you must have gone through, Harri.' Fritz couldn't hold back the tears now. 'But I'll make everything all right again. Everything will be all right again.' He kissed his son's forehead, then hugged him close once more.

Richard fought back his own tears of joy and relief. He looked over at Arthur. 'Thank you. I'll never forget what you've done here.'

'I had to call in seven old favours and tell three white lies to get him home,' replied Arthur. 'But to have witnessed this – well, it was all worth it.'

Deep in thought, he took out a packet of cigarettes and was about to light one, but faltered. 'Dammit, I'm supposed to be giving up.' He put the cigarette back in the pack. 'I keep lapsing! Can you get rid of these for me?' He handed them to Richard.

'But of course! For the sake of your health.'

'Right then, I've got to take the jeep back now and find a way of explaining to my bosses what I was doing out on Lüneburg Heath, why I had a flat tyre on the way back and used the spare.'

'That sounds like a problem.'

'Sounds to me more like calling in favour number eight.' He smiled. 'You'll hear from me again in the coming weeks when we tackle Krüger.'

Chapter 59

Fritz said very little about what had happened to him over the past year. He kept it to their disorderly withdrawal from France and their attempts to get back to Germany. He did disclose that the British had captured them in early April and they had surrendered without a fight. Fritz had been a prisoner of war at a Lüneburg Heath camp.

'The conditions were appalling,' he said. 'I saw to the sick and the wounded, but we had nothing, no bandages and no clean water. Many of the wounded died like flies and then dysentery got most of the others. I tried so many times to get medical supplies from the military administration, but they showed absolutely no mercy. It was easy to see how much they hated and despised us.'

'How did Arthur get you out?' asked Richard.

'No idea. Someone summoned me, said I was needed in Hamburg on the orders of the military administration and was to be released. I didn't immediately recognise Arthur, and told him I would rather die in the dirt there and then with my comrades than lift a finger to help the British administration. This was when Arthur dismissed everyone else from the room. They did exactly what he told them. Interesting, I thought. And then he told me Harri was alive, asked me to be so good as to play along and not wreck everything. I was dumbstruck, literally, so didn't say anything else. So I got my discharge papers and climbed into this terrible old jeep that Arthur had brought along. I still wasn't sure what to make of it all until soon after Lüneburg when we got a flat tyre. His casual manner slipped then, and I added some interesting words to my English vocabulary. He was absolutely desperate because he'd borrowed the car on the quiet from one of his colleagues but not told him he'd be taking it outside Hamburg. On top of that, he had not the faintest idea how to change a tyre. I think that was when I started to believe that he really had called in a few favours just to get me back to Hamburg. So I did a quick tyre change, showing him how to do it so that he'd know for next time! I've always enjoyed sharing my knowledge with others.' Fritz chuckled. 'I was so shocked when we got to Hamburg. I didn't recognise a thing.'

'St Georg Hospital is still standing, and I'm sure Professor Wehmeyer would be overjoyed to have you back,' said Richard.

'That sounds wonderful,' replied Fritz. 'First thing tomorrow I'll get registered and sort out my food coupons. Is there anywhere I can get coupons for something to wear? This uniform's all I've got, and Arthur told me all grey uniforms are completely forbidden now, even if you rip off the insignia and everything.'

Paula, ever practical, chipped in. 'We can dye your stuff for you. Clothing coupons are useless now. There's no material anywhere, not even for newborns at Finkenau. They get swaddled in newspaper if their parents can't provide baby clothes.'

'I've still got a spare suit,' said Paula's father. 'The trousers will be too short for you, but it'll do. At least you'll be able to go out in the morning looking halfway presentable!'

'Thank you. So, it really has come down to the final shirt.' Fritz shot Richard a sideways look, and his friend knew exactly what he was getting at. It seemed an eternity since their biggest problem had been getting hold of petrol coupons and they had joked about never having to share their last shirt because their next would be army issue.

'Still, we've got a roof over our heads. At least we're not living in some bombed-out flat or in a Nissen hut.'

'You're right there,' said Fritz, serious again. 'And I've got the biggest and best gift in the whole wide world.' He stroked Harri's hair, while the little boy snuggled in close. 'Everything else will sort itself out.'

◆ ◆ ◆

A fortnight later Richard closed the practice early one afternoon. Fritz was still at work, back in his old job as surgeon and as deputy to Professor Wehmeyer. Richard thought there had probably been an emergency, as Fritz usually came home on time to take care of Harri.

He turned up two hours late, grinning from ear to ear. 'Look what I've got!' He held out an old sack to Richard and took from it several bottles of beer.

'Where the devil did you find those?'

Fritz laughed. 'It was a bit of an archaeological expedition into the cellar of a bombed-out pub. I'd treated the publican this morning because he'd broken his arm in his efforts to rescue all his old stock. Once I'd got him in a cast, I told him he didn't need to stay in and it was time for me to pack up for the day, so I went with him to help retrieve his goods from the cellar. And here's my share! I've no idea what it'll taste like – it's been down there for a good two years, but the bottle tops are still sealed and not damaged.'

'I didn't think surgeons ever met anyone interesting, just stuffy doctors!'

'It's the interesting people who take the risks – they're the ones who end up in hospital,' Fritz said with a grin. 'Where's Harri?'

'He's gone down to the allotment with my parents and the twins.'

'And where's everyone else?'

'Paula's sitting on the balcony with Frau Koch, and her father's reading in his room.'

'Good! That means we can take over the kitchen and drink our beer without being disturbed.'

The beer was rather cloudy and it took a few gulps to get used to the taste, but it was drinkable.

'I'd say that either the time in the cellar and the heat of the firestorm have raised the alcohol content or I just can't take my drink any more!' said Fritz. The first glass had gone down a treat.

'It's pretty strong,' agreed Richard. 'So when was the last time we had a beer together?'

'Cherbourg. Four days before you were wounded.'

'That's it. I remember the shelling seemed quite far off then.'

'And now there's no shelling at all. The world may have been reduced to ruins, but at least there's peace.' Fritz poured more beer for both of them. 'Here's to peace.' The doorbell rang as they clinked glasses.

'So much for peace,' Fritz groaned as Richard went to answer the door.

'Arthur! This is a surprise! Come in.' He led Arthur straight to the kitchen.

'Hello, Arthur,' said Fritz. 'You've come at just the right time! Do you fancy a beer?'

Arthur looked at the bottles on the table in amazement. 'Where on earth did you get that?'

'Archaeological expeditions into dark caves have always rather appealed, haven't they? This item is in mint condition – mid-war ware, I should say, 1943, heated through once and then sealed under a pile of stones,' Fritz said with a grin. 'Pasteurised beer, you might say! Still drinkable. Help yourself.'

'No thanks.'

'What can we do for you?' asked Richard.

'I wanted to let you know that we're going to deal with Krüger on Monday and I'd like you to come with me, Richard. You know your way around the hospital and where the files are kept.'

'What time should I get there?'

'I'll pick you up here at nine.'

'Krüger will be overjoyed,' said Fritz drily. 'Pity I'll be in the operating theatre. I'd love to be a fly on the wall and see him get what he deserves.'

'He'll get that all right,' stated Arthur. He glanced at the cloudy beer in Richard's glass. 'You're really drinking that? I just hope you're still in the land of the living on Monday.'

Chapter 60

On Monday, Arthur collected Richard exactly on time, as promised. During the drive to Langenhorn he asked Richard to tell him again and in detail everything he knew about Krüger. When Richard was explaining what had happened during Georg's stay in the children's department, Arthur interrupted him.

'Your son's deaf? I didn't know that.'

'We've got used to keeping it secret so as to protect Georg. Krüger tried everything to make out it was a hereditary condition, and that would have had fatal consequences for both Georg and Emilia. He even reported me to the Gestapo.' Richard went on to tell Arthur everything. He told him about Alfred Schär and his unexplained death in Gestapo custody, about being summoned to appear before them, about Harms, who'd chosen to go to the Front rather than be forced to take part in the killing of the sick and the disabled and who had since disappeared somewhere on Russian soil. And he told Arthur how Paula had found Georg a home tutor in Göttingen so that officials wouldn't find out about his deafness. 'And hopefully, if the schools really do reopen next week, the deaf and dumb school will be one of them. My father's going to find out about that today. The building was destroyed in '43.'

'But your son isn't dumb.'

'No, he can speak, and if he can see your lips he can cover up the deafness for quite a bit and pass for hard of hearing. But that isn't enough to cope in a normal school. Lip-reading is very demanding. When it's just the four of us, we use sign language. It's mostly Emilia who does it for him – she's the quickest because she learned how to do it when she was tiny.'

They completed the journey in silence.

At Langenhorner Chaussee Richard gave some directions. 'You'll soon see the entrance on the right. Drive up towards the church and then bear left.'

'It's an impressive place,' commented Arthur.

'At one time it was a wonderfully modern mental hospital where the work really was about helping people. I worked here for twelve years, and for nine of those I was a consultant.'

Arthur parked in front of the directorate. This was where Krüger, as head of the children's department, had his office. Arthur put on his cap. 'I am not going to speak German for him. This man's getting the official British treatment.'

'So you're bringing out the McNeil in you?'

'I'm bloody good at that.'

'I can imagine. I remember the expression on your face in that tomb! Back then, I was glad it was me with the gun in my hand and not you.' Richard grinned ruefully.

'Yes, and then you went and put it away and wrecked my picture of the wicked Kraut.'

'Can't help it. I am a psychiatrist, after all.'

They both laughed then got out of the car.

Frau Handeloh was still Krüger's secretary and receptionist. When she saw Richard accompanying a British officer she was noticeably rattled.

'Good morning!' Richard greeted her in his friendliest voice. 'We want to speak to Dr Krüger.'

'Herr Doctor Hellmer! I didn't know you . . . er . . .'

'What's the problem?' Arthur's face and voice were so threatening that she took a couple of steps back.

'I don't know,' replied Richard, and addressed Frau Handeloh, still in German. 'You'd do well to let us see Dr Krüger before Lieutenant Grifford loses patience. This man can be astonishingly unpleasant.'

Looking scared, Frau Handeloh knocked on Krüger's door and cautiously put her head around to speak to her boss.

They heard Krüger's voice, brusque in the extreme. Frau Handeloh went right into his office and closed the door.

When she came out again she said, 'Please go in. Dr Krüger's expecting you now.'

Richard let Arthur go first and gave Krüger a long, hard look as they went into his room. His arch-enemy had got up from his leather chair and stepped forward. He wore an immaculate white coat and had clearly come through the bad times unscathed. His jowly face suggested he had been very well nourished either via the black market or by filtering off his patients' rations.

'Gentlemen, what can I do for you?' His eyes darted uneasily from Arthur to Richard and back.

'Do you speak English?' asked Arthur. There was a real arrogance in his tone that Richard had never heard before.

'A little bit,' stammered Krüger. Richard stifled a moment of mirth.

Arthur very pointedly placed his briefcase right on Krüger's desk and took from it the list of murdered children. He then demanded to be shown the corresponding files.

Krüger looked at the names on the list.

'These children are dead,' he managed to say in English. 'The files are in the archive.'

'Then have the files brought here.'

'Why?'

'It's not for you to ask the questions. You follow my orders, is that clear?'

'Yes, but—'

'Your English comprehension is obviously not very good. Dr Hellmer, would you please tell your fellow countryman in his own language what he is to do?'

Richard nodded. 'Herr Doctor Krüger, I would advise you to send Frau Handeloh to the archive immediately before you cause Lieutenant Grifford to lose his temper. That would only make this delicate matter worse.'

Krüger nodded and called for Frau Handeloh. He handed her the list.

'And what have you got to do with all this?' he hissed at Richard when he thought Lieutenant Grifford was busy looking around his office.

'I gave him that list because I have a problem with doctors who bring our profession into disrepute by murdering those entrusted to their care.'

'I have never murdered anyone,' said Krüger vehemently. 'This is insubordination.'

Arthur came over to Richard and asked in English what Krüger had said, although he had already understood the dialogue in German.

'He believes he is innocent.'

'We'll see,' replied Arthur with a wry smile.

It was a while before Frau Handeloh reappeared with the files. 'There were only twenty in the archives.' She looked worried.

Krüger then repeated this in English for Arthur's benefit. 'There were only twenty documents, not twenty-two.'

Arthur dipped into his briefcase again and took out the two missing files. 'Twenty-one and twenty-two,' he said, holding them up.

'He got those from me,' said Richard with uncharacteristic smugness.

'And how did you get hold of them?' Krüger said, rounding on him.

'That is none of your business.'

Arthur leafed through the files, which Frau Handeloh had now placed on the desk, then he looked Krüger straight in the eye and spoke to him in German. 'It is beneath my dignity to speak your own language with someone of your ilk, but your English is dreadful and I want to be sure that you understand exactly what I'm going to say to you, so today I am making an exception. Here is indisputable evidence of the fact that you murdered every single one of these innocent children with an injection of Luminal. Why?'

'That wasn't murder,' retorted Krüger with astonishing self-assurance. 'It was an act of mercy. If you were a doctor, you would be able to see from these files that all the children concerned were severely disabled or seriously ill. They were not viable. I released them.'

'I am a doctor and I understand fully what is in these files. A little girl with epileptic fits. That is not a fatal condition and, in any case, no reason to kill the child. If you had given her a suitable dose of Luminal, you'd simply have stopped her from suffering the spasms. Here's a case of infant hydrocephaly. You murdered him so early in his short life that it was too soon to judge what impact the water on the brain was going to have on his future development. In spite of this disability, he might have grown up to live a perfectly enjoyable life. And here's a case of . . . No, I'm not going to recite every case – that's for the courts to deal with – but we're plumbing the depths here and it makes me sick to the core.'

Then he turned to Richard. 'Do you want to take over here, or shall I do it?' He asked Richard this using deliberately informal German so that Krüger wouldn't miss the fact that they were close colleagues.

'What is it you want me to say to him?'

'Exactly what he said to you in 1941.'

Richard smiled. 'Krüger, you are summarily dismissed!'

Krüger was speechless.

Arthur continued in German. 'And not only that. Until the final court hearing you are banned from all medical work. Starting tomorrow, you must report for rubble clearing. Woe betide you if you are not there.'

'You can't do this!' shrieked Krüger.

'Yes, I can. And you should be glad that we don't have the same rules of law as the world you operate in.'

'This is just victors' justice!' Krüger was outraged. 'Hellmer, it doesn't surprise me in the least to see you hobnobbing with the occupational forces. You always were a blot on our national landscape.'

'One more word from you and you can forget the rubble clearing tomorrow because you'll be locked up instead.' Arthur was now at his most menacing. 'And we're taking all these files with us.'

Arthur fitted half of them inside his briefcase, gave the rest to Richard, and they walked together back to the car.

'Could you just drop me off at Hoheluftchaussee?' Richard asked Arthur. 'It's on the way to your headquarters.'

'I can take you all the way home,' Arthur offered.

'I thought it wasn't permissible – you know, driving a German around in an official vehicle without good reason.'

'I'll be the one to decide what is or is not a good reason.'

'Thanks, but it's fine if you drop me off at the Capitol. I've heard it's reopening soon, 27 July, in fact, and I want to book tickets in advance.'

'Whatever you want.'

They got in the car.

'I've dealt with two types of Nazi to date,' Arthur said as he started the engine. 'The whingeing, whining types who make out they knew nothing. Then there are all the others, and they're like Krüger. This is going to be tough.'

'Why's that?'

'Because the hearings of crimes against Germans take place in German courts, and I'm not sure that we've got all the old Nazi judges out yet.'

'We have evidence. Child murder has always been a crime.'

'I just wanted to warn you. It's not going to be easy.'

'Nothing's easy at the moment.' There was a deep breath from Richard as he leaned back in his seat. 'I'll give you an example. Did you know we're not allowed to receive any parcels from abroad?'

'No. What makes you think that?'

'My wife's best friend left for Switzerland nine years ago. It was my children's birthday last Thursday and she'd wanted to send them a parcel. The post office told her there was a directive preventing any parcel being sent to Germans so she sent a letter instead, but that had obviously been opened and read.'

'I didn't know any of that. If there's anything I can do . . .'

'No, Arthur, I didn't mean that. Please don't do a thing. You've already done so much. It might be better if you distance yourself a bit from us now. Look, we're not far from Hoheluftchaussee, I can walk the rest.'

'I'm not quite with you.'

'Then I'll be more direct. We both know that the occupying forces view Germans as the lowest form of life and that you're all supposed to avoid contact. If you don't stick to that, sooner or later you'll get into trouble and could even lose everything. I consider you to be a real friend, but our friendship could cause you genuine difficulties, so that's what I mean about you distancing yourself.'

'You're an idiot, did you know that?'

'If you were a psychiatrist, I'd give that some thought, but you only know about general medicine.'

'Richard, listen to me. It's true that lots of Brits see Germans as the lowest form of life, as you describe it – and you'll always get that when two countries have been at war – but there are a few who see things rather differently. Now here's an example: very soon we'll be providing school meals, and they won't require food coupons. I imagine that'll be a relief for a lot of parents. It's a lousy time to be alive, and it's worse for you than for me, but I can't change that. I can't change the injustices or the big picture in political terms. I can only do what you've been doing over the last twelve years, and that's help the people I care about but do it all on the quiet. And that's exactly what I'm going to do, whether it suits you or not.'

They'd arrived at the Capitol so Arthur pulled over.

'Now go and get your damned cinema tickets and then I'll drive you home. Is that understood?'

'Loud and clear!'

'Then you're not as big an idiot as I thought.'

Chapter 61

On the morning of 7 September Richard woke Paula with a kiss.

'Happy seventeenth anniversary,' he whispered, placing two cinema tickets on top of the bedclothes. 'Your father's standing in for us today at the surgery. We've got a date at three o'clock at the Capitol.'

'You've done something for our anniversary?' Her face lit up as she flung her arms around his neck.

'And that's not all. We've got the same box as when we went there together for the very first time in 1926. When I heard the Capitol was opening up again I just had to get these tickets!'

'And what's on?'

'Something fun – *The Punch Bowl* with Heinz Rühmann.'

The mere thought of going to the cinema with Richard and wrapping herself in that dream world buoyed her up throughout the day. She got out her best dress and tried to polish up her shabby shoes.

'Don't overdo it,' said Richard. 'The Capitol's lost its shine, just like we have.'

'And we haven't even got the tree frog to take us there, let alone our lovely Adler Standard 6.'

'Aha, but there's still the tram!' With a gallant flourish, Richard offered her his arm, and they set off.

'Thank God we couldn't see into the future,' commented Paula as they sat in the tram and looked out at the heaps of rubble. 'If we'd known what was going to happen, it would have poisoned our lives as youngsters.'

'We're alive, we're together, our children are fit and healthy, and I love you, Paula. That's all that matters.' He put his arm around her shoulders and she leaned into him, enjoying the feeling of security it gave her.

The Capitol had certainly lost its old glamour. Although the war damage had not been disastrous, a lot of its beautiful decorative old glasswork had shattered and been replaced by wooden boarding, the sumptuous gilding had faded and peeled, and the upholstery of the seats was as threadbare as the clothing worn by the audience. But it was a full house! Pleasure was a rare commodity and the cinema was still a place where you could forget your empty stomach for a while.

As they slipped into their seats, the same ones as nearly two decades earlier, when the world was still a place of glowing beauty, Paula tried to take herself right back inside the mind of the young woman she had once been. She remembered how she'd fallen head over heels with the most wonderful man, in spite of her father's doubts about him. She placed her hand on the arm of the seat, recalling how Richard had waited until the lights dimmed before gently placing his hand over hers – the first gesture of affection between them. As though Richard had read her thoughts, she suddenly felt his hand on hers, just like the first time, gentle, protective, attentive and yet overwhelming.

'Shall we make plans, like we did before?' he whispered to her, stroking her hand.

'Yes,' she whispered back. 'Tell me yours.'

'I have quite a few. First, we need to make sure we don't starve and freeze to death over the winter.'

'That's a good plan,' said Paula with a smile.

'Then we must do everything possible to get Krüger convicted and sentenced to the punishment he deserves.'

'Quite right.'

'And in three years' time, when it's our twentieth wedding anniversary, I want to have a camera again and take a photo of the party we'll have, with a huge cake to celebrate.'

'That would be just wonderful,' sighed Paula, leaning into him still as the opening credits rolled.

'But in 1953 it'll be our silver wedding, and we'll have another car by then. And we're going to drive to Rome in that new car and I'll photograph you in exactly the same place in front of the Colosseum, sitting on the bonnet, just like you did on our Adler Standard 6.'

'That's a lovely idea.'

'That's no idea – that's my plan.'

'You are an incorrigible optimist and dreamer, Richard darling. And that's why I love you so much!'

'You have to have the dreams in the first place for them to come true, my dearest Paula,' whispered Richard.

AFTERWORD

While the historical background to the novel is true, the main characters in this novel are fictitious. I created the story of Richard and Paula, two intentionally heroic figures, to present the broadest possible picture of psychiatry at that time and demonstrate the resistance offered by a substantial number of psychiatrists. It is well documented that some doctors spoke out against sterilisation and euthanasia and carried out acts of resistance in secret. Once it had leaked out that the registration process was not for financial budgeting purposes, as had been the official story, but was rather the first step towards the mentally ill and physically disabled becoming the first victims of the Nazi killing machine, many hospital doctors tried to protect their patients and started to falsify the registration forms. This led to the setting up of a supervisory commission that scrutinised hospital files where there was any suspicion of falsely positive records of patients' productivity. This left doctors in a dilemma. If they acted as Richard did in the novel and classified all patients as 'productive', it was noticed and they ended up saving no one. This meant they had to take tough decisions, like Paula did in Göttingen. There is documentary evidence of the work and actions of the Göttingen professor Gottfried Ewald. As an opponent of euthanasia, he tried to protect as many people as possible from removal and transportation and yet had to leave some to their horrific fate in order to save the others.

As early as 1920 Alfred Hoche, a medical doctor, and the lawyer Karl Binding published a book under the title *Allowing the Destruction of Life Unworthy of Life*, arguing the high cost to society of the unproductive mentally ill. The first part of their work features arguments in favour of assisted dying, the same arguments used today in support of active assisted dying, while in the second part it becomes clear that, in the end, this was all based on cutting public spending.

The Nazis took these views and further perverted them through their practice of killing on a truly industrial scale. They used gas to murder the disabled and the mentally ill and subsequently put this to further use in death camps such as Auschwitz.

All this grew incrementally, as there never was a comprehensive plan. However, even in his autobiography *Mein Kampf* in 1925, Hitler was already demanding the sterilisation of all those with hereditary diseases. When Richard leafs through the book, he notes with horror the original quote on this topic, as well as the Führer's original thoughts on it with regard to Jewish people.

Sterilisation was initially welcomed by many doctors. As described in the novel, the original draft law had come into being under the previous government but it was the Nazis who implemented it, and very swiftly, with one distinct and significant change. Gone was the clause regarding the patient's prerogative, or that of their legal representatives, to make a voluntary decision regarding sterilisation. From now on, the heads of hospitals, asylums and prisons had the right to determine whether or not their patients or inmates should be sterilised. The legal description given in the novel is abridged, but authentic.

The fact that the original law did not derive from the Nazis, even though the Nazis modified it to suit their own plans, had grave consequences for the people affected. It was precisely because the law was not considered to be a law decreed by the Nazis that surviving victims of their sterilisation policy fought for decades to be recognised as victims of National Socialism. They fought in vain.

The thirty-fourth sitting of the Bundestag's Reparation Commission took place on 13 April 1961 and found that the victims of forced sterilisation had not suffered harm and did not fall under the laws on compensation. These expert opinions were given by the same doctors who had presided over court hearings on hereditary disease during the Nazi dictatorship and who made the original decisions about forced sterilisation. There is documentary evidence that up to four per cent of those subjected to the procedure for forced sterilisation died as a result.

It was only in 1988 that the victims were permitted a one-off payment of 5,000 Deutschmarks. People still in financial need as a result of the consequences of forced sterilisation are permitted to draw a regular benefit of 291 euro per month. This benefit was still being paid to 482 survivors as recently as 2012.

In addition to the invented main characters and Professor Ewald, the novel tells of other characters who are historically documented. Alfred Schär, the teacher of the deaf and dumb, is a case in point. Although the friendship with Richard is fictitious, his story and fate have been faithfully presented here.

Another historical figure is Dr Carl Stamm, the Jewish doctor who was head of the children's hospital at Rothenburgsort. He died in 1941 but had been dismissed by the Nazis as early as 1933 and replaced by National Socialist Workers' Party (NSDAP) member Dr Bayer. The cause of Stamm's death is unknown. Many believe he took his own life to escape the threat of deportation, while others say he died of a brain haemorrhage. The Carl Stamm Park in Rothenburgsort, Hamburg, is named after him.

The children's hospital in Rothenburgsort really was bombed and the children evacuated to Langenhorn, as in the novel. Langenhorn is now the Asclepius Clinic – Ochsenzoll. I have a special personal connection to this incident as my father, now deceased, was a nine-year-old diphtheria patient at the hospital when it was bombed. As a child, he lived through the night-time bombings and the huge firestorm of 1943, and his grandmother had an allotment at Moorfleet. I took him as my historical model for Georg's friend Horst. He is further commemorated by my choice of birth date for Richard and Paula's twins, the same date as his. His reminiscences gave me a number of ideas for the children's perspective on their lives back then, one example being the children's dislike of the rubbery smell of their gas masks. And there was a reason behind the choice of Rothenburgsort. This was where my father lived as a child, and his own grandfather ran a big painting and decorating business there. During the bombings in July and August 1943 the whole district was destroyed, changing its face for ever.

Richard's nemesis, Dr Krüger, was inspired by the psychiatrist Dr Friedrich Knigge, a historically documented figure who worked at Langenhorn, first in the asylum, and later in charge of child euthanasia there. The hostility between Krüger and Richard made the two archenemies, and in this respect I have distanced the character of Krüger from that of Knigge. But it was Knigge who in real life murdered the twenty-two children and carried out dissection on six of them, exactly like Krüger in the novel. After the war ended, students reported the murders to the British. In August 1945 Knigge was dismissed and forbidden from further work in the field of medicine, as eventually happens to Krüger in the novel. Knigge twice stood on trial, the second time for child murder, although this second trial never fully concluded, as he died of polio in 1947 in St Georg Hospital.

The experiences of Richard and Fritz at the Front are also based on historical evidence. Medical facts such as the use of sulphonamides and Evipan are accurate, but I have adjusted locations to suit the novel's narrative, deciding to send Fritz and Richard through Italy to Cherbourg. This was not implausible because the field hospital system was fully reorganised in 1943, but for me this was far more about creating a snapshot of the Western Front and the emotional burden both men would have borne. Inveterate military historians are asked to forgive my poetic licence here.

The encounter with Maxwell Cooper and Arthur Grifford in the Egyptian tomb was always something I had planned. The location of the tomb is fictitious, but 1987 excavations of ancient Egyptian graves in El Alamein did indeed reveal evidence of previously unknown burial places on a large scale.

The post-war period did not come as a liberation for the German people, although it has at times been presented thus. It was actually a defeat, and once the concentration camps were liberated, the Allies' anger towards the German people was clear: it was now about punishing the Germans. For example, Germans were forbidden from receiving Care Packets until June 1946.

The conditions that Fritz describes in the prisoner-of-war camps are also taken from historical fact.

Under the British occupation, all enquiries and requests had to be presented in English and any submitted in German were simply not accepted. The ban on fraternisation was, however, quickly eased, as so many British did not adhere to it. However, the British continued to live in a somewhat elevated parallel society and there were still strictly divided British-only compartments on public transport until the late 1950s. The last residential property to be seized by the British was returned in 1957.

In spite of all this, friendships developed between British and Germans, such as that between Arthur and Richard. In August 1945 it was the British who organised school meals throughout Hamburg schools, something that saved many children from dying of starvation.

The Capitol Cinema on Hoheluftchaussee was among the first cinemas to reopen for Germans. Whether *The Punch Bowl* was on the programme, we don't know, but it was one of the last great films made by the German film company UFA and shown in German cinemas from 1944. I chose it because it is well known to cinema enthusiasts and, unlike any other film of that era, was ideally suited to lifting the mood in such dark times.

As far as Richard's and Paula's dreams for the future are concerned, well, currency reform came on 20 June 1948, and with it the Deutschmark. The shelves were suddenly full once more and the shops busy. Richard's dream of owning a camera again in time for their twentieth anniversary on 7 September 1948 may well have been fulfilled.

Even his plans for their silver wedding are likely to have come to fruition. In 1953 Germany's economic miracle was coming into full swing, the symbol of which is the most successful car of all time – the VW Beetle.

I'm sure that somewhere in Richard's photo album there's a photograph taken in '53 of a glowing Paula, laughing as she poses on the bonnet of a VW Beetle in front of the Colosseum in Rome.

But that's another story . . .

ABOUT THE AUTHOR

Dr Melanie Metzenthin was born in Hamburg in 1969 and still lives in the city. Her work as a psychiatrist and psychotherapist requires specialist insight into the mental state of traumatised patients, some of whom have committed criminal offences. When developing the characters in her novels, she enjoys drawing on her professional experience. She also writes psychothrillers under her pseudonym, Antonia Fennek.

ABOUT THE TRANSLATOR

Photo © 2016 Chris Langton

Deborah Rachel Langton was born in Reading, England, studied German and French literature at Cambridge, and has worked in Munich, Berlin, Milan, Abu Dhabi, London and Manchester. After a rewarding first career teaching and lecturing, she moved into translation while still working at Munich's Ludwig Maximilian University and loves translating fiction best of all. Deborah now lives in a rural location not far from London and translates in her study with views towards England's South Downs. She shares her life with her husband, Chris, and their two fine sons, Joseph and Samuel.

Printed in Great Britain
by Amazon